A SCENT OF LAVENDER

To Marion
Thanks for
all the
scrambled
egg!

Gillian
xxx

Other novels by Anne Willingale

The Key to the Street

Revenge

Between Classes

A
SCENT OF
LAVENDER

Anne Willingale

Matador
Unit E2 Airfield Business Park,
Harrison Road, Market Harborough,
Leicestershire. LE16 7UL
Tel: 0116 2792299
Email: books@troubador.co.uk
Web: www.troubador.co.uk/matador
Twitter: @matadorbooks

ISBN 978 1803136 004

British Library Cataloguing in Publication Data.
A catalogue record for this book is available from the British Library.

Printed and bound in Great Britain by 4edge Limited
Typeset in 11pt Minion Pro by Troubador Publishing Ltd, Leicester, UK

Matador is an imprint of Troubador Publishing Ltd

Alan Bricknell, for his proofreading, Mick Freeman, for his advice on courtroom etiquette, and the team at Troubador, who are always there on the end of the phone or e-mail with help and advice.

Western Morning News

13th February 1870

On Friday night last, an as yet unnamed woman was found murdered in Plymouth, her body left on the cobbles in the lane that runs behind Adelaide Street. It was a cold night and the body was soon iced and stiff with the cold. The body was discovered by Mr Draper of Well Street, after he had left his home earlier than usual for work, wanting to call in at the apothecary for a tincture for his child's cough. Doing his civic duty, Mr Draper reported it to the Watch House. The police are looking for witnesses.

1.

Kingsand

February 1870

'Sarah, come out of the chicken house, the postman's brought you a letter,' her aunt called from the back door. Most of her words didn't reach Sarah, as they were taken on a gust of wind coming off the sea, but she did hear *you* and *letter*.

Sarah ducked out of the wire chicken run at the bottom of her aunt's garden, picked up a basket that held three eggs, and secured the run with a twist of wire, saying over her shoulder, 'Who would write to me, Aunt?'

In the kitchen, Sarah looked at the envelope laying on the table where her aunt had placed it and asked again, 'Who would write to me?'

'I don't know, maid. Open it and find out.'

Sarah's hand shook as she lifted the letter and opened it slowly. Written on a scrap of paper, the letter held two sentences in her mother's scrawl, telling, not asking, her to return home. After three years, her sister Amelia was to take her place in their aunt's small cottage the next day. Sarah was in shock. Once again, her life was to change suddenly, at the demand of her mother.

Through eyes bleary with sleep, Sarah blinked at the torrent of rain hammering on the bedroom window and groaned. This was not the day for crossing the Hamoaze in a rowboat.

During the long winter, she had begun to believe that the sun would never again shine on the grey sea heaving at the end of the garden, and that she would become a pale-faced old maid, like her Aunt Jelly who she'd lived with for three years.

As she pulled the covers up to her chin, she could hear the gulls screeching, as they did when it was rough at sea; a high-pitched sound that stripped the very life from her and tore at her soul. It was all the fault of James Bellum, who told her one day when they were walking to school in Cawsand that all the men who had ever died at sea came ashore to see their loved ones in the form of gulls, and cried in anguish because they didn't want to be dead. From that day, she had hated their screeching.

Swinging her legs out over the side of the bed, she moved hurriedly across the small room. The warmth of her bed receded rapidly from her body as she poured water from the little green jug into the matching bowl on the washstand.

Washing quickly, she splashed her face and patted it dry with a small towel, while trying to ignore the letter from her mother that lay screwed up on top of the marble washstand. Screwed up so she couldn't see the words, yet as alive as the mother that Sarah Warrington was afraid of. A few scribbled words that would once again change her life.

Shivering in the cold, damp air, she dressed quickly before making her way down the steep, narrow stairs that led to the kitchen and warmth.

Her Aunt Josephine, her father's elder sister, was a small woman, with a kind eye and ready smile. Hard-working, until an accident left her with a broken leg that had not set properly, leaving her with a pronounced limp and an uncertain wobble. The children had renamed her Aunt Jelly, although not to her face.

Sarah, the eldest of five children still left at home in Plymouth, out of the twelve that her parents had brought up, was volunteered, against her wishes, to live with her aunt after their father died. Banished to Kingsand, to sleep in a small room with a pile of stinking fleece and a spinning wheel. That's how she'd seen it when she first arrived; left to grieve alone, missing her father and her siblings. At the age of twelve, she had felt that she was being punished; sent away without knowing why, the day after his death.

Over the three years that she had been here, she had come to realise that a widow without income could have her children taken away and end up in the workhouse herself. Now she felt that her mother and aunt had probably saved her and the family from a terrible fate.

She had cried as she read her mother's letter, but had understood when her aunt explained that her mother needed money to help with the younger children, and that she would have to find work.

Entering the kitchen with its distinctive smells of soot and cooking fish, she put on a brave face.

'Good morning, Aunt.' She tried to sound cheerful, for now she didn't want to go back to town living. She had grown to love the peace of the beach and the village, where everyone knew each other and everyone belonged. Where in the evenings, she sat beside the fire, listening to the click, click of her aunt's spinning wheel as she spun the fleece, her foot moving in a constant rhythm with the wheel, earning the money that she lived on. It was a skill that her aunt encouraged Sarah to learn.

This morning, as every morning, the wheel was pushed back in the corner of the room as her aunt prepared breakfast.

'Morning, Sarah,' her aunt looked over her shoulder as Sarah entered the kitchen, 'did you sleep well?' Her aunt looked up from the pan that she was watching and gave her a fond smile.

'I did, Aunt.' Sarah felt her lip tremble, realising that this would be her last breakfast in this tiny cottage with the aunt that she had come to love. A woman with a gentle disposition, like her father.

Noticing her niece's struggle with emotion, Josephine smiled encouragingly.

'You'll be alright. After all, you're going back home.' She scraped at the frying pan with a knife. 'Did you notice that they've moved? Your mother sent their new address,' she continued as flames encased the pan. 'It's on the back of the letter for when you arrive back in Plymouth.'

Sarah hadn't noticed it. Having read it, she'd screwed it up and thrown it onto the washstand. It was meant to fall into the rubbish box but had missed and been glaring at her ever since.

3

As she spoke, her aunt approached the table with a large black pan of smoked fish. The smell of oily fish would once have made Sarah retch, but now, as her aunt placed the fish on the plate in front of her, she realised that she was hungry.

'Your mother will hardly recognise you, Sarah. You've grown so much since you arrived here,' she smiled. 'You were the thinnest, greyest child I'd ever seen.' She nodded her head. 'The thinnest I ever saw,' she repeated, almost to herself.

'Really, Aunt? You didn't tell me that before.'

'Never came up.' Josephine shrugged and placed a portion of fish on her own plate.

Only the ticking of the clock on the mantelshelf, and the scraping of their cutlery, invaded the silence of the kitchen as they ate.

Sarah was remembering the first day that she had reluctantly arrived to live in the village of Kingsand. Her aunt had been waiting to meet her off the ferry, to lead a grieving child to what was to be her new home.

The cottage stood in a terrace built for fishermen and their families, on the main street above the beach, the back looking out over the sea.

She was given the only other room, a small single bedroom at the back of the cottage. A room her aunt used for storing boxes of fish, laid down in salt, and stored under the bed, and where bundles of fleece filled the empty spaces in the room. The smell of livestock was so strong that Sarah thought she would never be able to sleep.

'Sarah!'

She was suddenly brought out of her memory.

Her aunt sounded serious as she removed Sarah's plate from the table.

'You've grown, Sarah. Your clothes barely fit and you need something more suitable for your age, to return home in.'

'But I don't have anything, Aunt.'

'I know, maid. We have to do something about this.'

Standing up from the table, Sarah realised that her aunt was right. The sleeves of her top were halfway up her arms. Her skirt, no longer at ankle length, was partway up her shins and faded by the sun and salt air.

Now she realised how idyllic it had been living here. She hadn't to think about clothes, and for the first time wondered how to get new clothes without money.

'You came here as a child, Sarah,' Aunt Jelly was saying, as though reading her mind, 'but now you are a young woman. You can't go back to Plymouth still wearing the same clothes as a girl of twelve.'

Looking thoughtful, her aunt said, 'I'll see what I have of your cousin's upstairs in the chest. You wash the dishes, and I'll see what I have that will fit you.'

When she returned, her aunt had a chemise, a skirt, jacket and blouse hanging over her arm.

'Here!' She held them out to Sarah. 'Try these on. I think that they will just about do. Once you're earning, you can improve on them.'

Standing in front of the fire, Sarah removed her faded clothes and dressed in those of her unknown cousin. The skirt, a dark grey wool mixture, and the blouse, cream cotton with a high collar. The brown jacket she found comfortable with room to be done up.

Her aunt stood watching as Sarah dressed, her face giving no indication of what she felt seeing her daughter's clothes being worn again.

'They fit, Aunt.' Sarah sounded incredulous. 'I can't thank you enough.'

'Sarah...' Her aunt's voice had a break in it. 'You've been a pleasure to look after, you've brought this home back to life. Now,' she continued, 'let me try to get the comb through that thick hair and plait it. One plait down the back will be right for your age.'

When done, her aunt tapped her shoulder, sounding satisfied as she spoke. 'There you are, you'll do. I think your mother will have trouble recognising you.' Picking up Sarah's old clothes, she rolled them into a bundle. 'I'll keep these for your sister. She might need a change of clothes when she arrives,' she said thoughtfully.

Leaving Aunt Jelly standing at her door waving, Sarah set off uphill along a winding, narrow lane, edged on both sides by small cottages, each different in style from its neighbour. A large ginger tomcat that had been sitting on a wall jumped down and followed her, meowing loudly. It almost tripped her up as it pounced on the toe of her boot each time her boot appeared from beneath her skirt. Lengthening her stride, she eventually left it behind, sitting in the middle of the lane, still meowing loudly.

Her heart was pounding by the time she reached the top of the steep hill and set off along the main road that took her past fields and farms, through forested areas with views of farmland and a village far below to her left.

Eventually, she stopped on top of a hill looking out across the Hamoaze, dotted with ships. Many were moored, their sails down, resting, but some in sail were making for port, and in the distance, Plymouth, almost hidden beneath a thick, yellow cloud that hung above the town, hiding the rooftops and strangling the church spires.

Beyond the miasma that choked Plymouth, she could see the rolling hills of Dartmoor, glowing like a green jewel under a cloudless blue sky. A wild place that she had never been, nor did she know of anyone who had.

It had stopped raining before she set out, and she was thankful that her feet had not grown and that her boots still fitted, as she made her way downhill towards the quayside and the ferry.

On arrival, she was glad to see other people waiting, knowing then that she hadn't missed it, for there was nowhere to shelter if it rained again.

As the Cremyll ferry came alongside the wooden jetty, the men took in their oars and a boy jumped onto the landing stage with a rope, tying it to a post.

The small queue on the jetty waited as passengers, alighting the ferry, were helped off by the boy.

Sarah saw her sister Amelia being helped from the ferry and waited as the child, looking frail, walked towards her. It wasn't until she came abreast that Sarah spoke. 'Amy!'

Amy flinched. 'Sarah! I didn't recognise you,' the child said without smiling, 'you've changed.'

With hardly any time to respond, Sarah asked, 'Is everything all right at home, Amy?'

Her sister's eyes seemed to deaden as she nodded a silent affirmative. Then looking back at the ferry, she said quickly, 'You'd better go, Sarah, they're all aboard.'

'Do you remember the way, Amy?' she just had time to say as she moved down the slope.

'Yes! Go, Sarah.'

Giving her sister a quick wave and hurrying down the jetty to the boat, Sarah was helped aboard and took her seat.

Taking up the oars, the men rowed, pulling hard together, moving smoothly out onto the water.

Their muscles bulged beneath their shirts as the boat pushed through the waves, dipping and rising, the oars creaking in the rowlocks.

Sarah shivered and pulled the jacket closer around her body. It was much cooler out on the water.

There was nothing that she could do now but endure the journey, accepting the spray that showered her from time to time over the side of the boat, as her body jolted back and forth in sync with the rhythm of the oarsmen. To quell her fear of the crossing, she concentrated on the sound of the oars grinding in the locks.

For the first few minutes, she could see her sister's small figure making her way along the path, and then, when she became too small through distance, Sarah turned her thoughts to her mother, unsure as to what she felt about the parent who was the strict, no-nonsense authoritarian. It was as though the roles of her parents were reversed. Her father had been gentle, loving. It was he who

7

had understood his children. He who had made the world a better place to live in. It was her mother who wielded the strap, who denied them food as a punishment.

When at last the journey was over, she stepped shakily from the ferry, walked up Admiral's Hard and along Durnford Street, with its tall terraced townhouses, clean steps and railings onto the street. After the peace of Kingsand, the atmosphere was alive with noise. Visitors to a house being greeted with joy; a coach and horses being driven past; two men running to catch the return ferry.

After the heavy rain, everywhere smelt fresh and clean, the cobbles exhibiting their colours through the lingering wet on their rounded surface. But as she continued her walk along Stonehouse High Street, towards King Street, where her mother now lived, the streets became busier, noisier, dirtier. The cobbles, here, thick with mud and excrement, the aroma of horse and sewage mixing with the sharp chemical aroma belching from factory chimneys nearby.

Unused to crowds and noise, she felt overwhelmed by the people crowding the pavement, where small children and dogs ran loose in a street busy with traffic.

Walking slowly along King Street, she looked for 100, where it said in the letter that her mother and siblings were living. Eventually finding it, she stared at a tall building, trying to understand how her mother could afford to rent it, when the door opened and a man in a flat cap hurried out.

Surprised, she looked after him, wondering who he was and what he was doing in her mother's house.

The door was left ajar and, walking in, she found herself in a narrow, dark hallway. The walls smeared and dirty, the brick floor beneath her boots covered in dry mud. Above her, she could hear a woman shouting, a baby crying and feet running. About to knock on the door to her left, she stopped, hand raised, as the sound of pounding feet on the stairs above her came nearer.

Hand still raised, she looked up, waiting, until she saw the owner's little black boots and thin legs appear at speed, followed by smaller legs and shoes not far behind. The faces of two small boys, intent on escape, didn't notice her as a red-faced woman, her head wrapped in a turban, leant over the bannister above, shouting abuse. But the boys had already disappeared out of the front door.

As Sarah took the stairs upwards her boots made a hollow sound on the bare wood. On reaching the landing, she realised, noticing that each door had a number on it, that many people lived here. Her family had moved into a lodging house.

Looking again at the letter, she noticed a room number, 5, and it was right there to her left at the top of the stairs. Feeling unsure, she knocked on the door.

A woman's voice replied sharply. 'Go away.'

Recognising her mother's voice, Sarah opened the door, walked in and saw a woman who only vaguely resembled the mother that she remembered.

Gwen Warrington was sitting in a chair beside a weak fire. A thin woman with long, straggling strands of dirty hair, a bucket between her legs, her face almost grey with sickness.

As Sarah opened her mouth to speak, her mother retched. About to hurry to her side, she was stopped by an angry glare, just before her mother retched again into the bucket.

'Mother, you're ill, what can I do?' she asked from just inside the door.

'Have you got any money?' Gwen looked at her, mouth wet, eyes red and streaming.

'Yes,' Sarah nodded, taking the penny that her aunt had given her from her pocket. 'I have a penny.' She held it out towards her mother.

Gwen scoffed. 'A penny! What good will that be?' she gulped, heaving again into the bucket. This time, Sarah had moved close enough to see that all her mother was bringing up was water.

The door opened suddenly and the two boys that had run down the stairs passing her earlier ran into the room, slamming the door behind them.

They stopped dead at the sight of Sarah standing beside their mother.

'It's your sister. Well, what did you get?' she demanded, mopping her damp brow with the back of her hand.

The elder boy, who Sarah now recognised as her brother Samuel, reached into his trouser pocket and pulled out a bread roll.

His mother took it. 'And you?' She looked at Thomas, but before he could speak Samuel said, 'He didn't get time, the baker saw us.'

Turning her attention back to Sarah, Gwen asked sharply, 'Where'd you get that jacket?'

'Aunt gave me it,' Sarah replied, feeling confused at her mother's strangeness. 'I'd grown out of my clothes.'

'I could get a good price for that.' Gwen stretched out a dirty hand towards the jacket. 'Let me see it.'

Noticing a look that went between her brothers, Sarah said bravely, 'Some other time, Mother. These are the only clothes that I have and without them I can't work.'

Gwen stood up, blowing out her cheeks. 'I have to empty the bucket,' she said, leaving the room.

When she'd gone, Sarah asked the boys where their little sister Maud was.

They couldn't look her in the eye, and the colour drained from Thomas. In the silence that encompassed the room, a knock at the door made them all jump.

Samuel opened it carefully then pulled it wider, smiling at an elderly woman.

'Hello, Mrs Newby,' he greeted her.

'Ah, Samuel. I have a little something for your tea.'

The woman held out a newspaper parcel. Then, looking past Samuel, saw Sarah and raised one eyebrow.

'This is my sister Sarah. She's going to live here now, Mrs Newby.'

The small grey woman looked at the parcel that Samuel was now holding. 'I don't think there's enough for another person.'

'That's alright, Mrs Newby,' he said brightly, 'We can make it stretch.'

Sarah could smell fish and, taking the small package from Samuel, opened it, seeing two fish heads and two tails. She looked at the woman with a frown on her face, not understanding the gift at all.

The little woman's lips tightened and without another word she turned walking back to her own room on the other side of the landing.

'You upset her,' Thomas accused, when she turned back into the room.

'How did I upset her?' Sarah replied, still staring at the fish heads.

But the small boy didn't answer and went to sit on the end of the bed.

Samuel tipped the fish bits into a pan and poured water from a jug over them, before balancing the pan over the poor fire.

'Mrs Newby gives us what she can, it all helps.' He spoke like an old man. 'And I think you upset her.'

Taken aback, Sarah sighed. 'I'll apologise. I didn't mean to upset her, I was surprised. I didn't know what we were going to do with fish heads.'

'We make a fish broth. Just water, but Mum says it's good for us.' As he spoke, he placed the bread roll on the table and she wondered if that was all that they had to eat.

Humbled now, and getting an idea of how the family were not managing, she walked across the hall and knocked on the door opposite theirs.

The door was half opened by a large man who stared at her, saying nothing.

'I came to apologise to your wife. I think that I upset her.' Sarah felt timid, daunted by his size and not knowing him.

'She can't see you. She's not well,' he said sharply.

'Please. I've only been here a short time and I'm trying to understand what is happening with my family.'

He looked back over his shoulder. 'June?'

11

Out of sight, Mrs Newby must have agreed, as he opened the door wider and Sarah walked into a cosy red and green room, stuffed with potted plants. Mrs Newby sat at a table, her thin arms laid on a red velveteen tablecloth.

She looked upset.

'I'm sorry, Mrs Newby. I didn't know what to make of the fish heads.'

'I do what I can.' The woman sounded petulant, almost like a spoilt child. 'I know that it isn't enough, but we don't have very much ourselves. Jonas can't work long hours any more, nor can I. I clean for the butcher two hours a week and sometimes he gives me a little meat or bones on top of a small wage.'

'Can I ask you what you know of my family, Mrs Newby?'

The little woman shook her head. 'I'm not sure it's my place to tell you, but you'll find out soon enough that your mother's struggling to feed them. I'm not sure that she eats anything much herself since Maud died.'

'Died! The boys were upset when I asked them about Maud, but they didn't say that she had died,' she exclaimed in shock.

Sarah noticed the woman look at her husband briefly and then back at the table very quickly.

'I don't know that it's my place to say.' She spoke quietly.

'I have to know. Please tell me, it's affecting Thomas and, I think, Sam. Was it… cholera or typhoid?'

The little woman blinked rapidly and screwed her face up into a grotesque mask of wrinkled pain and, when her body began to shake, Sarah became alarmed.

'Oh!' she said out loud, looking back at Mr Newby.

'She's alright,' he said. 'It's the trauma of remembering.'

Now Sarah had a fearful feeling in her stomach. 'She was sick, wasn't she?'

'No, dear,' Mrs Newby sounded more like herself. 'She wasn't sick. Please sit down.'

She indicated the other chair at the table, which Sarah pulled out and sat on, waiting for some awful thing to be revealed.

Mrs Newby sighed.

'They hadn't been here long,' she said. 'Let's see. Amelia was about nine, that would mean Sam was about seven and Thomas five, and little Maud was about two. Just walking, it said at the inquest. We didn't know about you,' she said, looking at Sarah.

'Your mother had taken to working evenings and left the children to fend for themselves. She'd put them to bed before she went. In the night, Maud had got herself out of the bed while the others slept and had tripped and fallen into the fire, face first.'

Sarah took a sharp intake of breath. She had not envisaged anything like this, and the shock was visible in her eyes.

Mrs Newby continued but didn't look at her. 'I'm sorry, dear, but you did ask. Her screams woke the other children, who pulled her out of the fire, but she was covered in flames… her hair and her clothes. Sam, thinking to put the flames out, dropped her headfirst into a bucket of water. They left her like that until your mother came home and found her next morning.'

Sarah sat with her mouth and eyes wide open in shock. When at last she found her voice, it had no strength, but arrived in a whisper.

'She could have been burnt to death, or was she drowned?'

'Well,' Mrs Newby nodded, 'at the inquest, they decided it was misadventure and that was the end of it.'

'Misadventure? What does that mean?'

'It means,' Mr Newby said, 'that no one was to blame.'

'I see.'

Sarah suddenly felt as though she were floating. She couldn't feel the chair beneath her or the table in front of her.

'Jonas, get the rum. I think she's going to faint.' Mrs Newby's voice held a note of panic.

A small glass was put to Sarah's lips and a hot liquid reached her tongue. She coughed as it flooded her mouth and the colour came back to her face. The elderly couple gradually came back into focus.

Sarah wiped the tears from her eyes, saying, 'I'm so sorry, I've never done that before.'

'It was a shock to you, dear. I'm sorry that I told you.'

'No,' Sarah replied, swallowing the bile rising in her throat. 'I'm glad you told me. It'll help me understand what's wrong with my mother.'

'What your family need is money to live on. It's what we all need. Perhaps you can help them with that,' Mr Newby said, taking the used glass to a bowl sitting on a small table under the window.

'Yes, sir. I'll try and get a job tomorrow. Do you know of any jobs that I might do?'

Mr Newby walked to the door and opened it.

'If you ask up and down the street, I'm sure you'll find something.'

Taking her obvious cue to leave, Sarah walked to the door, thanking them.

Out on the landing, she could hear a man shouting and a woman crying. Otherwise, all the doors were shut and silent. Walking slowly back across the landing and into what was now her family home, Sarah smelt the fish cooking and remembered Aunt Jelly, who she'd left only that morning, and the peace of the little cottage. She almost cried.

~

It was getting dark. Gwen tipped water from their clean second bucket into a bowl and washed her face, before pulling her hair up, twisting it into a knot.

Sarah watched her as she secured it with a long-toothed tortoiseshell comb at the back, then checked her face in the mirror before pinching her cheeks to make them rosy.

'Where are you going, Mother?' she asked, alarmed at the colour of her mother's skin which, in the fading light from the window, looked yellow. 'Are you well enough to go to work?'

'If I don't work, then who will?' Gwen snapped.

'I'll get a job tomorrow, Mother. I'm sure of it.'

But she wasn't sure. And didn't feel like part of this family. She was uncomfortable in this room with its unfamiliar smells and furniture.

Gwen breathed out a long breath. 'Sure of it, are you? Well, we'll see.'

Picking up a small bag and hanging it from her shoulder, she walked towards the door. 'Give the boys the fish. I'll be back in the morning.'

Unsettled by what had happened to Maud in her mother's absence at night, Sarah asked, 'Where do you work, Mother? Just in case I need you.'

'You won't.'

Gwen pulled a black shawl around her shoulders, tying it at the front.

It suddenly occurred to Sarah that she didn't know any of the rules of living in one room with her family.

'Where shall I sleep, Mother?' she asked quickly as Gwen stepped through the door.

Her mother nodded towards the only bed. 'Top and tail with your brothers. They'll tell you.' The door shut behind her. No goodbye. No instructions.

Sam took a stub of candle from a wooden box on the windowsill and lit it. Like an old man, he held the candle over an old plate, letting the wax drip, softening the top of a wax mountain already stuck there. Lowering the candle, he pushed it securely onto the wax where he held it for a few seconds before placing the plate in the centre of the table. It gave off a feeble light.

Thomas pulled a chair across the room and, standing on it, reached up to take three bowls from the shelf in the alcove.

'I could have done that, Thomas,' Sarah said, feeling useless.

He shrugged.

It was obvious that the boys were used to looking after themselves, but it didn't make her feel any more at home.

'Put one bowl back, Thomas,' she instructed. 'I'm not hungry.' She had seen how little was left in the pan over the fire. Hardly enough for one.

Taking a small cup from the shelf, she filled it with water from the bucket.

That, she thought, *will have to do me until tomorrow.*

2.

In the early hours of the morning, Sarah was woken by the movement of the mattress on which she slept. At first, when she opened her eyes, she saw nothing out of place, until the mattress lifted again, just a little below her arm, accompanied by a groan and the sound of expelled air. Lowering her eyes, she saw that her mother was sitting on the floor with her arms below the mattress, pulling at Sarah's jacket that had been laid there on the direction of Sam.

'What are you doing, Mother?'

Gwen, startled, fell backwards. 'Go back to sleep,' she slurred.

But Sarah was already sitting up. 'That's *my* jacket, Mother, push it back.'

'I need it. Go back to sleep,' Gwen demanded, recovering her balance.

But Sarah had a grip on the material and pulled it from Gwen's hands.

'Leave it, Mother,' she said, with a determination in her voice that she had never used before to the woman she had always been afraid of.

Gwen raised her hand to strike her but lost her balance. Falling sideways, she lay unmoving on the floorboards.

Slipping from the bed, Sarah felt her mother's face and heart. She was breathing but smelt of drink.

Taking a pillow from the bed, she put it below her mother's head and, pulling the black shawl from Gwen's waist where it had been tied, she laid it over the prone body.

As she got up from her knees, she found herself looking into Sam's troubled eyes.

'It's alright, Sam,' she said, 'I'll look after her.'

He nodded and turned over, leaving Sarah wondering what had happened to her family while she'd been away. What had her brothers and Amy gone through in that time?

Woken next morning by the sound of movement in the room next to theirs, she heard the door closing and the sound of boots on the stairs. It made Sarah wonder how many people lived here and who they were.

Getting dressed and leaving the house, she walked to the nearest baker further up King Street where a large woman was filling the window with bread, her face and arms decorated with flour. The bread smelt good and Sarah's stomach was aching with hunger. The woman, having emptied her large wooden tray, noticed Sarah standing outside looking in, and raised her eyebrows before she turned to a second tray.

Sarah stepped through the door, removing the penny from her pocket.

The woman continued, emptying the second tray filled with pies onto the shop counter.

'Are you open?' Sarah asked.

The woman did not look at her but continued laying out the pies. 'Door's open,' she said.

'I need bread. I have a penny.' Sarah held it up. 'I know it's not enough. Could you let me have something?' Her face was hopeful.

The woman seemed to soften. 'S'alright, maid, half the street's starving. I'll cut you a third off a loaf for a penny.'

Sarah felt a huge gulf of relief and could have run around the counter and hugged the woman, but contented herself with watching her cut a piece from a large loaf with a small saw.

She handed it to Sarah, who took it with both hands, reverently, as though it were a precious bar of gold.

'Thank you,' she said tearfully.

The woman nodded and went back to arranging her counter.

Halfway back to the house, she saw Mrs Newby walking in front of her, struggling with a heavy bag, wood visibly sticking out of the top, and she hurried to catch her up.

'Good morning, Mrs Newby,' she said gently as she came abreast of her neighbour. 'Please, let me help with that bag.'

'Sarah! You're out early.'

'My brothers are hungry. I hoped to get something for my penny.'

'And did you?'

'I got bread, the baker cut me a piece off a big loaf.'

'Do you have anything to put on it?'

'I don't know.' Sarah felt deflated.

'Ah well, they will enjoy it as it is. How is your mother?' There was something in the tone of her voice that Sarah wasn't sure of.

'She's sleeping. She'll be better for eating some bread.'

The small woman nodded but did not comment further until they reached the front door of the lodging house.

'You know,' Mrs Newby said, stopping abruptly, 'if you get another penny, go to the greengrocer on the corner of Alice Street. He'll let you have some vegetables that are past their best for a penny. They're fine in a stew.'

'I will,' Sarah said, grateful for any information, and pushed the front door to the lodging house open.

Mrs Newby, Sarah noticed, struggled to climb the stairs, and when they reached the landing, the thin, wrinkled skin on her face was shiny and wet with the effort.

Handing over the bag of wood, Sarah asked, 'Would you like me to bring it in for you.'

'No!'

The reply was so forceful that Sarah almost took a step backwards.

'Sorry,' the little woman said, seeing the shock on Sarah's face. 'Mr Newby isn't up yet. We're not ready for visitors.'

As Sarah turned away, Mrs Newby said suddenly, 'Sarah, the butcher sometimes gives me bones or wood. He's a good man, he knows that we struggle. I would like to give you the wood. I have plenty.' She pushed the bag back at Sarah.

Stunned by the woman's generosity, Sarah mumbled a 'thank you,' taking the bag of wood held out towards her. 'Are you sure that you don't need it?'

'I'll keep the next bag. By then, I will have room to stack it in the corner. The weather is too warm now for a fire. I have the windows open.'

As Mrs Newby opened her door, they heard footsteps on the stairs coming down from the floor above. A woman, holding the hand of a child, descended slowly, followed by a man with a suitcase.

'Good morning, Mr and Mrs Salmon, are you leaving us?' Mrs Newby enquired, her door just ajar.

'I have a job up north, Mrs Newby. We're off to the station to catch the train.'

'Oh. I will miss you and little Carl, but glad that you are moving on. Good luck with the new job.'

As they carried on down the stairs to the front door, Mrs Newby entered her room and Sarah had a quick sight of Mr Newby's bulk still in bed before their door shut.

Today, Sarah noticed an unpleasant smell on the landing and made a face just as another woman came down from upstairs.

'It's the privies out in the yard,' she said as she passed. 'You should shut the landing window.'

She had continued speaking as she hurried on down the stairs, without even saying hello or who she was.

Sarah stood a moment on the landing, listening to the house that never seemed to be silent. Over her head, she could hear footsteps and children playing. A mother shouting, a man calling out for silence so that he could sleep. Someone coming in through the front door slammed it shut with some force, and the sound of heavy footsteps approached upwards on the treads.

Sarah hurried to her room. She didn't want to meet anyone else, not yet.

Her mother was on the bed, sleeping, covered with the blanket, and the boys were out.

She wondered vaguely where they went during the day.

Taking off her jacket, she hung it on the back of the door. Pulling some of the wood from the bag, she was still wondering at her neighbour's generosity as she lay some of it on the dying embers of their fire.

Looking around the room for the first time, she noticed how poor it was. The curtains, hanging in shreds, were yellow with age. The window, brown with dirt, filtered the light from outside, the lower windowpane was cracked, the paintwork on the walls peeling. Black mould hung around the ceiling like a decoration. The only furniture in the room was a double bed pushed against one wall, a faded and torn armchair, a table with four chairs of different heights and a small cupboard with one drawer, chipped and scratched. None of it did she recognise. What had happened to the furniture that she had grown up with? Where were all their things?

Taking the clean bucket from under the table, where it seems it was stored, she went down the back steps to the yard in which the two privies stood with the doors open. There was a washing line strung across the yard that Sarah ducked under, wondering if anyone had been beheaded on their way to the privy on a dark night.

A pump in a corner of the yard, green with algae, dripped precious water into a muddy puddle.

She placed the bottom of her bucket in the brown water and pumped the black iron handle, only filling her bucket halfway, realising that any more would be too heavy to carry.

After peering into the two foul-smelling privy cubicles, she decided to carry on using the china pot under the bed, as the concrete floor and wooden seats, of both privies, were thickly covered in excrement. The air from the closets was thick upon her tongue as flies swarmed about the floor and seats.

Retching as she stepped away from the open doors, she waved

the flies away from her head. Holding her nose with her spare hand, she turned away and jumped at the sight of a woman, her hair in rags, standing right behind her.

'Sorry, did I scare you?' she smiled.

'Yes, but not as much as that.' Sarah nodded towards the privy.

'I know,' the woman said. 'It's disgusting. But no one is going to clean it unless we do. The landlord won't pay someone.'

'When you say *we do,*' Sarah said, looking worried, 'who do you mean?'

'Why, the women who live in the house, of course. It's the men who make this mess. They don't even notice.'

'Oh, the smell!' Sarah gasped, moving further away. The young woman followed.

'I'm Jane,' she offered, smiling. 'Number 15.'

'Sarah, number 5.'

'Ah, you must be related to Sam and Thomas.'

'I'm their sister.'

'Ah!'

The young woman nodded, staring at Sarah, who now recognised her as the woman shouting over the banister at her brothers the day that she'd arrived. Sarah, not knowing what else to say, stared back in silence.

The woman seemed to make up her mind about something and frowned before saying, 'What will you do when your mother has the baby?'

The words struck Sarah like a physical blow. She felt her jaw drop and knew that her eyes had widened in shock.

'Baby? No, there's no baby.' Sarah shook her head.

The woman nodded again, weighing Sarah up, her tongue visibly moving behind her upper teeth.

'If you say so,' she said eventually. 'She's your mother.'

Jane walked to the pump with her bucket, while Sarah, who stood unable to speak, watched her. How could her mother be having a baby? Her father had died more than three years ago.

Back in their room, Gwen was still snoring. The air smelt of alcohol. Putting on her jacket, Sarah went back into the street to look for work.

Standing on the doorstep, looking up and down the street, she realised that King Street was a mecca of its own making, with almost every property having a shop on the ground floor. The road was busy with traffic as people skilfully crossed between carts and carriages. The pavement an eruption of movement, with all classes of people: housewives, workers, sailors, all denoted by their dress. After the stillness of their room, she felt overwhelmed by the movement and the noise. Taking a deep breath, she stepped out, thinking that she would look in the shop windows for any sign advertising the need for staff.

Walking slowly along the street, she looked hard at each window. An advert in the window of a greengrocer's only ten doors away drew her in.

The grocer was outside the shop, placing goods into a woman's basket from his display of colourful fruit and vegetables arranged on a table. He seemed jolly, and they were both laughing.

After the woman had paid and moved off, Sarah caught his eye as he turned to go back into the shop

'Yez, ma-dear, what can I get you?' He smiled.

'I'd like to apply for the job advertised in your window.' She swallowed as the nerves in her stomach fluttered.

'Oh! I'm sorry, maid, you just won't do.'

'Why?' Sarah asked, stunned by the suddenness of his decision.

'Because I want a boy or a man. Someone with muscles in their arms as big as you.' He smiled pleasantly.

'I'm stronger than I look,' Sarah offered in disappointment.

He shook his head, his face serious. 'I need a man to lift sacks of potatoes and other vegetables that weigh more than you do. Sorry, that's how it is. Yes, madam.' He turned away to another customer and Sarah, red-faced and embarrassed, walked further on up the street. Passing the undertaker's, with its brass plaque sitting in the front window on a polished piece of wood, Sarah shuddered and wondered if this was where her sister's little body had been brought.

23

At that same moment, a black horse, pulling a cart with a coffin in the back, appeared in the gap between the funeral parlour and the watchmaker's next door. Driven from the yard at the back of the undertaker's, it turned out onto King Street. And again, Sarah wondered if her sister had been placed on that cart.

Trying to shake the picture from her mind, she walked on until she came to a crowd gathered next to the railway arches. A woman, wearing a top hat, stood in the street beside her husband as he played a gay tune, winding the handle of a musical box.

A monkey sitting on his shoulder held out a cup for money as their daughter, dressed exactly like her mother, looked on.

A happy crowd stood around them listening, but when the monkey on its lead jumped down from the man's shoulder with the cup and hopped along the ground in front of them, the people stepped back, afraid.

The man's daughter ran and lifted the monkey, dressed like a soldier, up into her arms and smiling, said to the people in a strong foreign accent, 'Say hello to Jacko, he loves people.'

But as Jacko pulled back his lip and bared his needle teeth, it was clear that the people did not love Jacko, as they fearfully moved away from him.

A small boy, frightened to go near it with the coin his mother had given him, threw it at the monkey, who deftly caught it in the cup much to the delight of the crowd, who then fished in their pockets and purses and threw coins for the monkey to catch.

Noticing a portly woman standing outside the King's Head, holding glasses in her hands while watching the performance, Sarah approached her, smiling.

'Excuse me. I wonder if you would have any work that I might do?'

The woman, whose face had been soft, now turned towards Sarah, a hard expression changing her features. The grey eyes that explored Sarah were like pinpoints of steel.

'What's your name?' she asked sharply.

'Sarah Warrington.'

'How old are you?'

Sarah lied. 'Sixteen,' she said quickly, although she thought that she could be sixteen, as she didn't know in which year she was born. She was going by how many siblings were born before her, or after her, and although Aunt Jelly thought that she was fifteen, she could be sixteen.

'Sixteen!' the woman repeated. Taking in a deep breath, she twisted her lips into a pout and screwed her eyes up for a better look at Sarah. 'What work have you done before?'

'I haven't worked before,' Sarah replied, not realising that she would be asked questions like that. She felt unprepared.

'Do you think that you could wash glasses without dropping any? If you did, it would come out of your wages.'

'I can wash glasses.' Sarah nodded.

'Can you cook?'

'If you show me how,' she said enthusiastically.

The woman's attitude changed from interested to furious in a breath. 'I don't have time to teach you to cook. Damn it,' she shouted, her face reddening.

Sarah was shocked. She hadn't heard a woman swear before, and for it to be aimed at her because she was answering the woman's question, took her aback. She wouldn't take a job with this woman anyway, not now, not if it was the last job in the world. The woman had managed to make her feel small, insignificant, in front of people walking past.

She turned away, ready to walk on down the street looking for work.

'Where are you going?' The voice was sharp.

'To look for work,' Sarah replied, looking back at the woman, still standing with the glasses in her hand.

'I just offered you a job. Don't you want it? Eight to eight, start now. I'll trial you for today. If you don't work out, you'll be paid for the hours that you worked.'

Sarah stood with her mouth open, unable to understand that she had just been offered work.

25

'Well, do you want it or not? I'm not standing here all day looking at you.'

Sarah recovered quickly. 'Yes, thank you, I do. I do want the job.'

Following the woman through the doors with their beautiful coloured glass window squares closing behind her, Sarah entered her first public house. Inside, the dark room smelt strongly of beer, sweat and pipe smoke. A few men sat at tables and some at the bar. It was an old pub, with dark beams and upright wooden bench seats that she noticed had been covered in old carpet for a bit of comfort.

The woman made her way behind the bar with Sarah following, feeling interested, yet completely lost and out of place in this environment.

They entered a large square room behind the bar with a brick floor and, at its centre, an open trapdoor with a ladder leading down to a cellar. Heavy wooden barrels lined the walls of this room, some upright, others on their sides. The floor was wet, and the smell of beer was strong. The woman led the way through another door and into a room with two deep stone sinks and a table at its centre holding many dirty glasses and tankards.

'Phil, where are you?' the woman shouted. '*Philly?*'

'I'm here, Mother.'

A pretty girl with dark hair, a little older than Sarah, entered, straightening her skirt. 'I just needed the privy, for goodness' sake...'

She stopped talking, seeing Sarah. Eyebrows raised, she looked at the woman who she had addressed as Mother.

'This is Sarah, she's on trial. We'll see if she's suitable to give you a hand. We're going to be busy and it won't hurt for you to have help. Show her what she's to do.'

Placing the dirty glasses on the table, the woman left without another look at Sarah, who was glad that she had departed.

The young woman came forward. 'I'm Phillis. You can call me Phil or Philly, I answer to either.' She smiled pleasantly.

Sarah just nodded, looking around the room and wondering what there was for her to do.

'I'm called the pot washer.' Phillis expressed the title with a sweep of her hand over the dirty glasses and tankards waiting on the table. 'I wash the glasses and tankards here in *this sink*.' She pointed theatrically to one of the obvious and unmissable giants in the room. 'We have this contraption under the sink that heats the water accessed at this tap.' She indicated a tap that came out of a pipe on the wall, inches above the sink. 'Don't touch the fire box contraption,' she warned, pointing to a metal cylinder under the sink where flames could be seen through a little window. 'If it goes out, there will be an almighty discussion on what happened, and only James, my brother, can get it going again.'

Sarah nodded; there was no way that she was going to touch the fire box, as Philly called it. In fact, she was already afraid of it.

Phillis continued. 'You turn the tap on and let the hot water into the sink before you cool it down with the cold water from the bucket.'

Sarah concentrated as Phillis pulled forward two small wooden boxes that were placed in easy reach next to the sink. They held what looked like white wax flakes and small pieces of glass.

'Put a handful of these crystals in the water, and a little of this shredded soap.' Phillis demonstrated, by taking a little from each box and dropping the crystals and flakes into the hot water. 'Swill the glasses and the tankards around in the water,' she continued, 'then put them to drain on the rack,' she indicated a wooden box with bars, 'while you wash the second lot.'

Sarah nodded again, wishing the girl would speak slower.

'Then dry the first and put them on this tray, and Mother or Father will take them to the bar. We have to make sure that there are always some clean glasses on the table.'

'I can do that,' Sarah assured her.

'Good,' Phillis smiled. 'Now the other part of the job, for which I will be very grateful of help, is upstairs. Our first floor is for storage and for hire, meetings, parties and the like, the second floor is where we live and the third floor is let by the room, mostly one-night lodgers, like travelling tradesmen. Our job is to clean, change the beds, do the washing and remake the beds, so Mother can always show a room ready for occupation.'

Sarah was happy. She could do all that and could see that she was going to earn her money, whatever that was, and now realised that she had forgotten to ask.

3.

The work was constant, with both Phillis and Sarah washing glasses, tankards and plates in between changing the beds and washing the linen until, halfway through the morning, the atmosphere changed, with what Sarah at first thought to be thunder but which turned out to be a delivery of beer barrels arriving on the back of a cart pulled by heavy horses.

Asked to take a tray of glasses to the bar, she saw the horses, standing patiently in the road, through the open doors. The draymen with black leather shoulder capes carried the barrels on their shoulders, or the backs of their necks, accompanied by a young man in a striped shirt, sleeves rolled up, hefting the barrels from the cart. The barrels were carried to a trapdoor in the pavement, down which they were rolled, the sound carrying through the bar like thunder.

At lunchtime, she was almost faint from hunger when Phillis told her that she had a ten-minute break.

'Have you any food with you?' she asked. 'You can eat it now.'

'I don't,' Sarah replied. 'I didn't know that I would be starting a job today.'

The young woman cut her two slices of bread. Then walking to the other side of the kitchen, pulled a long tin from a shelf. Back at the table, she scraped the contents of the tray with a spoon, placing the beige mass into a colourful dish.

'Here,' she said, 'put this dripping on the bread and take the weight off your feet for ten minutes.'

'Thank you,' Sarah said, and almost fell into the chair at the table, her back and legs aching. She took the bread thankfully and spread the dripping on the slices. Her hunger made it difficult not to eat it as her mother would have said, "like a pig", stuffing it into her mouth, taking great gulps of desperate air. Somehow, she restrained herself, almost slipping into a dream world of flavour as she ate the beef dripping with her eyes momentarily shut. When she opened her eyes again, Phillis was looking at her.

'Hungry?' she asked.

'I missed breakfast. I didn't expect to get a job right away.'

Phillis just nodded. Although whether or not she believed her, Sarah couldn't tell.

Ten minutes later, the young man in shirtsleeves entered from the cellar room, where the delivery of barrels had been stacked.

Throwing a cloth, with which he had been cleaning his hands, onto the table, he grabbed the bread and, cutting a slice, spread it liberally with dripping. Turning his head, his bread halfway to his mouth, he saw Sarah staring at him and blushed.

'This is Sarah,' Phillis told him. 'She's on trial for today but might be joining us if she works out.'

When he didn't speak, Phillis looked at Sarah.

'*This,* Sarah, is my brother, James, and he will at some point speak to you when he gets over the shock.'

Sarah mumbled, 'Hello, James.' She noticed that he was a lot taller than his sister and whereas she had a small round face, he had angular features and grey eyes like his mother. To relieve him of his obvious embarrassment, Sarah stood and turned back to her job at the sink.

At eight o'clock, the landlady came into the room and handed Sarah a small brown packet. 'Your wage,' she said, not so sharply as she had spoken to Sarah in the morning. 'I will offer you the job on one condition, mistress. That you do not belong to a criminal family. That you are honest with me at all times and that you do not steal from me. If you can assure me that all is well, then I will employ you.'

Sarah agreed that she was not a criminal, nor knew of any criminals.

'Then I will see you tomorrow. Eight until eight. You won't work Sunday or Monday.' Turning to her daughter, she asked, 'You happy with that, Phil?'

'Yes, Mother. Sarah's worked hard and kept up the pace.' She smiled at Sarah. When her mother had gone, she said, 'It's been really lovely having another girl in the room. I seem surrounded by men, except Mother, of course, but she has to stay strict. She has all these men to deal with.'

'Men?' Sarah raised her eyebrows.

'Yes. Father, James, the victuallers, the deliveries, all men, and most of those drinking in the bar during the day. Men!'

She raised her eyes to the beamed ceiling, but Sarah didn't really understand what she meant.

'It's Mother they're afraid off,' Phillis continued. 'It's she that keeps the peace. We don't want to lose our licence.'

Sarah nodded. She didn't know what a licence was but it must be important. 'I have to go,' Sarah said quickly. 'I'll see you in the morning, Phillis.'

Outside, the street was still busy. The shops still open. There was an unpleasant odour on the air that seemed more polluted than it was in the morning. The stench was aggravated by a passing cart carrying tripe. Piled too high and not covered securely, some of its stinking load slipped into the road. And a cart filled with bones, collected from the local butcher's, moving in the opposite direction, towards the tannery, under a halo of flies, added to the stench.

Passing the Methodist church as she walked home along King Street, Sarah was surprised to see candlelight flickering through the windows upstairs and heard the sound of builders working inside. Reading a poster stuck on the door that informed the masses that the rooms upstairs were being turned into four classrooms, Sarah wondered for the first time why her brothers were not in school. Or should they have been, and their mother didn't know that they weren't going.

31

As she stood outside the imposing building, she decided to enquire within about lessons for her brothers. As the door was ajar, she stepped tentatively inside, just as the minister was approaching the door holding a candle high in front of him.

'Hello, can I help you?' he acknowledged her, frowning.

For a moment, she couldn't get her thoughts together, but as he continued to look at her with eyebrows raised in expectation of a reply, she asked, 'I wonder, when you open the classrooms, sir, would you have room for two small boys?'

He frowned, nodding his head as though weighing up something that was heavy on his mind. Eventually, he said, 'Are you Methodist?'

'I don't know,' she answered truthfully. They had gone to church when her father was alive, but she didn't know if she was a Methodist.

He nodded again, looking at her with a serious face that gave none of his thoughts away. He made a clicking sound with his tongue before asking, 'Are your brothers christened?'

Sarah felt that she was losing the battle, as again she had to say that she didn't know.

'Well!' he exclaimed. 'Go back and ask your parents these questions then get them to come and see me.'

'There's only our mother, sir and she isn't well. It might be me that brings them to see you.'

'Find out what you can,' he said, a little softer now. 'If they are Methodist, of course we will find room for them. If not, places may be limited, but I will do what I can.'

Before reaching home, Sarah opened the brown wage packet as she walked, and was delighted to find a shilling. Twelve pennies. The most money she had seen. Ducking into the grocer's, she bought bread, and a small amount of sugar, weighed out and put into a bag. Noticing a pile of metal jugs in one corner of the shop, she bought a small half pint jug to carry milk in the morning. Not knowing what else to buy, she returned home, her feet aching.

When she reached the landing, the smell was even worse than when she went out, and the landing window, she noticed, had been shut. Someone had to do something about the smell from the yard, although she had no idea who that would be. She would ask the next person that she met about who emptied the privies. How were they supposed to live like this?

Gwen was standing in front of a slice of mottled mirror glass, propped up on the shelf, combing her hair and pulling it up into a roll at the back of her head, anchoring her hair with her tortoiseshell combs.

The boys were on the floor playing with sticks, like she had with five stones when little. Throwing the sticks up and trying to catch them on the backs of their hands, they were laughing.

'Where have you been?' Gwen asked sharply, not taking her eyes from the mirror.

'I've got a job, Mother. I've been working. Washing glasses and bedding in a public house.'

'Have they paid you?'

'Yes, a shilling,' she replied lightly, feeling proud of herself.

'Give it to me. I'll look after it.'

Reluctantly, Sarah handed the pay packet to her mother and stood back while she counted it.

'You said a shilling. Where's the rest of it?'

'I bought food, Mother.'

Gwen looked annoyed. 'Next time, you hand it over to me without opening it. I'm the head of this house and it is I,' she dropped the money into a bowl on the shelf, 'who should be in charge of any money coming in here.'

Disappointed, Sarah had thought that she would receive some praise.

'Yes, Mother,' she said, pulling the food from the bag and putting it on the table, feeling as she had when small, that nothing she did was good enough.

Cutting the bread into slices, she sprinkled each slice with a little sugar and gave one to each of her brothers. They ate the food so quickly that she had to give them another, telling them that they could have more in the morning for their breakfast.

Her mother declined the bread and by ten thirty had gone out.

Sarah poured warm water into a bowl and watched as her brothers washed for bed and put on their nightgowns.

'Come and sit with me,' she invited, as she sat in the armchair beside the fire.

They sat on her lap without hesitation, cuddling into her body.

'Sam,' she said, sweeping his hair gently back from his forehead, 'do you go to school?'

'No,' came the sleepy reply.

'Would you and Thomas like to go to school?' She looked from one face to the other.

'What for?' Sam asked, frowning.

'What for?' Thomas copied, sleepily.

'So that you could read and write.'

'What for?' Sam asked again.

Thomas looked from her face to his brother's. 'What for?' he copied.

'You can get a job when you're grown up. You could earn good money and pay for food and a place of your own to live in.'

'But we get food now,' Samuel said, looking into her face, not understanding the gravity of stealing.

'Sam. Thomas.' She cuddled them to her. 'You mustn't steal from shopkeepers. One day, you will be caught and it will be very serious.'

'But they have lots,' Sam said. 'They don't miss it. It's a game. Mother said it's a game.'

'But if I arranged it and I came with you,' Sarah asked gently, 'would you go to school?'

Sam shrugged his shoulders and Thomas copied, shrugging his.

'Bed,' she said, quietly kissing both heads. 'Let's sleep on it and see what we think in the morning.'

They scampered across the room, throwing themselves onto the bed, giggling. Kissing them both, she tucked them in, before emptying the washing water into the dirty bucket.

Sitting in the chair, she wondered if this was how she was to spend her evenings, sitting alone in the poor light from the nub of what was left of a candle, with no one to talk to. Although tonight she was so tired that she laid on the bed not long after the boys and fell asleep, forgetting to blow out the candle.

It was the sound of a dull thump out on the landing that pulled her from her sleep in the early hours. Their room was completely dark. The candle spent. She stared at the door, on the other side of which someone was shuffling and cursing out on the landing, and she distinctly heard the sound of wood scraping wood.

Leaving the bed and crossing the room, she opened the door a crack and saw three men coming out of Mr and Mrs Newby's room. Two men were trying to manoeuvre a large coffin through the door, while the other held a candle to the dark landing. But the coffin had become stuck, and they were grunting and groaning with the weight and the effort of releasing it.

It was as though a bucket of cold water had been tipped over Sarah, as the fear of death swept through her from head to toe. Who had died? But that was soon answered as she continued to watch. When they were through the doorway, the men laid the box down on the landing floor before returning back into the room.

The third man sat on the coffin, waiting. It was only moments before the two men returned with another smaller coffin. Sarah caught her breath and shut the door quietly. Perhaps the smell on the landing wasn't entirely from the problem in the yard. Her eyes filled with tears as she hurried back to bed and, covering herself with the blanket, shivered. What had they died from? Was it catching? Even worse, what was she going to tell her brothers?

When she started to sob uncontrollably, she got out of bed and sat in the chair, pulling it up to the fire for the rest of the night, not wanting to wake the boys too soon.

What was left of the night was spent remembering her conversation with Mrs Newby and her saying that it was too hot for a fire. Of her insisting that Sarah had the bag of wood, and the smell on the landing.

Sam and Thomas liked Mrs Newby, and she was the first kind person, in fact, the only person, that had spoken to her kindly since she'd come back to Plymouth.

Their mother, who had crept in during the early hours, hadn't even noticed that Sarah wasn't in the bed as she'd undressed, and now lay in her chemise snoring.

As it got light, Sarah washed and dressed, hearing the voice of the milkman calling out loud and clear, '*Milk, Fresh Milk,*' as his cart rolled slowly over the cobbles, pulled by a large carthorse.

Taking a coin from the bowl on the shelf and picking up the jug, she hurried down to the street, joining the morning queue of women all holding jugs of various sizes. Eventually at the front, she handed up the jug. Dipping his measuring jug into the churn, he turned and filled her jug to the brim with milk. Paying him, she hurried back to their room.

Breakfast was already on the table when the boys woke up, and as they sat sleepily over their bowls of bread soaked in warm milk, Sarah waited for the right moment to tell them about the death of their friends, Mr and Mrs Newby.

When their bowls were empty, she could put it off no longer.

'I have something that I have to tell you.' She looked from one face to the other and saw how worried they looked. 'No, you're not in trouble,' she assured them, 'but I have some sad news.'

They waited. Two small, pale faces staring at her in silence.

'It's Mr and Mrs Newby. I'm afraid that they died in the night.'

Apart from Thomas blinking and looking at Sam, there was no reaction.

'Can we go now?' Sam asked.

Thrown by their lack of reaction to the news, she could only nod that they could.

Leaving her mother to sleep, she washed and walked to the King's Head to help them get ready for the day. She knew that she was early and was glad to have something to do and to be away from the family room.

The landlord, as proclaimed above the front door, was Mr Claude Augustus Gallaway, and he was busy behind the bar preparing for the day ahead as she entered. A short muscular man with a large stomach and bloated cheeks, he wore a stained cap of dubious colour that fitted tightly to his head. Excess orange hair stood out in tufts above his ears. Giving her a curt nod, he turned away, wiping down the shelves behind the bar with a filthy rag.

~

After six weeks, the atmosphere in the King's Head was beginning to feel familiar, stable, as Sarah took up her position at the sink and threw herself into her work. At lunchtime, she sat at the table and ate the food that she had bought at the baker's, a small pie. She felt more at home in the room at the back of the King's Head than in their room with her mother. It had become her escape, and the money earned was feeding the family. She still bought food on the way home with her wage, much to the chagrin of her mother, which, unless Gwen became violent, Sarah was able to ignore.

James and Phillis joined her at the table, where they liked to discuss the lives of their customers, which filled the lunchtime break with laughter. But today Phillis turned her bright eyes on Sarah.

'Tell us about yourself, Sarah. We don't know anything about you.'

'I don't think that there's anything to know,' she said, not liking the attention being placed on her.

'Tell us about your parents,' Phillis continued joyfully, not noticing that Sarah was uncomfortable.

'There isn't much to tell. My father died and my mother sent me to live with an aunt in Kingsand for a few years.'

Phillis looked shocked. 'So far away,' she exclaimed.

'Not really, Philly, it's only just into Cornwall by ferry.'

'You went on the ferry? That was very brave of you.'

Sarah ignored the notion of being brave and just nodded,

37

hoping that they could talk about something else, but Phillis was just getting started. James looked on, watching Sarah intently.

'Tell me,' Phillis said, 'do you have brothers and sisters?'

Nodding without any joy in her face, Sarah said flatly, 'I'm one of twelve. I don't know the older ones, but I live with my mother and my two younger brothers.'

'Twelve!' Phillis threw her hands up. 'How lucky you are. There's only the two of us, and we have so much work to do.'

Sarah nodded, understanding that these two people, whom she was becoming fond of, could have done with more siblings. In fact, it was strange to only have two children in a family. She could have turned the tables. Could have asked them why there were no other children and directed the questioning away from herself, if she hadn't suddenly felt very tired.

As Phillis opened her mouth to ask another question, Sarah stood up, hoping to finish their unwanted inspection of her life.

'I'll get back to work now,' she said quietly, moving away from the table. She didn't look at Phillis, but did notice a strange look being given her by James.

Surprised at her own reaction, she stood at the sink feeling that her safe and happy place had suddenly dissolved. She didn't want them to know anything about her. Didn't want home and work to mix, for then there would be no escape.

Phillis came up beside her and put an arm around her waist.

'I'm sorry. I didn't mean to pry. I just didn't imagine that it would upset you. Will you forgive me?'

Sarah sighed, and pushing her hands deeper into the water found herself holding back the tears. There was nothing that she could say, so nodded that all was well.

4.

During the following week, Sarah became more aware of James. He seemed often to be looking in her direction and even had the bread cut for their lunch before Phillis could do it. She began to feel a fondness towards him and even dreamed, in the night, that one day he would take her out. Just the two of them. The thought filled her with warmth. She had a secret that she didn't want even James to know and fell asleep dreaming of a brighter future.

At the end of the week, Sarah was putting her jacket on when Phillis approached, smiling.

'Sarah,' she said rather coyly, 'James and I have Sunday afternoons off and we often walk if the weather is good. Would you like to walk with us?'

'I would love to.' Sarah's quick response surprised even her.

'Meet us at Stonehouse Bridge. We will take the path alongside Richmond Walk and enjoy looking at the boats.'

Stepping into the street, with a heart lighter than it had been in a long time, she looked forward to the walk, something that she hadn't done before.

The street was still busy, especially around the railway arches where many of the street carts that were stationed around Plymouth during the day positioned themselves in the evenings to continue their trade.

The sound of music from the Italian family's hurdy-gurdy floated over all other sounds as Mr Pratt turned the handle, drawing a small crowd to watch the miniature manikin band playing their instruments within the black box. People tapped their feet to the tune, swayed arm in arm and smiled.

Avoiding the small children that jigged and jumped to the tune, she bought hot chipped potatoes, and although tempted by the ice cream, and knowing that her brothers would love it, she bought smoked herrings instead.

On her return home, the house was not silent. A child was screaming in temper and a woman was shouting. A man was yelling for silence and there were heavy footsteps on the floorboards above. As she reached the top of the stairs, she became aware of loud, argumentative voices coming from the room that had been that of Mr and Mrs Newby. Someone had already moved in and she wondered what they would be like, who they were.

At that moment, Jane came up the stairs behind her. 'Irish,' she said, tipping her head towards the door.

Sarah nodded acknowledgement.

'Come to dig up the road in Union Street,' Jane continued.

'Oh!'

Wondering how Jane got her information so quickly, she asked, 'Why will they be digging up the cobbles in Union Street?'

'Didn't you know! They're going to lay tramlines all the way from Derry's Clock to Stonehouse Bridge. The tramlines are going to run right along Union Street. I can't wait to have a ride on a tram.'

Jane's eyes were bright with excitement as she took the stairs up to her room in the garret, above the next landing.

In the early hours, Sarah was woken by the new neighbours shouting and arguing drunkenly on the landing outside her door. Unable to go back to sleep for the noise, she got out of bed and opened the door a crack to see what was happening.

Four men, their Irish brogue so thick that she couldn't understand them, seemed to be shouting angrily at each other. A thin, older man with sharp features leant against the door of their room, quietly singing, while the others yelled angrily at each other. One of the men suddenly hit the man standing next to him on the chin, spilling his beer over the floor. The man staggered backwards, blaspheming as he tried to balance the beer in his glass before he swung his fist into the first man's face. The small man leaning against the Newbys' door still sang, oblivious, until a fist caught him on the nose. Standing unsteadily, he joined the fight. The noise on the landing increased to such an extent that the residents were waking up.

As Sarah watched, mesmerised, a man in a nightshirt came down from upstairs, shouting at them to 'Go inside and be quiet, I 'aze to get up early.'

They pulled him into the fight just as the door of the room next to hers opened and the dockers lodging there joined in.

She shut the door quickly just before a body slammed into it, waking the boys.

Dragging a chair from the table, she rammed it under the doorknob to hold the door shut.

Shaking in fear as the noise outside escalated, Sarah looked across the room. Seeing that Sam and Thomas were sitting at the top of the bed, their eyes wide with fright, she tried to reassure them.

'It's alright,' she said, climbing onto the bed. She held them close until they heard a police whistle and heavy footsteps on the stairs. The fight continued with more force until the sound of scuffling boots, going down the stairs, accompanied by shouts of abuse and the slamming of the front door, finished it.

Peace enveloped the dark landing after they had gone and Sarah tip-toed across the room and removed the chair from under the door knob, knowing that the next battle would be with her drunken mother if she couldn't get in when she got home.

~

Sunday broke fair, although there was a strong wind blowing off Plymouth Sound that explored the streets with a vengeance. But by the afternoon the wind had died down and the sun glowed in a blue sky.

King Street became a different place, calmer, with all the shops shut and people arm in arm, promenading in their Sunday best, most having been to church.

No longer feeling the excitement that she'd felt when first asked to walk with Phillis and James, Sarah walked slowly towards Stonehouse Bridge. She had mixed feelings. Nervous about walking with the Gallaways, who had seen more life than she. What would they talk about? Would she have anything to contribute to the conversation? What did she know about life?

She was about to change her mind about the walk and turn around, when she saw Phillis waving to her from the bridge in the distance.

On reaching Phillis and James, she said, 'Sorry, am I late?' and smiled to cover the fact that she was about to run away.

'No, not at all. Come on, let's go down to the footpath and walk. We've been watching the boats coming under the bridge, haven't we, James?'

He nodded, hardly having eye contact before leading the way down to the grass bank and footpath below.

The atmosphere below the bridge was entirely different, warmer, quieter, as they walked on the grass bank next to the water.

The creek was full of boats, some moving but most moored with their sails furled. The air here was still, sheltered as they were below the bank. Sarah could hear birds singing, not the gulls, but birds.

A swan made its way slowly, almost regally, Sarah thought, towards the bank. But gasping fearfully, Phillis backed away.

'Don't let it come up on the bank, James,' she shouted, her body rigid.

He also looked fearfully at the large bird, which changed its mind and glided away as gracefully as a ballet dancer.

Sarah found herself walking between James and Phillis, the latter keeping up a rapid dialogue of all that she knew about the creek and the boats.

'Two years ago,' she said, eyes sparkling with excitement, 'James and I watched the regatta off the Hoe. I can't tell you how wonderful it was. People were cheering and waving, but we couldn't understand where the finishing line was, could we, James?'

When he didn't answer, Sarah asked, 'Would you like to sail on a boat, Philly?'

'I'm afraid of the water.' Her reply was sad. 'I fear that I will never be able to sit on the deck and watch the land pass by.' She sighed, then said more cheerfully, 'But I am happy to watch from a distance.'

'And what about you, James?' Sarah asked, feeling brave now that she had started. 'Will you stay working for your father for the rest of your life?'

'When you put it like that,' he turned his face away from the creek and looked at her for the first time, 'it sounds very dull. But yes. I will work for my father until I marry. And may even then work for him.'

There seemed very little joy in his voice and she wondered how many men stayed in a family business, even if their heart wasn't in it. It made her think about loyalty. Should she be more loyal to her mother? Did it apply to her? Wasn't she already doing her best to support her family?

She was deep in thought when she felt the back of James' hand brush hers. A shock of electricity ran unexpectedly through her body. Her breathing came faster as her heart pounded. She turned her head to look at him, but he was innocently looking straight ahead, his cheeks a deep pink, a small smile on his lips.

That night, she thought fondly about James. She had at times thought that he was watching her and now knew that it was because he liked her. She almost giggled out loud at the realisation that she had a real secret. James felt a fondness for her and she felt dizzy with happiness.

James continued in small ways to show that he felt something for her. Small things, like getting her a drink; setting her a place at the table at lunchtime. He openly stared at her and smiled, catching her eye whenever he passed through the room.

She almost ran to the King's Head on the days that she worked. All that she could think about was James. The secret love that was blossoming in her heart gave her a view of life that she could not have imagined before. She felt light. Nothing bad could take away the excitement, held so closely to her, her secret love.

5.

Heavy footsteps on the stairs came straight to Sarah's door. Two sharp knocks and, before she could walk to it, a police constable opened the door and walked in, pushing her brothers before him.

'These live 'ere, I believe,' he said stiffly.

Sarah's mouth became dry, and her heart pounded in her chest. 'What have they done?' she asked the constable, falling to her knees as the boys ran to her for safety. They clung to her, crying into her hair, their frail bodies protected in her arms, shook with fear.

Sam, who had one arm around her neck and the other around Thomas, was pressing his small body into hers. She could feel every bone in his body, every muscle in his tiny frame shaking, as he gulped in terror.

'We wanted to get you something nice,' he sobbed.

Sarah looked up at the policeman standing by the door, a question in her eyes.

'They were caught stealing oranges from the greengrocer. They often steal from him, but this time as they ran, his lad managed to catch them.'

Sarah shook her head.

'They still had the oranges on them when caught,' he continued. 'As they're local, I brought them here to let you know before I take them to the station. They'll be bound over until tomorrow when they will be tried. Mr Mathew, the greengrocer, and his boy will be there as witness. I brought them here,' he said again, indicating the boys with a nod of his head, 'to explain to their mother.'

He looked intently at Sarah. 'You're not their mother.'

'No!'

She found it hard to speak, realising the importance of the situation. 'I'm their sister. I'm sorry, sir. Please let them go. I can vouch that they won't do anything like this again. I'm trying to get them into a school.'

'Where is their mother?' he asked, ignoring what she had just said.

'I don't know, sir. Just popped out for some things.'

As she spoke, she couldn't believe that she had been reduced to lying to the police.

He nodded, an all-knowing look on his face.

'We'll be keeping them in a cell at the Guildhall overnight. They go before the judge in the morning. He will be holding temporary court, in the room above the King's Head, at ten, if you wish to attend.'

Sarah shook her head in disbelief. She knew that crimes were dealt with near to the place that they happened, but of all the places for the magistrate to hear the case against her brothers. The King's Head!

'You should prepare yourself and your mother for them to be taken to Exeter to the Assizes,' he continued, 'as this is a very serious case.'

Sarah felt faint as he pulled the boys from her arms and, with one in each hand, took them from the room.

She heard their feet stumbling down the stairs. Heard Thomas scream her name as she lay on the floor sobbing, her arms empty, their frail warmth ripped away.

It was as she got ready to leave for work that she realised her dilemma. Should she tell the Gallaways about her brothers, remembering what Mrs Gallaway had said about not employing anyone from a criminal family? She decided to work and say nothing, better to have one more day of work. It would all be obvious tomorrow and she would wait and see the woman's reaction. She might be kind.

Next morning, Sarah walked with her mother past Mrs Gallaway, who stood stiffly behind the bar watching them, her eyes as cold as steel.

They didn't look in her direction but took the stairs, heads held high, to the room where Judge Johnson was holding his temporary court.

Voices could be heard coming from an open door at the end of the passage. Entering tentatively, Sarah and Gwen were directed towards seats at one of the long tables that had been set out in a square, and where several people were already seated.

The room felt hot, oppressive, as they took their seats, and Sarah and Gwen had their first sight of the judge, a man of middle years with a pale, pockmarked skin beneath his wig. 'Who's next?' he asked the clerk.

'This is Elizabeth Axe, sir, of Summer Land Street,' the clerk, standing, said in a voice far too loud for the room. 'She is eleven years old and is charged with stealing a pair of earrings.'

The judge stared at the small girl, who gripped her mother's hand.

'And is the witness here?' he asked the clerk.

'Yes, sir. Mrs Gutrall, please come forward.' He turned to look at a tall woman who stepped forward and identified the earrings that had been placed on the table in front of the judge, as hers. Asked to tell the court what happened, she said that Elizabeth had crept into her house and had brazenly walked out wearing the earrings. She was caught on the doorstep by the woman herself, who called the police.

Sarah and Gwen sat rigidly, waiting to hear what sentence the girl would receive for stealing.

Judge Johnson looked at Elizabeth sternly. 'There is no doubt,' he said, 'that the earrings were stolen by you, Elizabeth Axe, as you were found wearing them.' He twisted his mouth into a bitter, tight rosebud and looked down his large nose at her.

The girl was as white as milk and looked as though her legs would give way.

'Elizabeth Axe,' he said, 'you are charged with stealing a pair of earrings and it has been proven. You will be sentenced to twenty days in prison and four years in a reformatory school in Exeter, where you will be away from all influences.'

He wrote in his book as the girl was led away crying. Her mother followed, weeping.

The clerk stood and called in a voice that cut Sarah through.

'*Samuel and Thomas Warrington.*'

The policeman, who had been standing with the boys handcuffed to him, walked forward to the judge's table, taking the boys with him.

Sarah thought that she was going to faint. There seemed so little air in the room. She looked at her mother, but Gwen's face was set in a mask that told nothing of what she was feeling. She didn't look at her sons but looked straight ahead.

The witnesses were called and came forward. Mr John Monk, baker, at number 5 King Street. Mr George Mathew, greengrocer, at number 53 King Street and Mrs Hoken, shopkeeper, at number 54. All told how they were often robbed by Samuel and Thomas. The policeman added that there were more people that had been robbed but that they could not leave their businesses to come to the court today, but had written letters.

The judge looked at Samuel and Thomas without any emotion on his face as he passed judgement.

'Samuel and Thomas Warrington. You are accused of persistent stealing and were apprehended *with* the oranges that you stole from Mr Mathew, the greengrocer, on your persons. And this has been proven. What have you to say for yourselves?' he barked angrily at the boys.

Flinching in fear, they gripped the hand of the policeman standing beside them as the judge stared fiercely down his nose at them.

The boys, wide-eyed in the presence of this man in authority, couldn't speak but shrank from him.

'You have no defence,' he continued. 'You were caught in the act of stealing, and I understand from what has been said that this is not your first misdemeanour against shopkeepers in King Street, as many have since testified. You will be taken to Exeter and imprisoned while awaiting trial at the Quarter Sessions. The charge laid against you is theft, a hanging offence. Take them away.' He nodded to the policeman.

'Mother!' Samuel cried, at last breaking down. 'Tell them you told us to do it.'

Gwen didn't look at her sons but kept her face impassive as they were led away down the stairs to the prison carriage awaiting them in the street.

As Sarah and Gwen reached the bottom of the stairs, James appeared from the barrel room. He stopped dead. Looked shocked, then confused, his face reddening before he turned around and went back the way he'd come. He said nothing. It was as though he hadn't seen her. Sarah wanted to cry.

Why hadn't he comforted her? Why did he say nothing to her? He acted as though she were invisible, as though he didn't know her.

As Sarah followed her mother through the bar, Mrs Gallaway stepped in front of them.

'You will not be surprised,' she said, addressing Sarah, 'that I don't want you working under my roof again.'

As she spoke, her eyes, filled with condemnation, had become slits above her podgy cheeks. There was no recognition of the girl who had worked so hard and so willingly for her. It was as though she were addressing a stranger.

'Your wage. Made up,' she snarled, as she pushed a tray forward on which a brown envelope lay, as though Sarah had some awful disease that the woman didn't want to catch.

'You will not show your face in here again,' she said sharply.

Gwen's hand shot out and took the wage packet and in the same movement was heading through the door. Sarah followed in silence, tears in her eyes.

As mother and daughter stepped out into the street, the horses were being encouraged to pull the black prison carriage away from the door. It already held Elizabeth Axe. Her mother was standing next to the carriage, silent tears rolling over her cheeks, her hand on its side, wanting to be close to her daughter in those last minutes.

'I'll come to Exeter, Sam. I'll be there for you,' Sarah shouted towards the barred window, high up on the side of the carriage, and heard Thomas' agonised cry.

'Sarah. Sarah.'

Gwen was silent for most of the day, staring into space, her blank face giving no hint of what she was thinking or feeling. Sometimes, her head leant against the back of the chair, her mouth open, snoring.

When later in the afternoon she was awake, she looked ill. Her skin had a grey tinge, the whites of her eyes yellow and bloodshot.

Sarah sat unmoving, her head resting in her hands at the table. She had been going over and over all that had happened since she came to live here. Berating herself that she had done little to take charge of her brothers. She knew that they were stealing. What had she done about it? Nothing. Was it not her fault that they were in trouble, shouldn't she have done more? Her father would have expected her to have done more.

Her mother's voice suddenly broke the silence of the room, stopping her destructive thoughts and self-pity.

'I'm not well, Sarah. You must find work.' Her mother's face was pinched, and her hollow eyes dark-rimmed as she poured water into a bowl and washed her face. 'The rent's due Friday and I have nothing,' she said, drying herself. 'There isn't enough in your wage packet from the pub.'

'You know that I looked, Mother, before I got *that* job. I can't invent work.'

'You must search in Frankfort Street, under the railway arch, or George Street. Try there.'

'And if I get a job? I won't have any pay until next week and we need the money in two days.'

'Then you will have to go to Union Street and stand in for me, Sarah.'

50

'Won't they mind?'

'Won't who mind?' Gwen looked confused.

'The people that you work for. I will have to be trained. I don't even know what you do.'

Gwen sighed. 'This is what you do, Sarah. You stand outside the apothecary shop, that's my pitch. If any of the girls approach you, tell them that Gwen is ill, that you are her daughter, and that you are standing in for me until I'm better. Don't let them intimidate you.'

'Who are they, Mother?'

'Other workers.'

'But I don't understand what it is that I have to do. Who is going to meet me and tell me what I am to do?'

'A man will approach you and you are to go with him. He will take you somewhere out of sight. He will tell you what he wants you to do. If you are nice to him, he will pay you. Do not let him go without payment. Some try.'

Sarah stared at her mother. 'This man will tell me what to do, but may try not to pay me at the end of the night.'

'No, Sarah!' Gwen was becoming exasperated. 'He will leave as soon as you finish being nice to him.'

The penny dropped, and Sarah stared at her mother in disbelief. 'You're a prostitute?'

The horror of this realisation hung for a second in the air between them, before the slap of Gwen's hand across Sarah's face knocked her sideways onto the armchair. As she fell, she felt her teeth rattle and tasted blood. Pain issued unbearably in her mouth. She'd bitten her tongue and it hurt more than the slap.

'I'm sorry,' her mother was saying, although she didn't sound sorry. 'It has to be you. You're young. You'll bring in more money than me. We have no choice, Sarah. If we are turned out of this room, it will be the workhouse, *if they have room,* and hard labour. If they can't take us in, it will be under Stonehouse Bridge with the lost souls, the drug takers and the murderers. We will be taken anyway. That, is what men do to vulnerable women. And we won't be paid, and we won't last long.'

Her mother's voice was raised on the last sentence as though it would have more force on her daughter's understanding of where they were headed.

Holding her burning face, Sarah stood shakily and dropped heavily into the armchair, knowing that she had no choice.

6.

It was after midnight in Union Street. Two women watched Sarah as she arrived and stood nervously outside the apothecary shop. She had never felt more exposed or fearful in her life. On legs that didn't want to carry her, she walked up and down, being careful not to encroach on the pitch of anyone else.

'Oi!'

A woman, with a heavily painted face and large earrings, seeing Sarah, shouted. As she approached, Sarah could smell the woman's cheap perfume before she reached her.

'Do you know what happens to girls who turn up to earn money in places they haven't earned?' She stood threateningly close.

A second woman strolled up behind the first, smiling with deep red lips and painted, cold eyes.

'You take our money, little girl, and you'll regret it,' the second woman said convincingly.

'I'm Gwen's daughter,' Sarah said nervously, stepping back. 'Gwen isn't well. She told me to take her place.'

Her limbs shook with the confrontation and she was in no doubt that these women would hurt her.

'Well,' the red-lipped woman said, looking Sarah up and down, 'you're an improvement on your sister. She ran as soon as she saw a policeman.'

'My sister?' Sarah was shocked. 'But she's only twelve.'

'Twelve?' The woman seemed startled. 'Gwen said she was fourteen. I have a daughter that age. I'd starve before I put her on the street.'

They looked disgusted and Sarah was frightened that they would blame her.

The woman with the red mouth asked, 'What's wrong with Gwen? What's she got? The pox? Has she seen a doctor?'

At this, the woman with the large earrings looked hard at Sarah, eyebrows raised, waiting for a reply.

'I don't know. My neighbour thinks she might be pregnant. But she can't be, my father's dead.'

For a brief moment they stared at her before throwing back their heads and laughing hysterically, bringing attention to themselves and to Sarah, who wanted at that moment to run away like her sister.

'Stupid cow!' The one with the red mouth laughed through teeth smeared with the colouring. 'I told her not to get so drunk that she'd forget to go to the apothecary for the cure. When you see her, tell her that Doxy says hello.'

Sarah nodded, and the two women moved off up the street, where they stood waiting, sometimes calling out to passing men and laughing loudly.

Sarah tried to be invisible by standing in the shadow of the shop front and jumped when a man stood in front of her.

'You'll do,' he said. 'Where do you usually go?'

Sarah had been prompted by Gwen to take him into the shop doorway and stepped back into the shadow between the two window fronts.

As she stood with her back to the door, his frame blocking out the street, she started to cry.

'What's going on here?' He looked shocked.

'It's my first time,' Sarah sobbed. 'I don't know what I'm supposed to do.'

'Bloody hell! Trust me, years away and I get a new whore.'

The slap that hit his face echoed around the door frame. For a second, he was stunned, before he grabbed her wrist so that she couldn't do it again.

'Well, aren't you the tiger. I don't want a new girl. Don't worry. I wouldn't take you against your wishes. I think you're in the wrong job, little girl. Go home to your mother.'

'My mother sent me here,' she cried, miserably. 'We've no money for the rent and no money for food. If we become homeless on Friday we will have to sleep under the bridge where we could be murdered.' She gabbled as the tears rolled over her cheeks.

'OK. OK!'

He held up his hands and stood back to see her better. 'If you do me a favour, I'll pay you, so that you can eat.'

Wiping away the tears with a shaking hand, she didn't know if she should believe him, but waited, fear in her heart, for what he was going to suggest.

He spoke thoughtfully, staring into the pale face, almost hidden in the shadow of his bulk. 'I've been away at sea for four years and I have two days' leave. I need to find my mother. She's moved, but the neighbours say she's still in the area.'

'I don't know many people, but I can try.' The relief was audible in her voice.

'She's Gwen Warrington. I'm Ned Warrington, her son. Have you heard of her?'

Sarah stood, open-mouthed and silent, looking at a brother that she had never met, who had left home two years before she was born. She had only heard his name mentioned when their father was alive.

'Well!' he said, frowning. 'Have you heard of her?'

Sarah could only nod that she had, but couldn't move, couldn't speak. All her limbs and her brain had frozen.

He shook her by the shoulders. Even though there was little light, he could see that she was about to faint.

'OK, little lady,' he said. 'Something tells me that you're not cut out for night work. Come on. I'll take you for a drink, to put some colour in your cheeks, and you can tell me what you know of my mother.'

As she moved, walking at his side, she tried to keep up but couldn't feel the ground beneath her feet. Her trembling legs were moving, but she had no idea how she was managing to walk.

Ned pushed her through the doors of a public house where she felt the immediate warmth on her face and shoulders, heard the voices, the laughter, but didn't feel as though she was part of any of it. He sat her down at a table and left her there as he went to the bar.

Coming back with two small glasses of rum, he pushed one at her. 'Drink this, it'll bring you back to life. I don't have long here before I go back to sea.' He looked across the table, staring into her eyes. 'It was fortunate that I met you.'

Sarah nodded dumbly, afraid of his reaction when she told him who she was.

He took a mouthful of his rum and then reaching over the table put the small glass in her hand and lifted her arm towards her face. 'Drink,' he demanded. 'You'll feel better and we can talk.'

She sipped and coughed. He nodded approval.

'There!' He smiled. 'The colour's returning already. What's your name?'

'Sarah,' she replied quietly, looking down at the table. 'Sarah Warrington. I think I'm your sister.'

Ned sat, eyes blinking, before the realisation of what had just been said showed in his eyes as they widened in disbelief, and then horror. Standing suddenly, his chair fell violently backwards.

As it crashed to the floor, the landlord shouted, 'Sit down or get out, I don't want no trouble in here.'

Ned held up his hands, apologised, picked up his chair and sat on it.

'You better tell me everything, little sister,' he said gravely.

As he picked up his rum, his hand was shaking with shock, or was it anger? Sarah wasn't sure. She told him everything. Of their mother's drinking, their father's death, about Maud, about Samuel and Thomas, their hunger and the change in their mother. How their mother had encouraged Samuel and Thomas to steal, and her lack of support for them at the trial, admitting nothing.

He sat in silence, arms stretched out before him on the table, chin down on his chest as he listened. When she had finished, he got up without saying a word, went to the bar and brought back a rum for himself and a lemonade for her.

Taking his seat again, he said, 'I've waited six months with the knowledge that I could get home and see my mother. I can't tell you how that hope kept me sane. Years at sea. The different foreign ports for trade. Sometimes, a little time on land to explore. The crew became my family, but I never forgot my mother.'

His head bent and he was silent again. When he looked up, Sarah could see the pain in his eyes. 'What happened to her?' he asked quietly.

'I don't know any more than I've told you, Ned.' Her own hand shook as she lifted the lemonade to her mouth and took a long drink. She needed the sugar. 'I remember her being strict and father being kind, comforting us when we were ill or had an accident. Mother never gave me the cuddles that Father did, and now I know that I loved him and was afraid of her. I'm still afraid of her, Ned.' Her voice trailed away as she spoke her truth. Yes, she was still afraid of this woman who had always managed to keep her distance from her children.

'Sarah!'

He looked at her with such pain in his eyes that if she had known him better, she would have thrown her arms around him and comforted him.

'I saved some of my wage to give to her. As a son, I've done little for my mother in all these years. But now, I think it best that I give the money to you. Don't tell her that I came looking for her, and don't show her the money. I think that she's gone down the road of drink and when it gets a woman, it's hard for them to break the cycle.'

Taking a drawstring purse from his jacket pocket, he pushed it across the table to her. 'Keep it hidden,' he warned. 'I have experience of women in drink, Sarah, and know that if she finds this purse she will spend it all. Let her think that you earned the little I think you should offer her. She will search your things for more. She won't believe that it's all you have. She'll think that you've kept some back for yourself. I suggest that you pay the rent, get that debt out of the way as soon as you can, and keep the purse on you at all times under your clothes.'

Sarah nodded, feeling more afraid of her mother now than she did when she left home earlier.

'I'll spend some of it on a ticket to Exeter, to support Sam and Thomas. I have to be there for them, Ned.'

Tears formed in the corner of her eyes as she remembered their small, frightened faces. Wiping her eyes with her hand, she said quietly, 'They were so afraid, looked so small, Ned. Sam's only ten and Thomas eight.'

'I wish I'd been there,' he said quietly. 'If I'd known about this and was here, I would have been.' He took a deep breath and, looking serious, qualified with, 'No, if I'd been here, they wouldn't have been in trouble.'

Sarah nodded. She believed it, but also that there was nothing that could be done. Justice would take its course.

'I've got a new merchant ship, Sarah. I'll be working closer to home, around the coast. My ship's out in the Sound but I don't sail until tomorrow afternoon. I'm staying at the Seaman's Mission. Can you meet me there in the morning? We could walk together on the Hoe and get to know each other. I'd like to have someone back home to think about when I'm away.'

For the first time since she'd left Kingsand, joy flooded her heart. 'I'd love to walk with you on the Hoe, Ned, and perhaps we could write to each other. You could write to me care of the post office,' she offered. 'You could let me know what exotic places you're visiting.'

He laughed. 'I don't think you understand about being at sea on a merchant ship, but yes, it will make me feel less alone to have someone back home to write to, not that Scotland and Ireland are exotic. There's an organisation that will try to get letters to me if you write, Sarah. Can you write?' he asked as an afterthought.

'Yes, Ned. I can read and write.'

He smiled. 'I'll see you tomorrow, about nine of the clock if that's not too soon for you, Sarah.'

When they parted company, she felt happier than she had in weeks, and for the first time since being back with her mother, she was looking forward to the morrow. She had a brother. He knew of her existence. She was no longer alone.

~

On the day of the trial, telling her mother that she was looking for work, Sarah took the train to Exeter and, asking directions from the station, walked to the courtroom.

Having sat all morning and heard the judgements of the Assize Court judge, Mr Hooper, against those brought before him, Sarah was worried by the severity of the punishments.

It was early afternoon before Samuel and Thomas were brought before the judge. Their heads had been shaved. They appeared frightened and small against the background of this room. She wanted to run to them and hold them tight and tell them that it would soon be over and that she had come to take them home. But this room was not like the room at the King's Head. This room was a real courtroom, and overwhelming.

She sat silently in the visitors' tiered seating, cut off from them, tears in her eyes, her heart pounding.

They looked for her in the gallery and, when they saw her, Sam nodded but Thomas cried. She tried to smile a reassurance but could only bite her lip and try to stop the tears rolling from her own eyes.

The statements of the witnesses were read aloud by the clerk, unwavering, one after the other. He ignored the whispers, expelled into the dusty air, from the gallery.

The judge, a rotund, elderly man, with several chins, sat unmoving while he listened intently.

Sarah waited with her fingers crossed for the sentence to be passed.

'By law, stealing is a hanging offence,' the judge said simply, staring hard at the boys. 'There is no excuse for taking from others that which does not belong to you.'

The boys shrank before him, looking confused, as voices in the room agreed and disagreed loudly.

'*Silence.*'

The judge shouted down the voices that grumbled for a moment more, as he looked from side to side, his face threatening.

'For stealing oranges, amongst other misdemeanours,' Judge Hooper's harsh voice rang around the packed courtroom, 'you will both receive a birching. Samuel Warrington. You will receive eight lashes of the birch. Thomas Warrington. You will receive six lashes of the birch. You will spend a further six hours of recovery in prison, before being taken to a reformatory school, where you will spend four years learning discipline.'

As soon as the sentence was given, they were taken away, down steps and out of her sight. They went quietly, not looking back. Perhaps not understanding what was about to happen to them. So small, so thin, she could see that they were confused, trying to understand the orders barked at them by strangers. Their individual personalities already gone from them.

~

It was a quiet, sad girl that caught the train back to Plymouth, having berated herself all the way to the station for not noticing that the boys were idle, knowing that she should have done more to curb them going out. She should have questioned what they were going to do with their day.

Sitting dejectedly in the corner of the train carriage, her hands folded on her lap, trying not to cry, she hardly noticed the spectacular seascape that passed by the window.

A family of five shared the compartment, sitting each side of the carriage door. And although she sat staring ahead, she noticed how the father held his hand protectively behind his son's back as the boy stood at the door looking out of the window, in case he fell backwards.

She noticed the young daughter sitting next to her mother playing happily with her doll and how the mother kissed the forehead of the gurgling baby in her arms.

What Sarah's family had lost was love, and she wondered when it had happened. For just one second, the face of James Gallaway floated before her eyes, and she realised that she had also lost love, so easily.

~

Walking down King Street, with all its life and clamour, she didn't want to go home, didn't want to face her mother. She wouldn't be able to tell her where she had been. Gwen would want to know where she'd got the money for the ticket. Despising what she was becoming, Sarah knew that she had no option but to be deceitful. Her father's voice was in her head: *Always tell the truth Sarah. People appreciate the truth. It will go better for you.* She couldn't help thinking that in this case he was most certainly wrong.

Calling in at the newsagent's, Sarah picked up the *Western Daily Mercury* to look in the job section. The front page had an item that made Sarah's blood run cold. A young woman known as Lillian Blatten had been murdered in cold blood by an unknown person. Charles Blatten, her brother, said that his sister went out about ten o'clock in the evening to buy something for a headache and when she didn't return he went to look for her. He found her not one hundred yards from their front door with her face and neck bruised. She was dead. He told a neighbour, who stayed with the body while Mr Blatten went to the police station to report the crime. The newspaper article went on to say that the police had no leads at present. Miss Blatten did not have a boyfriend but lived quietly at home with her brother. Plymouth police would like to speak to anyone with information that would bring the perpetrator to justice.

When Sarah got home, her mother looked better. She had washed and was combing her hair up into a bun.

'You look better, Mother,' she said, always worried by the reaction her mother had to the simplest things that she might say.

'I am feeling better. I'll be able to work tonight.'

'You're going to work? Is it safe?'

'It won't be any different to any other night, Sarah. It's never safe,' she said, her fingers exploring her hair as she added a comb to keep the bun in place.

'There's an article on the front page of the newspaper, Mother. An innocent young woman has been murdered just going to get something for a headache.'

'What are you saying, Sarah? That I shouldn't work every time someone gets murdered in Plymouth? There are reports of murders almost every day, and most of the people live together.'

'But this seems different, Mother. She didn't know her murderer.'

'They don't know that.' Gwen sounded scornful. 'She could have been going to meet someone she hadn't told her family about. In my opinion, young girls tell lies all the time. We would all starve if we didn't work each time someone was attacked.'

Feeling guilty, Sarah gave up showing that she felt anything for her mother's safety and, sitting at the table, opened the page at the job section.

Most jobs were for men, strong young men; there was nothing for women being advertised today.

7.

Like many streets in Plymouth, Frankfort Street was a mixture of old and new. Ancient, wooden-fronted buildings, some with exposed beams carved with flowers, animals or faces that showed the skill of past craftsmen. These buildings sat, old and worn, next to the newer, taller, stone-clad premises of shops and small enterprises. Today, Sarah would have been happy to work in a shop, as the thought of approaching a factory, as her mother had suggested, frightened her.

As she got closer to Russell Street, the terrible stink that always pervaded the air over Plymouth became stronger. The factory chimneys, in this small area, released gases that caused a permanent and noxious cloud over the town. If she got no work here, she thought, she would detour and look in Old Town Street on her way home.

By the time she arrived at the industrial site, she had already discounted two places of work: the saw mill and the smithy. If she got no joy at the sugar refinery then she would try the dye works, off Mill Lane. Although the dye works was hidden behind the flour mill, it was strongly present by its eye-watering fumes, and she wondered if she would be able to cope with the smell, working there.

The imposing iron gates of the sugar refinery felt intimidating as she walked through them. After all, what did she know about sugar or the making of it? Following the sign that led her to a separate reception building, she knocked on the door.

A woman's voice called, 'Enter.'

On opening the door, Sarah found herself standing in a room like no other that she had seen. A starkly cold, austere room. The walls lined with dark wood and locked cabinets. A large desk took up much of the office and the smell of polish was so strong, it clawed at her throat. A severe woman, with grey hair pulled back tightly behind her head, sat behind the desk surrounded by papers and books. At first, the woman did not look up. When she did, her eyes were enquiring.

'How can I help you?' she asked sharply, staring at Sarah through small glasses balanced on the end of her nose. The cold eyes trained on Sarah did not help her feel any more relaxed.

'I'm looking for work.' Sarah's voice held a croak of fear.

'You're looking for work, what?' the woman asked, almost spitting through thin lips that had formed into an even tighter line of disapproval.

There was nothing Sarah could say; she didn't understand. Her hands had become wet, and sweat ran down her back. Her face suddenly flushed with heat and still she stared at the woman, not understanding.

The silence in the room became heavy as the woman continued to stare. One hand was creeping towards the papers on the desk and Sarah knew that she was about to be dismissed.

It was then that she noticed a small brass plaque on the desk with the name Mrs Matthew inscribed upon it. And taking a chance, she repeated, 'I'm looking for work, Mrs Matthew.'

'I see!' Mrs Matthew nodded. 'I'm sorry,' she said. 'We have no work available at present.'

Defeated, Sarah turned to go.

'But... you could try the soap works at Mill Bay. I understand that they have a sudden vacancy and might need a worker.'

Grateful to the woman, Sarah thanked her, leaving the office as quickly as she could, needing air.

Discounting the dye works, she headed for Old Town Street, then carried on down George Street and past Derry's Clock, standing at the crossroads. Turning towards Mill Bay, she hardly noticed the crowds of people, the carriages and horses, as she hurried on.

A little later, she was standing before an imposing four-storey building and the tall chimney of The Mill Soap Works and felt uncertain about going in. It was quiet on the other side of the gates. The workers already inside. It felt like being late for school. The playground empty. Everyone already in class. Nervous fear jumped about in her stomach as she hovered at the gate. She could go home and tell her mother that there was no work to be found. But then… if they had nowhere to live, she would know that it was her fault, that she hadn't tried hard enough.

A grey-haired man, his spine humped so that his head was held stiffly before him, stepped from a hut beside the gate. Seeing her, he called out. 'Can I help you, maid?'

Sarah caught her breath but replied bravely, 'I was looking for work.'

'Go around that building.' He motioned with his hand, pointing to the building in front of them. 'You'll come to a group of small buildings. The first will be the reception, go in there.'

'Thank you, sir.' Nervous butterflies jumped in her belly. 'Do you know the name of the person I should speak to, sir?'

'That'll be Miss Denham.'

Relieved that she had a name, Sarah walked across the courtyard and around the corner, easily finding the reception building. Knocking on the half-glazed door, she entered an office with two desks where two smartly dressed women sat writing. They looked up as she entered, an enquiring look upon both their faces. They didn't smile.

Taking a deep breath, Sarah asked, 'Could I speak to Miss Denham?'

It was the older of the two women who answered.

'I'm Miss Denham, how can I help you?'

'I'm looking for work, Miss Denham. Are you needing anyone?'

Sarah noticed a look pass between the two women and it made her feel uncomfortable. Was she too dirty? Was she too young? Something went between them and she didn't know what it was, but it was to do with her.

65

'We do have a place for a woman. What work have you had before?'

'I washed glasses for a publican, madam. That is the only work that I have had, as I was looking after my mother.'

'And you don't look after her now?'

'No, madam. She is well now.'

The woman frowned while seemingly making up her mind. 'What is your name?'

'Sarah Warrington,' she replied, crossing her fingers behind her back, hoping that they hadn't read about her brothers in the newspaper.

'Miss McClary.' Miss Denham addressed the younger woman. 'Find the form and we will get Miss Warrington to fill it in. You can sit over there at that table while you do so, Miss Warrington.'

The woman nodded towards a small table in the corner of the office.

Sitting at the table, Sarah filled in the form and handed it back.

Miss Denham read what little was on it, sighed, and looked at Sarah with another frown.

'You will be paid weekly, Miss Warrington.' As she spoke, she handed the form to her colleague. 'File this, Miss McClary, and then take Miss Warrington over to Mr Rice and see if he can set her on today. Can you start today, right now, in fact, Miss Warrington?'

Sarah could only nod that she could and wondered what she had got herself into, what she would have to do.

Helen McClary got up from her desk and, opening the door, indicated with a nod of her head for Sarah to step outside.

Out in the yard, Sarah followed the young woman's black skirt and belted, cinched waist as they turned a corner, passing several sheds and workshops necessary for supplying the business with fuel. The area was busy with men going about their daily tasks, carrying boxes, pulling timber from a large pile and placing it on handcarts. Walking past the carpentry workshop, she saw that the door was closed, but the sound of sawing and the smell of sawdust still escaped. Outside the smithy, a large brown horse was having a shoe fitted by a man bent over, the hoof held between his legs. The sound of a hammer hitting an anvil railed above the rest of the noise in this area.

As they walked, one building in particular appeared not to have a roof and from which, the smell escaping was unpleasant. Her eyes watered and she was tempted to hold her nose, but didn't want the young woman to see her do it.

'That's the boiling room.' Helen identified the building with the open roof. 'You get used to the awful smell. It's the tallow and oil.' Passing two other buildings, she said, rather superiorly, 'That's the cooling room and that's the soda storeroom. Only men work there. The women work here,' she said, opening a door in a long building as they reached it.

The space they entered was, to Sarah, vast. Large stone pillars supported the roof under which two iron machines stood, and stretching away from them, long benches with women standing each side, working, heads down, their hands moving at speed.

The air, Sarah noticed, was fragrant, floral. A relief after the smell outside.

Helen led her towards a man standing halfway down the room. 'This is Miss Warrington, Mr Rice,' she said.

As Helen spoke, Sarah noticed a flush of colour bloom on Helen's cheeks. 'She would like to be put to work if you need a replacement,' she continued.

Mr Rice, a man of about forty with a large blond moustache and greying hair, looked Sarah up and down.

'Can you take orders?' He frowned.

'Yes, sir,' was all she could say, knowing that was what he wanted to hear.

'Thank you, Miss McClary.' Helen was dismissed without another thought.

'Follow me.' He addressed Sarah stiffly and, turning, walked towards the far end of the long bench.

She followed behind him, past the women wrapping squares of soap in paper and placing them into boxes. Aware that the women at the bench were watching her, although covertly, she felt embarrassed as she followed Mr Rice the length of the room towards a large woman who hardly raised her head as they approached.

'Mrs Malick. This is Miss Warrington, she will be Lillian's replacement. Show her what she is to do. I will be back to see you in half an hour to oversee the changeover. The next batch will be Rose, if you would get the new labels ready while Arthur cleans the cutters.'

He walked away, leaving Sarah standing beside Mrs Malick at the head of the table, feeling conspicuous. The woman didn't turn to her until her box was full. And Sarah diligently watched what she was doing.

'You can see what the women are doing,' Mrs Malick said, as she placed the last bar of soap in the box beside her. 'Wrap the soap in the square of paper like this. Sides and then ends.' She demonstrated. 'Seal it with the label that identifies the soap's fragrance. I will expect that you will be able to keep up with the others very quickly. You will stand here next to me so that I can watch you for ten minutes and then you will stand in Lillian's place.'

'Yes, Mrs Malick.'

Sarah looked uncertainly along the length of table at the confident movement of hands and fingers that seemed to her to be flying.

She was already feeling the pressure and she was yet to start.

The woman nodded, apparently pleased with her response.

After ten minutes, Sarah took the empty place at the table, wrapping and labelling the bars of soap, placing the items in the box beside her. Not as quick as the others, she was still wrapping while the women, having finished their work, were cleaning the space in front of them ready for the arrival of the next fragrant soap.

As they prepared, a boy climbed onto the iron machine that stood at the head of the table and cleaned the blades that cut the soap into equal sizes.

No one spoke to her or helped her finish. In one way, she was glad that none of the women wanted to talk to her. She didn't want the usual nosy enquiries about her family; she was happy to be alone. The most important thing was to tell her mother that she had work. But as they awaited the next instruction from Mr Rice, she heard a whisper.

'Lil's not cold in her grave yet and already her place is filled.'

Sarah couldn't see who spoke so quietly, but did see who replied and was disturbed by the bitterness in her voice.

'Who would have the nerve to come for her job? She hasn't been dead more than twelve hours.'

A small, thin woman with wrinkled features had replied out of the corner of her mouth, thinking that no one would hear, or not caring if they did, but Sarah heard.

'I was going to get our Flo to come for the job,' she continued, 'but thought I should wait until Lil was buried.'

'Will we hear when that will be? I want to go to the funeral.' A girl not much older than Sarah joined in.

'I expect we'll hear soon, Alice, but they might keep her till they find out who did it.' A woman Sarah had heard the others address as Grace spoke. 'It's worrying, though. I daren't go out at night now, I send my Bernard.'

They were standing ready at the table when the huge doors at the end of the room opened and a group of men wheeled in six huge slabs of soap on a large handcart. They stacked them onto pallets behind the machine where two men would feed the giant with the soap. The rest of the day was a blur. The soap kept coming and the filled boxes taken away and stacked by young Arthur onto flat carts that the men wheeled out through the large doors every half an hour.

By the end of the day, she could hardly move for the pain in her feet and knees. Limping home, she felt faint, having not eaten all day. She hoped that her mother would not be at home, that she would have the room to herself, so that she could sit in the chair and close her eyes.

Gwen was looking out of the window as Sarah entered. By the smell, and the aggressive way that her mother turned and looked at her, Sarah knew that she had been drinking.

'Where have you been?' Gwen snarled accusingly.

Sarah was about to explain when Gwen became abusive. 'I know you take the money and keep it for yourself. Don't think that I don't know what you're up to.'

Afraid of Gwen when she was drunk, Sarah tried to reason with her.

'No, Mother. I've found work and have been there all day.'

'Where's the money?' She held out a trembling hand. 'Give it to me.'

'I can't, Mother. I don't get paid until the end of the week.'

'You're lying,' Gwen shouted, as she launched herself from the window, staggering past the armchair, with her arm raised to strike her daughter. 'I know what you're up to,' she screeched, as she grabbed Sarah's hair, tripping on the small rug and pulling them both to the floor.

Tired as she had been, Sarah was now full of adrenalin-filled fear and was first to untangle herself and get to her feet.

Rushing from the room, leaving her mother on the floor, she fled down the stairs and out of the house.

Walking at speed along King Street towards the viaduct, she had no idea where she was going as fear replaced the previous tiredness in her legs.

The wind was getting up and it looked like rain, but not wanting to return to the room and face her mother, she wandered around for an hour before noticing the food vendors were setting up their stalls near the viaduct, ready for the evening.

Seeing a man holding up two skinned, cooked rabbits, she bought one with Ned's dwindling money.

Returning home, with nowhere else to go, she leant against the wall in the stinking back yard. Hiding from her mother, she ate one of the rabbit's back legs. Surrounded by flies, she tore at it, stuffing the meat into her mouth. Breathing deeply through her nose, she gasped for breath, aware that she was snorting as she desperately chewed and swallowed. She had never been as hungry, and became aware after a moment that she sounded like an animal. Gradually, she became calm and her breath returned to normal as she picked the bone clean.

When finished, she stared at her greasy fingers as hot tears erupted unexpectedly, and she cried bitterly where she stood. Tears for her brothers, for Maud, her mother and what had become of them. When the tears eventually stopped, she took the rest of the rabbit back to their room.

The landing was unusually quiet. She almost felt like creeping to her door, not wanting to disturb the fearful silence.

Turning the door knob slowly, she inched the door open, waiting for the reprisal. But there was no response from behind the door. Now another fear rose in her chest. What was she going to find? The room, when she stepped inside, was empty. This she found even more frightening, for now she had to wait to see what state her mother would be in when she came home.

Pulling the rabbit apart, she left it covered on a plate. Perhaps food would help Gwen to get over the drink when she came home.

It was the middle of the night when Sarah awoke to the sound of quiet groaning. Gwen was lying in the bed next to her, curled in the foetal position.

Putting her arm out, laying her hand on her mother's side, she realised that Gwen's body was cold beneath her nightgown.

'Mother, are you ill?' she whispered into the darkness.

'No! Go back to sleep.' The reply was immediate, the voice strained.

Afraid to say more, Sarah turned over and, still exhausted, fell asleep. In the morning when she woke, she had a vague recollection of having woken a second time in the night and her mother not being in the bed, and yet she was there now, covered with the blanket.

Moving carefully off the bed, not wanting to disturb her mother, she poured water from the bucket into a bowl. She was splashing her face to wake herself up when there was a knock on the door. She froze, staring at the door as though she could see through it. No good came from knocks on the door; she had learnt that. As the knocking became more demanding, Sarah glanced across at her mother before crossing the room.

Opening the door slowly, she was surprised to see a policeman and, standing behind him, Jane from number 15, accompanied by a grey-haired gentleman wearing a dark suit.

They all stared at her.

'I'm Police Constable Parrett.' The policeman spoke quietly, looking past Sarah into the room, and seeing Gwen still asleep in bed. 'I'm sorry to arrive so early, Miss Warrington, but we need to speak to your mother.'

Sarah looked beyond him to Jane, whose face was pale and serious, and wondered why Jane was with these men.

Opening the door wider, she indicated that they enter.

They looked uncomfortable as they walked across the room and stood quietly at the foot of the bed looking at Gwen.

'Will you wake your mother, Miss Warrington? I'm afraid that we have to speak to her. This,' the policeman said, indicating the elderly gentleman, 'is Doctor Pearce. And this your neighbour, Miss Salford, who lives at number 15.'

Sarah nodded, acknowledging the doctor, and felt confused.

'The body of a newly born baby has been found in one of the closets in the yard,' the policeman continued gravely. 'It was discovered by Miss Salford here,' he nodded towards Jane, 'who tells us that your mother is, or was, pregnant.'

'No, sir.' Sarah shook her head. 'My mother can't be pregnant. My father has been dead three years.'

The young constable smiled kindly but continued, ignoring her statement. 'Dr Pearce would like to examine your mother. He will be examining all the women in the house who are pregnant. One of them is the recent mother of this child.'

Going to the bed and placing her hand on Gwen's arm, Sarah shook her lightly. Gwen groaned. 'Go away, Sarah, leave me alone.'

'Mother, there are some people here to see you. Please wake up.'

Trying to blink the tiredness from her eyes, Gwen raised

herself up on one arm and looked sleepily at the three people standing in the room.

It was the policeman who spoke.

'Good morning, Mrs Warrington. I'm sorry to disturb you at this early hour. I'm Constable Parrett and this is Doctor Pearce. We are looking for the mother of a newly born baby found dead this morning in a cubicle in the yard. Doctor Pearce has been asked by the Inspector of Police to examine every woman, suspected of being pregnant, living in this building. We have reason to believe that you are, or were, pregnant.'

'I'm not pregnant,' Gwen said, fully awake now. 'Let me sleep.' She began to lower herself back on the bed.

'I'm sorry, Mrs Warrington.' The policeman looked uncomfortable. 'We have to examine you on the orders of our Inspector. We need to eliminate you from our enquiry. When that is done, you can go back to sleep.'

Turning to Jane and Sarah, he said quietly, 'Please step outside while the doctor examines Mrs Warrington.'

As Sarah and Jane stood outside on the landing, the door to number 6 opened and the five dockers living there left for work, their boots clumping loudly on the wooden stairs, as they did every morning at the same time. They didn't speak.

'I'm sorry, Sarah,' Jane said softly when she heard the door downstairs close behind the dockers. 'I didn't want to do this, but it was me found the baby, head down in the muck and paper.' Tears sprang into her eyes. 'It was a terrible sight. Poor little thing. I'll never forget it.' She wiped the tears from her eyes with a handkerchief.

'But why tell them that my mother is pregnant, Jane? You have no way of knowing that. I asked her about it and she denied it.'

'If I'm wrong I'll apologise but—'

'You *are* wrong, Jane,' Sarah butted in loudly. 'My father has been dead a long time. My mother is ill.'

'Then I'm sorry.' Jane shrugged.

Sighing, Jane turned away, walking along the landing to the stairs and, making her way up them slowly, didn't look back.

Sarah didn't watch her go. She stood forlornly outside the door feeling shut out and alone, yet totally exposed, standing at the top of the stairs.

'Please God don't let it be her,' she mouthed, and closed her eyes as the thoughts went around in her head. *She told me that she wasn't pregnant. She wouldn't lie to me.* Nervous energy surged through her body and to alleviate the feeling she walked up and down the landing at speed.

A baby cried somewhere in the house above her and a child shouted for its mother. A chair scrapped across a floor. A door opened and closed. The house was waking up as Sarah waited for the men to come out of her room.

She had just reached out towards the door, determined to open it and walk in, when it opened.

'Please come in, Miss Warrington.' The constable looked serious as he pulled the door wider.

Stepping inside, Sarah was surprised to see her mother dressed. Wearing her coat and hat as she stood before the mirror.

'Mother?'

Gwen didn't answer but kept staring into the mottled glass.

'We have to take your mother to the station, Miss Warrington. Your mother has been examined by Dr Pearce and has been found to have recently given birth.'

'No!' Sarah cried, shaking her head. 'She told me that she wasn't pregnant. She can't be. Mother! You can't have had a baby. Tell them.'

'I'm afraid that there is no doubting it.' Dr Pearce spoke quietly. There was a finality about the way he shut his medical bag, pulling the clips across to lock it. 'I'm sorry,' he said, picking his bag up and walking towards the door. 'Truly sorry,' he said again.

'Thank you, Doctor,' Constable Parrett said quietly as the doctor left the room, closing the door.

Constable Parrett turned to Gwen. 'Now, madam, please accompany me quietly or I will have to restrain you.'

Moving away from the glass, Gwen crossed the room, hesitating beside Sarah. Looking at her daughter briefly, her mouth parted in

74

a sad smile. She nodded but said nothing as she walked through the door, followed by the policeman, who closed the door behind them, leaving Sarah standing alone in the silence of the empty room.

Too stunned to cry, or make a sound, she stood unmoving, feeling hollow, trying to make sense of their lives.

Knowing that she had to go to work, she moved with staggered movements, like one of the Italian family's musical manikins.

Eventually, she shrugged on her jacket and, lacing up her boots with numb fingers, she moved on trembling legs towards the door.

Out in the street, everyone seemed to be walking at her, bumping into her, cursing her as she tried to walk with dignity and failed. Although the journey this morning was only half what it had been yesterday, she knew that she was not going to make it on time. Her brain seemed to have frozen. Time was standing still and she wasn't sure if she was moving forwards or backwards as she seemed to be getting no nearer the soap works.

When eventually she walked through the gate, she saw the elderly man in the gatehouse glance at the clock on his wall. He shrugged his shoulders and looked away. *Yes,* she thought, *I don't think they will want me after this.*

The air inside the workshop was filled with the smell of gardenia. She hoped to be forgiven for being late. Now more than ever she needed the job, needed the company. But the look on the face of Mr Rice as he approached her said it all.

'You are to report to Miss Denham. Go straight away,' he said, seriously.

She could only nod and, retracing her steps, made her way to the reception office and knocked on the door.

'Ah, there you are, Miss Warrington,' Miss Denham said. 'I have your wage made up for the hours that you worked. I expect you understand that lateness cannot be excused, as it affects everyone.'

As a brown envelope was handed to her, Miss Denham said, 'Shut the door on your way out, Miss Warrington.'

Standing in the courtyard, with this small amount of money, not enough for the rent, and no family, she felt lost. It was the first time she had ever been completely alone. For a brief moment, as she looked across Mill Bay, she considered going back to her aunt, but knew realistically it wasn't an option. There was only room for one other occupant in the cottage and Amy was safely there.

Back in the room, she spent her last day sleeping in the armchair or lying on the bed looking at the ceiling.

She ate the rabbit and let the fire go out.

8.

Up early next morning, Sarah searched the room for anything that might have been from her childhood. The shelves held five bowls and the same amount of plates, some cracked, but none recognisable from her past. The box on the windowsill only held a small stub of a candle but she took it and the matches, placing them on the table. She had hoped to find spare clothes, but it seemed that they all only had the clothes that they stood up in.

Searching under the bed, she found a bag covered in dust and in it discovered a small snuffbox that had belonged to her paternal grandfather. It was something that her father had held dear and she was surprised that her mother had kept it. The picture, painted on the lid of the box, was a portrait of a man wearing a white bedcap against a black background.

It brought memories of visiting her father in his little room at the back of the house, where he liked to escape his children and read. The little box always sat on his desk, out of the sunlight, a memory of her father's childhood holidays spent with his grandparents. Left to him in a will, it was something that no one was allowed to touch.

It was with a shaking hand that she stroked the lid and the picture for the first time. Then, hearing movement from within, twisted the lid and opened the box to find her maternal grandmother's silver thimble.

Sitting back on her heels, she wondered why her mother hadn't sold them. Had she just forgotten that they were there? Or could she not bring herself to sell the last of her memories, no matter how far she fell into drink?

Trying to think what else she might need, she took her mother's old shawl from where it lay on the bed and pushed it into the bag.

It was raining as she left the building, with no regrets other than that she had nowhere to sleep that night.

The rain, riding the wind off the sea, was cold, hitting her face like a million small needles, drenching the road, turning the street into a mire. But before she had gone far, the sun came out and steam rose from the wet ground, giving off a miasma of animal and human stink, as some of the open sewers and slurry, from pigpens in backyards and cellars, overflowed.

With nowhere else to go, she walked aimlessly towards the Barbican. Although it was early, the area was busy; cafés open for breakfast and bakeries selling warm loaves of bread. Fishermen with ruddy faces stood in groups, eating freshly baked pies, and although they looked tired, they joked with each other.

Trying to ignore the smell of food, she walked slowly, looking at the fishing boats moored along the sea wall. Their sails furled, they moved rhythmically with the sea swell. Empty crab and lobster cages stacked three high along the quayside smelt strongly of seaweed and fish as they air dried. Several women were loading boxes of fish onto carts attached to patient donkeys, who stood heads down, waiting. The cobbles were hard to walk on, digging into her feet through the soles of her boots, now worn thin. The people milling around were, she saw, workers of a different breed. They kept different hours and most, she suspected, were families with their own boats, as they all looked similar.

The smell of fish was stronger where a group of women wearing oilskin aprons, heads covered, were speedily gutting fish just landed from a boat in front of the Dolphin. Packing them into boxes, they worked cheerfully, their camaraderie making Sarah even more aware of her own loneliness.

Gentlemen in top hats stood in a group around boxes of gutted fish on the quayside. Bidding for the fish, they were waving their money in the air for attention. She walked past pony traps that waited quietly, some with servants, and some left standing unattended on the cobbles. She felt better amongst the hustle and bustle where she was anonymous, an onlooker, a drifter.

When she reached the end of the Barbican, at the Watch House, she sat on the harbour steps outside the Admiral McBride, watching a fishing boat approach surrounded by a cloud of screeching gulls. In an hour or two, all this would be gone, leaving only the stench of fish that would linger all day and then... where would she go?

Although hungry, she was uncertain whether to spend the last of Ned's money on breakfast. Walking back along the quay, she again felt each cobble under her foot pressing painfully through the thin soles of her boots and tried not to hobble.

As she drifted slowly back along the quayside, she noticed that the men gathered outside the public houses, standing with their beer, were all dressed alike. Even the young men had wrinkled faces and weathered brown skin. The conversations that she overheard as she passed was of fish quotas, the French and conditions at sea.

With a heavy heart, she walked as far as the steps outside the Harbour Master's House, before turning around to walk back, but had gone but a few paces when she saw a man in a suit waving. Ignoring it, she walked on in his direction, for she was sure that nobody knew her.

'Miss Warrington,' the man called, raising his hat as she was about to pass him. 'You don't recognise me?'

Shocked to be spoken to at all, Sarah stared at the man, who was now placing the hat back on his head and smiling at her.

'Constable Parrett?' she questioned, hoping that it was him, as he looked very different without his helmet and uniform.

'Ah, you have seen right through my disguise.' He laughed. 'And where are you off to so early?'

'I'm afraid that I have nowhere to be, as I'm now homeless.'

His smile faded and his expression changed to one of concern.

'I'm sorry to hear that. Have you eaten this morning?' He changed the subject quickly.

'I haven't. I was saving what I have, so that I could eat tonight.'

'I'm just going for breakfast here at the café. Would you join me?'

'As I said, I can't, sir.'

'Please. I hate to eat alone and I feel that it's partly my fault that you find yourself in this circumstance. I would gladly buy you breakfast.'

'It wasn't your fault, sir. You were doing your duty. It was the fault of my mother. It can't be laid at the door of anyone else.'

'But I thought that you had work.' He looked confused.

'I did until what my mother had done was discovered.' Sarah knew that she sounded bitter. 'It made me late for work. They dismissed me with one day's pay.'

Without her realising it, he had guided her as they walked to the door of a café and was holding the door open.

Her stomach roiled with hunger at the smell of cooked food. And before she knew it, her legs had walked her inside, and he had directed her to a table, where he left her sitting alone.

He soon came back from the counter with two plates. Putting one down in front of her, he said, 'I hope that this will suit you well, Miss Warrington.'

For a moment she was speechless as she looked down at two buttered muffins, each topped with two small fried fish. A wonderful feast.

Looking up from the plate, she was surprised to see the concern on his face. Smiling her thanks, she noticed a very young face behind the moustache. Without the helmet, he didn't look much older than herself.

'Thank you, Mr Parrett, I'm truly grateful.' And she was.

'Then eat, Miss Warrington,' he said, lifting his own fork.

As they ate, he asked, 'What will you do now?'

'I have to find work. But the difficulty is that I don't have anywhere to live and not enough money for a lodging. I thought that I might approach the Girls' Orphanage and see if they can take me in.'

He looked regretful saying slowly, 'I believe, Miss Warrington, that they are full. My colleague took a girl there yesterday, and she was the last that they will accept at present.'

'I see.' Sarah sighed, looking down at the table, disappointed. Her only plan now in tatters. She sighed again, a tight smile on her lips, saying quietly, 'Thank you for the breakfast, Mr Parrett, but I have to go. I have a great deal to do.'

He stood up as she stood.

'I do know of a couple who are looking for someone to work in their shop... so to speak...' he added quickly. 'The last person who took the position didn't last long. They are again looking to employ a young woman.'

Sarah sat back down and he followed, sitting back in his own seat.

There was a strange look on his face as he spoke. A softness in his voice. A connection so gentle that she felt that he might put his hand out and caress hers. She felt hot.

'I hope that you're not squeamish or of fragile emotion, Miss Warrington,' he continued. 'I believe, from what I have seen of you, that you are quite strong by nature.'

Sarah frowned and looked steadily at him, wondering what he was going to suggest that she do.

'Please don't dismiss this suggestion straight away and I will take you there myself. I have dealings with the family on almost a daily basis.'

She waited, wondering why there needed to be such an extended explanation.

Taking a deep breath, he avoided looking straight at her as he spoke.

'Mr and Mrs Cole own the funeral parlour in King Street. They are looking for a young lady to help them, and to live in. Do you read and write, Miss Warrington? If so, I think that you would suit them very well.'

Sarah paled, the hope that he had momentarily given her dashed away.

'I don't want to see a dead body, Mr Parrett, let alone sleep in a building where they're housed.' She shivered.

'I don't think that the bodies are kept in the house.' He frowned. 'I believe that they are kept in a separate building in the yard at the back.'

Her heart was racing, her mouth dry. What should she do? She needed work and somewhere to sleep and here was an opportunity to have both, if she was suitable. But the funeral parlour! The place that they took Maud and possibly the poor girl who was murdered, whose place, she now realised, she had taken at the soap factory. She expelled a long breath, her fear of the dead overwhelming any ability to think or to make a realistic decision.

'Why don't we speak to Mr and Mrs Cole?' he suggested kindly. 'See if you would suit them, and find out what you might have to do. You can always say no.'

As he stared at her expectantly, she knew that she would have to answer, but all she could do was nod an agreement. What other option did she have?

As they walked back towards King Street, her fear of the dead rose ever higher in her chest. Her feet wanted to move slower, but she found herself keeping up with his long stride.

They arrived all too soon outside the funeral parlour and Sarah had to take a minute before she could enter.

'Please, wait,' she gasped, needing time.

Once more, she was looking at the brass plaque, the black drapes and the small replica coffin sitting in the centre of the window. A tableau of the inside of the glass coach in which many who could afford it might travel to their last resting place.

Her companion had already opened the door and the little bell just inside was ringing manically, and wouldn't stop until the door was closed. Out of politeness, she hurried to join him inside.

'Good morning, Mrs Cole, Mr Cole,' he was saying, as Sarah shut the door.

A thin, bespectacled woman, dressed in black, sat at a polished desk. Standing behind her, holding a sheaf of papers, a distinguished man with white hair, also dressed in black, a gold watch chain visible beneath his unbuttoned jacket.

'Good morning, Constable Parrett, how can we help you today?'

The woman smiled, then noticing his clothes, she continued, 'Surely, sir, you are off duty.'

'I am indeed, madam, but I have brought you a young lady, Miss Warrington, who I have discovered is looking for work and who I think will suit you very well, if she is agreeable, once the duties are explained.'

Mrs Cole squinted at Sarah through her glasses. The thick lenses magnified her eyes in a most frightening way. In fact, just how Sarah imagined the face of the dead to look if they came looking for her. Staring. Manically.

She paled.

'Come here, my dear, and let me see you in the light.' Mrs Cole's voice was surprisingly kind.

Sarah moved reluctantly away from the door and stood in front of the desk to be inspected.

'Now, my dear. Can you read and write?' the woman asked.

'Yes, Mrs Cole,' she replied quietly. Her mouth had dried as she battled against the need to cough in the musty atmosphere.

'Let me explain the duties, and then we will know very quickly whether you would want to work here or not. And I will be equally frank with you, my dear, and will tell you if you are not suitable. Is that agreeable with you?'

Sarah nodded, surprised and relieved by the woman's openness and kindness.

'Now, Constable,' the woman was saying, 'while I explain to Miss Warrington, will you go and see Beth, and ask her to make tea. And yes, tell her that I know that it's early, and that I would like a plate of her biscuits put out.'

'Do you wish to stay for the interview, Mr Cole?' she asked the white-haired gentleman hovering near the door behind her.

'I will leave this to you,' he said, declining, as he turned towards the door.

The constable looked at Sarah, standing alone and obviously frightened. His heart swelled, full of admiration for her as he turned and followed Mr Cole.

When they had departed, Mrs Cole turned her attention to Sarah.

'Now, Miss Warrington,' she said, standing up, 'come around the desk and sit here. I will show you the ledger that you will fill in. It has been my job all these years but as you may have noticed, my eyes do not work as they once did. I am looking for a young lady to take over from myself. I have to stress that neatness in writing is paramount, as sometimes the police, or a surgeon, may have the need to read what is written here. As you can see, there are columns. Can you read what is written at the top of each one?'

'Yes,' Sarah said, interested in the neat writing on the page.

'Would you read it, please.'

'Date. Name. Address. Date of Death. Cause of Death. Doctor/ Surgeon. Initial.'

'Thank you, Miss Warrington, you read very well,' she said. 'Now I must test your handwriting. If it is not neat and you are unable to make it so, then I will not be able to employ you, as the authorities sometimes have to look at this book. Sometimes, the information has to go before the court.'

Sarah nodded, the responsibility beginning to seem overwhelming. 'Can you tell me,' she asked, 'what initials mean, Mrs Cole?'

'A good question.' The woman smiled. 'As you will see under the heading initials, there is what you might call a scribble. It doesn't tell you anything, and yet it tells you everything.'

Sarah didn't understand.

'As you look down that column, all the marks are exactly the same.'

Sarah had to agree, but was no clearer as to what it was.

Seeing this, Mrs Cole said, 'My name is Gertrude Alexandra Cole, and what I have written in this column are those initials, GAC. It doesn't matter that you cannot see any of the letters. What does matter is that I always write this in exactly the same way, so that it is clear that I am the person who wrote it.'

Pulling open a drawer and removing a sheet of paper, she said,

'Please write your name, address and age here. I would like to see your handwriting.'

Sarah wrote with difficulty, as her hand was shaking. She hadn't had to write anything since being in school.

'You haven't written your address, Miss Warrington.'

'Since this morning, I have no address, Madam.'

'No family?'

'No, Madam.'

It was a question that she answered before thinking about it. Of course she had family, but not here. That is what she meant, or had she just lied on purpose, telling the woman what she thought she wanted to hear?

'Would you be happy to live in?' Mrs Cole broke into her thoughts. 'There is accommodation if needed.'

'That would suit me very well.' Sarah could hardly believe the offer.

Mrs Cole seemed happy and asked, 'Do you have any questions, Miss Warrington?'

'I would like to know what I might have to do when there is nothing to write in the book.'

The woman stretched her back, obviously in some discomfort, yet she smiled, having guessed what was worrying Sarah.

'You will never have to see or touch one of the cadavers, Miss Warrington, I can assure you of that.'

Sarah frowned, not understanding.

'We refer to a body as cadaver, or corpse, Miss Warrington.'

'Oh, I'm sorry, I didn't know,' Sarah replied, wide-eyed.

'Why would you?' The woman smiled kindly. 'But as to how you will fill your days, Miss Warrington, you will deal with whatever problem comes through that door. People are grieving and need a comforting word. They will want to know about the coffins that are on offer and made here in the workshop. They will want to choose fittings and perhaps a nameplate. I will need you to go to the post office and sometimes you may take papers to the court, with information from this book that the judge, his clerk or a solicitor will need to see. Now, let us go and meet the rest of the staff while you decide whether you would like to work for us.'

'Would you *want* to employ *me,* Mrs Cole?' Sarah asked, surprised at the turn of events.

'You are, I believe, just the person that we have been looking for, Miss Warrington.'

'Then I would like to take the job, if you're sure.'

Smiling, Mrs Cole nodded. 'If you wish, you can try it for a week, Miss Warrington, and we will both decide then if we will continue. I think that might suit us both.'

Dizzy with the speed of this change in her life, Sarah followed her new employer down a short hallway to a substantial kitchen at the back of the house, which, apart from one woman, was filled with men talking. Mrs Cole clapped her hands for attention and the room became quiet.

'This is Miss Warrington, and she will be our new receptionist,' she said happily. 'I want you all to give her any help that she needs.'

The men, who were about to depart to their workshops, bowed in turn as Mrs Cole introduced them.

'This is Peter Lamb, our carpenter, and his apprentice, Sam Woodshaw.'

A man in his fifties nodded towards her. 'Hope you be happy here, miss.'

The apprentice, a boy of around ten years, nodded and looked at his feet, embarrassed. They left the kitchen, going out into the yard.

'This is George Banks.' Mrs Cole indicated a man who nodded to her, 'and Jack Williams and John Maple.' The three men were dressed identically in leather waistcoats, their cotton shirtsleeves rolled up. Each politely lifted his hat as his name was spoken. 'They look after the coach and the horses. They also do the collecting for us and lead the processions to the cemetery,' she explained.

Sarah nodded in their direction, recognising the three men who got Mr Newby's coffin stuck in the doorway of his room. Their hats replaced, the men left the kitchen.

'Beth.'

She addressed the woman who was clearing the table. 'This is Miss Warrington, she will be living in and will be taking her meals with us.'

Sarah smiled at Beth, who looked surprised but who nodded in greeting while wiping the table of any trace of those who had just left.

'My husband will be relieved that I may now take more time to rest, Constable,' she said, smiling at the young policeman as he placed his cup in the sink and prepared to go. 'Thank you for bringing this young woman to us, I'm sure that we'll get on very well.'

Smiling fondly at the small woman, John Parrett turned to Sarah. 'I'll leave you now, Miss Warrington, and I hope that you will be happy here. I will see you from time to time when I'm on duty. Mrs Cole.' He bowed and, placing his hat on his head, left through the yard door.

'Such a nice young man,' Mrs Cole said almost to herself, then sighed. 'Come, Miss Warrington, I will show you to your rooms.'

Rooms? Sarah repeated in her head, as she once again followed behind the woman, but this time to the first floor along a passage with several doors much like the lodging house further down the street.

The room that they entered was in darkness. A sharp fragrance of human sweat hung on the air. Mrs Cole found her way across the room in total darkness. Pulling back the heavy drapes, she revealed wooden shutters that she folded back against the wall. Having let in the light, she opened the window.

The room, when revealed, was large, and Sarah was surprised at the amount of furniture contained in it. Four large armchairs, each with its own occasional table at the side. There were other tables, some ornate, covered in lace and holding vases and knick-knacks. A large mahogany chest of drawers, on which ornaments and glass domes with dead birds in various poses, looked out through the glass, watching her.

87

On the walls, large pictures in ornate black or gold frames hung from the picture rail that ran around the room just below the ceiling. A mirror, in an equally large and ornate frame, hung in the same manner from the picture rail.

A long-case clock ticked loudly in one dark corner of the room and a second clock ticked a lighter note from the mantelshelf above the grey marble fireplace.

'These rooms were my mother's until her passing last year,' Mrs Cole said, as she walked to a door and, on opening it, revealed a bedroom. 'This is your bedroom. The bed hasn't been made up, but Beth will do it now you're staying.'

Sarah stood in the doorway, staring at a black iron bedstead standing in lonely splendour against a faded, and grease-marked, fawn wallpaper. The stained mattress, sunken in the middle, looked difficult to get out of once in, and afforded only one position for sleeping: the middle. It was the sort of bed, she thought, that had seen births and deaths over many years. But she wasn't about to complain, as she had nowhere else to sleep or shelter.

'I hope that you will find these rooms warm and comfortable, Miss Warrington. And if you need anything, please let Beth know.'

'Thank you. I'm sure that I will be very comfortable here.' Sarah nodded, not feeling at all comfortable in this alien environment.

'I will leave you now to put your things away.' Mrs Cole moved towards the door. 'Beth will bring your work dress for you to try on later. When you are done here, I will take you out into the yard and show you the workshops, as you will have to work with the men, letting them know the type of wood the client has chosen for the coffin, the style of handles, the colour of the satin lining.' She laughed. 'Don't look worried, it's all straightforward and you'll pick it up very easily. In a week, I can guarantee that you will be wondering what you were worried about.'

When Mrs Cole had gone, Sarah walked around the rooms, not feeling at ease. The sharp scent of the last occupant seemed embedded in all the fabric and she began to imagine that the woman had died in the bed. Her first elation about this position was wearing off. She would like a new mattress but wouldn't like to ask.

Mrs Cole had told her to unpack, but she didn't have anything to unpack, only having the clothes that she stood up in and her mother's shawl.

To pass the time, she sat on a chair beside the empty grate, her bag at her feet, then stood, straightening her skirt, ready for her introduction to the workshops.

It was as she was leaving to go downstairs that she noticed something unusual. Both the bedroom and the sitting-room doors had not only a lock with a key, but bolts, top and bottom, on the inside.

As no one was around, she walked quietly to the end of the passage and looked through the window into the yard below. As she turned back, she noticed a door with bolts top and bottom. Why would a door have bolts on the outside where whatever was within could be easily accessed?

9.

Sitting at the desk, dressed like her employer in a black dress, her hair pulled up in the style of her mother, Sarah was shown a catalogue of prices and how to write down the client's choices in an order book, including the cost, which was to be taken to Mr Cole in his small office next to the kitchen. It would be he who would work out how much the client was to be charged, for which Sarah was grateful.

As the two women sat together at the desk, going over all that she had so far been shown, the shop door opened and a man entered, not bent in grief but boldly, as though he owned the premises. A tall man, dressed casually, wearing a waistcoat over a shirt embroidered with flowers, dark trousers and a neckerchief of bright red. He didn't approach the desk but made for the door and the accommodation beyond.

'Mr Bronalski.'

Mrs Cole addressed the man, who stopped and turned to look at her.

'Mrs Cole!' he replied, a derisive tone in his voice that embarrassed Sarah. But Mrs Cole either didn't notice or ignored it.

'This is Miss Warrington, Mr Bronalski. She will be working here and sleeping in my mother's room. I will expect you to take all necessary precaution.'

There was something unsettling in the way she spoke to him, conspiratorial. Sarah could feel the dislike, the coldness that crept between them.

He didn't reply, or acknowledge Sarah, before he disappeared through the door.

Looking questioningly at her employer, Sarah wondered if she would get an explanation; after all, it seemed to include her, whatever it was.

Mrs Cole sniffed, then sighed. 'You will meet Mr Bronalski at mealtimes. He is my son's tutor and companion. He lives in. His bedroom backs onto your room, but sometimes, when Arthur can't settle, Mr Bronalski sleeps upstairs in my son's apartment.'

Sarah nodded in acceptance of the statement and wanted to ask how old her son was, as surely, she thought, the Coles were old enough to be grandparents, but it wasn't her place to ask. She would know in time.

The tour of the square back yard with all its different smells was brief, and involved the paperwork being given to the carpenter, informing him which wood to use for a coffin. The privy cubicle pointed out was clean and Sarah was relieved to learn that Beth looked after it daily. Then, beyond the stable and the dung heap, she was shown an area planted with lavender bushes and heard the peaceful sound of bees humming. This swathe of lavender was not what Sarah had expected to find in the middle of King Street. Mrs Cole pulled off a few flower heads and gave them to her. 'Squeeze them up and put them in your pocket. The smell, I think, helps to calm you when you feel stressed. I scatter a handful in each coffin, because it smells nice. A little luxury that some will not have had in life. I also distil a little oil, it helps my son.'

Sarah was moved by her kindness and was about to thank her when a large pig, snorting loudly, pushed against the low fence that divided them from the property at the back. The pig, standing knee-deep in its own stinking muck, tried to push its nose between the gaps in the spindle fence. Sarah took a step backwards as it snorted, stinking sludge running off its nose.

'We had better move or she'll have the fence down,' Mrs Cole said, looking flustered. 'She's had many litters and they get in here from time to time and it causes such devastation.'

'Can't you put up a better fence?' Sarah asked, seeing the frailty of the thin sticks held together with wire.

'It's their fence.' Mrs Cole pointed to the house that overlooked them. 'And they refuse to make it stronger. When it rains hard, all the slurry from their yard runs between the sticks and down into our yard. I think that's why it suits them. It's we that have to clear the mess up before it gets into the workshops.'

As they walked back, Sarah noticed that the back of the property had wooden steps leading from the ground to the top floor.

Mrs Cole, noticing her interest, explained. 'It's a fire escape. There are so many fires in King Street that Mr Cole thought it best to take precautions.'

'But it's made of wood!' Sarah commented.

'Yes!' Mrs Cole said, looking at it as though for the first time and frowning. 'It's what Mr Cole wanted, and our carpenters did the work.'

It was as she went to follow the woman to the back door that Sarah thought that she saw a face at the window under the roof. The features were not clear, but the face seemed large and white, like the moon. It pulled back quickly and Sarah was left wondering if she had seen a face or a reflection of the clouds.

Back in the kitchen, all the men had taken seats at the table and Mr Bronalski was leaving with two plates of food. He didn't acknowledge the women as they took their places at the table.

Beth served the lunch, and the men, who were too busy eating to speak, soon finished and returned to their work.

'As you can see, Miss Warrington,' Mrs Cole said, pouring cider from a jug into both their glasses, 'we have a happy working relationship with our staff. Hungry workers don't work well and we're more likely to keep them this way.'

The food, bread, cheese and pickle with the small glass of cider was more than Sarah could ever have hoped for. It seemed so long ago that Constable Parrett had bought her breakfast on the Barbican, and yet, it was this same morning.

At the end of the day, Sarah made her way downstairs and thought that she would be eating with her employers, but was surprised to see Mr and Mrs Cole leaving the kitchen with trays full of food.

'Ah, there you are, Miss Warrington.' Mrs Cole smiled as Sarah entered the kitchen. Mr Cole and I eat every night with our son in his rooms. You can eat in here with Beth or use the dining room. We'll see you in the morning.'

Beth, who had the meal ready, placed it in front of Sarah, saying, 'Hope you aren't fussy, I can't be doing with fussy.'

'No, I'm not fussy, Beth, I'm very grateful.'

Beth turned away to clear vegetable peelings from the small worktop, and to make conversation, Sarah asked, 'What was the girl like who did this job before me?'

Beth didn't reply. Thinking that she hadn't heard, Sarah asked, 'Why did the girl before me leave?'

When Beth turned back to the table, her face was hard to read, the expression sombre.

'I can't tell you that.'

Dropping the peelings into a bucket, Beth placed it at the back door. 'Not my place to have opinions,' she said sharply, almost like a spoilt child.

'Oh, I'm sorry, Beth, I didn't mean to pry. I was just interested.'

'If I were you, maid,' she said, removing her overall and hanging it on a hook by the door, 'I'd stop being interested and keep my own counsel. I'd mind my own business,' she said pointedly. 'Safer that way, in my opinion.'

Sarah was silenced by the woman's reaction and, when she had finished her food, Beth removed the plate, saying, 'If you want to go out, the key to the door hangs on that hook. When you return tonight, put it back and make sure that you lock the door.'

Sarah nodded.

'Did you hear what I said?' Beth asked pointedly.

'Yes, Beth, I heard you. If I go out, I will lock up when I get back.'

Beth nodded. 'I'm off to feed my own family now and put my kids to bed. I'll see you in the morning.'

Sarah was left alone, sitting at the kitchen table, unsure if the woman was just tired or didn't like her.

~

Over the next month, Sarah was surprised at how many children living in King Street died by fire, how many times people died in suspicious circumstances and how many times she had to walk to the court with her books.

There were several young constables who visited through their work, but it was John Parrett that she looked forward to seeing, feeling a fondness for him. After all, they had a past, he knowing her circumstance and getting her this job.

It was the last day of the month and the police were knocking on the front door early, before the shop had opened. A body, discovered in Union Street, needed collection. The hospital was overcrowded and the body would be brought straight to the funeral parlour. A doctor surgeon would arrive later to examine it. Usually, bodies were brought from the hospital and returned to families in a coffin, where they often lay on the dining-room table or in the front parlour for several days, while neighbours and relatives came to say goodbye.

There was nothing to write in the book until she had more information.

George and Jack had the horse and cart ready and went to get the corpse, which they were told they would find lying in the street, covered by a tarpaulin, a constable keeping guard.

Through the window, Sarah later saw them returning with Doctor Pearce sitting on the front seat next to George, and Jack sitting in the back beside the coffin.

A little later, the doctor walked into the office. 'Miss Warrington, how nice to meet you again.' He bowed.

Sarah smiled sweetly, but Dr Pearce was yet another reminder of her mother.

'I'll get the book,' she said, trying to keep hold of her emotions as she took it from the shelf and brought it back to the desk.

Doctor Pearce wrote the day's date. The name column was left empty, as was the address. He then filled in the column for date of death and the cause, murder by strangulation during a violent sexual act, and initialled it.

On her way to the post office, Sarah saw the headlines in the newspaper. The vicious murder of a prostitute in Union Street. Anyone with information should contact the police. But it was the smaller item of news, almost lost below the murder article, that chilled her. *Woman committed for the murder of her baby left in King Street privy.* It named her mother, and Sarah hoped that the Coles wouldn't see it.

As she walked back to the funeral parlour, she thought about denying that she was related to the woman in the newspaper, if she was asked. But would the Coles believe her? And then she remembered that PC Parrett wouldn't lie to them if they asked him.

All afternoon, she expected the Coles to say something; she knew that they received all the newspapers daily. When they didn't mention it, she assumed that they had just been too busy to read the news-sheet.

She had several customers that afternoon, but was not prepared for the man that entered as the doorbell jangled. Looking up from her books, her heart rate increased. She tried to smile, but her mouth had set in a grimace of fear, not the face of compassion that Mrs Cole expected.

The man who entered was tall, dressed head to foot in black, an older man with grey hair above his ears, his head a bare skull covered in a thin layer of waxy skin. As he walked towards the desk, his narrow eyes roved over her body and she shrank before him.

'Well, well,' he smiled, revealing yellow tombstone teeth. 'Who have we here?'

'Sarah Warrington, sir,' she croaked, her mouth dry with fear, for here was a dead person walking, dressed for its funeral and carrying its own flowers.

With a trembling hand, she rang the small bell for Mrs Cole, and thought that if he came any nearer she would scream, or faint.

'Ah, Mr Michaels,' Mrs Cole smiled as she saw him, 'I was expecting you. Come this way and let me see what flowers you can offer. Although I have to warn you that many who want flowers, want lilies.'

Mr Michaels followed Mrs Cole from the front office, but not without a sideways glance at Sarah that chilled her to her bone. He left an odd fragrance behind on the air.

It was just before five when the door to the street opened and a constable entered, accompanied by a woman and a girl of about nine, who carried a small child on her hip. The girl was reluctant to come in and stood near the door, fear showing in her eyes.

'This is Mrs Barrett,' the constable said. 'She's come to view the body. She believes that it might be her neighbour.'

Sarah went to fetch Mrs Cole, who took the woman to the small room opposite Mr Cole's office. The room had been set up as a chapel where relatives could, if they had no room at home, sit with their loved one.

Leaving the girl and the small child with Sarah, it wasn't long before the woman returned, the colour gone from her face. Taking the small child from her daughter, she turned to Sarah, saying, 'You must be very glad that your mother's no longer on the street. But she'll come to a sticky end anyway. I read the paper.'

Sarah gasped in shock, staring at the woman in front of her. How did she know so much about her and who she was?

'It's Doxy in there,' she continued. 'Could have been me, just a matter of chance.' She turned away. 'Come on, Annie.' She addressed the girl. 'Let's get home and get the babies fed.'

When they'd gone, Sarah realised who it was. The woman, Doxy's friend, looked very different without the makeup and revealing clothes. The air left behind in her wake held the accusation. If the space had been solid, its finger would have been pointing at Sarah.

Mrs Cole thankfully hadn't heard, as she had stayed behind talking to the constable, who she now showed out, locking the door behind him.

Sarah sat unmoving behind the desk, her limbs frozen. Mrs Cole was speaking but she heard nothing until the woman touched her shoulder.

'Miss Warrington.' Sarah jumped in fright. 'I've locked up, you can go and change before dinner, if you wish, and I will put the books away.'

Nodding her thanks, Sarah left the office on weak legs, climbing the stairs to her rooms, where she opened the window to let the air in and sat looking down on King Street. Gradually, the bustle of humans and horses brought her back to life. Her heart felt heavy. She was tainted. Didn't the priest say that the sins of the mothers were carried by their daughters, or something like that, on Sunday, when she went with the Coles to their church?

Washing her hands and face, she removed the awful black dress that the Coles had given her to wear in the office. She had thought it an old lady's dress, but Beth, reading the expression on her face, had pointed out that the dress was in keeping with her work, and in sympathy with the queen, who had lost Prince Albert.

Hanging the dress over a chair, she put her own clothes on and felt lighter in the cream blouse that had belonged to her cousin.

At the sound of heavy footsteps overhead, she glanced up at the ceiling. Over the weeks, she had heard running footsteps, thumps and things being dropped. Sometimes it sounded like someone jumping up and down on the same spot for so long that Sarah had to put her hands over her ears. And sometimes she heard the tutor raise his voice, and the following silence felt strange. She wondered why the Coles kept their son upstairs and why the tutor, Mr Bronalski, hardly spoke to anyone, not even his employers. Perhaps they spoke together when she wasn't there.

Seeing Mrs Cole on the landing with her tray, making her way to the door that Sarah now knew led to the next floor and their son, she took the opportunity to speak to Mrs Cole.

'Would you mind if I walked a little this evening, Mrs Cole? It's so nice outside.'

She hoped that the woman wouldn't have any objection, for she hadn't left the building, unless with work, in days, and she was getting very tired of looking at the yellowing wallpaper each evening with no one to talk to.

'Yes. You go, Miss Warrington,' Mrs Cole said kindly at the request. 'Of course you should get some air. Take the yard door key and let yourself back in. But you must be back before ten o'clock when we retire to our beds. It's when we pull the bolts across. Is that acceptable to you?'

'Oh yes, madam. Thank you.'

Hesitating in going downstairs straight away, Sarah ducked back into her room for something to put over her shoulders in case it turned cool. She returned to the landing with her shawl, just as Mrs Cole reached the door with the bolts on the outside. It was open now and she was stepping through it.

'Dada. Muma, Muma.'

The excited voice of a child floated from the open doorway and along the landing. It was the first time that Sarah had actually heard the voice of the Coles' son.

Mrs Cole's voice sounded rather frantic in reply as she attempted to shut the door behind her. 'Go back upstairs, Arthur, you'll have me drop my tray.' And more determinedly: 'Arthur, do as I ask, there's a good boy, and Muma will find those sweeties in a moment when we have eaten our supper. That's it. Good boy.'

Sarah ate alone in the kitchen, as Beth had gone the minute Sarah had picked up her knife and fork, with only a nod, not even a good night.

After she had eaten, Sarah placed her plate in the sink and, taking the key from its hook, hurried away from the building. But no matter how fast or slow she walked, she couldn't get away from the thoughts in her head, or the feeling that everyone knew everything about her, that she was as guilty as her mother, just by being her daughter.

Glad of the steep uphill stretch to the Hoe, Sarah joined the people walking arm in arm on the promenade, enjoying the evening breeze. The sky was still blue, although the colour was fading. The sea, as though in a state of meditation, rippled below her. Even the seagulls seemed quiet, strutting at a distance, though ever watchful.

Breathing in the atmosphere and trying to shake off the mood that had fallen upon her after her mother's night-time friend had recognised her, she began to relax. This was what she needed: freedom.

She thought of Ned, and how they had walked here before he returned to sea, and of John Parrett. She couldn't deny that she looked forward to the days that John might visit, after which, she felt different, happy all day.

The air on the Hoe was cooler than in the town, fresher, although that wouldn't last. When the tide was fully in, it would bring the stench of sewage with it.

Seeing two small boys with their father, rolling their hoops with sticks, she thought of Sam and Thomas. How different life would have been for them if their father hadn't died.

Halfway along the promenade she sat on a bench looking out at the sea and thought of Ned, who was out there somewhere. She should write to him. He had given her an address of a seamans' organisation that would eventually get mail to him. But should she tell him about their mother? She sighed. Ordinarily, she would have been happy to tell him what was happening in her life, but whether or not to let him know what had befallen their mother weighed heavily on her mind. What good would it do? He would be sad. Mother was his, their, flesh and blood after all, and they couldn't get away from that feeling of connection.

Watching the slow passage of ships with their sails fully up to catch the merest breeze, she forgot her troubles and her mind calmed. Eventually, the air on the Hoe cooled as the sun sank towards the horizon.

Standing up and pulling her shawl around her shoulders, she made her way slowly back to King Street with a lighter heart.

The yard was deserted, swept clean, ready for the morrow or the middle of the night, if the men were called out. Although it wasn't yet fully dark, there was a light in the window above the stable, where the stablehands lived, and it felt somehow reassuring in the darkening yard. One of the horses neighed quietly as they also settled down for the night.

The Coles had lit the lamp in their living room and its yellow light glowed dimly above the yard. In that moment, standing in the darkness, she felt the loss of family, of belonging. This wasn't home. No one here knew her.

Having located the door key in her pocket, she was pushing it into the lock when she felt goosebumps run down the back of her neck, and her hair creep over her scalp to stand on end. Something was hovering behind her. Fear clutched at her heart and her hand shook as she thought of the dead that lay in one of the outbuildings.

The key slipped into the lock and she was through the door and slamming it shut in one breath. Pushing the bolts home, she then locked the door with the key, before replacing it on the hook.

In the silent darkness of the kitchen, facing the door, she tried to quell her fear and understand what had just happened.

Her breath was laboured and her whole body shook as she passed quickly through the kitchen and up the stairs to her room, where she locked and bolted the door, before sitting in the armchair, watching the door knob, waiting for it to move. When nothing happened and the door stayed shut, she began to feel embarrassed and glad that no one else had seen her fear.

Derry's Clock had been showing nine twenty as she had passed it earlier. And although she had sat for a while at the window in her room before getting ready for bed, out of boredom, she thought that it was possibly still only around ten o'clock when she heard the familiar sounds of discontent coming through the ceiling above. It made her wonder why the boy was never allowed out for some air. Surely all children needed air. He must be as desperately bored as she was. Why had they never asked her upstairs to see him? It may have given him a bit more interest. She was good with children, especially boys like her brothers. She would ask Mrs Cole in the morning if she could visit him, perhaps play a board game with him tomorrow evening. It would be good to have company.

At breakfast, Mrs Cole asked if she had enjoyed her walk and Sarah had to admit that she had, and that she would never tire of watching the ships or the sun going down.

'I used to love the Hoe myself on a mild spring evening,' Mrs Cole sighed. 'I always felt that it was the herald of a good summer.'

'Would you like to walk with me one evening, Mrs Cole?' Sarah asked, only because the woman looked so wistful.

'Oh no, my dear. Thank you for asking, but I need to spend my evenings with my son, who doesn't see his parents all day.'

'Yes, of course. I understand. I had younger brothers once and know that they got bored in the evenings. I used to play board games with them. Would you like me to play a board game with your son, Mrs Cole?'

For a passing moment, the woman looked shocked but recovered quickly.

'Thank you for your offer, Miss Warrington, but my son is not well. He finds it difficult to relate to strangers. It upsets him, and if he can't sleep, poor Mr Bronalski will be up all-night coping with him. I hope that you understand, Miss Warrington, and thank you for offering.'

That, Sarah realised, was why he was never seen. The child was unwell and perhaps mentally unwell, hence the noise at night. Now that she understood, she would be able to sleep more easily, but still thought that the child needed air.

10.

Charles Blatten sat alone at the breakfast table, the silence of the house that he had shared with his sister, Lillian, pressing hard on his ears. Sometimes he thought that he heard her in the kitchen and, without thought, called out, 'Is that you, Lil?' and then, just as suddenly realised his mistake and cried, uncontrollably. It had been a few weeks since her death and her body still lay in the hospital mortuary. Although the police were no nearer finding out who had killed her, they were going to release her body for burial. It had taken a long while to convince them that she had only gone out because she had a headache. He was still angry that they had suspected him of her murder, and then that she was a woman of the night. They had spoken to some of the women who frequented Union Street and the police couldn't prove it, as none of those women knew her.

He glanced at the letter held loosely in his hand, received in the post that morning, telling him that Lillian's body had been released for burial. He knew that he had to pull himself together and go to the undertaker's and arrange her funeral, but it was hard. A year in age more than him, Lillian had always been in charge. It was Lil, just like their mother, who made the decisions and told him what he was doing, just like Mother had with their father. And now he was rudderless, would have to make his own decisions and he didn't know how. Suppose he got it wrong. Fear of failure was causing inertia. Pouring tea from the teapot, he realised that he had sat unmoving for so long that it had gone cold.

Standing, he put the letter on the mantelshelf. He'd think about it and try to decide what to do. At least while in the hospital, she was still in this world, but once he had arranged her funeral, she would be gone forever and he would be alone.

Later in the day, after going into work to claim the two days' leave that he was allowed, to make the necessary arrangements, he dressed in his best clothes and walked to King Street where he stood outside the funeral parlour for some time, thinking about what he would say. At twenty-two, he hadn't remotely thought that he would be in a position where he would be thinking that he should have asked his sister what sort of funeral she wanted. What sort of box she would want to be buried in. And the cost! That scared him more than anything. Could he afford to bury his sister? Until now, he'd had no time off work to grieve and that had made things worse. Sitting in the evenings alone in the silence of the house, and now, out in the street, he felt disconnected from the world.

He felt weak as he opened the door to the funeral parlour. His head swam, and the clanging of the bell over the door set his nerves jangling. Stepping quickly inside, he closed the door but held on to the door handle for a moment longer than normal, trying to get his balance. Was he going to faint! Men didn't faint; that was the prerogative of women. But he did feel very unwell.

He hardly noticed the young woman who was suddenly beside him, her arm around his waist, asking if he needed help. He let himself be led to a chair where he felt her hand on the back of his head gently pushing him forward, and still talking, pressed his head down towards his knees. He didn't realise that she had left him until she was holding a bottle of smelling salts under his nose. The strength and sourness of the ammonia fumes suddenly brought him round, and eyes streaming, he sat up rubbing his face.

'Are you feeling better?' The young woman standing in front of him looked concerned. 'You're very pale, but your colour is coming back now.'

Charles couldn't speak so nodded that he was feeling better. He wasn't. But that is what you did when asked if someone's help had worked.

103

'Sit there as long as you like, sir, then come to the desk and tell me who you are and how I can help you.'

'Thank you,' he mumbled.

As he began to feel better, he looked around, seeing the dark wood-panelled walls, the chairs, the desk with the young woman in black writing in a book. When she stood up with some papers and left, he made a hurried exit.

Standing out in the street, everything seemed to be moving past him at speed, and the noise of the street seemed heightened. He felt dizzy, tried to breathe, tried to move, but his knees buckled and he fell forward onto the cobbles.

The smell of ammonia brought him back to life again and, when he opened his eyes, he was laying on his back staring at a ceiling. The young woman was kneeling on the floor next to him, as was a street constable.

'He's coming around,' the constable whom he recognised was saying. 'Are you feeling better, Mr Blatten?'

Charles thought about it with difficulty. Was he feeling better? No, he wasn't, but he said, 'Yes, thank you, Constable Parrett.'

'Let us try and get him onto a chair, Miss Warrington. We'll take an arm each,' the policeman said. 'One, two, three, lift.'

This time, he was put on a chair in front of the desk, so that he couldn't fall forward. The door behind the desk opened and a rather severe woman in black came towards him, holding a glass. At the sight of her, Charles thought that he had died, that he was in God's waiting room, ready to be taken up to heaven, but why was the angel dressed in black? Surely he hadn't been bad. Why wasn't the angel in white? Tears rolled over his cheeks as he stared at what he believed to be an apparition. But when the angel spoke, her voice was gentle, like his mother's when he was ill.

'Drink this, Mr Blatten.' She held the glass towards him. 'I think that it will have you feeling better, and then we can talk, when you are ready.'

He took the glass with a shaking hand, supported by the constable so that he wouldn't spill it. The liquid was fiery. It made him cough and the glass was taken by the constable until he stopped coughing, then given back with the instruction, 'Sip a little more, sir, you don't have to drink it all.'

He did sip a little more and this time it wasn't so harsh. It seemed sweeter, even though still hot. He felt warmed. Feeling the colour coming back into his cheeks, he was able to take a breath and sit up straighter.

'Thank you,' he said, handing the glass back.

'I think, Mr Blatten, that you are here to make arrangements for your sister's funeral. Is that right?' Mrs Cole asked.

Charles nodded.

'Miss Warrington will help you. But take your time, Mr Blatten, you do not have to decide today.'

'Thank you, madam,' he managed. Then, turning to the constable, asked, 'Would you stay, Constable? I can't do this on my own.'

'Of course, sir, if Miss Warrington doesn't mind?'

Sarah, happy to have the constable stay, smiled. 'Please bring up another chair, Constable Parrett.'

Picking up a chair and bringing it to the desk, the constable sat next to Charles.

Sarah turned the pages of the catalogue, showing Charles the examples of wood and then the designs of coffin, but in this case, she didn't say oak or larch, only told him the prices. He chose the cheapest.

When it came to the coffin furniture, he decided not to have handles on the sides and became distressed again when asked what he would like written on the brass plate.

'It's all very expensive,' he groaned, almost to himself, tears appearing in his eyes.

'Perhaps,' Sarah said, 'I could ask our carpenter to make a wooden plaque with her name burnt into it. Would that suit you, Mr Blatten?'

'It would. Thank you.'

He appeared distressed, and he seemed to Sarah to have shrunk into a small boy. 'I'm sorry that I'm making this so difficult,' he said, biting his bottom lip. 'You see, I don't know if I have the money. My sister did the accounts, looked after everything. I didn't take an interest. I didn't need to.'

'Have you not been in contact with your bank, sir?' Constable Parrett asked.

'No. I didn't know if they would see me. I don't know the account number.'

'Your sister must have all the details written down at home. Have you not looked?'

Charles shook his head. 'I can't go through my sister's things. It wouldn't be right.'

'But you have to, sir. You can't live without knowing how to manage your affairs.'

Charles realised that he would have to take charge. That he would have to go into his sister's room, and would have to open her desk and look at her accounts and get involved in things he didn't understand. The colour drained once again from his face.

'When did you last eat, Mr Blatten?' Constable Parrett asked suddenly.

Charles thought, but couldn't remember. The days since the shock of his sister's death seemed to blur into nothing but one long torturous nightmare of loss and hopelessness.

The constable was speaking and Charles tried hard to concentrate.

'I'm about to finish my shift, Miss Warrington. If you could give us time, I will return later with Mr Blatten.'

Then, turning to Charles, he said, 'If you are agreeable, Mr Blatten, I would like to take you to the café for some food and then go home with you to look through your accounts.'

'While you're there,' Sarah said quickly, in case she didn't get another opportunity, 'could you also decide what you would like your sister buried in?'

'Buried in?' Charles didn't understand. He thought that they were deciding on the coffin.

Sarah blushed. 'The clothes, sir. It's most often their Sunday best.'

He nodded, a feeling of sickness overcoming him. 'I couldn't go through Lil's clothes, it wouldn't be right.'

'Do you not have a female relative that you could ask to go through her wardrobe, sir?' the constable asked softly, already knowing the probable answer.

'We were orphaned at the age of twelve and thirteen. Lil took over everything. She was like a mother to me. I don't know what I will do without her.'

As the tears once again flooded his eyes, Constable Parrett took over. 'Right, my lad. First off, let's get some food into you and then when you are stronger, we will go to your house and to the bank and get all this sorted out.'

After they'd gone, Sarah sat thinking about how unexpected happenings ruin lives. Perhaps she had been harsh with her mother. Perhaps Gwen hadn't been able to cope without the backing of her father, without his money. Was it he who looked after the finances, leaving her mother uninformed and perhaps penniless? She would never know the answer to that, but decided that she would try to think kindly of her mother in future.

The vision of Constable John Parrett offering to help Charles Blatten and taking charge of the situation softened her heart, and now she sat dreaming of him, a silly smile on her face, until the door behind her opened and Mrs Cole bustled into the room, saying, 'I'll lock the door now, Miss Warrington, as it's lunchtime. Go to the kitchen, Beth has it ready.'

In the kitchen, Beth had the table laid and the men, who had just finished their lunch, were leaving. Beth placed the food in front of Sarah and continued to clear the table where the men had been.

Sarah watched her moving about the kitchen, not speaking, and wondered why Beth didn't like her. What had she said or done to upset the woman, or was she always like this?

Then she remembered that it was since she had asked about the woman whose place she had taken, the one who had disappeared. Yes, that was when Beth changed, avoided her so as not to be asked again. What was the mystery? Why did she leave? What had happened to her?

As Sarah lifted the fork to her mouth, Mr Bronalski entered, followed by Mr Cole. Beth handed the tutor two plates of food. 'Will you manage them, Mr Bronalski? They're a bit hot.'

'I manage, thank you.' He nodded sharply, his accent stunting his words. Taking the plates from Beth's hands, he placed them onto a tray.

'How is my son today, sir?' Mr Cole asked. 'Settling down to his learning, I hope.'

'He is calm today, sir, and engrossed in making a model of a boat out of matchsticks.'

Mr Cole nodded. 'And his reading?'

'Yes, sir, that is coming along.'

'Hmm, I look forward to the day that he will read to me. Enjoy your meal, sir,' he said, as Mr Bronalski turned towards the door.

Mr Cole was taking his place at the table as Mrs Cole entered, saying, 'This looks lovely, Beth, thank you.' Her smile was warm and Beth's mouth, Sarah noticed, twitched in what was almost an accidental smile.

Turning to Mr Cole, his wife said, as she took her seat, 'We had that poor man, the brother of the murdered girl, in this morning to arrange her funeral.'

'How is he?' Mr Cole took his plate from Beth and placed it on the table.

'Not coping, sir. Not coping at all.'

'What did he order?'

'Well, Miss Warrington tried to help him but he doesn't know how much money he has, as his sister did the accounts and she didn't share the knowledge.'

'His own fault then,' he said dismissively. 'A man that cannot keep his own accounts is not a man in my opinion.'

'But he is not a man, my dear, he is a boy, left alone in this world without parents.'

'Like many others, madam,' he replied sharply. 'And they survive. I'm sure he will also.'

Mrs Cole kept a passive face as she replied. 'Constable Parrett has gone with him to the bank. He will help him talk to the bank manager and we will see then what he can afford.'

'Well, just remember, madam, we are not a charity.'

'No, my dear. We are not a charity. I know that,' she said quietly, picking up her knife and fork. 'I know that.'

~

It was the middle of the afternoon when the jangling bell announced the arrival of Charles Blatten, who looked much better than he had on his last visit.

'Mr Blatten,' Sarah acknowledged him. 'Is all well?'

'Yes, thank you. I'm ready to place an order.'

Sarah noticed his eyes fill with tears and ignored it so as not to embarrass him further. She reached for the catalogue as he took his seat in front of her desk and placed it in front of him. He still chose the cheapest coffin and the wooden name plaque that Sarah had offered before, and she wondered even more at his circumstance. She found that she was feeling a fondness towards him and wondered if it was because she had taken his sister's place at work, knew the women that she worked with and the work that she had done. She tried to distance herself from him, knowing that the Coles would not be impressed if she could not stay professional and aloof.

When all was done, he looked at her across the desk and said hesitantly, 'I wonder if you could help me, Miss Warrington. I have no one else to ask.'

Sarah frowned. She didn't mean to frown but was worried about the Coles' view of her work and what he was going to ask.

Biting his lip and screwing up his face as though he were in pain, he said quietly, 'When I was here earlier, you asked what my sister would be buried in.'

'Yes.'

'This is very difficult for me... I can't go into my sister's room and go through her clothes. It wouldn't be right.'

'I see.'

'Would you come to the house and do it for me?'

Sarah was shocked. Not only had she taken the girl's job, stood at her bench, made herself unpopular with Lillian's work colleagues, but she was now being asked to go through her clothes.

'Oh, I don't think…'

'Please, Miss Warrington.'

'Would one of her workmates not be more appropriate, sir?'

'No!' His voice was quite sharp. 'Lillian only pretended to like them. She found them nosy and prying. She hated gossip and tried very hard to keep herself to herself.'

'Oh!' Sarah was surprised; this wasn't the impression that she'd got.

'If you don't mind, sir, I will ask my employer if it's appropriate. I can't afford to antagonise them. I hope that you understand.'

He nodded but said nothing more. His shoulders had dropped and he looked so desolate that Sarah went immediately to find Mrs Cole to ask her permission.

She found her in the lavender patch, bending over the plants, picking the flower heads and placing them in a basket on the ground at her feet.

'Mrs Cole,' she called.

The woman straightened up, rubbing her back.

'I've been asked by Mr Blatten if I could go to his house and choose his sister's clothes for burial.'

'That's very unusual, and not appropriate,' she said. 'He's an unmarried man. He lives alone.'

'Yes, that is why I'm asking your opinion, Mrs Cole.'

'Umm, yes.' She looked uncertain. 'Let me speak to him.' Picking the basket up, she walked with Sarah back to the office.

'Mr Blatten,' she said kindly, as they entered the office. 'How can we help you?'

He looked shocked that Mrs Cole was there, and that he had to ask again, something that he was obviously mortified about.

'I need help, madam,' he said quietly. 'I cannot do it. I cannot go through my sister's things, it isn't right. She would be cross and embarrassed. The whole house seems so cold, so dark, so lifeless, and yet I feel that she's there watching me.'

The tears rose in his eyes again and Mrs Cole crumbled.

'Perhaps Miss Warrington can come in her dinner hour, but only if Constable Parrett will accompany her. I can't allow my employee to come alone to your house, sir. I hope that you understand.'

Nodding that he understood, he rose from the chair, saying, 'I'll ask the constable and let you know when… if it's possible.' He looked defeated as he nodded to Mrs Cole. 'Thank you, madam.' Placing his hat on his head, he left without another word, leaving them with the bell jangling above the door.

'Take the order to Mr Cole and the job to the carpenter, Miss Warrington. I'll stay here in case someone else comes.'

'Will I be helping Mr Blatten, madam?' Sarah couldn't deny that she didn't want to go through the murdered girl's wardrobe or even go to her house.

'Let's see if the gentleman can get Constable Parrett, or any of the constables, to accompany you. And it will have to be in your own time.'

'Yes, madam.'

The following morning, the rain was so heavy that King Street was awash with water and sewage that ran downhill from the streets above. The smell from the excrement, washed out of pig pens in back yards and from the twelve local abattoirs around the town, was overwhelming as it mixed with the sewerage from leaking privies, flowing in a slurry down alleyways and in some cases through the ground floors of some houses in King Street. After two hours, the rain stopped and the sun came out, causing a miasma of stinking steam to rise up from the road. Ladies held their skirts up above ankle height and men on tiptoe had rolled up their trousers as they walked.

Constable Parrett arrived, smiling cheerfully. 'I hear that you have offered to help Mr Blatten with choosing his sister's burial outfit, Miss Warrington. That's very kind of you.'

111

Sarah would have basked in the warmth of his praise a few days ago but now could only feel guilty.

'I'll see you at midday and walk with you to his house.'

'Oh, no!'

Her outburst surprised even her and she couldn't for the moment explain why she suddenly felt embarrassed, felt dread.

'Is something wrong?' He looked concerned.

Realising what was wrong, Sarah wanted to say, *I don't want to walk through the streets with a constable in uniform. People will think that I am like my mother, arrested.* She looked to Mrs Cole for help.

'We have the address,' Mrs Cole said, not knowing why Sarah didn't want to be accompanied. 'Miss Warrington will meet you there, Constable. I'm sure that will be best.'

He nodded. 'As you wish,' he said stiffly, looking at Sarah, the smile having gone from his face. 'I'll see you at the house, Miss Warrington.'

She could only nod an affirmative, feeling sorry for her outburst.

At midday, she arrived at a terraced house in Well Street. Constable Parrett was already there, talking to Charles, who was standing in his open doorway. The hall that they were invited into was clean and the whole house immaculate for a man living on his own.

'I try to live up to my sister's high standards,' he said, judging correctly what Sarah was thinking.

She blushed, not realising that her facial expression had given away her thoughts so easily.

'I'll show you to Lillian's room.' He started up the stairs and Sarah followed behind him, leaving the constable standing in the hall below. 'It's this one,' he said, nodding towards a door on the small landing, but making no effort to open it before he turned away, making a hasty exit down the stairs.

Sarah took a deep breath as she looked at the door and then touched the door knob. Lillian seemed very close, as though she was on the other side of the door, waiting.

Inside, the room was neat and tidy, the bed made, a sewing machine in the window, a chair before it. There seemed nothing out of place as she stepped into the cold room. Leaving the door open, she shivered. The bedroom held an emptiness, a silence, as though waiting for Lillian's return, and she could understand what Charles Blatten was experiencing. It did feel as though, in the heavy silence, Lillian was watching.

Trying to swallow her fear of the dead, she walked unsteadily towards the wardrobe.

Opening the door, she smelt the essence of Lillian on the clothes as she pulled out a dress and a velvet jacket. Closing the door with the clothes draped over her arm, she noticed a chest of drawers and wondered if she should look for undergarments. Opening the top drawer, she found a well-read bible lying on top of Lillian's white cotton drawers. Each item she noticed had a fancy L embroidered in silk in one corner. On the wall above the bed a wooden cross displayed a suffering Jesus, head bent, nailed to it. Sarah believed that this was, or must have been, a religious family and understood what trauma her death in this way must have caused. But why, she wondered, were the women of his church not helping him?

Taking what she thought was needed, she shut the drawer and, as she did so, noticed a small box with its lid open, in front of the mirror. Seeing an indentation of a cross in the mauve silk lining, she wondered if Lillian was wearing the cross when she was killed.

Downstairs, the men were talking quietly in the parlour and stood up as she entered. 'I have all that I think will be needed, Mr Blatten. Could I ask you something?'

He didn't answer but stared at the clothes hanging over her arm.

'I noticed,' she continued, 'an empty box on the chest of drawers, with the indentation of a small cross. Was Lillian wearing it? If so, would you want it back or would you want her buried with it?'

'Her cross?' He looked stunned. 'I'd forgotten it. She only took it off to sleep. Was she wearing it?' he questioned the constable.

'I don't know.' The constable frowned. 'No one has mentioned

113

jewellery. I'll find out for you. She's still at the hospital until the undertakers arrive. If she's gone, then Miss Warrington will have the information. But I'll walk over there now and ask.'

'Thank you, I would like it back. It was given to her by our mother. It belonged to our grandmother. It's silver, and has a blue stone at its centre, and an inscription on the back, "*Love thy Neighbour as I love you*".'

'Leave it with us, sir.' The constable stepped through the door into the street, leaving Sarah standing in the hall with Charles Blatten, who looked different in his own surroundings, standing in his shirtsleeves and carpet slippers.

Feeling awkward, she gave a little smile, saying, 'Goodbye, sir,' and, stepping out into the street, was glad to feel the air on her face, to hear horse-drawn vehicles and people passing at the end of the road. Relieved to be out of his house, she almost ran back to King Street.

Constable Parrett returned to the funeral parlour within the hour, saying that there was no sign of a cross when the body was taken to the hospital. 'The chain could have been broken as she was strangled, lost in the struggle,' he surmised. 'Perhaps someone has picked it up. We should put a notice in the *Herald*. Someone may know of its whereabouts.'

~

Lillian arrived in the back yard, travelling in a plain box in the back of the cart. Mrs Cole saw her taken into the mortuary and it was she who took charge of dressing her.

'Well, I've done my best,' Mrs Cole said to Sarah as she entered the office and sat heavily in the chair in front of the desk. 'Poor girl. Strangled and bruised. What is becoming of Plymouth?'

'Whoever killed her is still out on the streets, Mrs Cole, and it makes me feel nervous. I won't be going out at night.'

'No, better stay home, my dear.'

Sarah was shocked; Mrs Cole hadn't used a term of endearment to her before. It made her feel like she belonged, although she really hadn't come to terms with the lonely evenings sitting in that room. She wondered vaguely why she had never been invited to spend some time upstairs with them and their son in an evening.

Sarah's voice was hopeful as she asked, 'Has anyone handed in Lillian's cross and chain?'

'No.' Mrs Cole shook her head. 'The police can only think that when her body was removed it was still dark and it may have been on the ground for someone to pick up.'

'Could we put an advert in the paper? Perhaps someone has it. I think if they knew the circumstance of it being lost, then they wouldn't want to wear it.'

'I think that it's for her brother to do that, Miss Warrington, don't you?'

The endearment was gone; she was back in her place. 'Yes,' she said, 'I suppose that it is. But I have to say that Charles Blatten isn't a very capable young man, in my opinion.'

'Sometimes, Miss Warrington, it's best to keep our opinions to ourselves,' Mrs Cole countered quietly.

Sarah blushed, feeling admonished.

'Perhaps,' Mrs Cole continued, 'perhaps in normal circumstances, he is a different young man. He's grieving and that makes people say and do things that they wouldn't normally.'

Sarah might have replied but at that moment a woman entered with her husband. She was crying.

He helped her to the chair in front of Sarah's desk and then with tears in his own eyes stood back behind his wife, saying nothing.

'How can I help you?' Sarah asked the woman as Mrs Cole left the room.

It was a busy day and didn't let up until late afternoon. Sarah had noticed that three of those that had died were living in King Street and all had died with the same symptoms. Was it typhoid? Was this terrible disease coming back?

11.

The street was busy as Sarah made her way to the post office, intending to send a letter to Ned. Thinking that she heard her name called, above the street noise, she stopped, and turning, saw Jane hurrying towards her.

'Sarah, I thought it was you. How are you?' Jane was asking, smiling as she approached.

Sarah immediately felt uncomfortable. Here was a woman who knew far too much about her and her circumstance. But she smiled agreeably, saying, 'I'm well, thank you, Jane.'

'Where are you living and how are you surviving? You just disappeared. I didn't know that you were going, nor got to say goodbye.'

'I didn't have the rent, Jane. I left quickly. I had to find work.' As a cart carrying bones passed, they held their noses.

'And did you?' Jane asked, coughing.

'Did I what?'

'Did you find work?'

'Yes, I was very lucky and found work that same day. I live in with the job, so I wasn't homeless.'

'Are you a maid in a big house? That must be wonderful.'

'No, Jane. I work in the funeral parlour.'

Jane's face changed and she shivered. 'Oh, how can you bear it, Sarah?'

'It suits me very well, Jane. I have a parlour and a bedroom of my own and more space than many people.'

'What about the dead people, Sarah, do you have to see them?'

'No, never.'

Jane shivered again. 'I don't think that I could do it. But… I have to tell you. I'm so excited, Sarah. I have just been offered a job as a seamstress for Baxter and Simpson in their millinery workshop off Mill Lane.'

'That's wonderful, Jane, but I thought that you already had a job in the haberdashery. How did anyone know that you were sewing?'

'Just before you left, I'd been earning a little extra money by volunteering in the evenings at the theatre, making and repairing clothes for the performances.' She paused, as a passing wagon pulled by four horses made it hard to hear. 'Then one evening,' she continued, 'a gentleman came backstage while I was sewing. I'd made a dress for his mother and he asked if I'd like to work as a seamstress for his company. The wage that he offered was enough to cover my rent and food, so I accepted it gratefully.' There was a twinkle in her eye as she said, 'It had become difficult working from home, making dresses for elderly ladies who couldn't get up the stairs to my garret.'

The vision of large elderly ladies trying to get up three flights of stairs to Jane's room made Sarah laugh. She hadn't laughed in a very long time and it sounded strange, almost hysterical.

Jane stared at her and asked, 'When did you last go out?'

'Every day.'

'No, I mean to enjoy yourself.'

Sarah frowned. She had never been out to enjoy herself and wasn't sure what Jane meant.

Jane read correctly, from the confusion on Sarah's face, that she had never been anywhere.

'Sarah.' She smiled kindly. 'I have two free tickets for the theatre and you are coming with me.'

Sarah suddenly felt horrified. Theatre wasn't something that people like her did.

'I've never been to the theatre, Jane. I won't know what to do.'

'You don't do anything,' Jane said. 'You sit in a seat and listen and enjoy the story or the singing.'

'But what will I wear, Jane? I only have day clothes and working clothes.'

'You haven't bought yourself any clothes with your wages?'

'Well, no! I don't have anywhere to go to wear new clothes.'

'For a maid of sixteen, Sarah, you are a hopeless case. I will take charge of clothes for the theatre and we will go tonight.'

'Tonight! But I don't go out at night. There's a murderer roaming the streets at night.'

Jane tutted. 'He was probably off one of the ships, Sarah, and gone now. We'll be safe at the theatre where there are lots of people about when the theatre turns out.'

'I will have to be back by ten or Mrs Cole will lock me out.'

'Really?'

'Yes, they lock up at ten o'clock.'

'They wouldn't lock you out, would they?'

'I don't know.'

'We'll worry about that if it happens, Sarah. You can always come and sleep in my room. I'll see you later, at six fifteen. I will bring some clothes for you. The performance starts at seven.' She shouted the last sentence over her shoulder as she walked away, swallowed up by the crowd.

For the rest of the day, Sarah felt quite dizzy, with a mixture of fear and excitement running through her body.

The day dragged until Jane arrived at the back door at six fifteen.

Entering Sarah's room, Jane stood for a moment with her mouth open. 'All this is yours?'

'Well, not mine exactly. I'm only in here in the evenings and it is a little boring.'

'Boring! This room has no soul, Sarah, and the furniture is all in the wrong place.'

'I didn't like to move anything.'

'You should have a chair each side of the fire, for toasting our toes in the winter.'

'*Our* toes?'

'Yes, of course.'

Sarah smiled, realising that she was being taken over by Jane, and she liked it. It made her feel that she belonged to someone.

'You get changed and I will move some of the furniture, make it more of a home for a young woman who will have a visitor.'

In the bedroom, Sarah tried on the clothes, a pale blue dress and a dark blue jacket. When she went back into the parlour, she couldn't believe the difference that moving the furniture had on the room. Jane had also moved the rug, which should have been in front of the fire but had been placed partway up the room near the door, with an armchair on top of it. Jane was staring at the floor that had been uncovered.

'I can see why they moved the rug and put it here. It was to cover up that large brown stain.'

Sarah looked at the stain and wondered what had been dropped. But before she could talk to Jane about it, Jane was looking at the clock on the mantelshelf, saying, 'Come on, or we'll be late. They won't let anyone in after the bell.'

As they joined the throng of smiling theatregoers, Sarah pushed her arm through Jane's. The atmosphere around them was happy, excited, as people met friends, waving and calling out to them.

Sarah reflected momentarily on the difference here with the way that she spent her day, dealing with tragedy and death.

After the show, Sarah was glowing with happiness as they left the theatre until, looking at Derry's Clock, she saw that it was nearly ten o'clock. 'We'll have to run, Jane. I can't be late, they *will* lock me out.'

Lifting their skirts, they ran all the way back to King Street where Sarah said a breathless goodbye to Jane and carried on running down the passage and into the back yard.

The door was still unlocked and she almost fell through it in her hurry to get inside. Mrs Cole was sitting in her night attire, at the table, waiting. 'Mr Cole,' she said, 'would have locked you out, Miss Warrington, and if you had been any later, I would have had to lock the door.'

119

'I'm sorry, madam. I really am. I went to the theatre with my friend Jane and it was wonderful. But it finished later than I thought. Thank you for not locking the door.'

'To bed with you, mistress, and you can tell me about it tomorrow. And, Miss Warrington, lock your door.'

'Yes, madam. Good night.'

As she left the kitchen, she heard the bolts being pulled across the back door and, entering her own room, she bolted the door before throwing herself into an armchair.

Sitting with a silly grin on her face, she relived the evening at the theatre. How she and Jane had joined the crowd streaming towards the front of the theatre. And how she had been entranced by the singing, the bright lights. How she had laughed until the tears ran down her face at the comedy. She would never be able to thank Jane enough for taking her.

Kicking off her boots, she groaned at the pain the cobbles had inflicted on the soles of her feet. Wiggling her toes, she made up her mind that tomorrow she would get the boots mended in her lunchtime.

~

At noon, she walked across the road to the cobbler's shop and, removing her boots, sat barefoot on a stool in front of the tall counter while Mr Grose cut some leather to fashion into new soles for her boots.

As he worked at the end of the counter, near the light coming from the window, he said suddenly, 'Well, there he is again. That young man comes twice a week, sometimes more, and just stands looking at the funeral parlour. I wish I knew why. Perhaps he is deceased and can't bring himself to go in.'

Following his gaze, Sarah was alarmed to see James Gallaway standing with his back to the window, looking across the road to the funeral parlour.

Why? Was he looking for her?

'Dressed as always,' Mr Grose observed, 'as though he has just escaped from work. By his clothes, I think he must work in a public house or a brewery.'

She knew that James had liked her, and for a while she had held romantic notions about him, until the day that he had turned away, couldn't look her in the eyes, the day that her poor little brothers were taken from the trial to Exeter. *No!* She felt really strongly now that she would never marry a weak man, one who couldn't stand up to his mother and who would probably never take his wife's part.

Sarah slid off the stool and moved barefoot to the back of the shop where, hidden in the shadow, she pretended to look at the shoes and boots that were for sale, having been made by Mr Grose. Her horror was that James would look in the window and see her watching him. *Please*, she thought, *please be gone before I have to leave the shop.*

'Your boots are ready, miss.' Mr Grose broke through her silent prayer.

He was holding them out towards her and, to her relief, James was no longer standing outside.

Pushing her feet into the boots and buttoning them up, she was surprised at how much taller she felt in them and how she couldn't now feel the floor through the soles.

'My advice is, miss, that you don't let them get in that state again. They were nearly past repair.' He stared at her over the counter, bushy grey eyebrows raised, waiting for a reply.

'Thank you, Mr Grose. I will keep them mended.'

'They're good boots, nothing wrong with the uppers.'

'Thank you again.' She smiled sweetly as she walked towards the shop door.

Outside in the street, she looked up and down, hoping not to see James, before she crossed the road.

The afternoon was again busy with new deaths, amongst them a woman that she didn't know from number 100, the lodging house. An Emma Daniels, aged sixty-eight, who had died of asphyxia. Sarah had to ask Mrs Cole what asphyxia was.

'It's a condition that arises when the body is deprived of oxygen, causing unconsciousness or death. In other words, Miss Warrington, suffocation.'

~

On Friday night, she and Jane went again to the theatre, this time to see a melodrama.

'You will love it, Sarah.' Jane's eyes sparkled. 'It's so different from the music hall sing-along that we saw before. This is a melodrama. It's called *Murder at the Roadside Inn*. I think it's by Edward Fitzball, but I'm never sure about the authors or directors.'

Dressed in her own brown jacket, as they approached the theatre, Sarah did not feel out of place amongst the crowd going in.

Once they had taken their seats, she sat in anticipation and was amazed when the curtain went up to see the actors sitting and standing in a bar like the King's Head. There had been a murder. Sarah was entranced, completely lost in the story until the second act when Jonathan Bradford, the innkeeper, was in prison. He had been condemned to death for a murder he had not committed. In this scene he was being visited in his cell for the final time by his wife, Ann, and their two children.

Ann was saying to her husband, 'How shall I tell it to them – how will they understand? Home! Where is their home? No mother's voice. No father's admonition! Outcasts – abject – branded with the name of infamy. Shunned – degraded! Oh, my children,' she cried, wringing her hands, 'my children! What will become of them?'

The tears ran down Sarah's face. This could be her father, her mother, her brothers.

The anguish rising in her chest was almost unbearable. Jane, enthralled by the drama, didn't notice.

At the end of the show, after the audience had vigorously clapped and two encores taken with deep bows from the cast, the curtain was lowered. From the orchestra pit came the first, expected, strains of the *National Anthem*. The curtain was raised again to reveal the cast, standing stiffly in a line across the stage, joining the audience who had stood as soon as the first bars of *God Save the Queen* floated up from the orchestra pit, some of the audience singing with gusto, before gathering their coats to leave.

That was when Sarah saw John Parrett across the theatre. About to wave, she withdrew her hand as he stood, revealing who he had taken to see the drama. Phillis Gallaway. Sarah's world collapsed.

Because she and Jane had gone to an earlier performance, they were able to walk home slowly, Jane talking all the way about the play.

Then, stopping, she said, 'Did you enjoy it, Sarah? You're very quiet.'

'Yes, thank you, Jane.'

'Are you sure?' Jane was frowning.

'The drama didn't make me want to dance all the way home, Jane, not like the music hall.'

'No, you're right,' Jane conceded. 'A drama makes one think about life.'

Wanting to change the subject, Sarah said simply, 'Good luck with the new job, Jane. I hope that it goes well for you tomorrow.'

'Thank you, Sarah. We may not get another opportunity to go to the theatre for some time, so I'm glad you enjoyed the play. The actors were wonderful, weren't they? It was so real that it could almost have been true.'

She waved her hand as she left and Sarah walked slowly down the passage to the back yard, and entered once more through the kitchen. Relieved to find it empty, she went straight to her room and, sitting in the chair, contemplated the large stain on the floor.

But she couldn't keep the pain of loss at bay, and closing her eyes, she remembered the house that, as a child, she had been brought up in. How it had, as far as she could remember, been clean. Her mother had coped with her many children, although she had been, in Sarah's opinion, too strict. What had happened in the three years that she had been away? How had her mother fallen into what she had become?

Sarah realised, as she sat in the chair with her eyes closed, that a child would never be able to understand its parents. Would never be given the opportunity to know them as people, as they kept themselves so out of reach. All their trials and secrets securely hidden.

12.

Charles Blatten sat at his table, as he did every morning, and once again held a letter in his hand. It was from Crownford and Co, the landlord, saying how sorry that they were on hearing of the sad demise of Miss Lillian Blatten and that the rent had been missed by two weeks. Could he rectify this forthwith? If not, then the landlord would have to "take action", evicting him. The letter ended, *Please, accept our most humble respect and condolences on the death of your sister.*

It seemed to Charles that the world was against him. He couldn't remember, even though he had been told by the bank manager, how much the rent was, or on which day it was to be paid. At least the letter was on headed paper and he now knew the address of the landlord. It was as he held his head in his hands that he understood how his sister had disabled him by doing everything, keeping him in the dark. It had been so easy to just rely on her. The rent paid, the food on the table, the house clean, his clothes clean and hanging in his wardrobe. He hadn't once questioned how it all came about; it just did, as when their mother was alive. Now he felt the responsibility laying heavily on his shoulders. Thanks to the constable taking him to the bank, he did now know how much he had to live on. He must decide what to do. Pay the rent and live on what little was left for food and bills, or move to a more affordable property, a room in a lodging house.

Looking around the room in which he sat, he knew that his sister's standards had dropped. But he couldn't shift himself out of his self-pity. Crockery went unwashed in the bowl in the kitchen. He was unwashed, as were his clothes. All he could manage each day was to get up and sit at the table. He had been given two days' unpaid leave by his employer to grieve and arrange his sister's funeral, and after the funeral he had to return to work. He was panicking… he wasn't ready… he would never be ready. He needed Lillian to get him ready for work.

Two hours later, dressed in his Sunday best, Charles walked away from the church that he and Lillian attended on a Sunday. He was the only follower behind the funeral cart, making its slow journey towards the new Plymouth, Devonport and Stonehouse Cemetery, below Mutley Plain. He felt as lonely as the single pink rose, laid on the lid of the casket, that he had picked from their garden that morning. He hardly noticed the distance as he walked, head down, lost in thought, the only mourner following his sister to her place of rest. As he walked, he knew that his situation was desperate. Then suddenly, like a cloud lifting from the sun, he had some clarity that floated amongst the many other thoughts in his head. He would have to find a wife. Someone with money. After all, he couldn't live on his wage alone. He liked the look of the girl in the undertaker's, Miss Warrington, and she was earning a wage. But then he wouldn't like his wife to work. Other men would think less of him. Miss Warrington, he thought, must have some money put by to bring to a marriage, and she looked very capable when it came to finances. He was feeling quite satisfied with himself by the time they reached the gates of the cemetery and decided that he would start courting her at the weekend. He couldn't afford a thank you present, which would have been a good excuse, so perhaps just a walk to start with. But how could he move things on from there? He couldn't just ask her to marry him without them knowing each other better. He needed her to like him enough to talk about marriage. Perhaps the fact that she would be moving into a house would tempt her.

The horses were pulling the funeral cart slowly up the long drive towards the chapel on the right. A strange cemetery, he thought, having two chapels, one for Anglicans and one for Non-Conformists. He vaguely wondered why, for were they not all God's creation? He barely noticed the young girl standing by the chapel

126

door holding a flower as they made their way between both chapels to a dusty path where there were a few graves already in situ.

Lillian was buried in a spot behind the Anglican chapel, just off the path, where the sun shone most of the day. A quiet place. There was to be no headstone, so Charles tried to memorise the exact spot for when the mound of earth sank, leaving no indication of where she was.

George Banks, Jack Williams and John Maple helped Charles lower Lillian's coffin into the ground, as the vicar, standing at the head of the grave, prayed for her soul.

Charles followed the vicar's example, throwing a handful of earth into the grave at the end of the ceremony, not knowing why, but thinking that maybe it was something of himself going with her. He was then surprised when the young woman he had seen at the chapel door appeared beside him and threw her flower into the grave, just before the gravedigger started to fill it in.

Charles felt that his heart was as heavy as the earth leaving the man's shovel as it thudded onto the lid of the coffin.

He looked at the young woman, who put her hand on his arm in solidarity, the look of pain on her face reflecting his own. At the kindness of her touch, he could hold the tears back no longer and sobbed. Her arm went around his shoulders and he felt himself being comforted as though Lillian had her arms around him. As though Lillian had sent this young woman to help him.

'I'm Alice,' she said. 'I used to work with Lillian. She was kind to me when I started at the soap factory. I hope that you don't mind my coming to say goodbye. I got an hour off work.'

Charles leaned heavily on her and sobbed. 'Thank you,' he whispered through his tears to Lillian, although Alice, hearing his whisper, thought the thanks were for her.

George Banks took pity on the boy and offered them both a lift back to King Street in the back of the empty cart. The men didn't speak. What was there to say?

As Charles sat in the back of the cart in silence, with the comfort of Alice's arm around his waist, he was thinking, *Alice must earn the same wage as Lil. We could manage on that if she was good with finances.* He would have to find out more about her situation.

'Thank you for coming, Alice. It means a great deal to me that she had a friend.'

'Well, I don't know that we were friends,' she said quietly. 'We just worked together and she was nice to me. The others gossip, but not Lil. And I was so upset when this happened that my mum suggested that I come along today. I did want to come,' she said quickly. 'Mum told me to come if that is what I felt, even though I would lose some of my wage.'

'So, you live with your parents, Alice?'

'Only my mum. She is quite elderly now and not well.'

Charles nodded but was thinking, *If I married Alice the wage wouldn't feed three or pay for the woman's medication.*

'I'm sorry that your mother isn't well, Alice. How do you manage?'

'Mother has an income from an estate. Without that, we wouldn't manage on my wage.'

Charles frowned but asked innocently, 'Does this estate revert to you if anything befalls your mother, Alice?'

'I don't think so. It's something that my father worried about before he died.' She was quiet for a moment, seemingly lost in her own thoughts before saying, 'The house, though, is ours, all paid for. I just work to pay the bills.'

They went over a bump in the road and Alice removed her arm and held on to the side of the cart, steadying herself for a moment.

'Alice, would you consider seeing me again?' he asked. 'I'm very lonely without my sister, and I think that she would approve of our friendship.'

Alice blushed. Looking down at her hands now folded in her lap, she said quietly, 'I would like that, thank you, but I will have to ask Mother.'

Charles sat once again in silence, thinking. Perhaps the girl at the funeral parlour was a better option after all. Although, he had to admit, he didn't know anything about her.

13.

In Neswick Street, the bedroom door opened quietly and John felt his shoulder being gently shaken. He opened his eyes with difficulty and, in the semi-darkness, was aware of his mother in the room. As unsolid to him as a grey shadow, she had already taken the two steps from his bed to the window and was opening the curtains.

'Sorry, John,' she whispered. 'I left you as long as I dared, but you need to get ready for work.'

His response was a groan and the need to pull the covers back over his face to shut out the light. His head was pounding and his stomach roiling.

'It looks like you had a good evening, John, but your father and I expected you home before we went to bed. You know we don't like to leave the house unlocked with a murderer on the loose.'

John took a deep breath and let the air out slowly. He didn't know if he could get out of bed, let alone get through the day.

'I'll be down soon, Mum. I need to get out of bed in my own time.'

'Alright, son, I'll delay breakfast for half an hour, but your father won't be pleased.'

'I don't want breakfast. You and Father eat yours.'

When she had left the room, he turned onto his back staring at the ceiling, his thoughts in a sluggish maelstrom, accompanied by the banging in his head.

He groaned. He'd enjoyed the melodrama at the theatre with Phillis, and had walked her back to the King's Head where her father and mother had insisted that he stay and have a drink with them; and another, and another, until he didn't know how to leave. Each time he stood to depart, they filled his tankard and now he felt ill, more ill than he had ever felt in his life. He couldn't remember how he got home, or how he eventually got away from Mr Gallaway. What had they been talking about? It was all a blur.

At the station, Sergeant Norris took one look at him and sent him home.

'You can't look after the public looking like that, lad,' he said. 'You get home and go to bed. I will see you tomorrow unless you have something contagious.'

John, who could only nod gratefully, turned around and made his way towards home, wanting only to lay in his bed. As he passed the King's Head, the smell of beer churned his stomach.

Mrs Gallaway was outside washing the windows and, seeing John's pale face, exclaimed, 'You look a bit green, lad. But never mind,' she laughed, 'when you and Phillis are wed, we'll teach you how to take your drink.'

Feeling ill, he stumbled on towards home, her words ringing in his head. *When you and Phillis are wed.* Wed! What happened last night? He couldn't remember. Hard as he tried, he couldn't remember what they'd talked about. He wasn't old enough to wed! He didn't *love* Phillis. He only took her to the theatre. If only he could remember. Surely the woman was joking. Yes, she must have been joking. But if she wasn't, he was in trouble!

Feeling better in the early evening, John went downstairs to be with his parents, but still didn't want any food.

His father looked gravely at him over the top of his evening newspaper, before lowering it and giving John his full attention.

'What happened last night, son? Not like you to be the worse for drink.'

'It's worse than that, Father. Mrs Gallaway at the King's Head joked that I was to wed their daughter, Phillis. I don't remember. They kept filling up my tankard with beer. I don't love the girl. I never saw her before. Why would I ask their permission to marry her?' He leaned forward in the chair he had taken opposite his father. 'If it isn't a joke, Father, surely I can't marry without your permission, and I don't want you to give it.'

'I wish it were as easy as that, son. As the law stands, you could marry without my permission at the age of fourteen. But if you don't want to marry, why did you ask her father?'

'I don't think that I did. I can't remember. I feel so ill.'

'If I'm asked for permission, then I won't give it.' Shaking his newspaper, he pulled it up in front of him and continued to read.

Relieved, John ate supper with his parents and returned to bed, exhausted.

On his way to work the next day, John saw Mr Gallaway and tried to avoid him, but the man turned around just as John was going to cross the street.

'Morning, John. A fine morning and you're looking better than yesterday.'

'Thank you, sir. If you will excuse me, I have to get to work.'

'Course, lad. It will be good to have a son-in-law who has a conscience when it comes to work.'

'Mr Gallaway, sir?' John stopped and looked at the man. 'I don't remember asking for permission to marry Phillis. In fact, I don't love Phillis and she and I have never discussed it.'

'Well, of course you have. Otherwise, why would you ask me?'

'But I didn't. I'm sure that I didn't.'

'Well, John, if that is what you say then you will have to prove it in court, and that will cost you a lot of money and your reputation. You could lose your job. The force may feel that you can't be trusted.'

John was shocked by his reply. 'Can I see Phillis?' he asked. 'I'm sure that she will tell you that we did not speak of marriage.'

'I'm sorry, John, but she's gone to Exeter to buy her wedding dress. Nothing's too expensive for my daughter. We will hold the reception here. We'll have the banns read on Sunday.'

With that, he turned into the King's Head and the doors shut behind him, leaving John standing on the pavement, looking after him with a sinking feeling in his heart. Phillis was nice, but not what he wanted in a wife. He realised he would have to go through with it. He couldn't afford to go to court and fight his case and he didn't have any savings.

The duty sergeant looked up as John entered. 'Not so green today, John,' he paused, 'but still not your usual self. I'll put you on the Devonport route with William, there have been one or two thefts from the warehouses over there. Just show a presence and keep your eyes peeled.'

'Yes, sir.'

John picked up his uniform, truncheon and whistle from the shelf in the dressing area and, when dressed, without much enthusiasm, he joined William Best in the yard.

'What's wrong, John?' William asked. 'You look troubled.'

John sighed. 'I can't talk about it right now, Will, it's too…' He couldn't find the right words, so said, 'Perhaps another day.'

They walked miles that day, it seemed to John. They spoke to two warehouse men who confirmed what was missing and how often items disappeared. Although they had their suspicions, they could not prove anything.

In the afternoon, they dealt with a domestic – a woman attacking her husband with a chair leg – and a drunk who needed help to find his house.

John was going through the motions, but his heart was not in his work. His heart was heavy; his life was finished. He had missed the opportunity to tell Sarah Warrington that he loved her. He hadn't, of course, because they hadn't known each other very long. Not even been out for a walk, which now he regretted. He sighed. He would be expected to be a good husband and stay faithful to a girl that he didn't love and didn't know.

William Best had never seen such a change in a man. John seemed like a shadow, following him around, not taking any interest or the lead in anything found to be suspicious.

How, he wondered, could such a change come over a man almost overnight?

~

Edith Parrett stood at the table in her kitchen, rolling out pastry. She'd had a good marriage as marriages went, she thought. And what any mother wanted was a good marriage for her child. She knew her boy. If he had fallen for a girl and been wanting to marry her, he would have brought her home to meet his mother before this. 'No,' she shouted, hitting the pastry hard with her rolling pin. 'No! This is unlike John.'

Her thoughts were running around in her head. *I believe him when he says that he didn't ask this girl to marry him. But what can I do to help him?* She pushed the pastry into a tin that she had greased with lard. 'Something's very wrong here,' she said out loud, 'and I'm going to get to the bottom of it.' But she wondered how to talk to the girl without her parents.

Leaving the pie on the table, to be cooked later in the afternoon, Edith walked to King Street. She knew the pub, she often shopped in King Street, but how to see the girl, that was the problem.

Standing on the other side of the street, she observed the public house. People, mostly men, went in and out but no sign of a young woman. Should she go inside…? She had never been in a public house before. If she went in, what would she do? She would have to buy a beer, and may still not see the girl. She needed a plan. She was thinking of writing a note and getting someone to deliver it when a slim young woman came out of the pub and crossed the road to the baker's next door. Edith followed her inside just as the woman behind the counter spoke.

'Morning, Phillis, what can I do for you today? Usual?'

'Yes, please, Connie.'

The woman took a bag and placed three bread rolls inside before picking up a large loaf.

'Put it on Mother's slate, Connie. She'll pay you at the end of the month.'

Edith had stepped outside and, as Phillis came out of the shop, pretended to be going in.

'Oh!' she said pleasantly, stepping back, then... 'But how nice, aren't you Phillis?'

The young woman looked at Edith, obviously trying to place her.

'I should introduce myself,' Edith said lightly. 'I'm to be your mother-in-law, Miss Gallaway, and I wonder why my boy hasn't brought you home to meet me.'

Phillis reddened. 'I don't know,' she said, looking guilty.

'When did John ask you to marry him, my dear?'

She kept her voice gentle, not wanting the girl to bolt, and by the girl's reaction she was convinced that John had not asked this young woman to marry him.

'Have you forgotten such a wonderful moment already, Phillis?'

'He asked me after the theatre.'

'That is very strange, my dear. For you haven't been courting. John has been at home every night until you asked him to take you to the theatre, so when and where did you do your courting?'

The colour had drained from Phillis and, without warning, she stepped into the road, narrowly missing the back of a passing cart, and almost ran across the street, disappearing into the King's Head.

'Right,' Edith muttered as she was left standing outside the bakers. 'There is my proof, young lady. You look guilty, but my guess is that it's your parents that are behind this.'

14.

Sarah was feeling confident in her job and comfortable in her room since Jane had moved the furniture around. How strange it was that such a small thing made such a lot of difference to how she felt. She had decided that morning, when she woke up, that she should make more of an effort to be part of the team, and talk to the men working out in the yard, instead of delivering the paperwork and retreating back to the front office like a scalded cat. She really wanted someone to call her by her name. Always being called Miss Warrington was keeping her a stranger. The only time her name was used was when she was with Jane.

The morning was busy. One of the Irish men digging up the road in Union Street had died of a heart attack and his wife had been in to arrange his funeral.

Two children from different families had died, as had an elderly woman living at number 100. Sarah always felt connected when it was someone from her previous abode. She didn't know the woman, but then there were around sixty people living there at the time.

With the paperwork signed off by Mr Cole, she made her way to the carpenter's workshop and, opening the door, smiled at Peter Lamb as he looked up.

'Good morning, Mr Lamb,' she said cheerfully. 'I have some paperwork for you. Looks like we are going to be busy again after the rain.'

He looked up, the blade of his chisel half an inch from the wood, his hammer hovering above its handle. He nodded.

She laid the papers as always on a bench near the window. 'How are you today, Sam?' She smiled at the apprentice cheerfully.

'I'm alright, miss.' Sam blushed and looked at Peter, whose hammer came down with a gentle tap, tap, tap on the handle of his chisel, taking up chips of wood from the side of a new coffin. He had already forgotten her.

Back in the office, she was proved correct; they were busy, and she took four more orders in the afternoon.

When they were signed off and logged by Mr Cole, she again went to the carpenter's workshop.

'More, I'm afraid, Peter,' she said, as she laid the papers on top of those from the morning. Feeling embarrassed for taking the liberty of using his first name, she added quickly, in case he didn't like her familiarity, 'Would you call me Sarah? I might work in the office but I'm not any different to you.'

Peter nodded towards the orders. 'Thank you, miss... Sarah,' he corrected. It obviously didn't come easily to him after having called her Miss Warrington for so long.

She smiled encouragingly. 'I hope this is the last for today.'

He raised an eyebrow and looked at the pile. 'So do I, miss. If we get any busier, we may have to take on another carpenter.'

By the middle of the week, she could see that Peter was finding it easier to use her name so thought that she would ask the question that had been on her mind for so long. The question that Beth wouldn't answer.

After delivering the orders, she asked innocently, 'What was the girl like who did this job before me, Peter?'

He smiled as he thought, and his words were almost delivered on a chuckle. 'Oh! There was no one like Daisy May. She was bright and she enjoyed her job. She seemed happy here. We just don't know why she went,' he frowned. 'Something must have happened in her life that we didn't know about.' His voice had changed as he spoke. 'We're all mystified.'

The atmosphere of congeniality had disappeared, so Sarah retreated back to her office, having learnt nothing more about the girl other than her name and that she was friendly and liked her job. Why then did she leave?

The days continued to pass and Sarah wondered why they hadn't seen John, although in her heart she was relieved. She didn't know if she could keep her feelings of disappointment hidden and, as he didn't know how she felt, he might see the look on her face as dislike. There had been several other constables in the shop but she hadn't asked after him. It was none of her business after all.

On Sunday morning, having nothing else to do, she accompanied Mr and Mrs Cole to their church. They were a little late and joined the congregation by slipping in at the back. She found the church cold and wished that she had worn warmer clothes. Observing how people greeted each other quietly with waves and smiles, she wondered how they all knew each other.

Mrs Cole handed her a bible from the shelf in front of them and got her own bible out of her bag.

The service was long, and the vicar's voice droned on in a diatribe that Sarah could not hear as she sat looking at the back of a very wide man sitting in front of her. By the end of the service, she was more aware of her feet being cold from the drafts circulating from the ill-fitted door than of the uplifting of spiritual awareness.

'Amen,' the priest mumbled after the last prayer.

'Amen,' the congregation followed.

As they sat back on the pews, the vicar announced, 'It gives me great pleasure to call the banns of marriage for the forthcoming nuptials of Phillis Gallaway of this parish, and John Parrett.'

Mrs Cole gasped with surprise, and Sarah's heart almost stopped beating. John and Phillis! So, it was serious. Until seeing them together at the theatre, she hadn't even known that they knew each other, and wondered how long they had been going out. Not that it was any of her business... but suddenly she wanted to be somewhere else.

The pain that was building in her chest and throat, with the sudden and unexpected emotion, brought tears to her eyes. She sat, unable to move, gritting her teeth against the sobs that were forming. To cover her grief, she slowly put the bible back on the shelf in front of her and wiped her hand across her face, stood on weak legs, and followed the Coles from the church.

Her life was now derelict.

15.

Reginald and Edith Parrett sat in the Gallaways' parish church to hear the matrimonial banns read out for the first time. They could see that their son was not as happy as a young man taking this important step in his life should have been, as he sat, head bowed, beside Phillis and her parents.

As the banns were read, Phillis looked demurely down at the bible held in her lap, and after the service, when the congregation approached the young couple, congratulating them, John just nodded as Phillis blushed prettily.

But John's mother saw it differently. Her son had not asked Phillis to marry him and she would find a way to stop this farce. She believed that her son had been cleverly trapped into this situation by the Gallaways. Whatever their reason, she would do her utmost to get John out of it. But at the moment she had only one person that she could ask for help, if indeed that person was still alive after all this time.

Reginald was not happy with the situation but was even more unhappy when, outside the church, his wife turned to him, saying, 'You go on home, Reg. I'm going to find Marta Ellington. You go and get yourself something to eat. I'll cook tonight.'

His jaw dropped. He had never heard anything like it. 'But we always have Sunday lunch, Edith. Lunch meaning midday,' he pointed out sulkily.

Edith looked at him with such fury in her eyes that he took a step backwards.

'If you are telling me, *Reginald*,' she had raised her voice embarrassingly, 'that your stomach is more important to you than our son, I will *never* cook you a Sunday dinner again.'

And with that she turned and walked away from the church and her husband, in such anger that for a few minutes she just walked at speed without knowing where she was going.

Ten minutes later, Edith was standing on the doorstep of a house in Clarence Street. Taking a deep breath, she knocked on the faded front door. This her only hope.

The man who opened the door was only half dressed. His Sunday paper hung down the side of his leg, one finger keeping his place in the page that he had been reading. A look of annoyance crossed his face when he saw Edith, someone he didn't know.

Edith smiled, hoping to look friendly. Seeing this man, she was already beginning to think that she knew the answer to her question, as Marta Ellington was unmarried and lived alone. Although she could have married, or taken a lodger in the intervening years.

'I'm sorry to disturb you, sir, on a Sunday,' she said, as pleasantly as she could. 'I'm looking for Marta Ellington.' Her voice rose at the end of the sentence in expectation, or hope.

'Sorry, maid, no one living here by that name.' He started to close the door.

'Would you know where she moved to?' Edith said quickly, hoping that the answer wasn't that the woman was dead.

'Sorry,' he said again. 'I just rent here. No idea who owns it. If I did, I'd have some words to say to them. The rooms are damp, there's green mould growing on all the ceilings, the floorboards are soft and need replacing—'

Edith stopped him before he went on with his list of repairs.

'So you don't know where Miss Ellington might have moved to?' she repeated hopefully.

'No. Sorry. We've only been here a year, but if you find her, and she *is* my landlord, you tell her to come around and look at her property. It's going to cost her in the end, and more, if she leaves it.'

'Thank you, sir, for your help.' Edith started to walk away but said, 'I will tell her if I find her and if she is your landlord.'

He looked satisfied, relieved even, as he shut the door, and she wished that she could feel as relieved, knowing where Marta had gone.

Standing in the street, she wondered where to go next. She wasn't going to give in that easily. Then, setting off again at a fair pace, she walked north towards North Road Station before turning left into Denham Terrace. Breathing heavily from the exertion, she stood rather daunted in front of a large property that sat back in its own grounds in Clarendon Terrace, known as the Home for Orphans.

Walking up the short carriage drive, Edith stood in front of a dominating oak door and raised the knocker before bringing it down hard with a sharp bang. Its echo reverberated in the passage beyond the door. Waiting several minutes for someone to answer the door, she began to feel uncertain. Would they give her the address of Miss Ellington, if they even knew it?

She remembered standing right here with Reg, nineteen years ago, when they came to collect their son, who had already been named John. In the matron's office, they had decided to keep his forename in case he ever needed to trace his parents.

The door was opened slowly by a small girl in a grey dress that hung straight and loose. Untidy strands of hair were escaping from her braids and Edith noticed that the girl's hands were red raw.

Edith smiled. 'Hello. Do you think that I could talk to the matron?'

The girl looked worried and, when she replied, Edith felt that the words she spoke had just been rehearsed.

'She can't see anyone, it's Sunday.'

'Yes. It is Sunday. Can I see someone who could make me an appointment for tomorrow?'

The girl didn't seem to understand the question so, tearing a page from her notebook, Edith wrote down her address, writing that she would like an appointment to see the matron tomorrow. Holding it out towards the girl, she said, 'Would you give this to Matron?'

The child took it, pushing it into her pocket, and closed the door.

Edith wished, as she stood on the step, that she could have spoken to an adult, for now her hopes rested with a child of around six years.

There was nothing else that she could do today. Sunday was not the best day to call on anyone and now she would have to go home and make her peace with her husband.

Two days later, Edith was being shown into the current matron's office by another child in a grey dress, and was sitting in the same solid carver as nineteen years ago, in front of a solid oak desk, feeling small. The room with its leaded windows had not changed in all those years, and in fact also smelt the same, a mixture of wax polish and paper dust.

She could hear fleeting footsteps on the tiled floor on the other side of the door. Small, hurrying footsteps of children, echoing around the high-ceilinged hallway. When the door was suddenly pushed open, Edith flinched but held her nerve.

The woman that stood before her didn't have the gentle face of Miss Ellington, but was a hard-faced woman with a turned-down mouth encased by deep wrinkles of displeasure.

Taking her time to sit in the large leather chair behind the desk, she moved a book from left to right and laid a pen slowly on top of it, before looking up and acknowledging Edith with a long stare.

'How can I help you, Mrs Parrett?' she said slowly.

Feeling intimidated for a moment, Edith couldn't speak. She wondered how the children felt when they came up against this woman. But then, gathering her courage, she said, looking straight and without fear into the eyes of the woman opposite, 'Nineteen years ago, my husband and I adopted a baby boy from this orphanage and I wonder if you could tell me anything of his background before he came to live here.'

The matron's mouth squeezed into a wrinkled shape, reflecting someone who'd just sucked vinegar from a teaspoon.

'I am afraid, Mrs Parrett, that it is not for me to give out information regarding adoptions.'

'But I'm the person who adopted the boy. I need to know his background.'

The woman shook her head, a tight-lipped smile appearing and gone in an instant. 'I'm afraid, madam, that it's against the law for me to divulge that information, even if I had it.'

Edith nodded. She'd already weighed up this woman and knew that she would get nowhere, so changed tack.

'I've been looking for the last matron and find that she has moved. I wonder if you have a current address for her? I would like to invite her to my son's twentieth birthday,' she lied.

'Again, madam,' Matron's eyes flashed with annoyance, 'I cannot help you. I'm not allowed to give out personal details of staff, past or present.'

Edith nodded, realising that she would get nowhere with this woman.

'If that is all,' Matron stood, hands resting on the desk, 'I will get one of the children to show you out.'

And with that she walked to a sideboard and picking up a bell, rang it.

Within seconds, a small boy had opened the door and was looking at Matron for information.

'Show this lady out, Brian.' She gave a nod towards Edith as she spoke. A nod of finality. 'Good day, Mrs Parrett. I'm sorry that I'm unable to help you.'

Outside, Edith stood tight-lipped on the orphanage doorstep, fuming. The matron didn't look at all sorry and, if it wasn't against the law, she would like to have floored her, punched her in her unfriendly face. But that wouldn't have helped her get the information that she needed, or helped her son in his career. There had to be another way.

~

John and William Best had been friends since school and had joined the police force together. William knew that his father, Sir Geoffrey Best, had not been happy about his son taking a career in the police force. He had hoped that his son would become a lawyer and later perhaps, in older age, a barrister and Member of Parliament like himself. His son would never have to worry about money and would, of course, inherit from his father's substantial estate on his death. He had tried to talk William out of it, tried to get him to study for the law, but the boys had made a pact when young, and both John and William were determined on a career in the police force. Both wanted action, not exams.

Worried about John, William decided to speak to his father in the evening after work, if indeed his father was at home, for often he would be in London sitting in the House, fighting for a share of money for good causes in Devon.

At the end of the day, William had said goodbye to John and made his way home. It was a glorious evening. The blue sky was cloudless, the air warm and the leaves on the trees thick and green. The birds were singing, as though they too felt the difference in the temperature and were enjoying the warmth before bed.

When he reached home, the maid, Dolly, opened the door and took William's coat.

'Is Father at home, Dolly?' he asked.

'Yes, sir, you'll find him in his study. It's chicken tonight for supper, sir, is that alright for you? If not, Cook can make something else.'

'Chicken is fine, Dolly, you can tell Cook.'

As William made his way to his father's study, he was unsure what he was going to say. On the way home, it had seemed to him that his father could help him with anything, just as he had when he was a boy. But now he wasn't sure. He would have to find the courage to ask John again, and this time not be put off by John's gruffness and determination not to speak.

Overnight, William had an idea of his own. He had done two extra shifts covering for an injured constable and had the next day off in lieu.

Knowing that John was down at Mill Bay today, he made his way to Neswick Street and the home of John's parents, hoping that only John's mother would be at home.

Knocking on the door, he stood back and waited. When the door opened, Edith looked surprised and then worried.

'Has something happened to John, William?' She was already untying her apron in anguish.

'John's well, Mrs Parrett,' he assured her quickly, 'but I would like to talk about him if you have the time.'

'Come in, come in, Will.' Opening the door wider, she ushered him into her front parlour, indicating a chair for him to take.

'Tell me what's worrying you, Will.'

'I've noticed for some time that John isn't himself. Is something worrying him?'

Edith's hands began to shake as she tried to stop the emotion that she felt showing in her eyes.

'He hasn't told you, Will?'

'No, he hasn't told me. But I can see that it's affecting his work. I'm covering for him daily. Things that he misses, things that have to be reported. He seems in a fog. If you know something, Mrs Parrett, please tell me.'

'I shouldn't tell you, William. If he wanted anyone to know, he would have told them.'

'I think that he's too proud to tell anyone, Mrs Parrett, but to help him, I must know. I don't want him to lose his job. I know that he loves it.'

'If I tell you, Will, you won't let him know it was me told you.'

'No, I won't tell him who told me. I will leave that to you.'

Edith swallowed hard and wondered if John would think her disloyal. But also, she knew that she could not do this on her own, that she had run out of ideas.

'The Gallaways at the King's Head,' she said slowly, 'got him drunk and told him the next day that he had asked permission to marry their daughter, Phillis. Permission that they gladly gave. John says that he couldn't remember asking for her hand in marriage. And why would he? He doesn't love her. He doesn't even know her.'

'I remember the day that he came to work looking ill,' William said. 'That must have been the following day.'

145

'Yes. John was still drunk the next morning and feeling ill. It was on the way home that he bumped into Mr Gallaway, who told John how delighted he was that John was going to be his son-in-law. When John said that he didn't remember and didn't want to marry, Mr Gallaway told him that he would have to pay for breach of promise, and for the dress that Phillis was in Exeter buying. We have no savings, Will. I know that John doesn't want to marry her, but he's going through with it because he's a decent man.'

When William left Neswick Street, he was hopeful that his father could help John. John's mother had an idea that she was trying to follow up. To find the matron of the orphanage where John had been sent as a baby. A slim chance, but still a chance, although he might have to get his father to help with that. Would his father have the time, would he even agree? About that, William was unsure.

16.

On Saturday evening, with nothing better to do, Sarah walked on the Hoe with hundreds of other Plymothians, taking the air. She missed Jane. It would have been nice to have a friend to walk with, but since she had gone to work as a seamstress, she had heard nothing from her.

It was getting towards the end of June and, as the weather was warm enough not to wear her jacket, she had stopped at the flower seller and bought a single short-stemmed pink rose, which the woman kindly pinned to her blouse.

Her spirits were high as she nodded to a few people and glanced at the sea sparkling to her left. The water below was calm and a few men were swimming, naked. She could see the pink of their flesh just under the water. Not something a young lady should see before her marriage.

Turning away with hot cheeks, she strode out towards the steps that would take her down a level, to the sea wall, intending to walk back on the lower path. But as she turned, she saw John, walking deep in conversation with his friend William Best. At the sight of John, her heart skipped a beat, the world floated around her and for a moment she couldn't feel the ground beneath her feet.

She panicked. Her heart raced in her chest. She wanted to hide but she was out in the open. This was not the time to remake her acquaintance with him.

As she turned to flee back the way she had come, William pointed her out to John, who, seeing her, looked as though he had walked into a wall, stopping suddenly. He stared at her, seemingly angry, or confused, before turning away towards Elliot Terrace and disappearing at speed down the side street.

William stared after him, torn between speaking to Sarah or following John. In the end, without a word to her, he hurried after John.

Instead of taking the steps as she'd intended, Sarah stood facing out to sea, crying silently.

What had she done to deserve treatment like that? Rejected, not even a nod of recognition from John.

Taking a hard look at herself, she knew that she had been looking for love, had been ready to be loved by anyone. But then, she knew that she was telling herself a lie; she loved John with all her heart. The pain she felt at his rejection was so awful that if she hadn't been so afraid of it she would have thrown herself into the sea.

She sat on a bench until the evening air cooled enough for her to wish that she had worn her jacket. Shivering, she returned slowly to King Street, hardly noticing the pedestrians.

In the yard at the back of the shop, the boys were seeing to the horses, bedding them down for the night.

'Good night, miss,' they called, friendly now, since she had made the effort to speak to them.

The kitchen was empty and she made her way slowly up the stairs to her room. Sighing, she sat in the chair, lost in the silence that drummed in her ears. Closing her eyes, she visualised John, his hair like silk, shining in the evening sunshine as he walked deep in conversation with... her mind was trying not to make it Phillis. No! Not Phillis. With William. With William. The tears rolled unbidden over her cheeks.

At the sound of running footsteps above her head, she wiped her face with her hands and bolted the door. Mr Cole had raised his voice and the child had started to scream. Oh, how awful for the Coles, their precious moments with their son often marred by the child's moods. Perhaps after all they were right to deny her access to him.

Opening the window, she let the sounds of life float in on the evening air. People talking loudly, laughter, hawkers calling their wares. She became almost mesmerised as the constant moving scene below took her mind off her troubles.

Somewhere in the town a clock chimed the hours. It was ten o'clock. Closing the window, she got ready for bed.

Tomorrow was Sunday, the worst of days, with no one to talk to or to see. Tomorrow, she decided, she would take the ferry and visit Aunt Jelly.

~

Awaking to a clear blue sky next morning, she was filled with energy and excitement, looking forward to seeing her aunt.

In the kitchen, the Coles were having breakfast, sitting at the table surrounded by the Sunday newspapers.

Mrs Cole, engrossed in her newspaper, looked up as Sarah entered.

'Good morning, Miss Warrington. What are you planning to do today?' she asked cheerfully.

Mr Cole just nodded and continued reading his Sunday paper.

'I thought that I would visit an aunt who lives in Kingsand.'

'I didn't know that you had any family, Miss Warrington.'

Sarah didn't reply but took a bowl from the shelf and helped herself to porridge from the large black saucepan.

'You can have eggs if you would like. Beth collected them yesterday.'

'No, thank you,' Sarah replied, taking her seat at the table. 'This will be enough for me.' She knew that eggs and the movement of a boat would not mix.

'Which ferry will you catch?' Mrs Cole asked, pushing her own empty bowl away. 'Cremyll or Mill Bay?'

'Oh, definitely the Cremyll if it's running. It's a shorter journey.'

'That's true. But a longer walk.'

'I don't mind the walk. I enjoy it.'

Mrs Cole stood, moving her chair back. 'Well, enjoy your day. I'm going upstairs to see my son, help him get dressed. Mr Bronalski has the day off and I fear that Mr Cole and I will be very tired by this evening.' Her mouth moved into a tiny smile. 'Arthur's a lovely boy,' she reflected, 'and we are so grateful to have him. Oh, and Miss Warrington, you must read the article in the morning paper. Another woman was attacked last night but survived.'

As his wife left the kitchen, Mr Cole slowly folded his paper and, standing, followed her from the room without comment.

Sarah watched him go, unable to understand him. The only time that they spoke was about work.

As she ate her porridge, she found the article in the paper.

The young woman said that her services were procured by a tall man who took her to an alleyway where another man awaited her. It was the other man, who, while taking her, put his hands around her neck, strangling her. She feigned a faint, falling to the ground. The two men then hurried away, not even attending to see if she was alive. The woman told the police that the second man, the one who tried to strangle her, had a strong smell about his person. A scent of flowers, possibly lavender.

Collecting the bowls, Sarah washed them and left them on the side for Beth. Not her job, she knew that, and Beth would probably reprimand her in the morning, but it was giving her thinking time. She was looking forward to seeing her aunt and her sister but wasn't sure that she wanted to talk in depth about anything. Just to be with family, feeling their love and their connection would be enough.

~

The ferry was running and it was full. Sarah was the last on. It seemed that, on this sunny day, people were taking in the sights, dressed in their best clothes. Ladies, sitting with small parasols held up against the rays of the sun, chatted excitedly. The sea was flat calm. So different from the last time she'd taken the ferry.

When they reached Mount Edgcumbe, Sarah was first off the boat and had soon left the day trippers behind, making her way up to the main road. Deep in her thoughts and expectations, the walk seemed shorter as she quickly arrived above Kingsand and, walking down the steep lane between the cottages to her aunt's, she realised that she hadn't thought to send a message ahead and hoped that they would be at home.

Amy opened the door with a look of amazement on her face and then, throwing her arms around Sarah, held on to her for a few moments before Aunt Jelly's voice reached them from the kitchen.

'Who is it, Amy?'

'It's Sarah, Aunt.'

'Well, don't leave her on the doorstep, Amy, bring her in.'

Sarah followed Amy through the front parlour to the small kitchen where Aunt Jelly was placing a baking tray on the table.

'Just in time, Sarah. We've just cooked some Nelson's pudding. Would you like a slice?'

'I would, thank you, Aunt.'

As her aunt cut into the solid fruit-filled pudding, Sarah took a seat at the table opposite Amy, and was sad to feel like a visitor. The kitchen felt so different while she was living here. Then, like her aunt, she was part of the fabric of the cottage, eating every day at this table. But now she felt like an outsider. She didn't want to be a visitor and found it hard to hold back the tears.

Aunt Jelly pulled up a stool and, looking across the table, said, 'It's good to see you, Sarah, and looking so well. Did you get work and how is your mother?'

Sarah was at that moment rendered speechless. Looking across at Amy, whose face had drained of colour, she realised that her sister had possibly not told her aunt of the family troubles.

'What's wrong, Sarah?'

151

Her aunt's kind eyes were, for the first time, searching Sarah's face for an answer. Amy suddenly pushed her chair back and rushed from the room, taking the stairs two at a time.

'I think that you had better tell me what has happened, Sarah. Amy has said nothing about the family since she has been here. I haven't probed. I've been waiting for her to tell me. Waiting for her to feel safe enough to do so. It was obvious to me when she arrived in such a state that things were not right at home. Gwen was a strict woman, and would not have had a daughter travel in such condition. The girl was clearly ill.'

Sarah was trying to get her thoughts together. Her aunt deserved an explanation, they were family, and her aunt had twice picked up the fallout from her mother's actions. Probably saved the lives of both girls.

The pudding sat uneaten on the plate in front of her as she said, 'All was not well, Aunt, when I arrived in King Street. You wouldn't have recognised Mother. She appeared to be very ill and the boys, Sam and Thomas, were running wild, stealing from shops, encouraged by Mother.'

Aunt Jelly's mouth dropped open in surprise. 'I can't believe that Gwen could have changed so much. Do you know why?'

'They seem to have fallen on hard times, Aunt, and Mother was drinking.'

'That surprises me, Sarah. Your mother wasn't one for the drink. In fact, just the opposite, she deplored those that wasted their money on drink.'

'I can't tell you, Aunt, what the cause was, as I was here for three years.'

'Yes, of course. You're right, Sarah. The only person who can tell us what happened to your mother is upstairs.'

Getting off the stool and going to the bottom of the stairs, she called, 'Amy, come down to the kitchen right now.'

Sarah was surprised at the tone of her aunt's voice. She was obviously not going to take any nonsense.

Amy eventually appeared, looking frail, her eyes wet from crying.

'Come sit by me, Amy,' Aunt Jelly said, kinder now, seeing the distress in her niece. 'You're amongst family and you're safe. We need to know what happened to your mother three years ago, after your father died.'

Sarah got up and, putting her arms around her sister, led her to the table. She also wanted to know what had happened to the family while she was away.

Amy's voice was almost a whisper as she spoke, and both her aunt and her sister had to lean forward to hear what she was saying.

'At first, after Father died, nothing changed that we noticed. Mother was just the same, just as strict. But then one day she told us we were to have a visitor. We never had visitors and were excited. We cleaned the house top to bottom until the afternoon, when a man was shown into the front parlour. He was a docker.'

She swallowed and looked from her aunt to Sarah, as though they might comment. When they didn't, she continued. 'His name was Tudor Murphy. He had known Father. Mother was so different after that. She smiled, and she didn't shout at us as much. I heard her singing, and Tudor sometimes brought us gifts.' Amy blushed. 'Sometimes I crept downstairs and listened at the door. I used to do that before Tudor, when father was alive. I liked knowing what was going on... Sam said I was nosy.' She shrugged. 'One day, I heard Tudor asking Mother for money. He was telling her that he could double what she gave him, and eventually we would have enough to buy the house we were living in.'

Aunt Jelly took a deep breath and puffed out her cheeks, then rubbed Amy's hand encouragingly. 'Go on, dear.'

'Tudor came more and more often and Mother told us one day that he had suggested that he marry her. We had money coming in for clothes and new shoes and food. Life seemed so much better since Mother knew him.'

She stopped talking, looking from Sarah to her aunt, biting her bottom lip before continuing. 'But then he stopped coming and, having given him all our money, Mother had to sell things. Eventually, Mother received a letter giving her a week to find the rent or we would have to leave the house. She got a job at night in a public house, selling beer, but it wasn't enough. Mother couldn't feed four children and find the rent. We had to leave our home. Someone in the pub had told Mother of a room in a lodging house in King Street and that is where you found us, Sarah.'

'Ah, so now we know. Poor Gwen.' Aunt Jelly shook her head and sighed. 'Your mother was doing her best for her family. Unworldly, as are most women. Easily taken advantage of. Thank you for telling us, Amy. Don't you go worrying about it anymore. I want to see you get better, like your sister did while living here. Now, both of you, eat your Nelson's pudding and we'll go to the beach and get a bit of air.'

Sarah was relieved that she had not been questioned further and glad to know what had happened to her family while she'd been away. It helped her understand the circumstances that had driven them from their home, but still didn't reconcile her with the fear she had of her mother.

Their aunt sat at the top of Cawsand beach while the girls paddled at the edge of the water, lifting their skirts so as not to get the material wet. It was as they approached the rocks that Amy said, 'Thank you for not telling Aunt what Mother asked me to do. I expect she asked you to do the same if you couldn't find work.'

Sarah felt awkward speaking of it to her little sister but felt that they did have something in common.

'I did find work at first,' Sarah said, 'but when I lost that job, Mother did make me go to Union Street. She was so ill that she couldn't go to work herself. I didn't understand what the work was.' Blushing, she looked quickly up the beach to make sure that their aunt was still out of earshot. 'I didn't know what her work was,' she repeated, 'or how I could do her work. I thought that she had a job. I also know that she sent you to do the same.'

Amy stopped walking and shielded her eyes against the sun. 'Oh, who told you?'

'One of the street women. She was murdered a few weeks later.'

'Murdered!' Amy almost fell backwards into a small rock pool and Sarah grasped her sister's arm to stop her falling over.

'I was so frightened, Sarah.' Amy's hand was shaking as Sarah took it. 'When a policeman came along the street, I ran away. Mother gave me a good beating for that.'

'I'm sorry, Amy.'

'No, I'm sorry. If the queue for the ferry had been longer, I might have had time to warn you.'

'There wouldn't have been time to warn me about the change in our mother, Amy. Let's go back to our aunt and, Amy, tell her what it was like living in King Street if she asks.'

'I can't, Sarah.'

'If she asks me, would you mind if I tell her what I found when I arrived in King Street?'

Amy nodded her head in agreement. 'I just can't say it, Sarah.'

As they walked back to their aunt, Sarah said, 'There's so much that I haven't told you, Amy, and perhaps I should. The three of us are the only family that we have now.'

Amy stopped walking and Sarah turned to look at her, noting that the colour had drained from her cheeks and that her eyes were full of fear.

'We can't be all that there is. Where are the boys and Mother?'

On impulse, Sarah wrapped her arms around her sister, knowing that she would have to reveal it all to both Amy and their aunt eventually.

Aunt Jelly was already standing, brushing the sand from her skirt, as the girls reached her. 'Time to head back, I think, girls.'

Sarah and Amy followed their aunt in silence along the main street to Kingsand. When they arrived at the cottage, their aunt ushered them into the parlour, telling each where to sit. Then looking directly at Sarah, she asked, 'How is your mother, Sarah?'

Even though she had already made up her mind to tell her aunt, it was a shock. Where should she start?

'As I said, Aunt, Mother was drinking and not looking after the boys.'

Her aunt nodded; that much she had ascertained from what Sarah had said earlier.

'And has something happened to your mother?'

Sarah blew out her cheeks, finding the questions hard to answer without emotion. Looking at Amy, she said, 'I'm sorry, Amy, but I discovered something that you didn't know. Mother was pregnant and has been sent to Exeter for trial. Her baby's body was found in the yard, pushed down the privy.' She couldn't look at her aunt as she said, 'It might be murder, if they can prove that the baby had taken a breath.'

Silence filled the room as both Amy and Aunt Jelly tried to digest what Sarah was saying. Aunt Jelly nodded, taking it in. 'And the boys, Sarah, where are they while you are here?'

'They were caught stealing, Aunt. It had been going on a long time. Mother led them to believe that it was a game. When they were caught, I went to both trials. They were eventually sentenced to several lashes of the birch and then sent to a reform school for four years.'

Aunt Jelly was speechless, blinking at Sarah, trying to take it all in.

'You're alone in Plymouth, Sarah. How are you managing to live?' she said eventually.

'I have a job in the office of the funeral director in King Street, Aunt. I live in, above the shop. Mr and Mrs Cole have been kind. They feed me and give me a wage each week.'

'Mr and Mrs Cole?' Aunt Jelly nodded. 'I see.' She frowned.

'It's very sad, Aunt. They have a son who never sees the outside world, there's something wrong with him. They are very good parents. They have employed a tutor who looks after him during the day and they spend their evenings and Sundays with the boy. I haven't seen him, they're very protective of him.'

Aunt Jelly nodded. 'Well, Sarah,' she said, standing up slowly, 'it's been lovely to see you and to know what has happened to my sister-in-law, but it's time for you to head back home.'

Shocked, Sarah felt the pain of being dismissed. Standing up, she bent and hugged Amy, nodded to her aunt and stepped out of the front door, unsure of how she was feeling. Her only family had asked her to leave.

As she made her way up the steep street to the main road above, she felt confused, abandoned. She had never expected anything other than support from her aunt.

By the time she reached the main road, her emotions had turned to anger. Stepping out, she didn't see the trees, and didn't hear the birds, as her feet pounded the road, going over the conversation again and again in her head. Her aunt had wanted to know, and she had told her. And then she was dismissed.

The embarrassment of it, after telling Amy that they would support each other. That they were family.

17.

On the following Sunday afternoon, Sarah walked down King Street to the lodging house and, with some trepidation, pushed the familiar front door open. Today, as she climbed the stairs and stood on the landing, outside the room in which she had lived for such a short time, she had the strangest feeling of familiarity. That her mother was inside.

Hurrying up the next two flights of stairs, she hesitated outside Jane's door. Now that she was here she was uncertain whether she should knock. Was Jane still living here? Was she ill? Worst still, was it because she was with someone that she had not been in contact?

She had changed her mind, was about to creep away, when she heard someone coughing on the other side of the door. Sure now that it was Jane, she knocked and heard a groan. When after a few minutes the door was still not opened, she knocked again. When Jane still didn't answer, Sarah opened the door slowly and quietly so that she would be able to withdraw without Jane knowing that she had been there if she had company.

The room was in darkness, the curtains pulled. An outline of Jane's body could be seen in the bed beneath the blanket and, just as Sarah was backing out, Jane coughed again. Sitting up to take a drink from a glass, she saw Sarah and stared, blinking.

'Sorry, Jane,' Sarah whispered, wishing the floor would open and swallow her up. 'I didn't mean to disturb you.'

'Come in, Sarah,' Jane croaked.

'Are you sure?' Sarah whispered, shutting the door behind her.

'What time is it?'

'It's afternoon, Jane. Are you ill?'

'No, Sarah. Just exhausted.'

Pulling back the covers and standing, Jane pulled the curtains, grimacing as the light flooded the room.

Sarah looked around the room that she had not been in before and wondered if it was always this untidy.

'Would you get me some water, Sarah, while I get dressed?'

'Of course.'

Lifting the empty bucket, Sarah noticed that the inside was dry, and wondered how long Jane had been without water.

Downstairs, she hesitated at the door to the yard with all its bad memories. As she crossed to the pump, she avoided looking at the closet, and was soon pumping the cold black handle, filling the bucket.

Struggling to carry the bucket up three flights of stairs, she regretted having filled it so full and realised how soft she had become, with Beth doing all the manual work at the Coles'.

She was breathing heavily as she entered Jane's room with the bucket.

'Leave it there by the table, Sarah. I'll wash my hands and face.'

'Do you have any food, Jane?'

Jane shook her head as she scooped some water out of the bucket into a small bowl.

'While you get dressed, Jane, I'll get you something to eat. I won't be long.'

'Where will you get food on a Sunday?'

But Sarah was already on her way out of the door and on her way back to the funeral parlour.

The Coles were upstairs with Arthur when she arrived, and Beth didn't come on a Sunday, as she went to church with her family.

Alone in the kitchen, she cut a thick slice of bread and then a slice of ham from a cooked joint, before hurrying back to Jane.

When Sarah returned, Jane was dressed and ate the food with gusto.

Sarah got straight to the point, asking, 'What has happened, Jane? Are you still employed?'

Jane wiped her fingers and straightened the towel hanging on the rail at the side of the washstand. 'I am still in work, Sarah. But it wasn't what I thought it would be. I don't get the chance to design anything. I sit at a sewing machine with other women, packed into a long shed. We work for hours without a break. I have to put my hand up to go to the privy and my time away from the bench is timed. I'm chastised if I take longer than the forewoman thinks that I should, and they take money from my wage if they're not satisfied with my work. I want to leave, but my old job at the haberdashery has gone.' She stopped talking and closed her eyes. 'I'm so tired, Sarah.'

She did look tired. There were dark rings under her eyes that should have belonged to someone much older. Not knowing what to say that might help, Sarah said the first thing that came into her head.

'Now that you've eaten something, Jane, I think you should get some air. Let's go for a walk, you're very pale.'

'Exercise is something that I don't get, Sarah. I know that I need it, but I'm always so tired, I just want to sleep when I get home.'

They walked, arm in arm, through the town until they reached St Andrew's Church. Entering the graveyard through the gates, they walked slowly along the main path edged with gravestones, some upright, the oldest leaning, some with ivy creeping over them, obscuring the names of those long gone. An atmosphere of calm and silence fell about their shoulders; the busy road and clamour of human life, on the other side of the wall, did not disturb the peace of this sacred, ancient ground, where Plymothians had been laid to rest for hundreds of years.

Seeing a bench, they sat down, neither speaking, lost in their own thoughts until Sarah said, 'What will you do, Jane? Will you stay there until you are old?'

Looking horrified, Jane replied slowly, 'I hadn't thought that I would stay there for the rest of my life. And now you've pointed it out to me, I don't know how I can get another job, as I work such long hours.'

'Could you make dresses for the women that used to be your clients?'

'No.' Jane shook her head. 'They will have moved on, and there wasn't enough money in it to pay the rent and bills.' She sighed. 'No, Sarah, it's not possible. I am where I am, and that's it.'

They sat once again in silence, each deep in their own thoughts, until Sarah said, 'Jane, I didn't tell you before but I met my brother not long ago, after not knowing him as I grew up. He's away on a merchant ship and misses family. Would you do me a great favour and write to him?'

'But he doesn't know me!' Jane sounded shocked. 'And I don't get time for writing, Sarah.'

'I know, Jane, but please, it's so wonderful when you get a letter. It would cheer you, and Ned, to receive letters. I will write to him and tell him that you are my friend and that you would like to write to him.'

'But I'm not sure that I do want to write to him, Sarah.'

'You can write, can't you, Jane?'

'Yes, of course I can write. I did go to school.'

'Then please, Jane, write to Ned. He really needs a friend.'

'What would I write to a man? I have no life to write about.'

'Of course you do, Jane. Tell him about what is going on in Plymouth, he's a Plymouth boy. Tell him how much you hate your work, that you used to go to the theatre with me. What we saw. There is so much to write about.'

'You write to him first, Sarah.' She sounded unsure but, Sarah noticed, was not saying no. 'Give him my address and, if he replies, I will write back if I can. Maybe just a line.'

'Thank you, Jane. I know that it will make my brother happy to have someone else to write to and to have something to look forward to. Years away from Plymouth, without family, has left him feeling empty and alone.'

'In that, Sarah, we have something in common.'

'I'll write today, Jane, as letters may take a long time to reach him. Now,' Sarah said, standing up, 'let us walk up on the Hoe and get some fresh air. It will bring the colour back into your cheeks.'

As they walked, Sarah realised that she couldn't tell Jane of her own troubles, of her feelings for John, of missing him. Jane had enough pain in her life without carrying her pain also.

18.

Sarah still hadn't seen John going about his work, patrolling the streets. Other constables came to the shop but not John. And Sarah felt that Mrs Cole also missed him. She was very fond of John and always asked him into the kitchen for a bite to eat or a drink on a hot day. She didn't extend this welcome to any of the other constables.

On her way to the Guildhall to see the town clerk, she almost bumped into Phillis coming out of the baker's, with her mother's order of bread.

Both girls acted in the same way, shocked.

'Oh, Sarah!' Phillis almost dropped her bag of bread.

'Phillis!'

For a moment, both stared at the other until Phillis had to get out of the doorway to let someone else in.

'How are you, Sarah?'

'Well, thank you. I hear that congratulations are in order.'

Phillis blushed. 'Thank you, Sarah.'

'When's the big day?'

'Not set yet. But it will be within three months of the last reading of our banns.'

Although it was breaking her heart, Sarah asked, 'How did you meet your husband-to-be, Phillis? You hardly leave the washroom.'

'That's true, but Father came to me and told me that a young man wanted to take me to the theatre. And that evening, after the performance, he asked Father for my hand in marriage.'

Sarah found herself gaping at Phillis before pulling herself together, asking, 'Why would you agree to marry a man that you don't know?'

'I was surprised. But Father tells me that John loves me. That he has a good job and will be an asset to our family.' Then, looking across to the King's Head, she said quickly, 'I have to go. Mother is waiting for her bread order. Goodbye, Sarah.'

And with that she stepped out into the road, skipping daintily between people, horses and carts, before disappearing through the doors of the King's Head, releasing the sound of laughter from within, before the doors shut behind her.

Sarah stood looking after Phillis, realising that Phillis hadn't asked about her life.

As she turned, deep in thought, to continue her journey to the Guildhall, she almost bumped into a woman who was walking straight at her.

The woman was taller than Sarah and, on first impression, very grey. Her hair, her skin and her coat. At first, Sarah prepared to step out of the woman's way but the woman's eyes were focused on hers to such an extent that she felt that she had done something wrong and was going to be chastised in the street. The woman did not change her direction.

'Forgive me for approaching you in the street, mistress, but I saw you speaking to Phillis Gallaway and wondered if you were friends.'

'We are not friends, madam. I'm sorry. I can't stand and talk, I have to get to the Guildhall.' She waved a file of papers in front of the woman.

The grey woman nodded her head, accepting that Sarah was on her way somewhere with work.

'I'm Mrs Parrett,' she offered. 'My son is about to wed that young lady and I don't know anything about her.'

Sarah was taken aback at the woman's directness. This was John's mother and she could see the concern on her face, but she didn't know what to say.

'Can you help me with any information about the family? I don't know them, and they haven't arranged a meeting of the two families as is the normal custom.'

Sarah was struck dumb and could do no more than stare at John's mother. Recovering a little from the shock of speaking with the mother of the man that she loved, Sarah could only say, 'I'm sorry. I don't know anything about the marriage and was asking Phillis about it myself.'

'Do you know John?' his mother asked with such enquiring eyes that Sarah could feel the blood rushing to her face, as her own pain of loss rose in her chest.

'I do know John. Through work,' she qualified quickly. 'As a constable, he comes to the funeral parlour, or used to,' she added.

'I'm very worried.' Mrs Parrett's face seemed to drain into a deeper shade of grey and Sarah felt the need to help her.

'If you have the time, Mrs Parrett, you could walk with me to the Guildhall.'

'Thank you.' John's mother sounded so grateful that she was almost wringing her hands, and in that moment it was clear to Sarah, for the first time, that all was not well.

As they walked, Sarah asked, 'Why would John ask Mr Gallaway if he could take his daughter to the theatre, if he didn't know her?'

'But John didn't ask him,' Mrs Parrett said very strongly. 'Mr Gallaway asked John to take his daughter to the theatre, because there was something that she really wanted to see and had no one to go with.'

Sarah stopped walking and Mrs Parrett had to turn around to look at her. 'What's wrong?' Mrs Parrett asked.

'I think that we're getting somewhere, Mrs Parrett. Phillis told me that her father told her that a young man, that she didn't know, wanted to take her to the theatre. Yet John says that Mr Gallaway told him that Phillis needed someone to go to the theatre with. And asked him to take her.' It was beginning to make sense. 'Mr Gallaway is at the heart of this. A very nasty man. I know, because I worked for

165

the family for a few weeks. But I can tell you that if John goes ahead with this, Phillis is a gentle girl, not at all like her parents.'

'Thank you for your help.' Mrs Parrett looked relieved. 'You've given me the information that I needed to help my son. I will never be able to thank you enough. Miss…?'

For a moment, Sarah was tempted to hide her identity, but replied shyly, 'Miss Warrington.'

Mrs Parrett placed a hand on Sarah's shoulder before turning away into the crowd.

Sarah stood looking after her, still able to feel the heat of John's mother's hand on her skin beneath her blouse. It was like having a part of John with her as she entered the Guildhall looking for the town clerk's junior.

That evening, Edith Parrett made her way to the home of Sir Geoffrey Best, hoping to see William.

The house was substantial, standing in its own grounds with views of Dartmoor behind it. Knocking, she stood back, not knowing who would answer the door and hoping that she would be able to speak about her findings without crying.

A pleasant-faced maid answered the door and instead of shooing her away or looking down her nose at Edith, she smiled, and asked how she could help.

Tears filled Edith's eyes and a lump formed in her throat as she managed to say, 'Is Mister William Best at home? He's a friend of my son.'

To Edith's relief, the door was pulled wider and she was invited into a wide hallway with a marble-tiled hall, the like of which she had not seen before. She noticed an armchair, upholstered in pale blue, which looked as though it had never been sat in, and a large mirror on the wall which she tried not to look into, but in which she could still see her dowdy reflection out of the corner of her eye.

The maid indicated the chair. 'Please take a seat, Mrs…?'

'Mrs Parrett,' Edith replied, her throat dry, her heart palpitating. Unsure now if she was doing the right thing.

The maid nodded and turned away as Edith sat nervously on the edge of the pale blue chair.

As she sat in the silence of the grand hall, she looked at the pattern on the tiled floor while she waited. Her stomach started to lurch. So far out of her normal mundane comfort, she had to question what she was doing sitting in a Member of Parliament's hallway. What if William wasn't there and she had to speak to his father? Would she be able to convey her fears to him, and tell him what she now saw as evidence?

It was with great relief that she saw William walking towards her with the maid. 'Has something happened to John?' He looked and sounded alarmed.

As she stood to greet him, her legs almost collapsed with the emotion and fear of this evening. And for a moment she held on to the arm of the chair.

The maid rushed forward and both William and the maid helped her to a room where a fire glowed in a large stone fireplace. A cosy room warmed by shelves of books that lined the walls.

'Shall I bring tea to the library, sir?'

'Yes, Dolly,' he said over the top of Edith's head. 'And some refreshment, perhaps some of Cook's cake.'

He helped Edith to sit in a chair next to the fire. Then, going to a table holding many carafes filled with liquids in various shades of amber, he poured them both a glass of one of his father's expensive whiskies.

Edith waited until William was seated in front of her before sipping the liquid. She was not a drinker. They couldn't afford drink unless it was Christmas, when they bought a cheap port. She expected to cough and show herself up, but the liquid was smooth and warmed her.

Leaning back in the chair opposite, William waited.

As Edith placed the glass on the occasional table next to her chair, she looked at William, who still said nothing.

'I met a young woman today,' she started, 'a Miss Warrington, who knows John and Phillis Gallaway through work.'

William nodded, waiting.

'She was talking to Phillis Gallaway in the street and, after the maid had gone back to the King's Head, I approached Miss Warrington and questioned her about the Gallaway family. She told me that Phillis had said, that her father told *her*, that John had asked if he could take Phillis to the theatre. Yet John says that Mr Gallaway asked him to take his daughter to the theatre. It seems that Mr Gallaway is at the heart of this. He then got John very drunk, as you know, and told him that he had asked for the hand of his daughter in marriage. What are we going to do, William?'

The door opened and Dolly walked in with the tray, placing it on a small table and left, leaving them to talk.

William poured the tea while he thought and, after handing a cup to Edith, he sat back in the chair looking grave.

'The problem is, Mrs Parrett,' he sighed, 'I can hear my father saying that we have no evidence.'

'But!'

'No.' William shook his head. 'I'm sorry, Mrs Parrett, but word of mouth isn't enough. It isn't evidence. But I think that the constables can make life difficult for Mr Gallaway. Show that we suspect foul play until we have some evidence.'

Edith frowned. 'Surely, William, if John has no evidence, then Mr Gallaway has no evidence.'

William was impressed. 'That is true, but he will probably be able to get many of his customers to say that they heard John ask it.'

'But is that evidence, William? Isn't that still word of mouth?'

'It's at times like this that I realise I should have taken more interest in the law as my father wanted. Please be assured that even if you don't hear from me, I am working on John's behalf to try and stop this marriage.' He took a sip of his tea and then, holding the cup with both hands, frowned across the top of the dainty porcelain at Edith. 'He could, of course, stop it himself,' he said suddenly.

'How?' Edith was filled with sudden hope.

'By telling the priest that he was tricked into this marriage. That he doesn't love the woman.'

'He won't do that, William. He has no proof that he didn't ask it. He's a decent soul and not a man to go back on his word.'

With her hopes dashed, Edith walked home slowly. There had to be a way out of this, and if not, where were the young couple going to live, or was that another secret up the sleeve of the landlord of the King's Head?

19.

The next day, Claude Augustus Gallaway looked up as his wife entered the bar with the clean drinking vessels ready for the day ahead, and commented on the lack of customers that had been in that morning. There were just the two regulars, that always propped up the bar, talking rubbish and putting the world to rights in their own archaic opinions. Which, boringly, had not changed in many years, to the extent that all the Gallaways had to do was agree without listening.

'I s'pect,' said Bill Overcoat, the eldest man sitting at the bar, as he sucked at his beer, drawing it in over his toothless gums, 'that it's the fault of them constables standing outside your door.'

Stepping out into the street, Claude was surprised to see two constables standing each side of the entrance to the King's Head.

'Is something wrong, Constable?' Gallaway asked the nearest.

'I don't know, sir, you tell me,' Constable William Best replied, with a look of such interest on his face that Claude was unnerved.

'Your standing outside my premises is stopping my customers coming in.'

'Why would customers, with nothing to hide, not just walk past us and into your premises?' William asked, frowning.

Claude had no answer to that so tried a different tack. 'Why are you standing here outside my door?'

'It's our job, sir, as you know, to keep watch on the streets, to keep everyone safe.'

'Yes, yes, but why here?'

'This is as good as anywhere to keep watch on this part of King Street.'

Claude's face was suffused with a sudden anger that he couldn't hide. 'I want you to move on, and I want you to do it now, Constable.' He emphasised the title.

'Are you threatening us, sir? Are you trying to interfere with the law as it goes about its duty?'

Claude Gallaway stood with his mouth open, trying to think of something more to say, as two men that he recognised as customers crossed the road and entered the Royal Oak.

William, on seeing two more constables making their way under the viaduct towards him, said, 'Well, it's time for us to look at the rest of the street. Good day to you, sir.'

As the two policemen walked away, Claude felt that he had won the battle. Returning to the bar, looking satisfied with himself, he missed the next two constables arriving to position themselves each side of his door minutes later.

When his next customer arrived an hour later asking why there were constables outside, Claude went to investigate.

'What are you doing here?' he demanded.

'Our duty, sir,' the older constable replied. 'Keeping an eye on the villains.'

'I already sent two of your kind away today. Now I'm telling *you* to move off.'

'Are you trying to interfere with the law, sir?' The constable, who was taller and older than Claude, looked down on the man's drink-swollen face, staring into his eyes with such intensity that Claude felt intimidated for the first time in his life.

'I'm not putting up with this,' he blustered. 'I'm going to see your superior and let him know what you're about.'

'And what might that be, sir?'

'Interfering with a decent man's livelihood, that's what, Constable, and I will have you removed from the force.'

Turning away, Claude stomped off under the viaduct, elbowing anyone who got in his way.

When Claude was out of sight, the constables walked away.

~

Twenty minutes later, two men entered the King's Head, the tallest carrying a small but heavy sack, while his shorter companion stumbled behind as he searched in his pockets for money.

After Margaret Gallaway had served them, she noticed how they spoke quietly to each other as they leant on the bar.

Margaret had seen enough customers in her time to know a couple that were up to no good and wondered what it was that they'd done, or were going to do. Edging nearer, pretending to be arranging a shelf under the bar, she listened intently, wishing that the two old fools in the corner would stop talking so that she could hear better.

'What do you think?' she heard the tallest whisper, his eyes flicking from side to side as he made sure that no one was listening.

'I think that someone could make a lot of money out of it. If they had the right set-up,' his companion muttered out of the side of his mouth.

The first nodded. 'Can it be traced?'

'No. All barrels look the same. It won't be traced. That's the beauty of it.'

'What should we ask for it?'

'Not sure. Perhaps we should ask someone who knows the price of rum to give us an idea. It's going to make someone a fortune and I can get another, if it's wanted.'

Unable to hold back her curiosity, Margaret spoke up. 'I couldn't help overhearing you, sirs. I know the price of rum and could help you.' She spoke quietly, matching their tone.

Both men stared at her for a moment, looking shocked, before looking about the bar as though they were about to be arrested.

'Well, gentlemen, what do you have that needs a price?'

The tallest man hefted the sack from the floor and, putting it on the bar, pulled one side of the sack down, revealing a small barrel. 'The best Jamaican rum,' he whispered, to enlighten her of its contents.

'Where did you get it?' Margaret asked, using the same conspiratorial whisper as the men.

'Can't say.' The man pulled the sack up over the barrel, hiding it from sight. 'Best you don't know, madam,' the smaller man whispered, looking uncomfortable.

'I see,' Margaret said, wondering if she should offer to buy it. After all, it could make them money at the wedding.

'How much would you want for it?' she asked, looking at its size and trying to work out how much they could charge a nip.

The tall man sucked at his teeth, making a squelching sound. 'Well, that depends...'

'Depends on what?' Margaret now wanted the barrel, having worked out a huge profit.

'Depends on whether you can be trusted, madam.'

'Trusted? Of course I can be trusted. I can hide that barrel amongst a hundred barrels and it wouldn't be found.'

The men looked at each other. 'We're not used to dealing with a woman. Do you have a husband?'

Put out by this question, Margaret hissed, 'Yes, I have a husband, we're joint owners of this establishment.'

'Aha.' The smaller man nodded. 'Does that mean that you are allowed to buy what you want without him knowing?'

Margaret was incensed at their implying that she took orders from her husband. She, who was joint owner of the King's Head, and it had been her money that had bought it. Yes, she could do as she damn well liked without the "by-your-leave" of Claude Gallaway.

~

Sergeant Norris was behind the desk in the front lobby when Claude Gallaway entered the police station, shouting that he wanted justice. Recognising the landlord of the King's Head, Sergeant Norris ignored him and carried on writing in his book.

'Do you hear me?' Claude shouted, banging his fist on the desk.

Sergeant Norris sighed. 'Please take a seat, sir, and I will see you in a minute.'

'You will see me now, Sergeant. It's about your constables.'

'Please sit down and await your turn, sir.'

Claude looked around him. There was no one in the lobby but himself.

Sergeant Norris carried on writing, slowly.

'I'm going to report you to your superior, sir,' Claude shouted in frustration. He had never been treated like this before. The man before him may be wearing a uniform but he was a paid servant, a servant of the law to which Claude paid his taxes.

'For what reason will you report me, sir?' the sergeant enquired calmly.

'For not listening to my complaint.'

'Sir.' Sergeant Norris' voice held a threat. 'I will listen to your complaint when it's your turn. Now, take a seat and wait to be called, or I will arrest you for disturbance of the peace.'

Claude looked once more around the empty lobby and then back at the sergeant, a look of disbelief on his face, before walking over to a row of empty chairs and sitting down.

A woman came in saying that a man had tried to make off with her purse in George Street and gave a description in great detail to the sergeant, who wrote it all down slowly. In the next half hour, several people came in and were dealt with straight away.

Exasperated, Claude went to the desk in an angry mood. 'I was here first. I demand to see your superior officer.'

'Ah, well, there's the rub, sir. Our inspector is in Exeter today on vital business. I'm afraid that I'm the most senior here. Perhaps you could come back tomorrow.'

'You made me wait all this time, knowing that the inspector wasn't here?'

'Well, sir, I didn't know that you only wanted to speak to him until just now, or I would have told you. I was prepared to write down your complaint when it was your turn.'

'But it was my turn an hour ago.'

'Well, sir, that's your opinion and you may have it. But I am the law and my opinion seems to be at variance with your own.'

Claude realised that he was going to get nowhere today and stomped out shouting over his shoulder.

'I'll be back, sir, and I will have your job.'

~

His mood had not improved on arrival back at the King's Head, and the drinkers went quiet as he stomped through the bar.

James, seeing his father's face before his father saw him, disappeared out the back door. Phillis was shouted at for working too slowly and Margaret stood her ground in front of him as he came behind the bar, his face red with anger.

He gave her the full account of what happened at the police station, loudly. The customers listened, staring into their beer, agog, as Claude ranted, threatening to have the sergeant dismissed, and some of the constables.

Margaret gave him a small glass of rum and listened until his ranting subsided. Frowning, he looked at the glass that he'd just drunk from. 'This isn't one of ours. Where'd you get it?'

'Come to the barrel room and I'll tell you.'

When they were deep in the room, Margaret whispered, 'Two men came in with a small barrel for sale. They wanted far less than it's worth, so I bought it off them. We will make a great profit.'

'Where is it?' he said, sounding suspicious.

'Where's what?' she frowned.

'The barrel, woman.' His temper flared. 'What have you done with this barrel?'

'I hid it in one of the empty barrels.'

'Now why would you hide it, madam?'

Pulling him to the end of the room, she whispered, 'Because it could be contraband.' She smiled excitedly. 'They didn't know its worth. But I did. We will make a fortune.'

'If we're found with it, we'll be locked up,' he hissed.

'How will they identify it? There are no markings on the barrel.'

'Let me see it.' He sounded more interested.

175

Margaret went to a large empty barrel at the end of a row of barrels awaiting collection by the brewery and lifted the lid, taking out the small barrel.

Claude inspected it all over. There were no marks to identify it. Perhaps they could make a profit. And how could he get rid of it now even if he'd wanted to? He couldn't sell it to other publicans. They would want to know where he'd bought such a good rum and why he was selling it. No, now they had it, they would have to keep it.

'We will have to be very careful who we sell it to. I wouldn't trust all our customers.'

'But most wouldn't know, Claude.'

'They'd know. The price will be more than a glass of the cheaper rum.'

'Of course,' she replied thoughtfully. 'Then we will sell the best only to those who can afford it and who won't ask questions.'

Claude pushed the small barrel back into its hiding place and lowered the lid. Turning to his wife, he said, 'And, Margaret,' the threat barely disguised in his voice, 'don't do this again, unless you ask me first.'

20.

A storm had been brewing out at sea all day; the low grey clouds that had covered the town had now turned black above the rooftops. Sarah could hear the distant thunder getting louder and guessed that the storm would soon break. She prayed that, if it came inland, it would bring the rain and relief from the humidity.

The air inside the shop was too warm and stale; her clothes were beginning to stick to her, but she was afraid to leave her position and wash, as they had been so busy all day.

Mrs Cole came in with a bowl of lavender heads, placing the bowl on the desk. She had been distilling her lavender oil and also brought a few drops, floating in water, in specially designed pottery that took a small nub of candle that, when lit, heated the water from below, giving off the fragrance of lavender, refreshing the reception area.

They had taken so many instructions that there had been no time for lunch. The storm broke with flashes of lightning about four o'clock, the rain so heavy that it bounced with force off the fetid cobbles outside.

Mr Cole arrived, carrying two bags filled with earth and sand, placing them in the doorway outside before shutting the door. 'Best we can do,' he said, looking worried. 'Best we can do.' And returned to his office, saying to Sarah over his shoulder as he went, 'If the water comes in through the door, call me.'

'Yes, sir,' she replied, feeling anxious, wondering how deep the water might get.

No one else came into the shop and Mrs Cole returned, telling her to go to the kitchen and get some food. Taking Sarah's place at the desk, Mrs Cole stared at the floor in front of the door, waiting for the first trickle of water.

In the kitchen, Beth was in a sour mood as she pushed a plate of meat and bread onto the table. 'Everything's at the wrong hour,' she mumbled.

Sarah didn't answer, not wanting to fuel Beth's frustration any further, and noticed the sweat standing out on the woman's skin and her damp hair.

Pulling the plate towards her, she ate the meat, discovering that she was hungry and that if Beth had been in a better mood, she might have asked for more.

As the storm continued, they closed early, knowing that there would be no more custom until the drenching rain stopped.

Jagged lightning flashed above the rooftops, illuminating the street below and a passing carriage and horse. Another flash highlighted the shops on the other side of the street and a person hurrying, head down against the rain, the presence of life there and gone in a second, followed by thunder that boomed immediately overhead. The street was becoming empty of human life. The dead could wait until the rain stopped.

Beth had the evening meal ready at the usual time. Sarah ate with Mr and Mrs Cole who then went to visit Arthur, taking his supper up with them, leaving Sarah to go to her room.

Unable to take her evening walk, she sat looking through the closed window at the empty street below as the rain hammered against the glass. She sighed, it was going to be a long evening. Looking around the room for something to do, she took all the unopened wage packets and put them in her mother's bag with her father's box and her grandmother's thimble, telling herself that she must buy a coat before winter.

She had so little, there was no point in spreading it about the room. This task being so quickly over, she sat in the chair and thought of Jane, deciding to call on her next Sunday.

It was an hour before Sarah noticed that the storm was abating, and that the rain had stopped. Opening the window, she breathed in the fresher air, feeling the tension leave her body. The empty street below was awash with the detritus of everyday living, some of it washed down from the streets above. The distant thunder, having moved on, now rumbled over the moor.

She could hear Mr Bronalski opening and closing drawers in his room on the other side of the wall, she supposed getting ready for bed. It made her feel uncomfortable being able to hear this man, who after all this time had not spoken two words to her, completing his ablutions. She also wondered why he wasn't upstairs with the child, remembering how she had hidden under the stairs in fear of thunder and lightning when she was small.

As she thought of getting ready for bed herself, she heard the child upstairs shouting. Had it woken needing company? As she opened a drawer and lifted her nightdress out, she heard the child screaming loudly, and soon after, the sound of furniture being moved, dragged, or so it seemed, before the sound of smashing china. What was happening? The boy must have woken and found himself alone, frightened of the storm, even though it had retreated.

Hearing the Coles' door open, she opened her own door onto the landing in time to see Mr Cole disappearing up the stairs, chased by his shadow reflected onto the wall from his candle, and Mrs Cole, her hair half brushed, and she in her nightwear, hurrying after him, holding her lighted candle in front of her.

Mr Cole's voice came from upstairs, louder than Sarah had ever heard it, shouting at Arthur to 'Put it down.' He repeated, 'Put it down,' again, this time with a threat in his voice. Mrs Cole's voice joined that of her husband's, louder than usual, but with a gentleness as she spoke to her son with words that Sarah could not hear over Mr Cole's shouting.

Mr Bronalski's door opened suddenly and he rushed, pale-faced, to the door opposite his, tucking his shirt into his trousers as he went. Noticing Sarah, he shouted, 'Go back in and lock the door.' He didn't stop to see if she did it, as the most terrible scream came from upstairs and Mr Cole was yelling with a strained voice, *'I told you to put it down. Now look what you've done. Oh my God!'*

Sarah couldn't move. One foot on the landing and one in her room, she stood frozen to the spot, holding on to the doorframe for support.

Mr Bronalski's voice joined that of Mr Cole. Voices that blended in anger, fear, determination, before the sound of a fight. Men grunting, cursing and a louder diatribe of foreign words from Mr Bronalski. Then several horrific screams, before silence.

The air around Sarah felt cold as she clung to the doorframe, listening for a sound. The silence, and her rising fear, had fused her bones, her muscles. Unable to move, she stood, wide-eyed, waiting for someone to come back, wondering what had happened. Why was no one talking to the boy? Should she go to the foot of the stairs and call out?

But at that same moment she heard a soft noise on the stair. A slow step, and then another, hardly audible, so soft, so muffled, it filled her with renewed fear. Who would descend that slowly and why?

She was breathing hard, her mouth dry, when a foot appeared in the doorway, followed slowly by the body of a grotesque man.

Her eyes widened in horror, and she would have screamed if she had not been filled with such terror. A thickset man with long arms and a huge, deformed white head stood facing her from the doorway. One of his eyes opaque, the other, a large eye, sat unblinking, low on his cheek above a crooked mouth and swollen bottom lip from which spittle dripped. But it was his nightshirt, soaked in blood, that held her in a grip of fear. What had he done? Where were the Coles and Mr Bronalski?

He raised his arm as though in greeting and she saw the bloody knife held in his hand.

'Za rah,' he said slowly, in a small voice.

For a second, she couldn't move. Her eyes holding the spectacle that began to move towards her. She had no breath. Her limbs had frozen with fear as she still clung to the doorframe.

Movement came back to her with a jolt.

Ducking into her room, she slammed the door, turning the key in the lock with a shaking hand as he reached the door, hammering on it.

'Za rah.'

His high-pitched voice reached her through the door as he hammered on it with his fists, so hard that it seemed to buckle.

Forcing her muscles to move against her fear, she slipped the bolts across top and bottom. Then stood back, wondering if it would hold. Who was it? She didn't know. How did he know her name? Where were the Coles and what had happened to their son, to all of them?

Going to the window, she opened it wider and screamed for help into an empty street. The sound at the door changed. No longer hammering but huge thuds. He was throwing his body at the door and the screws in the top bolt were loosening. In panic, she screamed out of the window, 'MURDER, MURDER.' Her small voice floated on the air of a street where the occupants heard screaming every night, and, it being so normal, they ignored it.

A shadow on the other side of the street moved in the doorway of the shoe mender. A vagrant sleeper stepped slowly into the street, looking up at her.

'They've all been murdered,' she shouted. 'Help me. He's coming for me.'

The man stood, mouth open, for some moments, then called back, 'I'll go to the Watch House for a constable.'

It was her only hope. But how long would that take? The Watch House was on the Barbican, and the constables walked the whole town at night.

With the sound of wood splintering, she brought her head back into the room. An arm was through a jagged hole in the door and his bloody fingers were feeling for the key left in the lock. Her only escape would be to jump from the window. Looking down, she knew it would hurt, break her bones. Kill her.

His arm was feeling for the upper bolt, pushing a bigger hole in the fractured wood to get his shoulder through.

Sarah ran to the bedroom, locked and bolted the door. Opening the bedroom window, she again contemplated the drop.

The crash in the other room alerted her to the fact that he was through the door. Pulling the bedclothes from the bed, she started to tie the ends of the sheets and blanket together, making a rope, before tying one end to the iron bedstead. But it hardly crossed the gap between the bed and the window.

With the strength of someone whose life depended on it, she pushed the heavy iron bed towards the window, driven by her fear. Now her emergency rope fell across the windowsill and a few feet down the wall, but was still far too short.

As she climbed across the bed, the hammering started on the bedroom door. Climbing out through the window, she sat on the windowsill contemplating the drop as she held on to the first knot. She could see that, from the last knot, it was still a long drop to the street below. It would still hurt.

She hadn't noticed that people were gathering on the other side of the street, until a woman screamed, and a man shouted, 'Jump, maid.'

Turning her head in the direction that the crowd were looking, she saw the grotesque man easing himself out of the other window and starting to stand on the sill. Holding on to the window frame, he leaned across the gap between them, and the woman in the crowd below screamed again.

Sarah tightened her grip on the knot in her hands. It seemed impossible that he could reach her over the gap between the two windows.

He was holding one arm out towards her, the other still holding the edge of the window frame. Something was swinging below his fist, held tightly in his bloody fingers. When she realised what it was, she almost fell, as her hands loosened on the first knot. There was no mistaking what it was. A cross with a blue stone at its centre, swinging in the evening air between them. Lillian's lost cross and chain. He was offering it to her; how did he have it?

Fear hammered in her chest and the next that she knew he was no longer at the window but was breaking down the bedroom door.

The crowd below in the street were shouting, 'Jump, jump,' with such fervour that she turned her body and, holding on to the first knot, slipped over the edge of the sill, her feet fumbling desperately for the next knot. Sliding her hands down the sheet, she found the courage to let her feet leave the safety of the knot and search for the next one. The crowd began to shout and scream in earnest.

Looking up, she saw the deformed head and face of the grotesque, hanging over the bedroom windowsill above her, grinning. His hands were on the first knot. His spittle dripped on her face as he began to pull her up towards him.

Closing her eyes, she let go of the rope.

21.

A sharp pain shot through her arm and right hip as she fell with a jolt onto something otherwise soft. But the pain hardly registered, as the fear still held her in its grip. She heard herself screaming as she stared up at the white face hanging out of the bedroom window, still holding the makeshift rope. Moments later, the misshapen head jerked backwards and disappeared before a constable hung out of the window, looking down on her. She was safe. But not from the trauma, as her body began to shake uncontrollably.

A hand smoothed her hair gently back from her face and it was then that she realised she was lying on top of someone. Someone had caught her, breaking her fall, and they were both lying in the bottom of a cart. A voice that she recognised, although she had never heard it so soft, was whispering in her ear.

'I thought I'd lost you. I will never let you out of my sight again, Sarah. You mean so much to me.'

'John?'

She sank into John's arms and cried. 'What *was* that?' she asked, her voice barely audible.

'I don't know,' he whispered. 'But right now, you are my priority. I'm taking you to the hospital for them to examine you. And then we'll see what the constables have found out. Someone must know who that is.'

It was the last she heard as she passed into oblivion.

Sarah awoke next morning in an unfamiliar bed. The mattress hard beneath her back. Her mind in those seconds between darkness and wakefulness, trying to work out where she was. As the horror flooded back, she tensed, her eyes widening, a scream forming in her throat. Someone was in the room with her, sitting in the shadow, only feet from the bed.

At that moment, the door opened, flooding the room with light from a corridor. A nurse, smart and stiff in her uniform, approached the bed and, seeing Sarah awake, opened the curtains, revealing John, sitting in a chair, looking haggard. Puffy bags had formed beneath his eyes, now red from lack of sleep. He looked different, older, a beard forming along his jawline. She had never seen him looking so dishevelled.

He was out of the chair and beside the bed in an instant, looking at the nurse, his face etched with worry.

'She's fine, Constable,' the nurse said, as her fingers rested on Sarah's wrist, taking her pulse. 'The doctor will see her soon and I think that he will say that she can go home tomorrow.' Looking satisfied, she patted Sarah on the arm and bustled from the room.

As the door closed slowly behind the nurse, Sarah looked at John, and in the silence, tears formed in her eyes as the words echoed in her head. *She can go home.*

John shook his head. 'You can't go back there. You can't live in a house with all those men and no other woman.'

The words struck her as strange. 'Mrs Cole?' she questioned.

'I'm afraid that Mrs Cole was killed.'

Sarah stared at him, her mouth open, trying to take in what he had just said. Then remembering Mrs Cole's scream, she sobbed uncontrollably.

John went for the nurse, who returned with him to Sarah's side. She again held Sarah's wrist and nodded, satisfied.

'This is good,' she told John. 'She has to let out the horror of what she has been through. I'll tell Doctor. He'll be happy.'

When she'd left the room, John sat next to the bed, holding Sarah's hand. He couldn't speak, he was so distressed. He wanted to put everything right for her, now that he knew how much he loved her.

'I'm homeless again,' she sobbed. 'I can't go back there.'

'You must come and live with me and my parents, Sarah. We have a small box room and Mother will look after you.'

Sarah shook her head, horrified at the suggestion. 'I can't live with you, John. You are about to get married. You and Phillis might be living with your parents.'

Stupidly, he replied, 'There will still be room for you, Sarah.'

For one moment, she had thought that he had feelings for her, but now! How did he think that she could live in a room next to him and his new bride when he and Phillis were married?

With the tears still running over her cheeks, she nodded solemnly, before speaking in a quiet, reserved voice that reflected her feelings.

'Would you leave me now, John? I would like to wash.'

'Yes, of course.' He looked embarrassed. 'I'll be outside.'

'No, John. Please go home. I will get my things together and go and live with my aunt.'

'Oh!' He looked surprised. 'I didn't know that you had an aunt.'

'Goodbye, John.' She kept her face passive, not letting it reflect the huge emotion of loss that she felt.

When he'd left, she collapsed back against the pillows and cried. At first, all that she felt was the grief of loss, but gradually she realised that she had to get her life back together. She would go back to Kingsand and her aunt. Then she would get a job and perhaps a room like Jane. She knew now that she could look after herself. Knew what she was capable of.

~

Later that morning, the coroner, Mr James Blendall, walked with twenty-four jury men and a Plymouth surgeon, Mr David Hopkins, to the funeral parlour in King Street that was now closed off because of the incident. Here, they viewed the body of Mrs Cole, who had been left there all night, and the damage to the room, while the surgeon examined her body, pushing his fingers into the wounds.

The unconscious bodies of Mr Cole and Mr Bronalski had already been removed last night to the nearest hospital.

The jury men then looked at Sarah's rooms and the damage there, before walking back to the Guildhall, where, after taking their places in the courtroom, the coroner addressed them.

'We are here this morning, gentlemen, to determine what happened in the rooms above the King Street Funeral Parlour. We have seen the site for ourselves and we will hear from the occupants of that establishment in due course. But first, I call the surgeon, Mr David Hopkins, to tell us of his findings.'

The surgeon, a small man with a dominant orange moustache, stood to give his evidence. 'I have,' he said, 'examined the body of Mrs Cole, who lay in a pool of blood on the floor of the room that must have been their upper living room. She was quite dead and presented a fearful wound across her neck. The wound was very deep. Death resulted from the severing of both her left internal jugular vein and left external jugular vein. Also, gentlemen, the force by which the knife blade was delivered cut the common carotid artery. It was the blood loss from the wound that caused her death.'

The coroner thanked the surgeon and, turning to the jury, said, 'Gentlemen. We have visited the premises where the murder took place and viewed and examined the body of the victim, Mrs Cole. Without any witnesses today, as all are in hospital, I will close this session and we will reconvene at ten o'clock tomorrow morning.'

~

An official letter, addressed to Miss S. Warrington, was handed to Sarah that day as she lay in the hospital bed, by the matron. On opening it, she read that she was called to give evidence at the inquest of the deceased, Mrs G. A. Cole, at ten o'clock, at the Guildhall the following morning.

She lay back on the pillows thinking how kind Mrs Cole had been to her. She had not been invited to feel like part of the family, it was true. But the woman had always been civil and caring, seeing that she ate her supper and her breakfast, and hadn't locked her out when she was late back the first time that she went to the theatre with Jane.

~

Still feeling fragile, the following morning, Sarah sat in the courtroom wondering why she was there. When the door opened and John entered, her heart exploded with love, then embarrassment, followed swiftly by regret. As the usher showed him where to sit, she kept her eyes cast down, unable to look at him.

When Sarah was called to tell what she knew of the evening that Mrs Cole died, she told the court of the storm, and of the Coles rushing upstairs to their son at what sounded like someone smashing the furniture. Of the shouting and the screams. Of Mr Cole exclaiming, *My God, look what you've done*. Of Mr Bronalski shouting at her to go into her room and bolt the door, before he went upstairs. Of his voice joining that of Mr Cole's, and the sound of a fight. Of the silence that followed and how she was about to go and look up the stairs when she heard slow footsteps coming down and waited to see who it was. 'I was,' she added, 'very frightened.' And once again felt the tears welling up and had to take a moment before carrying on.

'When a man that I had never seen before stood before me on the landing covered in blood, I couldn't move. And then, when he called my name and began to move towards me, I ran into my room and bolted the door. He was trying to break it down, to get into the room when I opened the window and called for help. The street was empty because of the storm, but a vagrant sleeping in a shop doorway stepped out and I asked him to get the police. I told him that there had been a murder, although I didn't know who, and believed that I was to be murdered.'

She stopped once more, taking a deep breath. 'The bloodied man was almost through the door,' she continued, 'when I ran into the bedroom and pulled the bolts across top and bottom. Then, opening the window there, I made a rope of the bed covers to escape. It was a long drop and I feared that I would die from the fall if I jumped and be killed if I stayed. It was then, as I sat on the windowsill, that the man stepped out of the first window and I saw that he held the cross and chain that belonged to Miss Lillian Blatten, who was killed earlier in the year.'

She stopped speaking. Her mouth had become dry and her legs had begun to shake as she remembered sitting on the ledge and her fear of falling. Taking a deep breath, she continued. 'The next I knew, he was hammering with his fists on the bedroom door. When I heard that door giving way, I held on to the rope and, slipping over the edge of the sill, I lowered myself to the first knot. A crowd had gathered on the pavement and they were screaming for me to let go of the rope. Not understanding why, I looked up and saw that the grotesque man was leaning out of the bedroom window and about to pull me back up.' She stopped speaking and shuddered.

'Do the jury have any questions?' the coroner asked.

A portly man raised his hand. 'Jonathan Armour, sir. Miss Warrington,' he frowned, 'can you tell the jury why there were so many bolts on the doors, in fact, three to each door?'

'No, sir, I can't.'

'How often did you hear the child upstairs crying or shouting?'

'Fairly often, sir. I understand that he was not well.'

'In what way unwell?'

'I don't know, sir. When once I asked Mrs Cole if I could see her son, and perhaps play a board game with him, she said that he didn't do well with people that he didn't know.'

'Thank you, Miss Warrington,' the coroner said, not asking to be told more.

'Excuse me, sir,' she said quietly. 'I keep thinking that no one has mentioned Arthur. What happened to their son?'

The coroner smiled kindly at her. 'That will be answered in due course. You say that you were never introduced to their son, Arthur, Miss Warrington?'

'No, sir.'

'Did you see who killed Mrs Cole?'

'No, sir. I was on the floor below.'

'Thank you. You can return to your seat.'

When John was called upon to speak, he told how he had been approached by the vagrant and, after telling the man to go to the Watch House and raise the alarm, he had run all the way to the funeral parlour.

'Seeing the situation,' he said, 'with Miss Warrington hanging from a sheet rope halfway down the wall, I ran to the back yard of the funeral parlour, and with no time to attach the horse, the stable boys and I pulled the cart up the passage to the front of the shop to shorten her fall. We had only just got it in place, and I had just jumped onto the back of it to catch her, when she fell.'

He described the terrifying face of the murderer looking down at them and the relief when Constable Hayes looked out of the window, exclaiming, '*We have him.*'

He didn't know, he said, what had happened to the Coles or their son. His only thought was to get Miss Warrington to the hospital. His colleagues dealt with the murderer.

When Constable Hayes was questioned, he told the jury that the constables went into the property via the back yard and, arriving at a room on the first floor, they found the man hanging out of the window, holding on to the rope that held Miss Warrington. The man fought them when they pulled him back inside the room. The constable that was trying to disarm him was stabbed in the arm, and the man had the strength of ten men. 'Eventually, sir,' he said, looking proud of himself, 'the man was overpowered, arrested, and taken to the secure wing of the hospital.' He looked expectantly at the jury. When no one had a question, he carried on speaking.

'We found the bodies of Mr and Mrs Cole and Mr Bronalski upstairs,' he said. 'There had been a fight. Much of the furniture was broken and we found the three people on the floor in different parts of the room. Mrs Cole was dead, stabbed in the throat. Mr Cole and Mr Bronalski were bleeding, stabbed and unconscious.

The two men were taken to hospital, where they are still recovering.'

'And the child?' the coroner prompted.

'There were signs of a child, sir, in the form of games and toys, but no sign of the boy Arthur Cole. An advert has been placed in the paper offering a reward for his return, or for information of his whereabouts. But so far, sir, no one has replied.'

The coroner in addressing the jury remarked that under a different set of circumstances it might have been necessary for him to have gone very minutely into the case and heard more witnesses. But the evidence had been clearly given, and he did not think that he needed to detain these witnesses any further.

The coroner closed the inquest, which would be continued again at a later date when Mr Cole and Mr Bronalski were both well enough to be present.

22.

The young woman that stepped from the ferry that afternoon was emotionally different from the girl who had boarded it some months earlier, not wanting to return to her mother.

Walking along the main road to Kingsand, Sarah didn't know if her aunt would take her in. Not after the strange way that they had parted on her last visit. And this time she was going to ask if she could stay, even though she knew that there was little room.

Encased in thought as she walked, she hardly noticed the sound of a horse, and the rolling of cartwheels, coming along the road behind her, until it pulled up alongside.

'Hello, Sarah.' A cheerful male voice greeted her. 'You visiting your Aunt Josephine?'

'Mr Tucker!' she greeted the shopkeeper. 'Yes, I'm visiting my aunt.'

'Would you like a lift?' He smiled down on her.

'Thank you, Mr Tucker. I would like a lift.'

'Climb up then, maid.'

The horse moved restlessly and the cart jolted forward as she put her foot on the step. 'Whoa, Sal. Stand,' he called, pulling on the reins. The horse obeyed, snorting.

Sarah climbed up next to him, holding on to the seat beneath her skirt as they jerked forward.

'How are you?' he asked unexpectedly.

'I'm well, thank you, Mr Tucker.'

'Ah ha.' He nodded, and flicked the reins to encourage the horse up the hill between the trees. 'I read in the paper that you had a fright,' he continued tactfully.

When she didn't reply, he said, 'Sorry. I hope you don't mind my saying, but most of the people in Kingsand know what happened. I thought I might warn you.'

He again made a clicking sound to encourage the horse. Not looking at her, he said again, 'Just thought that I would let you know.'

Sarah anxiously bit her lip. Of course. She should have realised it would be reported in the local papers, which he sold in his shop. She wasn't sure if she was happy that her aunt already knew of her trouble. Suddenly all the emotions of the past days welled up in her once again and she had great difficulty in hiding it from Mr Tucker.

Twenty minutes later, it was with a tentative hand that she knocked on her aunt's front door.

She'd hardly finished knocking when the door burst open and Aunt Jelly stood in the doorway, her arms open, having already seen Sarah approaching.

'Sarah,' she cried in heartfelt welcome, and Sarah fell into her aunt's arms.

Shutting the door, Josephine called out, 'Amelia, bring small glasses and the rum. It's Sarah come home.'

Hearing these words, Sarah broke down, sobbing uncontrollably. With her hands covering her face, she was lowered into the nearest armchair. From feeling alone and abandoned, she now felt the love and inclusion of being with family.

Amy arrived with three small glasses and a bottle of navy rum, placing them on the occasional table in front of their aunt.

'Pour the rum, maid,' Josephine directed Amy. 'We have our Sarah back, safe and sound.'

Amy filled the three small glasses and handed one to her aunt. Sarah took hers with a shaking hand.

Sipping her rum, Josephine said, 'Welcome back home, Sarah, you must stay as long as you need. Amy and I will change rooms. You two can both sleep in my bed and I will have the single. We're very glad that you came back to us, Sarah.'

'You're the only family that I have now, Aunt,' Sarah muttered, hardly able to look at the two women sitting with her.

'When you're ready, Sarah, you must tell us all that happened. But I don't want to make you relive it now. We want you to feel safe here. To get better.'

Nodding, Sarah lifted her eyes and saw that what had happened to her had affected all of them; Amy looked pale and about to cry, and her aunt's face was etched with worry.

'I do need my family.' She spoke quietly, trying not to weep again and failing.

Her sister and aunt came to her. Wrapping their arms around her, they all wept together.

Now that the horror was over and she was home, exhaustion claimed her; her limbs shook uncontrollably.

Amy took the glass from Sarah's hand before she could drop it, and wrapped her own shawl around her sister's shoulders.

Alarmed, but realising that it was the shock showing itself, Josephine filled a stone bottle with hot water and placed it in the bed, before getting Amy to help her sister up the stairs, and to undress her.

Sarah slept the rest of the day and didn't stir until halfway through the next morning when she padded slowly, barefoot, downstairs to the kitchen in her nightdress, her hair hanging loose and unbrushed about her shoulders.

On hearing her moving about upstairs, Josephine had food ready on the table.

As Sarah entered the kitchen, absorbing the familiar smells of soot and cooking, she felt safe. And half an hour later, she was sitting in the tin bath, in front of the fire, with Amy washing her back and her hair.

When dressed, she sat quietly in the garden looking at the sea and feeling the sun on her face. Although she felt safe, she couldn't relax; there were so many thoughts swirling about in her head, unanswered questions that wouldn't leave her alone. Who was the murderer? How did he know her name? How did he get in? Had he broken in before? Was this the reason for the Coles' obsession with the bolts on the doors? Why had John said that he would never let her go and yet was marrying Phillis? This last question brought her the most pain and, try as she might, she could not stop feeling the gentleness of his hand smoothing her hair. His breath on the side of her face.

~

It was several days before Sarah felt ready to speak about her life since leaving Kingsand the last time. The evening was cool, and her aunt had built up the fire in the parlour and lit the lamp that now sat cosily on the occasional table. As she sat in the flickering light from the fire, she felt the need to talk, felt safe. The pressure in her head was becoming too much to bear alone. But where to start? The visions and the traumas were tumbling about in her head, all screaming to get out, each bringing back the fear.

'Take your time, Sarah,' her aunt said, gently.

A few moments passed before she could speak. 'I might be repeating what I've already told you, Aunt.'

'That doesn't matter, Sarah. Just tell me it as you want to.'

'After Mother was arrested, I didn't have a job, or money for the rent. I gathered a few things from the room and left, walking to the Barbican, needing to be with people. I knew that I had to get work but had nowhere to live, even if someone gave me a job. I was desperate, frightened and homeless when I met the constable, John Parrett, on the Barbican. Even though he had arrested both my brothers and then Mother, he was kind when he realised that I was homeless, and bought me food. Then he took me to the funeral parlour where he knew that the Coles wanted a receptionist, as Mrs Cole was suffering with her back and the last girl had run away.'

Once she'd started talking, Sarah couldn't stop. It all came tumbling out. How lucky she felt to have a job where she was fed and could live in. The strangeness of the rooms having bolts on all the doors and the tutor who didn't speak to her, and how good the Coles were with their son, who was unwell and kept on the floor above.

195

Her speech began to slow. She was getting to the place that she didn't want to revisit, where she had heard the noises upstairs after the storm. The screams that she still heard in her head, that still woke her in the night. Of being told by the tutor to bolt her door. Of hearing the voices, the cries. The following silence.

She told it all, staring straight ahead, before she stopped talking. Couldn't get her thoughts together. Couldn't remember in what order anything after that had happened. Exhaustion suddenly overtook her and she knew that she had to lay down. She had to sleep. *Immediately.*

Once again, she was helped upstairs to bed, where she fell asleep before Amy had pulled the covers up over her.

~

Sarah slowly regained her health, enjoying the peace and protection of Kingsand. The constant nightmares and visions that she endured at first began to recede, and the memory of that awful night did not invade her mind as often. Although when she went to bed, she still thought of John before sleep, of seeing him in the courtroom telling the coroner how he had found her hanging from the rope and of the man pulling her back up to the window. How John had saved her from injury or death, and his whispering into her hair that he would never let her go.

Silent tears of regret rolled from her eyes to the pillow and had to be wiped away.

23.

Sarah left Kingsand on the early-morning ferry. Her thoughts had been in turmoil for two weeks, ever since receiving an invitation to be a bridesmaid at Phillis and John's wedding. A little note on the side of the invitation implored, *Sarah, you are my only friend, please say yes.*

Sarah had written back very quickly that she was unable to attend. The invitation had played on her mind ever since, and she'd found herself counting off the days to the wedding and falling into a deep pit of despair.

On the day of the wedding, she told her aunt that she was going to visit Jane, and bought eggs at the corner shop to take as a present, remembering her last visit when Jane had nothing in her room to eat.

But deep in her heart a morbid curiosity had formed. She desperately wanted to go to the wedding, to see John, to secretly and strangely be part of his day. In the days leading up to it, she had known that it was stupid, that she would not be able to cope with the pain. And as she sat on the ferry, her heart was pumping with anxiety. No, she couldn't do it; she would walk around until it was a good time to call on Jane.

Getting off the ferry, she walked up Admiral's Hard and made her way towards King Street, and yet she only crossed it, her feet walking in a direction that she didn't really want to go. She made her way slowly to the church, telling herself that she would only look at it. Three times she walked past it. All was silent, cold, locked up, like her heart. When men and women began to arrive, she hid amongst the gravestones, out of sight, watching.

She saw Phillis and her parents arrive, and then John, looking smart in his uniform, soon afterwards with his parents. When all were inside and the first hymn was being sung, she slipped into the church, sliding onto an empty pew at the back, where she concealed herself behind a pillar, not wanting to be seen and yet needing to be there.

~

Early every morning, Amy went to the corner shop to get her aunt the *Western Morning News*. Aunt Jelly liked to look at the obituaries. She'd been brought up in Plymouth, went to school in Plymouth, and lived there until she married her husband. The reading of the obituaries was a way of finding out who still lived and who had died. Then she would think about how she had known them. It also told her if they'd had children, grandchildren, what trade they had gone into and what they had done with their lives.

Amy had left her aunt reading the paper while she scrubbed the kitchen floor and put the washing to steep in the tub. She was just pushing the clothes below the surface of the water with the washing stick, when she heard her aunt shout, '*Oh no!*' And then heard the front door slam. When she went to investigate, her aunt had gone, leaving the newspaper crumpled up on the floor. Amy picked it up, straightening it and folding the huge paper, so that the columns her aunt had been reading were visible in the folded square headed, *Births. Marriages. Deaths.*

As she placed it on the table, she wondered what her aunt had read that had made her leave the house in such a hurry.

~

At the end of the long church service, John and Phillis stood together before the priest, and the congregation fell silent. Phillis was wearing a cream dress, edged with lace, and with long buttoned sleeves. John stood stiffly in his uniform next to William, who looked as strained as the groom.

Mr and Mrs Gallaway sat in the front row on one side of the church and John's parents on the other. The Gallaways looking proud and jubilant. The Parretts looking serious, stiff and unhappy.

The priest spoke for an age about the sanctity of marriage, telling the congregation of his own matrimonial bliss and the joy that children brought to his marriage. That the happy couple would have to face all the trials of life. That not all would go well but how important it was to support each other through adversity. By the time he got to the marriage ceremony, people were moving restlessly in the pews.

Looking at Phillis, the priest asked her if she would take this man, John Parrett, for her husband. She said, coyly, that she would love, honour and obey him. The priest turned to John.

His parents and William held their breath, each praying that he would say no.

'Will you take this woman, Phillis Gallaway, for your wife?' the priest asked John.

John didn't answer straight away and his silence seemed to cloak the expectant congregation, who looked at each other with questioning eyes.

The priest spoke the words again. 'John Parrett, will you take Phillis Gallaway for your wife?'

John turned his head to look at Phillis and could see that, under her veil, she was looking horrified by his hesitation.

Turning back to the priest, John opened his mouth to speak just as the main church door crashed open. The sound reverberated through the congregation and up into the rafters.

Like everyone else, Sarah looked towards the door and was amazed to see her aunt and Mrs Tucker stride into the church.

Annoyed, the priest frowned as two women, one robust, the other walking with a rolling movement, made their way down the central aisle.

'I object to this marriage,' the small woman shouted. 'It's against God's will for a man to marry his sister.'

The priest's mouth fell open in shock and the congregation gasped and craned their necks to see who had spoken.

The Gallaways, who had stood up, now sat down, and the Parretts, who hadn't moved, looked shocked and relieved.

No one seemed to know who this woman was and the question floated about the church, at first in whispers, and then outright brazen enquiries and gossip.

'I ask for time to speak to the priest,' Josephine said loudly, now standing at the front of the church facing the congregation.

'This is highly irregular.' The priest's voice no longer echoed around the church, it being barely heard above the clamour of voices.

'No, sir,' Josephine came back strongly. 'If you continue with this wedding after what I have told you, then, sir, you may spend the rest of your life in prison.'

She didn't know that, but hoped it would scare him enough for her and Marta to speak with him privately.

The priest's face was flushed with anger as he moved past the two women and addressed the congregation.

'There will be no wedding today,' he said, his bible held tightly in front of him. 'I ask you all to return home while I speak with the parents of the bride and groom.'

As the congregation rose noisily and made their way towards the door, the priest indicated with his head that the two women, and the wedding party, should be seated.

'Thank God,' Edith whispered to Reginald. 'I think that's Miss Ellington with that woman.'

When they were alone, the priest looked at the mystified faces of the wedding party assembled before him and sighed deeply.

'A serious accusation has been made by this woman.' He pointed at Josephine as he addressed the people seated in front of him in the pews.

Phillis sniffed tearfully as she sat between her mother and father.

Claude, red-faced with anger, could hold his tongue no longer and shouted in exasperation.

'Who is this woman who comes here with such lies and spoils my daughter's day?'

'That, sir, is what we are about to find out,' the priest replied, looking at Josephine.

William spoke quietly to John and his parents. 'Is this possible? That John and Phillis could be brother and sister?'

'We adopted John as a baby,' Edith whispered back. 'And the lady with the small woman is the matron who ran the orphanage, Miss Ellington. She would know.'

William looked at John. 'You might be saved,' he whispered, 'from the biggest mistake you could make in your life.'

John sat in silence looking at his hands. Life was moving too fast. He had no control over it. He was sorry for Phillis, yet hoped that these women had not made a mistake. That he was saved from living a life without the woman that he loved. And then he realised that he had already lost her; she had made that very clear.

Josephine and Marta stepped forward and Josephine addressed the group.

'My name is Josephine Helbridge and I grew up in Plymouth. I went to school in Plymouth.' Josephine looked at Claude. 'My name then was Josephine Warrington.'

Claude scowled, clearly trying to think back to those days.

John looked up, taking an interest at hearing the name.

'When I was a young woman, I knew Claude Gallaway and Gertrude Vallace. We, the children in their school year, believed that they were more than friends.' She blushed. 'There was a whispered scandal and Gertrude left school. She didn't come back. We didn't know what happened or where she went. This lady,' Josephine indicated Marta, 'is Mrs Tucker, who was at that time Miss Ellington. She knows what happened next.'

Marta smiled at the assembled. 'My name is Marta Tucker. Gertrude Vallace was brought to the hospital where I was working, by her mother. I was only six years older than Gertrude in age, and I think that she was lonely in the hospital while she waited for the birth of her child. She had her baby, a boy she named

John. After the birth, she wouldn't tell the nurses who the father was, and the birth certificate was left blank under *Father*. But one night when I was on duty, I found her crying. She wanted to see her baby. He was being taken into care the next day. I shouldn't have done so but took her to the nursery to hold him one last time. I asked if he looked like his father. She said that he didn't. She held John so tenderly that I also cried for her loss, and that is when she told me that he was the son of Claude Gallaway, the young man that she had been seeing. The only man that she had been seeing. There was no doubt. She asked me if I would let him know that he had a son.'

'It's an untruth, a lie.' Claude shouted. 'There's no proof of this.'

'Oh! But there is, sir,' Marta replied. 'You see, that night while she fed her baby for the last time, I got her to write a letter, one to her son and one to the authorities. I agreed that I would hold the letters in case they were ever needed.'

'Preposterous,' Claude shouted.

Phillis sobbed.

Her mother put her arm around her daughter while looking at her husband with raised eyebrows.

Marta continued. 'I was offered another job as assistant matron at the orphanage where John was taken and where, later, he was put up for adoption. He was adopted by a young couple who couldn't have children. Mr and Mrs Parrett.'

John gasped and looked at his parents.

'When, ten months later, Gertrude had married Mr Cole, they came wanting the baby but he'd gone, and I couldn't tell them where. It broke my heart. Mrs Cole was so distressed. I have kept those letters and they will now be used as evidence that this couple are brother and sister.'

She held them out to the priest, who took them with a trembling hand and read them, nodding in agreement as he did so.

'The authorities will have to see these if the wedding is contested. It seems that this young couple are brother and sister,' the priest said solemnly.

'What have you got to say for yourself, Claude?' Margaret Gallaway asked, sharply.

'Not here, Margaret,' he returned stiffly. 'We're leaving. Come, Phillis, and you can stop that snivelling.'

Grasping Phillis by the arm, he marched her through the empty church. His wife, following at his heels, looked furious.

As the Gallaways emerged from the church, the police, who were waiting at the side of the path, stepped in front of them, asking, 'Mr and Mrs Gallaway?'

Both stopped walking, eyes wide in shock, having noticed the police presence on the way in, but thought that they were there to celebrate the marriage of Phillis to their colleague and had thought no more about it.

'We are arresting you both on the matter of receiving stolen goods found hidden on your premises. You will accompany us to the station. Please make your way to the wagon.'

For a moment, the Gallaways were stunned, before Claude shouted, 'I will not. And I will be complaining of undue harassment from the police department.'

'We can do this in one of two ways, sir,' the policeman replied, ignoring Claude's outburst. 'You can ride in the carriage or you can walk handcuffed through the streets. The choice, sir, is yours.'

The Gallaways both held out their arms to be shackled. Margaret Gallaway looked terrified, and Claude Gallaway was still threatening to have them removed from their jobs as they were taken to the black coach waiting in the street outside the church grounds.

Margaret climbed into the carriage with help, but Claude had to be pushed in, his abuse continuing, leaving Phillis standing in her wedding dress, alone, outside the church.

The Parretts, who had let everyone else go before they left, found Phillis outside, crying.

Edith put her arm around her, saying, 'We'll take you home in our carriage, Phillis. You can't walk home alone in your wedding dress.'

Phillis walked silently, with Edith's arm around her waist, to their waiting hire cab, thankful for the rescue and the kindness of John's mother.

John did not go with them, needing to walk and clear his head.

As he walked away from the church, he wasn't sure what he felt other than relief and emptiness.

William followed him at a distance.

24.

Sarah slid out from the shadows, feeling guilty and ashamed that she had witnessed something that she shouldn't. She couldn't risk being seen as an eavesdropper when it all unfolded and, after the revelations, couldn't walk out with the congregation. Her only saving grace was that no one in the wedding party knew that she was there.

From the shadow of the church doorway, she saw John's mother put her arm around Phillis and take her to their carriage. She saw John walk off without speaking to anyone and saw William, his friend, going after him. It seemed to her that John was devastated, either with the knowledge that he and Phillis were brother and sister, or that the wedding had been cancelled.

She felt even more confused as she made her way to Jane's and the lodging house in King Street, a dark, filthy building that held so many bad memories for her.

Pushing the door open, she faced the stairs and remembered. The boys running hell for leather away from Jane. The Newbys being carried down them in their coffins. Her mother being taken away, down those stairs.

Taking a deep breath, she ascended them, not looking at the door of number 5 with all its bad memories. At the top of the garret stairs, she waited a moment outside Jane's door before knocking. Her feelings were running riot and she knew that her emotions were out of control. As Jane opened the door, Sarah broke down sobbing.

Alarmed, Jane put her arms around her and pulled her inside, shutting the door. 'What has happened? Have you been attacked?'

In reply, Sarah could only shake her head and cry louder, unable to stop the flow now it had started.

Jane led her to a chair and held her hand until the crying lessened, becoming the odd sob.

'What has happened?' she asked quietly.

'My life is ended, Jane. I don't want to be here anymore.'

'In King Street?'

Sarah shook her head. 'I'm finished with life, Jane. I can't take any more of it.'

Jane was shocked. 'Things can't be that bad. Are they?'

Sarah broke down again while Jane sat with her arm around her shoulders.

'Shh, shh. Tell me what's happened.'

'Where can I start, Jane? I've lost everyone. I have no one. I have nothing.'

'That's not true, Sarah. You have me, you have Ned and your aunt in Kingsand.'

Sarah nodded. That was true, but not what she needed. It would make no difference to them if she wasn't here. She needed someone to love, someone who loved her. As she thought it, John's face miraged before her eyes. Then the picture of him walking away from the church, head down, shoulders hunched, grieving. Yes, she had heard it all. The whole sorry story from her aunt's lips in the church. That John was the son of Mr Gallaway and Mrs Cole, who didn't know that John was the child for whom she had grieved all those years. Another terrible sadness that brought the tears to her eyes.

Then she remembered the feeling that she'd felt when John had said that he loved her as they lay in the cart. That he could never let her go. A closeness that she had never felt before. An opening of her heart that flooded her being, a feeling that she had wanted to last forever. Yet how could he love her? He had said nothing to her in all the months that she had worked for the Coles. Not until she was in mortal danger had he told her how he felt. But he hadn't loved her enough not to go through with the wedding to Phillis.

She was on the verge of telling Jane, but something stopped her talking of her love for John. This was her secret. Bittersweet as it was, this was hers, and she couldn't share it. She didn't want the opinion of anyone else tarnishing her love.

'I know what happened at the funeral parlour,' Jane was saying quietly, her voice breaking into Sarah's thoughts. 'It was the talk of the sewing room. Is that what has brought you so low?'

'Oh, Jane! I was never so frightened in all my life. I thought I was going to die.' Tears welled up in her eyes. 'The man was the most frightening person that I've ever seen.' A sob erupted from her chest as Jane's words brought it all back and she shuddered.

'He was going to kill me, Jane, and he didn't even know me. And to think that all that time I was afraid to go out at night because there was a murderer roaming the streets, not knowing that he could get into the premises and come from upstairs.'

'Is that what has brought you so low, Sarah, because I don't think that I could have come through that without feeling different. Nobody would. In time, you'll get over it. It will fade, and in the meantime you have me.' She smiled impishly.

Sarah had to grin. Yes, she had Jane. She had never had a friend before and yes, Jane was her friend. A true friend.

Pulling herself together, wiping her eyes, she remembered the eggs and, taking the small box out of her bag, gave them to Jane.

'I brought you a present. I almost forgot.'

'You are my saviour, thank you. Shall we have a couple now?'

'I'm so hungry, Jane, I could eat the whole chicken, feathers an' all.' And for the first time in days, she laughed.

Later, after she had left Jane, she walked to the Watch House on the Barbican. The sergeant at the desk acknowledged her with a nod of his head as she entered.

'I'm Sarah Warrington. I used to live in King Street, at the funeral parlour.'

He seemed suddenly interested, as he took a long look at her before speaking.

'How can I help you, Miss Warrington?'

'I wondered if it would be possible to go back into the funeral parlour premises. I left my bag in my room and everything that I own is in it.'

'Just a moment, Miss Warrington. Take a seat,' he said, before leaving the desk and going through a door behind him.

When he returned, he had a policeman with him, a man of about forty, not one of the young constables.

'This is Constable Leavland, Miss Warrington. He will go with you to the property and make sure that all is well.'

'You'll be alright with me, miss,' the constable said kindly. 'It might be difficult for you going back.'

They walked through the town together and for the first time Sarah didn't feel that everyone was looking at her. Perhaps Jane was right. What had happened had made her stronger. She was her own person, not a child in the shadows, carrying the sins of her mother.

They entered the King Street property through the back yard, and Sarah was surprised that everyone was there, working as normal. When the constable opened the back door for her, she was even more surprised to see Beth in the kitchen. For a moment, she felt as though she was going mad. Was Mrs Cole about to appear and ask her why she'd not been at work?

'Quick, catch her, Constable, she's going to faint.' Beth's voice floated urgently in the space in front of Sarah.

The room was fading. She felt dizzy as everything swam before her eyes.

Beth and the constable led her to a seat and pushed her head forward onto the table. She couldn't breathe and felt hot.

Beth pressed a damp cloth to her forehead as she spoke to the constable.

'She's coming around, Constable. I'll look after her now.'

'If you're sure, madam?'

'Yes, I'm sure. She belongs here. We'll look after her.'

Sarah heard the door close as a glass of water was pushed in front of her face.

'Sit up and drink this, then you'll feel better. You only fainted.' Beth's voice was the kindest Sarah had ever heard it.

Sitting up slowly, she drank a little of the water.

'The colour's coming back into your cheeks,' Beth said. 'Drink some more of the water.'

'Why are you all here?' Sarah asked.

'We're burying Mrs Cole today.' Sarah recognised the usual tension in Beth's voice. 'There's still the second inquest hanging over our heads,' Beth qualified. 'Mr Bronalski isn't well enough to attend yet, but we've had permission to bury Mrs Cole.' Beth removed the glass, saying, 'Mr Cole isn't really well enough but he's here.'

These were the most words that Beth had ever spoken to her, and Sarah was now unsure of Beth's personality. Was this caring person the real Beth, or was she really the offhand woman that Sarah had known all those months that she had worked here?

Then it dawned on her. *They were burying Mrs Cole today.* 'Is anyone putting lavender in her coffin?' Sarah asked.

Beth looked confused. 'No one said anything to me.'

'Could I do it for her, Beth?'

'Oh! I don't know.' Beth hesitated. 'I'm not sure what Mr Cole would say.'

Standing up and walking to a cupboard in the kitchen, where she knew that Mrs Cole kept the linen bag filled with dried lavender and the little bottle of oil, Sarah left the kitchen and carried them towards the mortuary.

As she got nearer, she knew that, if she went inside, she would be faced with her first dead body. Fear ran through her veins and she had to take a deep breath before she could open the door.

The room was as cold as ice. The hairs stood up on her arms as she stepped inside and closed the door.

In the dimness of the room, Mr Cole was standing at the side of the coffin looking down at his wife, his face bruised and stitched, a wide bandage around his throat. Feeling that she was intruding on his privacy and that she shouldn't have been so bold, she began to back out.

Disturbed by the sound of the door, he looked up and saw her. 'Come in, Miss Warrington.' His voice was quiet, with an emotional tick that surprised her, bringing a lump to her throat.

'I thought that I would bring lavender,' she said softly. 'Mrs Cole always put it in the coffins.'

She couldn't bring herself to say, *with the bodies*, or, *with the dead*; it frightened her too much.

'You're right,' he said. 'I had forgotten. Thank you. It would have been awful to remember when it was too late. That we hadn't treated her with the same dignity that she showed to others. I see that you've brought it with you.'

He was looking at the bag that she was holding. 'Will you do it, lay the lavender in the coffin?' he asked. 'I will administer the oil to her forehead. It's the least that I can do for my dear wife.'

Sarah stepped forward slowly, shots of hot fear running through her body as her dread of seeing a dead person grew. With every step she took, a little of the body was revealed. Mrs Cole's forehead and some of her hair. Her nose, her face; white and waxy. Her neck, covered by a thick band of lace hiding the injury at her throat. Her body, dressed in a crisp white cotton nightgown. It was Mrs Cole, and yet not Mrs Cole. She was silent. No longer here.

Sarah's heart was pumping as she placed her hand in the linen bag and brought out a handful of dried lavender. Not sure what she should do with it, she sprinkled it over the nightgown and in the coffin.

Mr Cole took the oil from her and, dripping some on his index finger, smeared it gently over his wife's forehead.

Sarah cast her eyes downwards and pulled on the drawstring to close the bag and to give him some privacy.

Opening the door as silently as she could, she left him saying goodbye to his wife.

Back out in the yard, she was shaking as the tension of what she had just done stayed with her.

'You all right, Sarah?'

It was Peter Lamb, standing in the doorway of the carpentry shed.

'I don't know,' she said honestly. 'I've just seen my first dead body.'

'You get used to it, I suppose,' he shrugged. 'Mrs Cole treated them all like they were asleep and she was their mother.'

At that same moment, George and Jack brought the heavy horses out of the stable, the sound of their hooves echoing around the yard. Their coats shone as though they'd been polished.

They tied the horses to rings set in the stable wall before going to join John Maple in the carriage shed.

There was a long pause before all three men reappeared, physically pulling the glass carriage out of its storage and into the yard. Like the horses, it was gleaming.

Seeing her watching, John Maple called, 'Afternoon, miss.'

The others noticed her now as they untied the horses and led them to the carriage shafts.

'Good to see you back, miss.' Jack nodded to her, while encouraging one of the horses to walk backwards between the shafts.

The horses secured, the men then went into the mortuary and, a few moments later, carried the coffin from its resting place, out into the yard. They were taking much more care than they had with Mr Newby, Sarah noticed, as they gently pushed the coffin into the carriage and closed the glass door.

Beth arrived in the yard, having changed into her Sunday best, and handed Sarah a bag.

'You'll be wanting this,' she said, holding it out towards Sarah. 'I found it when I was trying to put your room straight, but I didn't know where you lived. I knew you'd come for it at some time.'

'Thank you, Beth.' She took the bag gratefully, relieved that she didn't have to return to the room.

'You can walk with me, Sarah, if you wish,' Beth offered.

Sarah hadn't realised that she would be included in the funeral procession and, in her floating state of mind, she followed Beth, standing beside her as she took her place behind the carriage.

Mr Cole took his position ahead of the mourners, directly behind the carriage, and the rest of the staff walked behind him.

George Banks and Jack Williams sat up front, in smart uniforms and top hats with a feather in the side. As always, they were in charge of the horses as the cortege made its way along the passage and turned slowly out into King Street.

People had lined the street, standing in silence. Women cried, men reverently removed their hats and bowed their heads as the carriage and coffin slowly passed by. King Street was giving Mrs Cole the recognition that she deserved, having looked after so many of their relatives in death.

The silent procession walked through Plymouth, towards Pennycomequick and along Cemetery Road.

The horses walked slowly as the carriage rolled between the stone pillars that held the black iron gates of what was still thought of as the new cemetery. The mourners followed the carriage up the slight incline and along the main path, edged each side by graves adorned with stone angels, ornate headstones and crosses. The cemetery's two chapels, standing side by side, came slowly into view.

A minister was waiting at the door of the chapel on their right, beneath its grand portico, to receive Mrs Cole.

As the horses came to a stop under the shadow of its roof, Sarah was surprised to see the same minister who, this morning, was to marry John to Phillis. He had started that part of his day with a smile and finished in anger. Now his face was sorrowful, to match those suffering the loss of a loved one, and she wondered if he really felt what his face showed, or was it just a job and, like an actor, he inhabited the different roles as needed?

The service was short, the minister reading from his bible and then speaking a little of Mrs Cole. 'A fine upstanding woman, a pillar of the community,' he said, 'whose kindness will be greatly missed by grieving families.'

After the service, the coffin was carried by Peter Lamb, George Banks, Jack Williams and John Maple, out into the sunshine, to a place where a hole in the ground, already dug, awaited her.

Sarah wanted to cry. Her throat was tight with emotion, but the tears wouldn't come. Her eyes stayed dry.

As they gathered around the grave, Sarah had a sudden thought. Had anyone told John that they were burying his mother this afternoon?

Standing behind the mourners, she looked across the surrounding graveyard, hoping to see him. But apart from the funeral party and a flock of noisy crows, there was no one in the huge empty space.

Now the tears flowed freely as she cried for John's loss and for Mrs Cole's cruelly lost motherhood.

25.

The postman brought a buff envelope, addressed to Miss S. Warrington. She had been expecting it. The rest of the inquest, she learnt, was to be held two days from the date on the letter.

Sarah, her aunt and Amy took the ferry to Plymouth so that Sarah could buy some clothes for the event. Aunt Jelly had already made her feelings clear about the clothes that Sarah should by now have bought with her wages, if for no other reason than for her Sunday best.

They shopped in the large department store Spooners, where Sarah bought a teal green dress, also the coat that she should have bought ready for winter but had not got around to doing.

~

The following day, her aunt accompanied Sarah to Plymouth and, on arrival at the Guildhall, Sarah and her aunt were approached by a robed court usher who asked their names before telling them that Sarah was to make herself ready in case she was to be questioned again as a witness.

The outer landing was busy and, as they made their way towards the courtroom door, Sarah saw the same robed official walk over to, and speak with, John and his parents.

Entering the courtroom, she looked up at the crowd in the gallery and recognised Beth, who was sitting with Peter Lamb, the Coles' carpenter, along with the boys from the stable. They looked worried as they sat in silence, watching all who entered.

It occurred to Sarah that since the funeral of Mrs Cole, she hadn't given them one thought, and that they may have lost their jobs. Who was running the parlour? Who was burying the dead?

John and his parents took their seats. Mr Cole and Mr Bronalski, then entering, were shown to their seats at the front of the courtroom, where they sat with their heads bowed, not looking at the people in the room.

Her attention was diverted away from them as the twenty-four male jurors filed in to take their places on the long benches, along one side of the chamber. Sarah felt cold. Overcome by the seriousness of the situation, daunted by her surroundings.

A side door opened and, as the coroner entered, the assembled stood until he had taken his seat.

'Is everyone here?' the coroner, Mr Blendell, addressed the clerk of the court.

'Yes, sir, all present,' he replied, standing before the bench.

'We are here,' the coroner said, looking around the courtroom, 'to establish what happened to Mrs Gertrude Alexandra Cole on the night of July the nineteenth and the motive and personality of the murderer. Members of the Jury,' he continued, looking at the twenty-four men sitting on the long benches, 'you may ask questions of each witness. Proceed,' he instructed the clerk.

'My Lord.' The clerk bowed. 'I call Mr Sidney Albous Cole, to tell us what he knows of the events of the night of the nineteenth of July.'

Sarah watched as Mr Cole left his seat and moved slowly to the front of the court, where he stood looking frail, yellow bruises around his eyes. A long scar visible, stitched, red and angry, down the side of his face, stretching from his ear to his mouth.

'Are you Sidney Albous Cole of 45 King Street?'

'Yes, sir, I am.'

'Are you the owner of the funeral parlour?'

'Yes, sir, I am.'

'And do you live over the premises?'

'Yes, sir, I do.'

'I understand that you lived and worked there with your wife, the deceased, Mrs Cole.'

'Yes, sir.'

'In your own words, sir, tell us of the happenings of the nineteenth of July.'

'Yes, sir.'

Mr Cole swallowed loudly and hesitated, a pained expression on his face, as he tried to recall the horror of that night and the events in the order that they happened.

'A thunderstorm had raged all day,' he said slowly. 'And I had gone upstairs several times to see that Arthur, my son, was alright. But Mr Bronalski had everything under control and the boy seemed happy. After the shop was closed, my wife and I ate our supper with Arthur, in his room as we always did. All seemed well. We were getting ready for bed when we heard the noise.'

'The noise?' the coroner questioned.

'Arthur was having one of his outbursts, but it sounded far worse than we had ever heard it before. We could hear the furniture being thrown about and his screaming with temper.'

'I see.' The coroner nodded and made a note in a book on the desk. 'Carry on.'

'Yes, sir. When my wife and I got upstairs, Arthur was raging and breaking the furniture. He had a knife and my wife was trying to coax him to put it down when he stabbed her in the throat. I was trying to wrestle it from him when Mr Bronalski arrived to help me. But the boy was very strong and overpowered us both. He stabbed Mr Bronalski and then myself. I fell over a broken chair trying to stop Arthur stabbing me again. I can tell you no more, sir.'

Sarah was shocked. Was the grotesque man Arthur Cole? She thought him a small boy. But she didn't dare to speak to her aunt as the room was silent, everyone taking in what they had just heard.

'Jury!' The coroner looked at the twenty-four men. 'You may ask questions now.'

'Can you tell us about your son?' A thin man with a crooked nose asked. 'How old is he?'

'He's seventeen, sir,' Mr Cole replied.

'And still playing with toys?' the gentleman questioned with a look of mirth on his face as he turned to look at the other jurors, who smiled or giggled, as he expected.

'My son has been unwell since birth, sir.' Mr Cole blushed slightly, in defence of his son. His body seemed to sag with tiredness as he bore the onslaught of the ridicule he and his wife had tried to shield their son from.

His face, Sarah thought, was now as white as his hair. She could see that this man, who had always kept her at arm's length, as employer and employee, even when the shop was shut, had suffered greatly since she saw him last.

'Perhaps, sir,' the coroner said, 'you could explain to the jury how your son had become ill at such an early age.'

Mr Cole stared into space, almost as though he hadn't heard, a look of pain on his face. Taking a deep breath, he spoke reflectively, looking at the coroner and ignoring the jury.

'My wife, sir, gave birth to a baby out of wedlock. This was before she knew me and which she told me about when we first met. She had been forced to give the baby up for adoption and it had affected her greatly. After we were married, we tried to get him back, but it was too late. He was already living with another family.'

He stopped and took a moment before he could speak. 'It broke her heart.'

Sarah turned her head for a quick look at the Parrett family and saw Mrs Parrett place her hand on John's. She looked tearful.

'We were overjoyed,' he continued, 'a month after our marriage to find that Gertrude was to have a baby.'

He stopped talking; it looked as though he was thinking, turning something over in his mind.

'Mr Cole?' the coroner prompted.

Mr Cole nodded. 'The birth was difficult, sir, the baby so large that after many hours the nurse had to use a contraption – an instrument around the baby's head – to release him.'

He stopped talking again, seeming to be reliving the moment. He rubbed his chin with his hand and licked his lips.

'Mr Cole?'

'The baby's head was badly misshapen. The nurse said that as he grew, it would come back to shape. But it didn't. Gertrude loved him and didn't seem to notice the deformity. As he grew, it became clear that he had a violent streak and should be in an institution where he would be safe. But Gertrude couldn't give another son away to the authorities. Couldn't lose another child. We took the decision to hide him.'

He swallowed hard and tears were visible in his eyes as he took a deep breath and continued. 'When we could no longer cope with Arthur, we engaged tutors. Most couldn't manage Arthur's outbursts, his destructive personality. Mr Bronalski was the fifth tutor to be employed, and the best. He was able to manage Arthur. He made life interesting for the boy, trying to teach him to read and to write. He gave him paper and pencils to draw and paint. He devised games and we saw an improvement in Arthur as he grew. Until this last year, when his moods escalated and were triggered more often.'

He stopped speaking.

The coroner nodded, seeming to understand the difficulty that the man before him was having. 'Would you like to sit, sir?' the coroner asked softly.

'No, thank you, sir.' Mr Cole continued. 'Mr Bronalski pointed out to us that Arthur needed to go out, to have exercise. Of course, we couldn't let that happen. If people laughed at him, at his appearance, we didn't know how he would react. Gertrude was afraid that he would be taken away, put in an institution, sectioned, and we would never see him again and...' his voice cracked, '...and that he would never again feel loved.'

He coughed and a steward brought a chair for him to sit on. He sat, nodding his thanks.

Aunt Jelly pushed her arm through Sarah's. 'I'm so glad you're safe,' she whispered.

218

Sarah could only nod at the thought of Arthur's horrific face, at his violence, as what she had lived through played out before her. Then of how John had saved her from injury or death. How he had revealed his love, even though he was betrothed to be married. She closed her eyes tightly and sat in silence.

The coroner was speaking again. 'Are you able to continue?' he addressed Mr Cole.

'Yes, sir, thank you. In the knowledge of how many fires there are in King Street, and how many child deaths by fire, it was very easy to convince my wife of the need of a fire escape. I asked my carpenter, Peter Lamb, to build the steps up the back of the house with access to all floors. But, in reality, it was so that Mr Bronalski could take Arthur out at night, his form hidden beneath a cloak with a large hood. At first, Arthur became calmer as his life expanded. He drew or painted what he'd seen on these outings with his tutor. But sadly, he became more demanding, wanting to go out more often and became angry if he was denied.'

'In what way was this anger shown?' the coroner asked.

'Screaming, like a child that can't get its own way, sir, and breaking things.'

'But he wasn't a child.'

'Not in his body, sir, but in his mind, yes.'

'Do you put the violence in Arthur, on the night his mother was killed, down to his wanting to go out?' the coroner asked.

'I don't know, sir, this is something that you will have to ask Mr Bronalski.'

'You may step down if the jury have no relevant questions.'

'No, sir,' the jury foreman said, looking around at the other jurors sitting on the benches.

'Call Mr Bronalski,' the clerk shouted when the coroner looked in his direction.

Mr Bronalski limped to the front of the court and stood, looking tired, his arm in a sling and a large bruise on his cheek.

'Are you Mr Mikiel Bronalski of King Street Funeral Parlour?' the clerk asked.

'Yes, sir,' the tutor replied strongly.

'Thank you.'

'Mr Bronalski,' the coroner said, looking up slowly from a piece of paper on his desk.

'Were you employed as tutor to Arthur Cole?'

'Yes, sir.'

'Did you find this post difficult?'

'I did, yes, sir, sometimes.'

'Please tell us of your duties and how things changed in recent times.'

'I was able to keep Arthur amused and learning a little. He enjoyed it. But he was becoming a young man, sir, with a young man's desires. Without the knowledge of his mother, I sometimes took him out at night wearing a hooded cloak. I would hide him in an alley and procure a prostitute for him. They didn't see him properly, as his head was covered by the large hood.'

'And did this help his moods, Mr Bronalski?'

'Yes, sir. At first, it seemed to be the answer, although I noticed that his needs were becoming more violent and the prostitutes complained of his holding them around the neck.'

'Did they not see his disability, Mr Bronalski?'

'No, sir, his hood kept him hidden.'

'Continue, sir.'

'His needs escalated. He wanted to go out every night. But it was dangerous. If we were not careful, he would be found out and taken away. But he didn't understand this. And his moods increased with growing violence.'

'Did you witness the violence?'

'Yes, sir. I did.'

He looked across the room at Mr Cole. 'I'm sorry,' he said, his face full of regret. 'I have to speak.'

Mr Cole stiffened, almost imperceptibly, with just a small movement of his head and eyes.

'One morning,' he continued, 'Arthur noticed Daisy through the window. She was in the yard. From that day on, he seemed distracted, constantly looking towards the window. It was harder to get him to be involved in learning or play.'

'Who is Daisy and why did you think that this was?'

'Just interest in something new, sir, I suppose.'

'Please tell the jury about Daisy.'

'Daisy May was the receptionist employed by the Coles, as Mrs Cole was suffering with her back. Arthur had become devious. Something that we didn't think him capable of.'

'How did you learn this, Mr Bronalski?'

'Beth, the housekeeper, complained that food was missing from the kitchen, and Daisy mentioned that she thought we had rats, as she could hear scratching at her door in the night.'

'And what was it that was happening?' the coroner asked, frowning.

'We didn't know that Arthur had worked out that he could go down the fire escape and get into the house through the window on the floor below. And this is what we believe he did. Sadly, one night, Daisy hadn't locked her door and he got into her room. Being afraid, she fought him off when he tried to undress her, or at least that is what we thought, as her clothes were ripped down the front. I was sleeping in the next room to Daisy. I was the first to enter the room and pulled him away from her. I held Arthur, but it was a struggle. He fought back until his father arrived.'

He stopped talking, screwing up his eyes as though reliving the scene. 'It was too late. Daisy was dead. Strangled and bleeding from a head wound.' He had a croak in his voice.

There was an audible groan and whispering from Beth and the funeral staff sitting at the back of the room.

'Quiet, please.' The coroner glared at them. 'And what did you do next, Mr Bronalski?'

'Mr and Mrs Cole had heard the noise, as they sleep on that floor. Mr Cole helped me take Arthur upstairs. We gave Arthur a sedative, a powder, before we went back to Daisy's room.'

'Where was Mrs Cole?'

'She was sitting with the body in a state of shock. We rolled Daisy in her bed sheets and took her to the mortuary where a coffin, prepared for the next day, held a cadaver ready for burial.' He shook his head, seemingly in disbelief at what he had done. 'Mr Cole and I,' he continued, 'placed Daisy in with the dead man and nailed down the lid. It was easy, then, to tell everyone that she had run away.'

'Did they believe you?'

'They were surprised, as Daisy was so full of life and loved her job.'

'I see. Was anyone else involved in the cover-up of the murder of Daisy May?'

'No, sir.'

'Who cleaned up the mess in her room?'

'Beth was asked to scrub the carpet, sir.'

'Who is Beth?' the coroner asked.

'The Coles' housekeeper, sir.'

The coroner turned to the jury.

'Do you have any questions for the tutor, Mr Bronalski?'

The foreman answered. 'Yes, sir. Mr Bronalski,' the foreman looked grave, 'would you say that Arthur Cole had a violent nature?'

'I would, sir. But he wasn't always like that. He was a sweet boy when younger.'

'Would you say, sir,' the foreman continued, ignoring Mr Bronalski's opinion, 'that as he killed Daisy May and his mother, he is a danger to the public?'

'I would agree with you, sir. He did kill both his mother and Daisy and we know now that if he escaped his rooms again, that he would be a danger to the public.'

'Thank you. We have no more questions.'

The coroner looked around the room. 'We will reconvene in one hour when the Coles' staff will give evidence.'

Sarah walked around the shops in Old Town Street with her aunt, passing the time until they could return to the Guildhall. Although normally walking around the shops would have been a great adventure, neither could concentrate on anything but the inquest. And Sarah, stunned by the admission of Mr Bronalski, was feeling chilled. She remembered the look exchanged by Mr Bronalski and Mrs Cole on that first day. They knew that she was in danger. Knew what Arthur was capable of and yet they didn't warn her, still employed her.

An hour later, they were again seated in the courtroom, but this time the funeral staff took up the front row and Sarah, Josephine, John and his parents were seated at the back.

Everyone stood until the coroner took his seat. He nodded to the clerk as they all sat down.

Sarah glanced across the aisle. John was looking at her. As their eyes locked, she felt the energy of love almost overcome her and had to look away, casting her eyes down into her lap.

'I call Mrs Elizabeth Almour, housekeeper employed by Mr and Mrs Cole at their funeral parlour in King Street.'

Beth stood up. Looking worried, she walked slowly to the stand. She gave her name clearly and agreed that she was the Coles' housekeeper.

'Who asked you to clean the carpet in Daisy May's room and when did they ask it?' The coroner spoke to her in a gentle voice.

'It was after breakfast, sir. Mrs Cole told me that Daisy had left and that she had left a terrible mess in her sitting room. She asked if I would go and clean the carpet.'

'And when you saw the type of stain that you had been asked to clean, what did you do?'

'I scrubbed it, sir.'

'And what did you think caused the stain, Mrs Almour?'

Beth shrugged.

'Is that your answer, Mrs Almour, a shrug?' the coroner asked sharply, staring hard at Beth. 'I will ask you again, madam, and this time I expect an answer.' He scowled and Beth looked chastised. '*What* did you *think* was the cause of the stain?' There was an edge to his voice that Sarah noticed made Beth pale.

'I thought that it was blood, sir,' she said feebly, 'but it wasn't my place to ask about it.'

'A young woman who loved her job runs away, Mrs Almour, her floor is soaked in a pool of blood and you do not question the cause?'

'No, sir. I keep my job by keeping my nose out of other people's business.'

'Were you able to remove the stain, Mrs Almour?' he asked, ignoring her outburst.

'No, sir. I covered it up with a small rug when it was dry and Mrs Cole and I put an armchair on top of it, to stop the rug moving.'

'So hiding the stain.'

'Yes, sir.'

'Jury.' The coroner looked at the twenty-four men sitting silently listening. 'Do you have any questions for the witness?'

A small blond man held his hand up.

'Mrs Almour, did you like Daisy May?'

'I did, sir.'

'But not enough to question your employers about the blood in her room.'

'I need the job, sir. It's long hours and convenient to where I live.'

'Did you ever see Arthur Cole?'

'No, sir.'

'But you knew that he was unwell?'

'Yes, sir.'

'Did you not think it strange that you didn't see him?'

'No, sir.'

'Why not?'

'It isn't my place to ask questions, sir. I just do my work.'

'And what is that work, *madam*?' His lips had tightened into a thin line, his eyes flashed.

'Cooking and cleaning, sir.'

'Thank you.' He nodded towards the coroner. 'I have no more questions, sir.'

The clerk stood up as Beth returned to her seat.

'I call Peter Lamb.'

Peter walked forward, holding his cap nervously between both hands. As he faced the court and the jury, his shoulders were trembling.

'Mr Lamb.' The coroner spoke gently. 'We are here trying to

understand the motive for the killing of your employer, Gertrude Cole, and the personality of her son, Arthur Cole.'

'Yes, sir.' Peter nodded.

'Did you ever see Arthur Cole?'

'I did see him once, sir, when erecting the fire escape.'

'And did you witness any strangeness or violence?'

'He was a frightening sight, sir. I realised that there was something wrong with him when I saw his misshapen head and that he was playing with a small wooden horse, like a small child would, but he was a large boy, old enough to be at work.'

'Did you speak to him?'

'No, sir.'

'Did you ever see him come down the steps after you had built them?'

'No, sir. I didn't see him again after that day. Mr Bronalski put a black curtain up at the window while I was working.'

'On the morning after Daisy May's disappearance, did you find anything strange about your workshop?'

Peter turned his cap in his hands, looking nervous, and replied, 'No, sir.'

'You didn't think that the lid already screwed down on a coffin was strange?'

'No, sir.'

'Why not?'

Because I make the coffins. I don't fill them.'

'Who does that?'

'The bodies are kept in the mortuary next door and the coffin for the burial is taken into the mortuary on the day that it's finished. Mr and Mrs Cole place the dead in the box and screw the lid down. Mrs Cole likes to place dried lavender in with each corpse,' he added.

'And Mr and Mrs Cole didn't say anything to you the morning after Daisy May left?'

'No, sir. There was no need to tell me anything.'

'What happened on the day of the funeral, the morning after you were told that Daisy had gone?'

'George, Jack and John put the coffin on the cart. The stable boys attached the horse and the body was taken to the chosen cemetery.'

'And in this case?'

'The Plymouth, Devonport and Stonehouse cemetery, sir, in Cemetery Road below Mutley Plain.'

'I see. Questions from the jury?'

The jury men shook their heads. 'No questions, my Lord.'

The coroner looked at Peter Lamb, who stood trembling before him. 'Mr Lamb. You can take your seat.'

Peter nodded. 'Thank you, sir.'

The coroner waited until Peter had taken his seat before summing up. Looking around the room, he spoke slowly.

'We are here today to hear the circumstances in which Mrs Gertrude Alexandra Cole died. In summing up, I can see that Arthur Cole's conduct, for some time past, had been strange and progressive in its violence. I am satisfied that Arthur Cole murdered his mother and that he would have gone on to murder his father and his tutor if they had not become incapacitated on that night. That he would possibly have murdered Miss Sarah Warrington. That it was possible he had become increasingly insane as he became older. That Arthur Cole's action was triggered by a sudden impulse of which we may never be certain. The jury and I have read the report on the state of Arthur Cole's mind, written and submitted to the court by Doctor Evans, after Arthur Cole was examined at the secure hospital, where he resides, during this inquest. It is Doctor Evans' opinion that Arthur Cole is a danger to the public and in particular to women. It is the doctor's opinion, and that of his colleagues, that Arthur Cole should never be released. Doctor Evans recommends that Arthur Cole be sectioned and kept in a secure hospital for the insane for the rest of his natural life.'

Mr Cole put his head in his hands and sobbed.

Ignoring him, the coroner continued. 'It has become clear during this inquest that there is another case that has to be answered. The covering-up of the murder of the young woman known as Daisy May. I believe,' the coroner said, 'that it is beyond the power of this jury to decide that question. However, this jury were sworn to do their duty and it is for them to make the verdict, not for me to decide.'

The coroner and the jury left the room and were gone for an hour. On their return, the jury indicated that they had come to a decision.

The foreman stood, nodding to the coroner that they were ready.

'We are in no doubt that Arthur Cole murdered his mother and should be in a secure accommodation for the rest of his life,' he said slowly. 'But during this inquest it has become clear that there is another case to answer and we have decided that it is beyond the power of this jury to decide that question. It was,' he said, looking at those sitting in the courtroom, 'for a jury in another place to settle the matter of the apparent murder of Daisy May and by whom.' He took his seat.

The coroner looked silently at those sitting before him in the room for what seemed to Sarah a long time.

'The notes from this inquest,' the coroner said eventually, 'will be made available to the Crown. Mr Cole, Mr Bronalski, you are to be detained until the court in Exeter convenes at the quarter session.'

The funeral staff appeared stunned and Sarah saw that Beth was being held upright by Peter Lamb.

'Mrs Almour.' The coroner looked at Beth, who had clearly worked out that she might have a case to answer. 'You will keep yourself available for that trial.'

Beth could only nod in agreement.

It was over. Sarah, while feeling relief, also felt loss. A great empty hole filled with nothing ahead of her.

Outside in the street, she took a deep breath.

Her aunt rubbed her back. 'Come on, maid, let's go home.'

At the word *home*, Sarah broke down.

Josephine was holding her as John and his mother walked from the building. John approached them, looking worried.

'Can I help?' he asked, while his mother looked on.

'No, thank you, sir.' Josephine smiled. 'I will get her home and look after her. Oh! And, sir, thank you for rescuing my niece. She would have been killed but for you.'

'If I can do anything to help.' John sounded sincere, almost pleading, Josephine thought briefly.

Sarah raised her head, looking up into John's worried face, and a fusion of energy, of love, passed between them. Something they both knew to be futile. Never to be given or received.

With his heart broken, John turned back to his mother and walked away.

26.

Sarah sat in her aunt's garden, watching the waves swell and roll towards the land, breaking upon the rocks or gently rippling over the wet sand. She would, she thought, never tire of the sound of the sea.

Relaxing though this was, it didn't wash away her thoughts. She'd heard nothing of John since the inquest, and wondered what he was doing. She had been tempted many times to catch the ferry and walk the streets of Plymouth looking for him. To bump into him, quite by accident, yet she hadn't. And she wasn't really sure why, or what was holding her back. Nor had she visited Jane. Why would she, what had they to talk about?

As the sun descended slowly below the horizon, the last rays caressed a ketch out at sea, turning its sails from cream to a warm apricot. A warmth that, in her sadness, Sarah was unable to feel. Just behind the boat, the sun, it seemed, was drowning, just like her.

~

It was now mid-November and Josephine was worried about her niece. Although Sarah helped her sister around the house, she hardly spoke. Her eyes were dull and she sat for many hours in the garden looking out to sea.

Josephine had asked Amy what ailed her sister, but Amy didn't know and was as worried as her aunt.

'We have to do something, Amy. This can't go on, she's disappearing before our eyes. I know that she's been through a great deal with the loss of her mother and the boys, and who would recover quickly from nearly being murdered, but she has been here for weeks now and isn't recovering. There has to be more to this than she is letting on. Maybe she needs to face her fears. I'm going to see Marta, see if we can't think of something.'

The following day at breakfast, Aunt Jelly suddenly said, 'Amy and I are visiting Mouse this morning, Sarah, taking her some broth. Amy will carry some wood for their fire, as Moth can't cut any himself and the evenings are getting colder. We won't be long. Come along, Amy.' The door shut and they were gone before Sarah had time to answer.

Sitting in the kitchen, she felt at a loss now. Although she didn't want to talk, she missed the company and the sound of her aunt and sister moving about the cottage.

They had been gone no more than five minutes when Sarah answered a sharp knock at the front door.

Opening it, she was surprised to see Marta Tucker standing on the step looking anxious.

'Is your aunt at home, Sarah?' she asked rather brusquely.

Worried by the look on Mrs Tucker's face, Sarah blurted, without even a good morning, 'No, Mrs Tucker. Aunt and Amy have gone to visit Mouse. Moth is too sick to cut wood for the fire, so they took some of ours and some broth.'

Marta looked crestfallen. 'Oh dear.' Her face crumpled and worry lines appeared on her forehead. 'I was desperately hoping for her help today.'

'Can I help, Mrs Tucker?'

The woman's face lit up and there was such a look of hope in her eyes that if she had asked Sarah to jump in the sea at high tide, she would probably have done it.

'I wouldn't normally ask, but Mr Tucker and I are desperate. We have to go to Plymouth. Mr Tucker has to visit the bank and I have to pick up our order from the grocer's warehouse. I need someone to go to the haberdashery to pick up my order before they shut at midday. I just can't do it all, as the haberdashery and the warehouse are at different ends of the town.'

Her voice had risen on the last sentence and Sarah, understanding her distress, agreed to go with them.

Ten minutes later, she was sitting in the back of the Tuckers' cart, passing along the road above Kingsand at such speed that her eyes watered. It was the first time that she would travel on the Tilt Ferry, and it wasn't anything to look forward to.

The horse and carriage ferry was larger than the people ferry, and Mr Tucker's cart swayed alarmingly as the horse and cart were led aboard. They stayed sitting in the cart, high above the waves, for the journey, the movement of the sea feeling more pronounced from the cart.

By the time they arrived at Admiral's Hard, she was feeling distinctly green. The horse stood quietly during the crossing, for which Sarah was thankful. On reaching land, the tilt was lowered and the horse pulled the carriage up the wet slope with so many jolts that Sarah was almost sick and was planning to do it over the side of the cart when thankfully it resumed its normal movement.

In town, Mr Tucker and Sarah alighted outside the bank in Old Town Street. Mrs Tucker took the cart onwards to the warehouse in Ebrington Street, while Sarah walked slowly in the opposite direction to George Street, on legs that shook as though they were still at sea. She was not looking forward to the return journey.

It felt strange to be back in town after so many weeks, but instead of feeling a part of it, as she had when she worked in Plymouth, she now felt like a stranger.

Walking without acknowledging the shops or the people, encased completely in her own lonely world, she eventually opened the door of the haberdashery.

Standing just inside the door, she was assaulted by the colour and smell of the fabrics. Shelves, on both sides of the shop, reached up to the ceiling, holding bolts of cotton, linen, muslin and silk, in a kaleidoscope of colour. A glass-fronted display cabinet to her left held cotton reels in every colour imaginable. Curtains of lace hung on poles from the ceiling, where the delicate woven designs could be appreciated by customers.

Turning her head, she saw several racks holding coloured ribbons. There were feathers, large and small, some dyed in hideously unpleasant shades of mauve, red, orange and green.

The two counters that ran down both sides of the shop had chairs at each end where ladies could sit while waiting to be served.

The four shop assistants, standing behind the counters, were busy cutting material to length or speaking with customers. One assistant was showing a customer gloves from a drawer pulled out from under the counter. There were cotton and satin bodices, petticoats and nightgowns. There were hats in an area near the window, balancing in a display, each hat sitting in turn upon its own hatbox, also beautifully designed, either in stripes or with large ribbons to match the colour of the hat above.

A young assistant approached Sarah and asked what it was that she would like to look at, and that an assistant would be with her very soon.

'Please take a seat, madam,' she finished.

Overwhelmed, Sarah gave the girl Mrs Tucker's list, which she had carried, carefully folded, in her pocket.

'Oh! I can do this for you, madam,' the little assistant said, reading the list after taking it from Sarah's hand. 'Three pairs of lace gloves, two cream and one pair white.'

Going to a drawer behind the counter, she brought back the gloves and, laying them on the counter for Sarah to see, asked, 'Do you like these gloves, madam?'

When Sarah said that she did, the girl looked at the list again, reading, '*Seven ribbons of varying colours.*'

Pointing out the stand holding the ribbons, she asked Sarah to choose what she wanted while she went for the nightgowns next on the list.

While Sarah chose ribbons in colours that she would like to wear, the three nightgowns, in different sizes, were laid on the counter. And soon, twenty cotton reels, in different coloured threads, were laid on top of the purchases.

'One of our small boxes of mixed buttons,' the assistant continued.

Taking a small ladder, she reached up to several boxes stacked on a shelf on the other side of the shop. Bringing a small box back to the counter where Sarah stood, the assistant carefully opened the lid and counted out the buttons in front of her, to be sure that, before they left the shop, all were accounted for.

Sarah was mesmerised by the designs and colours of the buttons, some very small and six pale blue hexagonal buttons her favourite.

Everything was wrapped carefully in a brown paper parcel and tied with string.

After being given the invoice for Mr and Mrs Tucker, Sarah left the shop carrying the large parcel. It wasn't heavy but was a little large for her small frame.

As she was making her way back to Old Town Street and the bank, she noticed Jane on the other side of the street. Her first reaction was to wave, her second was to hide, but in the end she did neither, as a man approached Jane and stood very close in front of her. They were talking and Jane was smiling. As the man enveloped Jane in his arms, Sarah realised that it was John, not in uniform, as she had expected to see him if she bumped into him, but in his ordinary clothes. Her heart sank.

She wanted to run away yet was transfixed by the sight of the only person in her life that she could have called friend now locked together in joy with the man whom she loved.

Turning around, she walked away without noticing the direction until she was outside number 100, with all its bad memories.

Crossing the road, she walked down Alice Street and onto Union Street. Again, the bad memory of that night rose up before her.

If only she'd had word from Ned. Where was he? The brother whom she had tried to shield from all that had happened. She did know why she hadn't told him; she didn't want to worry him with information that he could do nothing about. But now she had need, like Jane, to be in the arms of someone who loved her.

Mr and Mrs Tucker were sitting in the cart outside the bank when Sarah arrived. She mouthed sorry, getting into the back of the cart, and was silent for the rest of the journey home.

When they arrived back in Kingsand, the Tuckers thanked her for her help and Sarah walked slowly from the shop to her aunt's.

Opening the door, she went straight to her bedroom, leaving Josephine and Amy looking at each other with raised eyebrows. The plan had obviously not worked.

After half an hour, Josephine suddenly threw down the copper stick and, wiping her hands on her apron, said to Amy, 'I can't put up with this any longer. We have tip-toed around that maid for far too long. I'm going to get to the bottom of this, right now.'

Amy was open-mouthed in shock as her aunt marched from the kitchen and stomped up the stairs.

Josephine found Sarah laying on the bed, staring at the ceiling, tears flowing from the corners of her eyes.

Standing next to the bed, she spoke with such a determined voice that Sarah turned her head to look at her aunt.

'Sit up, maid. I want to talk to you.'

Sarah obeyed, sitting up, wiping her eyes.

'I want to know, *right now*, Sarah, what ails you. I know all that you have been through, but I think that this is something else. You live under *my* roof and I *demand* to know what is going on in your head.'

Shocked by the way her aunt spoke to her, the tears that she needed to shed flowed uncontrollably, and she howled, to such an extent that her aunt went to the window and shut it so that the neighbours couldn't hear.

Sitting on the bed, she put her arm around her niece and wondered if, had her daughter lived, she would have been going through this scenario with her, whatever it was.

When the crying seemed as though it would never stop, Josephine said quietly, 'Enough, maid, you must tell me what's wrong. I can't help you if I don't know what is causing you this pain.'

'I can't speak about it, Aunt. Please don't ask me to explain.'

'I am asking you, Sarah, and you will tell me what ails you.'

'But it's embarrassing, Aunt.'

'At my age, Sarah, there is nothing that you can say that will embarrass me.'

'I had a friend, Aunt,' she started, 'Jane, the only friend that I have ever had. I thought that we would be friends for life. I really liked her.'

'Liked her! What has she done, Sarah, to upset you?'

'She hasn't knowingly done anything, Aunt. I'm sure that if I'd told her that I had fallen in love with someone, that she would have been supportive. But she didn't know.'

'You are in love? I don't understand, Sarah. Is he married?'

'No, Aunt!' She was shocked. 'Nothing like that.'

'Then what?'

'When I was in town, I saw Jane in the distance. I was about to wave to her, when I saw her swept up in the arms of a man. It was John, the man I love. She didn't see me.'

She began to cry again, unable to help it, the pain of loss so great.

'I don't want to live anymore, Aunt.' She sniffed, wiping her face with the bed sheet. 'But I don't know how to end my life.' She sobbed, her eyes and nose streaming, her cheeks wet with tears.

Josephine was shocked. 'No!' she said sharply. 'No, maid. Nothing is so bad that you should lose your life. A life that could change in the blink of an eye and you would have lost that opportunity.'

Sarah sighed and wiped the tears from her cheeks. She had known that no one would understand that her life was finished.

'Thank you for telling me,' Josephine said quietly, pulling her niece to her and wrapping a supportive arm around Sarah's waist. 'You were brave to do so, Sarah. I know that it was difficult, but it's always good to share tragedy with a friend. I know I'm your aunt, but I'm also your friend, Sarah.'

She cuddled the girl to her, thinking how much, even in grief, Sarah looked like her own daughter, lost so long ago.

~

The following day, Amy was groaning in pain. Josephine was short with her.

'Stop that noise, Amy. Anyone would think that you were the first to become a woman. Pain is what we have to get used to.'

Amy, who was holding her belly, groaned again and rushed from the room, disappearing through the back door and into the closet in the yard.

'Sarah.' Aunt Jelly shook her head, looking through the window into the empty yard. 'Cut up some cloths to make pads for your sister. We will have them ready for when the blood breaks. I don't think it'll be long. I have to go and see Marta. I'll be back soon. Put the pads in the drawer ready. If it starts before I get back you will have to show her how to attach them. The pins are in a little box on the shelf.'

'Yes, Aunt.'

Sarah was glad to have something useful to do and sat quietly composed while cutting and folding.

Amy's face was pale when she re-entered the kitchen. 'I have to go to bed,' she mumbled, and made her way slowly upstairs.

Sarah put hot water in the stone bottle for Amy to curl up around with it near her stomach, and was sorry that it wasn't softer.

When Josephine came home, nothing else was said, as Sarah had finished Amy's chores.

During the afternoon, Marta arrived with a letter addressed to Sarah. On opening it, Sarah paled. It was from Jane, asking if they could meet at a tearoom in Old Town Street.

Josephine, watching her niece closely, saw her fold the letter after reading it and put it in her pocket without saying who it was from. As Sarah started to leave the room, Josephine asked, 'Who is the letter from, Sarah?'

Sarah stopped and turning to her aunt, said, 'It's from Jane, Aunt.'

'Ah! Jane, your friend.'

'Yes, Aunt,' she said quietly.

'And what does Jane say, Sarah?'

'She wants to meet me, Aunt. She has something to tell me. I don't want to go. I already know what she has to tell me and I think the pain will be too great for me to hide what I feel. How can I let her think that I'm happy for her, when my heart is breaking at her news?'

'Sarah. You *will* go, and I'll go with you. I'll look after you. This has to be faced, you cannot go through the rest of your life a bitter maid. And if you don't address this now, in the future, you may marry an unsuitable man and be desperately miserable for the rest of your life.'

'That, Aunt, is what I will be, for the rest of my life, whether I see Jane or not.'

'You owe her this meeting, Sarah. She still believes you to be her friend. We'll go on the morning tide tomorrow. Now write to Jane and take it to Mrs Tucker. She'll send the message with the courier for you.'

'What will I say, Aunt?'

'That you will meet her at midday. You will see her on your own, Sarah, but I'll be at another table if you need me.'

~

Jane was sitting at a table in the tearoom window, watching the street. Seeing Sarah approach, she was so excited that she didn't notice that she was with an older woman who followed Sarah into the café and secreted herself at a table in the corner.

As Sarah entered the tearoom, Jane jumped up and rushed towards her, beaming and flushed with happiness. Leading Sarah to the table, she held on to her hand across the tablecloth. 'Oh, Sarah,' she said, eyes gleaming. 'I have been asked if I would marry someone so special that I think I am going to die with happiness. Please say that you are happy for me, and that you will be my maid of honour when we marry.'

Sarah sat silently, shocked at Jane's glowing happiness. She knew that she should speak, but nothing was coming from her mouth.

'Are you not happy for me, Sarah?' Jane let go of Sarah's hand and sat back in her chair, frowning.

'Oh, Jane.' Sarah had been practising with her aunt. 'I'm very happy for you. It was a shock. I didn't know that you knew anyone well enough to marry them.'

'Well, I didn't, and it's all thanks to you that I met this person.'

'Me?' Her heart thumped in her chest.

'You are all that he and I have in common.'

Tears rose into Sarah's eyes as she chewed at her bottom lip, desperate to run out of the tearoom. Desperate to escape the happiness that could have been hers.

'I hope that those are tears of joy, Sarah, as I am to be your sister-in-law.'

'My sister-in-law?' Sarah's eyes widened at Jane's unexpected words.

'Yes. Oh, Sarah! Your brother is the most marvellous man. We fell in love through our letters and when we met I knew, as did he, that we were meant to be together for the rest of our lives.'

Sarah was so stunned that all she could utter was, 'Ned! You have met Ned?'

'Yes, he comes home each month with this new ship. Sails from Plymouth to Wales and Ireland, then up to Scotland and back. I see a lot of him and we are so happy, Sarah. Please say that you are happy for us.'

'I can't tell you, Jane, how happy I am. It's the best news and of course I will be your maid of honour.'

'Then I will buy tea.'

'Jane, that lady over there in the corner is my aunt. Can she sit with us and be included in your good news?'

'Oh, Sarah, how wonderful. I would love to meet your aunt, for am I not going to be part of the family?'

'Yes, Jane, you are and I could cry with happiness for you.'

On the way home, Josephine asked, 'Did Jane not say anything about John?'

'No, Aunt.'

'And you didn't ask her?'

'No, Aunt.'

'Her flinging herself into John's arms in the middle of the street means nothing to you now?'

'She doesn't know how I feel about John, Aunt, because I have never told her. I can't tell her now, it would make her sad.'

'How does she know him?'

'I can only think that it was when he came with the doctor to examine Mother to see if she was the one who'd given birth to the dead baby. Jane was with them because it was she who found the body.'

Josephine winced. 'I see. But was that short acquaintance enough to throw herself at him in the street? You said he had his arms around her.'

Sarah frowned. She had to agree that it was a strange way to behave with someone Jane hardly knew. Was Ned making a mistake in marrying Jane?

Josephine was not going to let this go. Ned was her nephew and she had to know if he was making a mistake. Whether or not she would tell him and risk losing him was something weighing heavily on her mind.

~

Jane and Ned were invited to tea on Sunday when Ned was to be home. Sarah could not settle all morning and was in such a nervous state that her aunt sent her into the garden before she could ruin the tea, having already dropped the flour and an egg.

Amy was icing the cake and suffering nerves in a different way, being excited to meet a brother that she had never met. Every ten minutes she ran to the window and looked out at the street, not knowing which ferry they would catch. When eventually there was a knock on the door, Amy almost fell over her own feet rushing to open it.

'For goodness' sake, Amy,' Aunt Jelly's voice followed her through the parlour, 'calm down, maid, or he will think you demented.'

Amy took a deep breath and opened the door to the smiling couple on the doorstep.

'You must be my sister Amy,' Ned said. And was almost knocked over as she threw herself at him, holding him around the waist and burying her head in his chest.

'You smell just like Father.' Her muffled voice emerged from his jacket. 'I love you.'

'I love you too, Amy, and thank you for the warm welcome. Can I introduce my fiancée, Jane?'

Josephine came to the door at that moment, having caught up with her niece.

'Ned dear, Jane, how lovely to see you. And welcome to my home. The girls have been making a special tea. Come in, come in. We can't leave you on the doorstep.'

They were settled in the parlour and, looking around, Ned exclaimed, 'It's so long since I came here with Father, Aunt, when I was small. It hasn't changed at all.'

'Is Sarah here?' Jane asked.

'Oh yes. She's just seeing to the chickens. Amy, go and get your sister. She doesn't know that our guests have arrived.'

Amy frowned and was about to say, *But I saw to the chickens this morning, Aunt,* when the glare her aunt sent in her direction left her with her mouth open and no words escaping.

Hurrying from the room to where she knew that Sarah would be hiding in the garden, she found her sitting on the bench, staring out to sea.

'Sarah,' she called. 'You have to come in. Ned and Jane are here.'

Sarah acknowledged her with a sigh and, standing slowly, followed Amy inside.

'Ah! there you are, Sarah.' Ned stood holding out his arms.

She stepped forward and allowed herself to receive a cuddle from her brother.

'You're looking very pale, sister. I can see that you've not yet recovered from your ordeal.'

Again, Sarah smiled and nodded to Jane in greeting.

Jane seemed confused by the lack of warmth and friendship

240

coming from Sarah and looked apprehensively towards Ned who, in catching up with his family after so long away, didn't notice.

Sarah escaped, with the excuse of helping Amy in the kitchen. Eventually, she had to return to the parlour and carried the tea tray, while Amy carried the cake. Aunt Jelly had her fingers crossed, hoping that the child wouldn't drop it.

Over tea, Ned told them that he had been writing to Jane and that when eventually they met, he had fallen in love with her. Jane blushed and Amy looked at the pair, her face alight with amazement.

Sarah didn't say anything.

'Tell me, Jane,' Josephine said sweetly, 'how do you know John Parrett?'

'Oh!' The unexpected question caught Jane off guard. She looked shocked but recovered quickly.

'It's a bit of a story really. You see, John is my, sort of, cousin.'

'Sort of?' Josephine commented, giving Jane one of her raised-eyebrow looks. 'How can he be a sort of cousin? He either is, or he is not.'

'Yes, I can see how that would sound.' Jane smiled. 'You see, there were three sisters: Edith, Silvanne and Dorothy. My mother, Silvanne, married and had me.'

Jane lifted her hands as though this was an enlightening moment. When all the faces before her did not change, she continued. 'After Edith married, she discovered that she was barren. Couldn't have children,' she qualified, as though it was needed. 'She and her husband adopted John and of course as children he and I played together. But when I was five, my father died of the consumption and I went to live with my Aunt Dorothy in Plymstock to keep me safe.' She sighed. 'My mother caught the disease two weeks later and before I was six I was an orphan.

'My aunt, also barren, told me that she didn't have a maternal bone in her body and had thought that she would have me for only a short time. Apologising, she sent me to a home for orphaned girls. In some ways, it was nice. I had lots of company. But no family. I was taught to read, write and sew. When I was old enough, I had to leave.'

She smiled sadly. 'They arranged for me to have an interview for the job at the haberdashery and, from then on, I was on my own. I can't tell you how overjoyed I was at meeting John again when he visited your mother, Sarah.'

As she spoke those words, Jane grimaced as she looked across the room at Sarah, who was sitting silently with her plate on her lap, her cake uneaten.

'I'm sorry, Sarah, I know that memory must hurt you,' she said, looking guilty.

'So!' Josephine paused, trying to understand what Jane had just said. 'You and John Parrett are cousins through adoption.'

'Yes, yes, exactly.'

'You are family, although not related,' Josephine continued.

'Yes. I feel so lucky to have him. I have no other family.'

'But you're wrong, Jane,' Ned said, reaching out for her hand. 'We are going to be your family as well as John.'

Jane smiled at him and, squeezing his hand, looked at Sarah, who had sat silently through tea and the conversation.

'Yes, Ned, I hope so,' she said, still looking at Sarah.

'Right,' Josephine said, standing. 'Amy, you will wash up with Ned and then show him the garden, while I think that Sarah should show Jane Kingsand and Cawsand, as she is going to be a constant visitor here.'

Sarah, who was still sitting in silent shock, wanted nothing more than to run to the bedroom and shut the door until they'd gone.

'Sarah!' Aunt Jelly's voice had a stern edge to it. 'Get going, maid, and show your friend, and soon-to-be sister, around. I know that you have a lot to talk about,' she said, pointedly.

Putting her plate on the occasional table, Sarah stood up and walked to the front door, not looking at Jane or waiting for her.

In the street, Jane asked, 'What's wrong, Sarah? I thought that you would be very happy for us. But instead you are silent.'

Without replying, Sarah walked away, unable to speak. What could she say, where would she start? Her love for John had been her secret. She had told her aunt but didn't want anyone else to know. Even though painful, her love for John still felt like her possession. Once told again, she would have nothing. Nothing to hold on to, nothing that was hers.

27.

Marta was outside the shop, cleaning the bench, put there for the elderly to sit on in the shade, or the sun, at different times of the year. Moth, who lived at the top of the hill, often sat with his friends, chatting about the past or putting the world to rights before he attempted to shuffle back home.

As she completed her task, Marta stood and stretched her back. Noticing Sarah approaching, she was about to raise her hand in greeting when she saw the look on the girl's face and lowered her arm. The young woman with her was trying to keep up with the fast pace, and it looked like Sarah was trying to get away from her.

It made Marta sad. She knew what Josephine had been up to and it looked like her plan had gone disastrously wrong.

Stepping inside the shop, Marta watched Sarah turn down towards the beach, striding down the slipway, before walking with more difficulty when reaching the sand.

The young woman that, through Josephine, Marta knew to be Jane, was here to be welcomed into the family. Things were obviously not going well. She could see that Jane was red in the face from the exertion of trying to keep up with Sarah and had removed her hat.

Marta watched as Jane followed Sarah down the slipway and onto the sand, where she too had difficulty in walking.

Sarah strode on, her legs aching from the drag of deep sand beneath her boots. All the time she could feel that Jane was behind her. She wished that she could rise up into the air and get away.

Rise above the rocks. Float across the land where no one could follow. Inside, she was screaming, *Leave me alone, leave me alone, let me be.*

Eventually, when she reached the end of the beach, unable to go further, she sat on a rock, looking out to sea. She could hear Jane approaching. Could hear her heavy breathing. And wished she had not come this way but gone along the coastal footpath where she would have been able to outpace Jane and get away. But then she knew that she would eventually have to come back and face her aunt.

Jane arrived and, without speaking, sat heavily on a rock next to Sarah, trying to get her breath back.

Neither spoke as the gulls wheeled and screeched overhead, filling the silence that sat heavily between them.

Eventually, Jane said, 'I know, Sarah, that you've been through a great deal. We spoke about it. But this is something different, something else, and you won't feel better until you speak your truth.'

'Speak my truth, Jane?' Sarah exploded. 'What do you know about my truth?'

'Isn't that the point, Sarah?' Jane returned, just as forcefully. 'I don't know your truth and so can't help you unless you talk to me. I want to help. Something is very wrong. You are changed, Sarah. I see a great difference in you.'

Sarah sighed.

Diamonds of light danced on the sea as the sun's rays touched the waves, eventually trickling ashore and gently lapping the shoreline. Squinting, Sarah looked out to the horizon, wishing that she was anywhere but here.

Jane waited in silence, seeing the struggle that Sarah was having, yet not knowing why.

Eventually, Sarah said, 'I don't want to speak about it, Jane, it's too painful.'

'Yet if you don't tell me, Sarah, surely the pain will increase and will change you. You are already changed.'

Sarah shook her head. She was not changed. She was just the same as she always was; it was just that they couldn't see it.

'There's nothing for you to know, Jane,' she said, keeping her eyes on the pinpoints of light shimmering on the sea.

'Then why have you not welcomed Ned and I today?'

Sarah lowered her head. Jane was right. She had sat in the parlour only because she was expected to. She had not welcomed her brother after all these years. Was not joining in the celebration of his love for Jane. Why? Why did she feel so dead inside, that even her brother and Jane's good news could not lift her out of this dull state of mind?

Knowing that she was trapped, Sarah sat thinking how she could start telling Jane. For in reality, she didn't know herself what was wrong. But then, she did know. All she could think about was John. How she loved him. How he had said that he loved her, yet had still been going to marry another woman. How bad she felt when she saw him with Jane, believing that he was now involved with her. Would she not be better off on her own, where no man could tear her emotions to pieces? What sort of life could she have with a man who she could not trust? Trust, she realised, was the bedrock of a relationship, and her trust had been stripped away before a relationship had even begun.

'When I first met you, Sarah,' Jane was saying quietly, her voice only just heard above the gulls, 'you were a young woman who, unprepared, supported your family. Impossible though your mother made it for you, you did your best, never complaining, always believing that you could make their lives better.'

Sarah tried to think back to the time she lived in King Street. Tried to find the girl that Jane remembered. But it seemed so long ago that she could no longer recall the nature of that girl.

'You never gave up, Sarah,' Jane persisted. 'Even when your mother was taken away and you became homeless. You didn't give up. You were determined to survive. And you did. You found a job and found that you were capable of great responsibility.'

'Your cousin found me the job, Jane. I didn't find it,' she conjectured dully.

246

'But can you deny that you were not good at what you did, Sarah?'

'I can't deny it,' she shrugged. 'I enjoyed the work and I liked the people. They were different. People who have work are different to those struggling with empty bellies.'

'I think that you've learnt that we are all capable of many things, Sarah, given a chance. And my cousin gave you that chance.'

'Yes, he did.' She had to agree that from the day she met John, her life had improved.

She remembered the day that she had met him on the Barbican, when she was lost, desolate. How he had bought her a meal and then taken her to the Coles', and instead of being homeless, vulnerable, she had everything; money, food and somewhere safe to sleep.

But then the grotesque form of Arthur Cole flooded her mind, moving towards her covered in Mrs Cole's blood, his odd eyes staring at her, a look of lust on his face. He was mouthing her name, *Za-rah*, and she was still frozen in the doorway, unable to move.

Overcome by the vision, she shook her head as though she could dislodge it.

'I can't do this anymore, Jane,' she said sharply. 'Leave me alone. I'm no one. I have no life and I don't want a life that has to include another person.'

Jane was shocked by Sarah's sudden outburst. 'What sort of life would that be, Sarah, and where would you lead this life alone? In a convent? Do you envisage becoming a *nun*?'

Again, Sarah shook her head. She didn't know what she wanted other than to be left alone in the grief that she felt at John's loss.

'I think, Sarah, that you are in love with my cousin.' Jane had suddenly put into words the reason for Sarah's wretchedness. Words that came so unexpectedly from Jane that Sarah felt that she had been dealt a physical blow, losing the breath from her lungs.

She gasped, and shook violently, before the tears came. Covering her face with her hands, she sobbed.

Jane held her tight. Frightened to let her go in case she ran off. As the gulls became quiet, moving away out to sea, Jane sat watching them while holding Sarah to her chest.

'John tells me that he loves you, Sarah,' Jane whispered into Sarah's hair. 'He knows that he's made mistakes. Mistakes that he can't take back. He's young. He knows nothing of life other than the trauma that he sees every day suffered by the people of Plymouth. Mostly by their own hands,' she qualified. 'But I can tell you, Sarah, that if you give him a chance, he will love you to the end of his days, and that he is suffering just as you are.'

Sarah raised her head, her eyes red with crying. Nodding, she pulled away from Jane and sighed. With shoulders slumped in submission, she said slowly, 'He was going to marry Phillis, Jane, even though he didn't love her. *He's* a weak man.'

'You're wrong, Sarah.'

And Sarah heard the disappointment in Jane's voice.

'He is a man of great principle. If he were older and more worldly, he may have acted differently. He would have challenged that man. I'm sure of that. But he's young and felt it his duty to go through with it, if he had asked her father for her hand in marriage. He didn't know the Gallaways. He didn't know that they would lie to get their daughter wedded and to have, as they saw it, the police in their family under their control.' She laughed ironically. 'Of course, John would have been a great disappointment to them, as one thing he is not, even though young, is in any way a criminal. He has seen too much of that in his short career. Seen too many lives destroyed.'

Sarah took in all that Jane said, but shook her head.

'Too late now, Jane.'

'It's never too late, Sarah. Do you want to lose him?'

'I've already lost him, Jane.' Her voice held a note of irony. 'The love I had for him feels different now. He no longer has a place in my heart.'

Standing, she held out a hand to Jane, saying, 'Let's go back and I'll congratulate Ned on his coming marriage. And Jane... I am very happy that Ned is marrying you, even though I haven't shown it.'

'You will be my maid of honour, won't you, Sarah?'

'Yes, but I'm nervous. I've never been part of a wedding, let alone had an important role in one. What will I have to do?'

'Help me choose a dress and shoes and, on the day, help me with my hair. Just be with me as my companion, Sarah, for I also have never been to a wedding.'

As they passed the shop, walking arm in arm, Marta, who had been looking out for them, felt greatly relieved seeing the girls looking happy.

Perhaps Josephine's plan was working.

~

The weeks passed quickly and Aunt Jelly was the happiest that Amy and Sarah had ever seen her as she joined in with the excitement of the wedding plans.

Jane, now supported by Ned, no longer had to work and was making her own wedding dress and Sarah's bridesmaid dress. She came regularly to Kingsand for fittings and, with some material left over, made Amy a dress with the silk and lace.

On the Saturday before the wedding, Ned and Jane arrived, their faces glowing with excitement.

Aunt Jelly looked at the pair, saying, as they entered the kitchen, 'You look like you had the cream off the top of the churn.'

Ned picked her up and swung her around, to the delight of Amy and the surprise of everyone else.

'Put me down, you silly boy, or I won't be able to stand up straight.'

Still grinning, he stood her back on the floor, where she held on to the table to get her balance.

'We have great news, Aunt,' he said, smiling, as Josephine recovered. 'I've bought a farm on the outskirts of Plympton. I've given up seafaring. There's plenty of room in the farmhouse and a small cottage besides, if you would like to come and live with us.'

Josephine had her mouth open, staring at him, speechless for the first time in her life, and Amy was jumping up and down, saying, 'I want to live with you, Ned. Please say that I can live with you, and can I have a dog?'

'If you come to live with us, Amy, of course you can have a dog. We'll need a dog to help with the sheep.'

'Sheep! You're going to have sheep?' Amy's eyes sparkled.

'Yes. There are several barns. We thought that we'd start off with a couple of pigs and a few sheep.'

'What do you know of farming, lad?' Josephine asked, eyes now squinting at Ned, her eyebrows raised.

'While away in different parts of the world, I've seen many types of farming, Aunt, and have always fancied not living in a town but maybe on the outskirts of a village. We'll pick it up as we go along.' He looked at Jane and smiled. 'I think that there are farmers locally who will help us with their knowledge.'

'And what about you, Jane?' Josephine asked. But the answer was already written on Jane's face.

'I'm so excited to be living away from the noise, the smells and filth of town. I know we'll be happy and that I'll love it as much as Ned.'

'Away from the smells and the filth.' Josephine looked hard at Jane. 'Are you sure that you know what happens on a farm?'

Everyone laughed, even Sarah, who in reality had no idea why they were laughing, and wondered how it would be to live in the middle of nowhere. She tried but couldn't imagine having no one living in the next room, or even not having another house in sight.

She wasn't sure that she would feel safe being so isolated, but as she looked at Jane, glowing with health and love, she knew that it would suit her.

Jane was saying, 'I'm going to continue dressmaking, and that will bring in some money until we get started.'

Ned was looking at his aunt, and noticing that she was no longer smiling, he asked, 'Will you live with us, Aunt?'

'No, lad. I don't think that I will. I have a life here and friends, people who know me, and at my age, I don't want to move away. This is my home, and one day soon the farm will feel like yours, and you will be unable to think of living anywhere else.'

'Then you will always be welcome in our home, Aunt.' He bent and kissed her on the cheek. 'Isn't that right, Jane?'

'Yes, Ned.' She looked at Josephine. 'I don't have a family and I want you to visit us. It'll make our house feel like a family home if we have family visiting.'

'Then I'll visit.' She frowned. 'Although I don't know how I'll get there. Plympton is a long way from Kingsand.'

Ned grinned at his aunt and Jane. 'We'll work that out when the time comes, Aunt. You may be happy to stay for a few days, and we'll be happy to have you stay. There's going to be a lot of work to do.' He smiled. 'But I won't ask you to pick up a pitchfork or muck out the pigs.'

28.

Sarah was in a constant state of flux as the days drew nearer to the wedding. She got involved in the preparations and was as excited as Jane, but always there lingered the thought, in the back of her mind, that John, being Jane's cousin, would be there with his parents. But she couldn't ask. She didn't want anyone to know that she still had feelings for John, didn't want them to see the sparkle that might come to her eyes when she saw him. Didn't want them to see her disappointment if he looked away.

On a fine, frost-free Saturday in January, the bells of Charles Church rang a constant peal of celebration. A weak sun, shining in through the gothic windows, cast patterns on the flagstone floor and warmed the interior as Ned and Jane stood before the stained glass window and altar at the core of the church.

A small but happy gathering sat in the front pews. Three girls from the sewing room and two of Ned's naval friends. Mr and Mrs Parrett, Aunt Josephine, Amy and Sarah.

The minister was a pleasant man who smiled and made everyone feel part of the service and the celebration of Ned and Jane's marriage. Aunt Josephine cried, and that brought tears to Sarah's own eyes as she handed her aunt a handkerchief.

The bells continued to ring as the wedding party emerged happily from the church and walked arm in arm through the graveyard, to the gate in the wall, and out onto the busy street.

People passing paused to congratulate them and women stopped to admire the bride. And through all the laughter and happiness, Sarah looked for John. Perhaps he'd had to work? Perhaps he was unwell? Why was he not at his cousin's wedding? But she couldn't ask, couldn't show that she cared, didn't want anyone to know how she felt, didn't want their pity.

A jolly party, they walked the short distance to the Minerva Inn on Looe Street. Ned bought them a celebration drink and had arranged with the management for a meal of belly pork and vegetables to be served.

Until her aunt was ready to make the return journey home on the ferry, Sarah sat apart from everyone, sitting in the tavern window watching the happy couple and their friends.

Suddenly aware of someone approaching, she looked up to see Mrs Parrett taking a seat at the table.

'Miss Warrington,' she said, smiling, 'isn't this a wonderful day? And they look so happy.'

As she spoke, Mrs Parrett looked towards the happy couple, who were talking to their friends and laughing.

'Yes,' Sarah smiled fondly, 'they're so happy.'

'And isn't it just surprising that you and I are now family, Miss Warrington. After all that we have been through together.'

Sarah's heart missed a beat. Yes, it was strange, and ironic, that they were now family.

'As we're now family,' she continued, 'may I call you Sarah? Miss Warrington is a mouthful.'

Sarah had to laugh; her surname was a mouthful. 'Please, do call me Sarah, Mrs Parrett,' she replied quietly, thinking that had she married John, his mother would have been using her Christian name, and that this was indeed ironic.

'I'm sorry that John's missing this celebration. I'm sure that he would have loved to be here.'

Every part of Sarah's body seemed to shrink as his mother spoke. John would have *loved* to be here. Then why wasn't he? And why was she speaking in the past tense? Had something happened to him and no one had told her?

'You've become very pale, Miss... Sarah, are you ill?'

'No, I'm very well, thank you. Just a little tired. It's been a long day, even though a very happy day.'

'And, of course, you have the long ferry ride home. It must be difficult living in Kingsand. It is Kingsand, isn't it?'

'Yes, Kingsand. It's a lovely place to live. Very quiet. A village really. Everyone knows everyone else. A real community. Not at all like Plymouth where people don't always know their neighbour and many go hungry.'

'I haven't been to Kingsand, it's true,' she said, 'and I can see the attraction. You make it sound a friendly place to live.'

'I live with my aunt and my sister in a small cottage that backs onto the sea. On a sunny day when the sea is calm, it's the best place on earth to be living.'

'And when there are storms?' Her face twisted into what Sarah thought might be mock fear.

'Then that is more challenging,' Sarah said sagely. For she was still afraid of the unpredictable moods of the sea.

Looking hard at John's mother, Sarah thought that she didn't look like someone grieving the loss of her son, wasn't wearing black, so not in mourning, and was just summoning the courage to ask about him when Aunt Jelly approached with Amy.

'It's time we went home, maid.' Aunt Jelly smiled. 'It's been a glorious day. Have you enjoyed it, Mrs Parrett?'

'I have. It's been so long since we had a marriage in the family.' For just a second, she frowned, realising what she had said, but recovered quickly. 'I couldn't be happier than I am today that our families are now joined.'

'If you're ever in Kingsand, Mrs Parrett, please call in and we'll sit in my garden and look at the sea.'

'Is the sea that close, Mrs Helbridge?'

'Please, call me Josephine, we're in-laws now, and yes, it is close, just below my wall.'

'Then I'm Edith, Josephine. And if I can find the courage to travel on the ferry, I would like very much to sit in your garden.'

'Then that's settled. Come, Sarah, we must make our way home.'

254

After saying goodbye to Ned and Jane, they made their way to the ferry, Aunt Jelly and Amy talking all the while about the day and the service. Sarah had never seen her sister looking so well. She was blossoming into a beautiful young woman and Sarah vaguely wondered who she took after. Was it their mother? Her mother must have been young once. And what had attracted her father to such an austere woman? Someone so stern and unfeeling.

~

As they alighted from the ferry, Sarah noticed James Bellum sitting on the front of his buggy at the top of the jetty.

'Good evening, Mrs Helbridge,' he called, smiling. And Sarah noticed for the first time what a very good-looking man he had grown into.

'Good evening, James, and what are you doing here?' Aunt Jelly asked, walking slowly towards the cart.

'I brought some people to the ferry and thought that I would hang on to see if anyone wanted a lift back. It's a long walk for some.'

'That was very thoughtful of you, James. I know that I would be glad of a lift. I seem to have been on my feet all day.'

James got down and helped them into the back of his buggy with its worn leather seats. Sarah noticed Amy blush as James helped her up the step and inwardly she smiled.

Weren't they all looking for love?

Western Morning News

March 1871

EXETER – The trial of SIDNEY ALBOUS COLE & MIKIEL BRONALSKI of 45 King Street took place on Tuesday last, at the Exeter Crown Court, before Mr J Mountford, concerning the death of Miss Daisy May, also of 45 King Street, who was unlawfully killed and her body hidden on 16 February 1870.

The jury of twenty-four men took very little time to find both Mr Cole and Mr Bronalski complicit in the covering-up of the murder of Daisy May, who lodged and worked at the same address. The jury were told that Arthur Cole, aged 17, the delinquent son of Mr and Mrs Cole, and who resided at the same address, killed Daisy May when he escaped from his secure accommodation on the top floor of the same premises. Mr Bronalski, his tutor, told the jury that he believed that Arthur Cole had entered the house via the fire escape in the middle of the night. Miss May, who had been encouraged to bolt the doors to her rooms at night, had not done so on this occasion and Arthur Cole had entered those rooms.

Miss May was strangled while fighting off the unwanted advances of Arthur Cole, who could not defend himself in court, having been sectioned by Mr Evan Broadbent, Plymouth surgeon, for Arthur's own safety and that of others. Mr Cole and Mr Bronalski, with the help of Mrs Cole, now deceased, covered up Miss May's murder by putting her body into a coffin with another cadaver, both being buried the following day.

Mrs Elizabeth Almour, servant at the same address, who had been asked to clean the carpet, was acquitted by the jury. She said that she had not questioned her employer but had carried out her duty as she saw it. She had nothing to do with the cover-up and indeed believed what she had been told, that Miss May had had an accident and had run away. Mrs Almour said, when questioned, that she liked Daisy May.

Mr Bronalski was asked by the jury why Arthur Cole had a sudden interest in Miss May. He told the jury that his charge had the mind of a child but the developing body of a young man with all its frustrations. He had the boy's best interest at heart when he took him out at night, his deformed head covered by a hood, to have relief with a prostitute. The disadvantage was that he had to leave Arthur alone in an alley while procuring the services of a prostitute. On one occasion, he returned to find Arthur missing. He dismissed the prostitute and later found Arthur Cole pulling at the clothes of Lillian Blatten, who was on the ground and dead. They returned home. Leaving the body to be found. He found out the woman's name next day in the newspaper. The foreman of the jury questioned, 'Yet you did not report this to the police, Mr Bronalski?' Mr Bronalski admitted that he had not, for the sake of the young man in his charge, and that the only way to keep the boy happy was to take him out at night when he became fractious. Mr Bronalski was asked how often this was. Mr Bronalski answered that he had to take him, unknown to his parents, more and more often, and that Arthur's sexual appetite was becoming more and more violent by strangulation. After the death of a prostitute at the hands of Arthur Cole, Mr Bronalski said that he was trying to find a way of telling his employers about their son, whom they still treated as an infant.

Mr Cole was sentenced to five years' hard labour, for covering up the murder of Daisy May. Mr Bronalski received ten years' hard labour for knowingly covering up the murder of Miss Daisy May and for allowing Arthur Cole to murder Lillian Blatten and Mrs Dorrett Browne, otherwise known as Doxy.

29.

Kingsand

September 1874

It had been three years since the wedding of Ned to Jane, and after the first three months living on the farm, their visits to Kingsand decreased until they visited no more. Having two small children and a farm full of demanding animals, they found that they could no longer get away. Aunt Jelly visited once, and Sarah and Amy went four times in that first year, but after several winter storms stopped the ferry running, somehow the trips dwindled away.

Aunt Jelly's health was deteriorating. She was finding it hard to breathe and could no longer visit Moth and Mouse, unable to walk up the steep hill. It was Mouse who now visited Josephine.

They sat in the garden in summer or the parlour during the winter, sitting in front of the fire, talking about the past. Mouse brought homemade herbal concoctions to help ease Josephine's breathing condition, which they did for a short time, but weren't a cure.

Sarah and Amy were doing everything in the house, as their aunt had taken to her bed during the third winter. She had local visitors, but Edith Parrett, although now an in-law by marriage, had never risked the ferry.

It was the end of the month. A serene day without a wind. The sea flat calm, and a gentle warmth promised a late summer day.

They'd just brought the washing in when Amy, who had been very quiet all day, asked, 'Sarah, would you mind if I went out this evening? I know it leaves you with Aunt, but I really would like to have some time to myself.'

Remembering how she had felt cooped up in the room above the funeral parlour in King Street, Sarah understood the need to get away.

'Of course you can go out, Amy, but be back before dark, and don't speak to any strangers.'

'I promise. I won't speak to any strangers or go off with them. That's the next thing you were going to say.'

Sarah had to smile, for it was exactly what she was going to say.

'Before dark, please,' she smiled.

After supper, Amy came downstairs in her new lemon dress and Sarah noticed how she smiled, how her eyes sparkled, and thought idly, *I don't think my sister is going to be alone.* She was about to ask, when the thumping of Aunt Jelly's walking stick came from the floor above.

'I'd better see to that.' She was torn between Amy and her aunt. 'Don't be late.'

'I won't.'

The door shut quickly, leaving Sarah looking at the wood.

As the knocking on the ceiling became ever more demanding, Sarah took the stairs two at a time.

After getting Aunt Jelly ready for bed, Sarah sat with her, reading. It wasn't until the light had faded so much that she had to light the candle in the glass lamp, that she realised that Amy wasn't home.

She closed the book slowly, not wanting to disturb her aunt with her fears.

'I'll leave the candle lamp alight until you're asleep, dear,' she said, pulling the bed covers up. 'I'll see you in the morning, Aunt, but if you need anything just knock.'

'I will. Is Amy coming up?'

'Oh, I'm sure that she will.'

Once downstairs, Sarah looked out of the parlour window. It was dark. She lit the lamps and, pulling on her coat, went to the front door. It wasn't as dark outside as it was in the cottage, but it was dark enough that Amy should have been on her way home.

She walked up the street in the direction of Cawsand, not knowing where Amy might have gone. When she got to the corner shop, she knocked on the side door. Marta answered, looking concerned when she saw who it was.

'Is it Josephine?' she asked quickly.

'No, it isn't anything to be worried about but have you seen Amy?'

'Yes, I saw her earlier. She was with James Bellum, they were walking towards the beach.'

'James Bellum?'

'They seem to have a friendship. I thought that you knew.'

Sarah sighed, 'No, I didn't know. I would have liked to have known but I've been busy concentrating on my aunt, who needs a lot of help.'

'I know, dear. I don't know what she would do without you girls to help her. Do you want me to come with you to look for Amy?'

'No, I want her to believe that I'm just out for a stroll. I don't want her to think that I'm looking for her. But I did ask her to be home before dark.'

'If you need us, Sarah, just knock on the door.'

As she walked down the slipway to the beach, the smell of seaweed was strong in her nostrils, a fragrance that she loved and would normally have stopped to breathe in. But not tonight. She carried on along the edge of the water on the wet sand, where the walking was easier. As she approached the end of the beach, the rocks didn't look as friendly as during the day. What she saw were black shapes, humped like dead people, people drowned, washed up on the beach. She shivered, turning away towards the back of the beach, hoping that she wouldn't find Amy and James in a compromising situation. But the back of the beach was empty. She sighed, getting a little annoyed, for it would soon be too dark to see.

At the top of the beach she took the track that would take her up onto the coastal path. It was lighter here, strangely, and she felt a cool breeze that hadn't been on the beach below.

261

She decided that she'd walk as far as the memorial bench, and then she would turn around, as Amy might, by then, be home.

About to sit on the bench for a few minutes to get her breath back, she heard a scream carried on the wind. Was it a gull? Then a shout for help, a sound of panic in the tone.

Walking on, she saw, ahead of her, the shape of someone on their belly, lying flat on the path edge, their upper body hanging over the drop. She wasn't sure if what she was seeing was real, or if it was her brain playing tricks, like it had with the rocks on the beach. Then she clearly heard another cry for help.

Running to the spot, she found James Bellum on his stomach, head and arms hanging out into space above the drop into the bay below. Panic rose in her chest. Where was Amy?

She fell onto her own belly beside him.

'Thank God,' James uttered. 'I can't hold her much longer.'

Looking down, Sarah could see that he had Amy by one hand, her body hanging over the rocks below.

'Stretch out your arms and hold her wrist.' His voice was strained. 'She's too heavy for me to haul up on my own.'

Following his arm down, she found Amy's wrist and held the cold flesh with both her hands.

'Can we pull her up now there's two of us?' he said, almost to himself.

There was no sound coming from Amy, and Sarah thought that she must be unconscious.

'Pull,' he demanded.

Sarah did her best and although Amy may have come up a little, it wasn't sustainable. There was no way that they could get her all the way up. If only he'd had hold of both hands. Sarah was trying to think how they could rescue Amy, when a man sat down beside her, saying, 'Hold on.'

Mr Tucker had arrived out of nowhere. 'Can you hold her, James, while Sarah removes her coat?' he asked.

'God, I hope so.' James spoke through gritted teeth.

'Quick, Sarah, take that coat off.'

While he was speaking, Mr Tucker was removing his own coat.

Letting go of her sister's wrist, Sarah struggled out of her coat and handed it to him, before laying down again, reaching over the edge, following James' arm down to Amy's wrist.

Mr Tucker tied one of his coat sleeves and one of Sarah's coat sleeves together.

'James,' he said, breathlessly, holding out a sleeve to the boy, 'I want you to hold this sleeve with one hand. You will still have to keep hold of Amy's hand and take my weight in the other. Wrap it around your wrist. Don't let it go.' As he spoke, he was wrapping the end of the sleeve around his own wrist.

'I'll go over the edge, holding on to the coat sleeve,' he was saying. 'If I can reach her other arm, we can pull her in and pull her up. Ready, James?'

'Ready.' James braced himself for the extra weight.

Going over the edge, holding on to the coat sleeve, Mr Tucker disappeared.

James groaned. Still holding Amy's hand and the sleeve of the coat in his other hand, the weight was pulling him forward towards the edge. The toes of his boots dug into the soft earth rucking up the grass, but the ridge they made wouldn't hold him back for very long.

Sarah couldn't breathe. She could feel James slipping forward. The weight of her sister was pulling her arms from her shoulder sockets. Her muscles were screaming in pain, and she too felt herself slipping towards the edge.

'I can't let go. I can't let go.'

She didn't realise that she was saying it aloud, until James said, through gritted teeth, 'You're doing fine, Sarah. Just hold on.'

Suddenly the weight was released, as Mr Tucker leant out and grasped Amy's arm, pulling her into the side of the cliff and taking some of the weight from them.

James brought himself to a kneeling position, still holding on to Amy's hand and the coat sleeve.

Sarah, still on her belly, had hold of her sister's wrist with both hands as she and James pulled at the command of Mr Tucker, who shouted, 'I have a foothold, pull her up.'

As Amy's head and then the top of her body appeared above the edge of the cliff, James and Sarah pulled her up onto the grass by her clothes.

Sarah rubbed Amy's ice-cold flesh, as James helped Mr Tucker up over the edge by reeling in the coats.

The shopkeeper sat on the grass, recovering next to Amy, who was unconscious.

'Is she alright?' James' voice held the tension that they all felt.

'Why isn't she recovering?' Sarah asked, looking at Mr Tucker.

He shook his head. 'Was she alright before the fall, James?'

'Yes.' James was kneeling beside Amy, rubbing her arm. 'Wake up, Amy, you're safe. It's all over, wake up. Please wake up.'

It was then, Sarah realised, that Amy meant a lot to James, and that maybe they were more than friends. But she didn't say it, concentrating only on bringing her sister back to life.

Mr Tucker was asking, 'How did it happen, James?'

James seemed startled but raised his eyes from the prone body, answering, 'We were on our way back from a walk. We were thankfully holding hands and talking when the earth gave way beneath her. It was so sudden. Thank God we didn't both go over or she would be dead.' He looked at Sarah. 'I'm so glad you came looking for her. If you hadn't found us when you did, she'd be gone.' A sob escaped him as he stroked Amy's hair. 'Amy, Amy, please wake up.' He was crying.

It was the first time that Sarah had seen a man cry and to her shame she was embarrassed.

It was Mr Tucker who cut through their shock and took control. 'Let's get her back to the shop. She needs warming up and we may have to send for the doctor.'

James picked her up and carried her as Mr Tucker led the way in the semi-darkness along the uneven path and down into Cawsand.

As they entered the living quarters at the back of the shop, Marta gave a little gasp.

'What happened?' She looked from her husband to James.

'Sit her in the chair next to the fire,' Mr Tucker directed James, ignoring his wife's question, before saying, 'Is there water in that kettle over the fire, Marta?'

She lifted the kettle, shaking it. 'Yes, there's hot water.'

'Then fill the bottle and put it in her lap. I'll get the brandy.'

'What happened?' Marta asked again, looking at their strained faces and dirty clothes.

'I'll tell you in a bit,' Mr Tucker said, coming to the table and putting the brandy bottle down, along with five glasses.

'You two get near the fire,' he addressed Sarah and James. 'You're both shivering, if not from the cold then the shock.'

Sarah and James sat each side of the fire, James placing himself in the seat beside Amy and, taking her hand, he examined her bruised wrist and arm.

Marta placed the bottle, that would normally warm the bed, in Amy's lap and covered it with a blanket. Shaking her head, she stepped back, looking at her husband. 'Why isn't she waking up?'

'I don't know,' he frowned, 'give her time.' Turning to James, he asked, 'Did she bang her head, James?'

'I don't know, it all happened so quickly. One minute we were walking, on our way home, then she just disappeared over the edge. *Amy*,' he whispered, near her face, 'wake up, you're safe now.' But Amy didn't respond, sitting white and floppy in the chair.

Sarah had a sudden flashback of Mrs Cole in her coffin and started to cry. 'She can't die. She's too young.'

As the tears flowed over her cheeks, she remembered Maud and all the children that had died in King Street. Her body suddenly racked with sobs. Sobs for them all.

'Shh, maid.' Mrs Tucker put her hand on Sarah's back. 'Give her a little time to warm up and to come around. I'll count to ten and if she isn't back then, it will have to be the smelling salts.'

After the count of ten, Marta waved the little brown bottle of smelling salts under Amy's nose.

265

Amy screwed up her face against the fumes of ammonia emanating from the bottle, then took a breath, holding her hand in front of her face to ward off the smell.

Mrs Tucker had already removed the bottle, putting it back in her pocket.

'Does it every time,' she said, satisfied.

As Amy opened her eyes, she looked confused, disorientated, and then, remembering, she gasped and clung to James, who put his arms around her, holding her to his chest.

'I thought that I'd lost you,' he cried into her hair.

Amy's body began to shake; her face became grey as she pulled away from James, suddenly looking desperate.

'Get the bucket, Mr Tucker,' Marta shouted, holding the blanket up to Amy's mouth in case he wasn't in time.

Just as the bucket was placed on her knees, she retched. James rubbed her back as she retched again. When finished, she took a deep breath. As the colour crept slowly back into her face, she leant slowly back into the chair.

'She'll be alright now,' Marta said with confidence. 'I've seen it many times, it's the shock coming out. She'll be fine now.'

'Can I take her home to her bed, Mrs Tucker?'

'Aye, Sarah, best place for her, in her own bed. Get the cart out, Mr Tucker. The maid hasn't the strength to walk.'

Half an hour later, James and Sarah were helping Amy down from the back of the cart and saying goodbye to Mr Tucker, with heartfelt thanks for saving her life.

Sarah and James supported Amy as they took her into the parlour, sitting her in the chair by the fire.

As Sarah left them alone, going to the kitchen to put hot water in the bottle for Amy's bed, she reflected on how the evening had changed everything. She had been so caught up in her own sadness. In the extra work in the house, of looking after the needs of her aunt, she had completely missed that her dear sister had fallen in love. Not once had Amy spoken about it. Not once had she complained about the extra work and that she would rather be seeing James.

As she climbed the stairs to their bedroom, she remembered how, when she felt so alone, she had held her deepest wish to herself, her secret, not wanting anyone else to know it, tarnish it. It was her secret joy. And Sarah understood it.

When James had gone and Amy was in bed, Sarah looked in on her aunt. She was breathing raggedly but looked comfortable and warm. Blowing across the top of the lamp sitting on the bedside table, her breath extinguished the candle.

~

Sarah watched Amy for delayed signs of stress. She seemed physically weak for a day and then was back to her old self, glowing. Sarah knew that she must speak to her about James, and their relationship, but their aunt had taken a turn for the worse. The doctor had been called and, after examining Josephine, shook his head.

'Make her as comfortable as possible,' he smiled sadly, when they were alone in the parlour. 'I'm afraid that she has a deep lung infection and, at her age, she may not recover from it.'

After the doctor had gone, Sarah went back to her aunt's room to see if there was anything that she needed.

'Can I get you anything, Aunt?'

'Would you mind, dear, getting me the paper?' She laughed weakly. 'I just want to see if I'm in it.'

Sarah laughed, glad that her aunt still had her sense of humour. 'I'll get the paper, Aunt, and you are *not* in it. Nor will you be for some time yet.'

'When it happens, Sarah,' she became serious, 'will you make sure that I am?'

'Of course I will. But let us hope that event is a long way off.'

Kissing her aunt's head, Sarah walked to Cawsand, to the corner shop, to get her aunt's paper.

~

267

A month passed and Sarah saw a change in Amy. At first, the trauma of that night seemed not to have affected her, but in these latter weeks, she had become quiet, unresponsive to anything said. It was as though she had retreated into her own world.

Sarah was worried, and also worried about her aunt, who was not responding to the mixture that the doctor had prescribed.

~

The rain, falling in sheets, started to creep under the front door. Amy and Sarah raced around the cottage finding cloths to put on the floor to keep the water out, or at least soak it up. They raised all the chairs that they could lift onto the tables in the parlour and onto the table in the kitchen.

Sitting on the stairs, Amy said quietly, 'I'm going to have a baby, Sarah.'

For a moment, Sarah was speechless, staring at her sister as though she were a stranger, trying to take in what she had just said.

'Why didn't you tell anyone, Amy?' she said eventually.

'We have told James' mother.'

Sarah stared at her sister, unbelieving. 'You told Mrs Bellum before me. Why?'

Amy screwed her face up as though feeling pain. 'Because she's had children and you and aunt are old maids.'

Sarah was speechless. She didn't know whether she was upset because she hadn't been the first to know or that her sister thought her an old maid.

'James and I would like to be married,' she continued. 'If Father were alive, James would have asked him.'

'And would James want to marry you if you were not pregnant?' Sarah had to ask.

'Yes, Sarah, he would.'

She sounded so grown up and in charge that Sarah again wondered how she had missed the change in her sister who, it was now obvious, had become a woman.

268

'Can James support you?'

'Yes,' she nodded. 'His father's a fisherman and James a partner in their business. They split the profits. We're going to live with his parents until a cottage comes up. We don't want to rent one of the cottages owned by the Edgcumbe family. We'll save until something comes up.' She stopped speaking and, looking at Sarah, said cautiously, 'I would like your blessing, Sarah.'

'Yes, of course you have my blessing, Amy,' Sarah heard herself saying, although still stunned by her sister's sudden news.

'We have to organise a wedding. James and I had been talking about getting married before we knew I was going to have a baby.'

Sarah could only nod, and Amy was so carried away with her plans that she didn't notice Sarah's lack of enthusiasm.

'Will you tell our aunt, Amy?'

'I thought that you could do it, Sarah.'

'No, Amy, if you're old enough to have a baby, then you're old enough to take responsibility for it. Telling our aunt your good news is something that you should do.'

Amy nodded and, standing, made her way up the stairs to their aunt's bedroom.

In her heart, she had known that Sarah would say that she should do it, and she also knew that Sarah was right. But as she climbed the narrow staircase, she didn't feel like an adult, and standing in front of her aunt, confessing, she knew that she would feel like a naughty child.

~

The banns were called on the next three consecutive Sundays in Rame Church. Although she and Ned could not get away from their farm, Jane had made Amy a dress for her wedding.

And, on the day, Sarah helped Amy dress, then stepped back, looking in awe at her. At sixteen, Amy had grown into a beautiful woman. There was a part of Sarah that, without saying it, thought, *You are too young, you've had no life.* But then also, what life was there to be had other than to be looked after by a husband? And, in fact, Amy was fortunate that she had met a man that she loved and one that loved her, adored her even.

Aunt Jelly couldn't make the journey to Rame Church, and instead Amy had visited her aunt, in her bedroom, to show her how she looked in her wedding dress.

Aunt Jelly, although frail, was all smiles and encouragement for her niece, saying, 'You will be a good wife, Amy. Visit when you can and bring the baby to see me.'

Amy kissed her and left the house in James Bellum's buggy with Sarah, as her maid of honour, sitting beside her.

The buggy was driven slowly through the village for maximum effect by James' elder brother, Eden, who acted like a celebrity, waving to those that lined the streets to see the bride.

Amy and James were married. The congregation was made up of fishing families that had known James all his life, teachers, past pupils from the Cawsand School and Cawsand villagers. The happiness of the couple, and everyone who witnessed the marriage vows being taken, was so infectious that Sarah could only smile along with everyone else. It was the happiest day that she had been a part of in a long time. Since the marriage of Ned to Jane three years ago, when their aunt was with them in their celebrations.

Mr and Mrs Tucker came to witness the wedding and had shut the shop for an hour. There was music and food in the pub in the square at Cawsand. The celebrations would go on all evening, but Sarah couldn't stay.

And now, back home, she was missing her sister. The cottage seemed empty with Amy gone to live with her in-laws and her aunt upstairs in bed.

She sat in the parlour, her eyes closed, as she relived the day, and for the first time in a long while she thought of John and sighed. If only things had been different.

Going to the kitchen, she pushed the kettle over the fire and prepared to go upstairs and tell her aunt about the celebrations.

30.

The days were getting shorter, the weather cooler. Sarah kept the fires built up as her aunt was feeling the cold, especially when a sea mist surrounded the cottage and moved through the streets, leaving everything salty damp, dripping.

She'd moved the spinning wheel into the kitchen, where it was warmer for her to spin, and had chicken and vegetables cooking in a pot over the fire. Her mind was in a calm, meditative state as she reflected on her life. She knew that she was fortunate to have somewhere to live and enough earned from the spinning to support them. She had to put in more hours now that her aunt could no longer sit at the wheel. After all these years, her spun yarn was as good as her aunt's. Josephine still insisted on doing her bit and worked, propped up in her bed, carding the fleece. When all the fibres were straight, she pushed each batch into a large wicker basket kept beside the bed.

"I can still be useful. I'm not dead yet!" her stock phrase, as every morning Sarah asked if she felt well enough to do it.

Sarah replied as always, 'You'll still be doing this at a hundred, Aunt.'

Josephine chuckled, saying, 'You get me in the paper, maid. And make it sound good.'

'I promise. I have a warming stew in the pan, for your lunch. When I take this fleece downstairs, I'm bringing the stew up. Will you want bread with it?'

'No,' she replied, sounding weary.

Pouring water from the little green jug on the washstand into the matching bowl, she got her aunt to wash the lanolin from her hands. 'Are you warm enough, Aunt? You're looking a little pale.'

'I'm alright.' She sounded tetchy. Her manner had become brusque in these last few days, but she insisted that there was nothing wrong with her. Sarah saw beyond it, knowing how terrible it must be not to be able to go downstairs in her own home and to have everything done for her.

'The stew smells good.' Josephine smiled, closing her eyes. 'I'll have a sleep before you bring it up.'

Sarah took the basket of carded fleece down to the kitchen and placed it next to the spinning wheel.

She washed her hands and ladled some stew into her aunt's favourite dish. But on entering her aunt's bedroom, she knew that something was wrong. Josephine looked to be asleep, but her chest wasn't moving, and one arm hung down over the side of the bed.

Placing the stew on the bedside table, she felt her aunt's face. She was barely warm. Instinctively, she pulled the covers up under her aunt's chin, as a mother might for her child in the night.

Shock suddenly overtook her. She began to shake. The colour left her face and she knew that she was about to retch. Taking the stairs down, two at a time, she only just made the back door before she heaved.

Her face was still wet and her skin grey as she arrived at Marta's shop.

'My God, what's happened?' Marta exclaimed as she came around the counter, seeing Sarah standing just inside the door.

'I think my aunt has died,' she mumbled through bloodless lips.

'Mr Tucker!' Marta shouted, holding Sarah's arm.

As he appeared from the back of the shop, she said, 'I'm going back with Sarah to look at Josephine.'

And with that she led Sarah out of the shop and back along the road to the cottage.

The mist that had persisted all morning was thinning, drawing back from the land. The sun, almost visible through a muslin veil, was trying to break through. Its autumnal heat would eventually dry the road, the cottage walls and roofs.

As they entered the silent cottage, Marta went first up the stairs, Sarah following a few steps behind, not wanting to see her aunt in death.

'Josephine,' Marta whispered as she approached the bed. But Josephine didn't appear to hear. Standing next to the bed, Marta lifted Josephine's arm, placing it back under the covers. 'Josephine,' she said a little louder. When there was no response, she felt Josephine's neck for a pulse. Then, sighing, pulled the cover up over Josephine's face and turning to Sarah, said softly, 'I'm sorry, Sarah, you were right, she's gone. You'd better go for the doctor.'

'Isn't it too late?' Sarah asked, naively.

'You have to have a death certificate, Sarah.' Marta smiled sadly. 'You can only get it from the doctor.'

Sarah's feet dragged on the road. Her legs felt heavy, as though she were walking through deep sand.

The doctor's double-fronted house, built on a corner, had an undisturbed view of the sea. Yet it was angled in such a way that it was protected from the worst of the storms.

Knocking on the door, Sarah was asked in by the maid and taken into the front room with its view of the sea. While she waited, she stared out at the water, unable to hear it lapping through the glass, or the waves breaking. Everything seemed strange. Unreal. This morning, her aunt was alive, hearing the sounds of life that they both knew. Now she was gone and everything seemed silent and dead.

The doctor walked back with Sarah. People noticing them walking didn't ask but looked troubled, some turning to their neighbour, whispering.

Aunt Jelly was dead.

Sarah howled like she had never howled before. Like an injured animal, she sat alone in the parlour with her grief, her body curled up around her pain until the door flew open and Amy was there, holding her in her arms as though she were a child.

Inclusion in the births, marriages and deaths section of the Western Morning News read:

> *It is with great sadness that the death of Josephine Helbridge, née-Warrington, formally of Plymouth, but for many years of Kingsand, was reported. Mrs Helbridge died peacefully in her sleep. She leaves two nieces, Mrs Amelia Bellum and Miss Sarah Warrington also, her nephews Mr Edward Warrington and Samuel and Thomas Warrington. She will be missed by all that knew her.*

Josephine's funeral was held at Rame Church. James and Ned, along with four other strong fishermen, carried the coffin up the hill and into the church.

Sarah was bereft and realised, now that she no longer had it, how much she had come to rely on her aunt's company. How she had enjoyed looking after her.

Amy was getting near her time and she and James moved in with Sarah, there being more room than with James' parents and two brothers.

Sarah took the small room and Amy and James the larger bedroom. Once again, Sarah had someone to share the chores with, and company. James spent every day at sea with his father and brothers; it caused a lot of washing. But Sarah was grateful to have the silent cottage filled with life once more.

~

An official letter was delivered addressed to Miss S. Warrington. Sarah took it from the courier with a tentative hand, frowning at the man.

'Postmarked Plymouth,' he said, as though that would be useful knowledge.

Sarah paid him and took it into the kitchen, showing it to Amy.

'Better open it,' Amy said, staring at it with the same worried expression as Sarah. 'No good trying to guess what it is.'

Nodding, Sarah took a knife to the paper and unfolded it. Her mouth became dry. She didn't understand. A letter from a solicitors' office in Plymouth. The letter was headed in a heavy script at the top of the page, **Constant, Samuels and Best, Solicitors.**

'What's it about?' Amy asked.

'It says that I am mentioned in the Will of Mrs Josephine Helbridge.'

'Aunt Jelly made a will?'

'Yes.' Sarah stared at it. 'I wouldn't have thought of doing that.'

'Nor I,' Amy said, taking the letter from Sarah. 'What do you think they'll say?'

'I hope that it isn't that someone else owns the cottage and wants us out.'

'So do I. I'd hoped that James and I could live here with you. I don't relish living with James' mother, nice as she is. There just isn't enough room, and with a baby taking up space, it would be unbearable.'

'Don't worry, Amy, I'll be with you. We'll live together somehow, somewhere. I'm able to work and help James with the cost. We'll be alright.' She smiled reassuringly.

Turning away, the smile slipped from her face. She wasn't sure, and didn't want to go back to the way they'd lived with their mother. She could not bear to think of her sister having to work in Union Street behind her husband's back to survive. But then she stopped worrying. James came from a large family and they would support the couple, come what may.

*

The narrow entrance to the office of Constant, Samuels and Best was wedged between two shops and identified only by a polished brass plaque on the wall beside the door. The clean steps, gleaming door

275

furniture and black railings that reached down to the pavement unnerved her.

She was about to take hold of the railing when the door opened and a portly man with grey hair came hurrying out, followed by a young man, who helped him into a waiting cab. As the cab left, the young man returned to the building, not noticing Sarah.

Following him inside, she found a young woman sitting at a desk in a small reception area surrounded by potted plants.

Looking up as Sarah entered, she enquired stiffly, 'Can I help you?' in a voice that wasn't Devonian.

'I had a letter,' Sarah held it up. 'An appointment for today with a solicitor.'

The young woman made great issue of looking down a list and asked, without looking up, 'Can you give me your name?'

'Sarah Warrington,' Sarah answered just as stiffly, thinking that this woman wouldn't be any good in the funeral office, where a receptionist needed to be gentle and helpful.

'You were to see Mr Constant, but he's been called away. You will be seeing one of his juniors. Follow me, please.'

Sarah followed the young woman up a flight of stairs, their footfall loud on the wooden treads. Opening a door to an office, the young woman told her to take a seat inside, before she turned away and Sarah heard the sound of her boots retreating back down the stairs.

Everything in the room was brown; the window frames, the panelling, the desk and the seats. It was most obviously a male domain; it smelt musky, and of cigars and hair cream.

Sitting in a smaller chair in front of the desk, she felt diminished in this extravagant room with its brass and blue glass desk furniture. From the corner of the room, the slow clunk, clunk of the grandfather clock's pendulum held authority, as she nervously watched the dust mites floating on the air in front of the window. The large leather chair on the other side of the desk seemed to dominate the room, and her. As she tried not to look at it, the nerves began to jump in her stomach. She had never felt more out of place in her life.

When the door opened, she kept looking forward, nerves rising in her chest, and when the young man, stepping around her, came into sight, she thought that she was going to faint.

'Miss Warrington.' He spoke quietly.

'John!' she blustered. 'I thought you were dead.' Tears rose in her eyes and she didn't know where to look. This was truly awful. What was he doing here?

'I'm sorry, Miss Warrington. It must be a shock if you thought me dead.'

'Your mother didn't explain, when she came to Ned's wedding. She just said that you were no longer here.' A sob escaped her; unable to keep it at bay.

John stared at her across the large desk. Blinking, he said, 'I've been away in London for three years.' He smiled sadly. 'Studying law.'

'I see.' She didn't know what else to say.

'Are you well?' he asked suddenly.

'Yes, thank you. A little worried by this unexpected letter.'

He nodded, taking up a copy of the letter that had been sent to Sarah. 'Your aunt, as you know, made a will, and in it she has left her cottage and all its contents to you, Miss Sarah Warrington.'

Sarah nodded. 'I hadn't known until I received the letter that my aunt had made a will.'

He looked at her across the desk, a serious look on his face. A slight flush on his cheek as he spoke. 'I have to ask, Miss Warrington, are you about to marry or have any intention to marry?'

Sarah stared at him, unable to believe that he would ask her such a thing.

She sighed, biting back her feelings. 'No, sir. I am not about to be married. Nor do I have any plans to marry.'

He nodded and almost smiled. 'I'm sorry. I had to ask, as it would affect the will.'

'Do you mean that if I marry I lose my aunt's cottage?' She felt aggrieved at that.

'No. No,' he returned quickly. 'I would just advise that you also make a will. If that were the case.'

'Well, I can assure you, sir, that you have no need to worry on that score.' Her eyes flashed with emotion, as she'd spoken almost before he'd finished his sentence.

He looked sad as he replied, almost in the same vein as she, 'Then I will arrange for your name to be put on the deeds of the cottage, and I will send them to you, Miss Warrington.'

He took a sheet of paper from a folder, saying, 'If you would kindly sign here and here, I will make this as painless for you as I can.'

As she took up the pen, her hand was shaking so much with emotion that she was unable to sign, and put the pen down.

'Are you ill?' He half stood, looking concerned.

She had to take a moment before she could answer. Everything in the room was suddenly out of focus.

'Seeing you has been a shock, John, as was my aunt dying.' She could no longer deny that his being so near her, after so long, was not affecting her. 'Your mother should have told me.'

His face was filled with regret as he spoke. 'My mother didn't know how I felt about you, Sarah. She only knew that I didn't want to marry Phillis.'

'And yet, John,' she said forcibly, 'you were going to marry her, even though you had expressed your love for me.'

He nodded. 'I regret that, Sarah. More than you will ever know,' he said quietly.

Taking up the pen again, she scribbled her signature on the paper. 'Then you may regret it no longer, sir.' Staring into his eyes, she said, 'Is that all, Mr Parrett?'

'Yes, Miss Warrington. I will get the paperwork sent to you.'

'Good day, sir,' she said shakily, getting up from the chair and walking unsteadily to the door.

He reached it before her and looked as though he was going to open it, but instead held the door shut.

'Sarah, I'm sorry,' he said gently. 'If I had that part of my life again, I would have asked for help from the law. But I didn't know any more than that the Gallaways were going to sue me. Neither

278

my parents nor I had any money. I didn't want my parents to lose their home. Which I believed would happen. Please, Sarah, could you find it in your heart to forgive me?'

He was so close that she could feel the heat from his body, smell the fragrance of his soap. As she put her hand out to open the door, their hands met. She looked up into his face and all the years of love that she had held so close rose to the surface. As he looked longingly down at her, she raised her face to his and their lips met.

'Oh my God.' He lifted her away from the door and back into the room. 'I love you so much, Sarah. I haven't looked at another woman in all these years. I've kept you in my heart all this time, my love.'

Overwhelmed, she allowed herself to be in his arms. All the years of loving him in secret fell away. She knew now that she was a child when she blamed him for going through with the attempted marriage service with Phillis. But now she had grown up and realised how short life was, and that to find a man who loved her, as she loved him, was a miracle.

'Sit down, Sarah. I'll get Nelly to bring tea and we can talk.'

When Nelly the receptionist had gone, he poured the tea, saying, 'I joined the police force with my friend William Best. His father had always wanted William to take up law, but William, like I, had thought policing more of an adventure. But after not being able to help me when I needed the help, through his lack of knowledge, William decided to give up policing and do as his father suggested, take up law.'

He passed her a cup and offered the milk jug. 'It meant moving to London,' he continued. 'With nothing left in Plymouth for me, I went also. His father paid for me. For my exams and for my lodging with Will. But after three years I knew that going to court was not for me. I found it dull, whereas Will found it stimulating. It was Will's father who suggested that I knew enough of the law to join his firm of solicitors here in Plymouth and, in truth, I'm glad to be back. London wasn't for me. I know Plymouth people. I know their roots, what hardships they face. I believe that I can be of more help here than in London.'

Staring at him across the desk, she could only wonder, almost disbelieving, that she was talking to John and that he had expressed once again that he loved her.

'What are you thinking?' he asked suddenly, breaking into her thoughts.

Taken off guard, she could feel the colour rising in her cheeks. She found it hard to speak and wished that he hadn't asked.

'I realise,' she said coyly, 'that I haven't told you how I feel, John.'

He nodded silently and sat back in the chair, as though waiting for the axe to fall.

'I've loved you, John, for so many years. I buried you deep in my soul, hiding you from everyone, just in case I lost you. If that happened, I wanted to grieve in private. And I did. Believing you gone forever, you became my secret, one that no one could sully or remove, because they didn't know. I think, John, that I'm going to find it difficult not to have the secret.'

He smiled. 'Do you mean that you love me, Sarah?'

'Yes, John, forever.'

'Is it too soon to ask you to marry me, Sarah? For I think that we have wasted too much time already.'

'Are you asking me, John?'

He came around the desk, pulling her up into his arms. 'Will you marry me, Miss Warrington?'

'I will, Mr Parrett.' She giggled.

He swung her off her feet and around the office. 'I'm so glad that Mister Constant was called away and that I was asked to deal with your aunt's will. For I don't know how we could have met again.'

Sarah, although swept off her feet, had to ask, 'John, when we marry, where will we live? My sister is about to have a baby and needs to be living with me, and I want to be with her. She and her husband have nowhere but the cottage.'

'I have to confess, Sarah,' he said, putting her back on her feet, 'that I knew that you lived in Kingsand and I've bought a house there that's been empty for many years. It sits above the village, off the main road. I was going to repair it, make it a home, and if you were to be married, I was going to sell it and make a little money. It's a family home, Sarah, large enough for a few happy children, and I know that they will be happy.'

'But how would you get to work in Plymouth, John, when the ferry doesn't run regularly in the winter?'

'I'm getting a position in Cornwall. William's father is opening a new branch.'

'And my brothers, John? They will be coming home soon and I want to offer them a home.'

'I've already been in touch with Ned, and between us we have decided to ask the boys if they would like to live with Ned on the farm, where he would put them to work. We could now ask them if they would like to live with us, when the house is ready and after we are married.'

There were tears in her eyes as she spoke. 'Then we will let the boys decide where they would like to live. And they will have family to support them for the rest of their lives.'

~

The barred windows and large green door of the reform school in Exeter opened onto an extensive yard, surrounded on all sides by a high wall. It was the day of their release, and as Samuel and Thomas, now taller and with their heads shaved, stepped out into the yard, they stood stock-still, mouths open in disbelief.

Standing in a row before them, Sarah, Amy and Ned smiled and opened their arms. Samuel and Thomas ran to them without hesitation, and as Sarah and Amy held their brothers close and Ned looked on, Sarah knew that this family would never again be parted, or be without love.

Author's Note

While looking for my characters, I found Samuel Warrington, aged eleven, and his brother Thomas, aged eight, of 100 King Street, Plymouth, who were put on trial in 1870 for stealing oranges. Both were sentenced to a birching; Samuel, eight strokes, Thomas, six strokes, followed by six more hours in prison to recover, before being sent to a reform school in Exeter for four years, where they were to learn discipline. These two boys governed the start of this novel. Who, I wondered, were their family? Why did they steal the oranges? From there, the family took shape and my main character, their sister Sarah, was born onto the page.

During my research, I also found Elizabeth Axe, aged eleven, of Summerland Street, Plymouth, who was accused of stealing a pair of earrings in 1870 and sentenced to twenty-one days in prison and four years in a reformatory school. Also, the trial of a woman who gave birth to a baby that was found dead, head down, in the toilet of the back yard of a boarding house. The woman had previously denied being pregnant when asked by her mother. Blood spots were found on her kitchen floor and spots of blood led from there to the toilet in the yard. She was arrested. An inquest on the baby's body could not show that the baby had taken a complete breath, even though one lung seemed to hold a little air. Without the proof that it had taken a full breath, and so lived, even for a second, the woman got off. I gave this story to Gwen.

The Plymouth that I wanted to write about is no longer there due to the damage caused by the bombing of the city during the Second World War. Many of the buildings and streets not obliterated by the bombing were then pulled down by the council to make way for the city we know today. In my research, I walked around the city looking for its lost past many times, following old maps to understand where the old roads were and where they went.

The town of Plymouth was well known as a dirty town; in fact, a survey taken in the 1840s rated the health of the population as the 7th worst in England. I tried to weave into the novel as much as I could of what was there in 1870, what my character Sarah would have seen and experienced at the time. There was the fear of disease, and many factories belched out clouds of noxious fumes that became trapped in the town by low cloud, smoke from fires and mist from the sea. Where the shops of Mayflower Street, Cornwall Street and New George Street are today, there was a sugar refinery, a dye works, a flour mill, a smithy and a saw mill. What we now know as the middle of the town was, at that time, industrial.

The New Cemetery, now known as Ford Park Cemetery: A group of leading citizens of Plymouth met in August 1842 for the purpose of forming a cemetery company. These men were deeply concerned at the scandalous state of the overfull churchyards and other burial grounds, which were proving to be a health hazard. In June 1846, the Plymouth, Devonport and Stonehouse Cemetery Company was incorporated, and the company initially purchased 18 acres of land. The first burial took place in December 1848.

Assizes. The courts of assize, or assizes, generally dealt with the most serious crimes (e.g., murder, theft, treasonable activities, infanticide, rape, assault, coining and forgery). These cases were committed to the assizes by the justices after sitting locally, usually in the nearest public house.

Inquests Taken into Suspicious or Unexplained Deaths for the County of Devon.

Coroners' inquests were usually held within the space of forty-eight hours following a death that appeared to be of a suspicious or unexplained nature. They were usually held in a local public house, alehouse, municipal building or parish workhouse, but sometimes in the building where the death occurred. The coroner usually came from a legal or medical background and, more often than not, was appointed for life by the respective county. The coroner and a jury of between twelve and twenty-four persons, usually men of substantial standing, were empanelled to examine the body, hear witnesses, and the jury then to come to a verdict as to cause of death. The account of the inquest, appearing in local newspapers, included the name of the deceased, where they died and how they died. Sometimes, age, occupation, parish or address, and other relatives' names can be found. In later years, when hospitals appear, people can be dying away from their parish after having been admitted to that institution, and the inquest is therefore conducted where the death occurred, rather than where the person was living.

The Marriage Act. The Marriage Act of 1753 made it illegal for those in England under the age of twenty-one to get married without the consent of their parents or guardians. However, the consent requirement was repealed and replaced in July 1822. Therefore, from 1823, the age at which a couple could undergo a valid marriage, without parental consent, reverted to fourteen years for boys and twelve years for girls.

In England and Wales until 1970, a woman whose fiancé broke off their engagement could sue him for breach of promise, while a woman, historically regarded as the weaker sex, was permitted to change her mind without penalty. The last prominent case was in 1969, when Eva Haraldsted sued George Best, the footballer, for breach of promise.

Theatre: Edward Fitzball was one of the most prolific and popular melodramatists of the Romantic and Victorian periods. The peak of his success was in the 1820's to the 1830's. Fitzball reportedly wrote for at least 25 theatres and produced about 170 melodramas, opera librettos, burlettas, tragedies, comedies, and farces. He wrote, The Murder at the Roadside Inn, a melodrama in two acts.

Dialect. I considered putting more Devonshire dialect into this book, but after reading several books on the dialect, I realised that there was a possibility that those reading this novel would be unable to understand it and that it would make for difficult reading. I showed some of the Devon dialect to people born and bred in Devon, and they couldn't read it either. For clarity and enjoyment of the story, it is as it is.

Acknowledgements

This was not an easy story to find. I was ready to write my next book when COVID-19 struck, and for the life of me, I could not get my head into the writing space that I needed. And so, a year passed in fruitless thought. Eventually, I was asked to set my next book in Plymouth, and this also became a struggle for me, as I didn't know the city well, although I have lived in the area since 2006. But knowing a city as it is today was not the same as reliving it as it was before it was destroyed in the Second World War.

Because the old pre-war Plymouth is still within many people's memory and families can trace their lineage back to the 1800s and beyond, I had to make up some names. Although there were many public houses in King Street, I was sure that someone would be able to trace their family back to one that I might use, so I made up the King's Head, although a public house of that name did exist in another street. As I started my research, I became more and more interested in the social history of Plymouth and shared it with my friend Alan Bricknell, who, being an historian, became as excited about Victorian Plymouth as myself. It has been a great joy wandering around the streets, visiting the new Plymouth museum "The Box" and the Plymouth Central Library with Alan, and having the many discussions that went with each visit. I got to a point in the book, as I often do, where I was out of my depth with legal jargon, and here my friend Mick Freeman, a retired solicitor – advocate in the Magistrates Court, helped me with how a coroner should be addressed.